SEQUENCE ALIGNED

THE HEART OF THE OCEAN

BOOK 2

LORRAINE M.L.M

TO MY HUSBAND, SIMBA

For all the sacrifices you make each day. You think
of others first before you. You bring joy, laughter and
humour in everything you do. Thank you from the
bottom of my heart for being such a loving husband.
I can never imagine my life without you.

TO MY CHILDREN, NATASHA & NATHAN

You're beautiful bundles of joy, great gifts from God,
and bountiful blessings to everyone around you.
Live all you can. Love all you can. Learn all you can.
And never forget that you have a family that loves you
dearly on the other side of the world. Distance
is nothing. Family is everything. We always,
always take care of each other.

This book is affectionately dedicated.

Love,
Lorraine

CONTENTS

Moon-Day Two
My Felradian Gift
to you...

A Game of Sequence

A Game of Sequence is as complex as a pyramid and as simplistic as a triangle. A Sequence is a natural order of elements, thoughts, and beliefs that brings about a nation. It is a journey from birth to death, a path from genesis to exodus, a number from one to infinity. A Sequence never ends. It rekindles, rejuvenates, and refreshes with time. When the Sequence gains total control of the Game, the players have no choice but to align with the Sequence.

Signed,
Halkateiy Valeima Mautilus
of House Regai-Rallias

PREFACE

Dante's Chain of Thought

In a Game of Sequence, when you're faced with certain death, there are only two options to you—Zeneshians and humans alike. Be bold, or cry yourself to sleep, but neither makes you a hero, for death is, without question, the master of all life.

Each moon-day that you're alive, you're running from him—death, such is his nature to chase...like a hunt...only this hunter is unyielding, unmerciful, tenacious. For as long as you can, you dodge this unalterable shadow or try to...but relentlessly, death pursues you. You stop, and he, too, takes a breather, watching you from a distance.

You pick yourself up, stagger across the land, running when you can, plodding, crawling, feeling as if your breath is being sucked out of you. Succumbing to your fate, you finally trip and fall. Death stops and appears to feel your pain.

Again, not wanting to concede defeat, you find your willpower. You wobble to your feet. At that time, the rain is thumping so hard you feel each bruise. A moment after, the sun is scorching the life out of you, but still, you carry on. Why? Because you have a path to follow, a destination to reach, a Sequence to fulfil. With hope and faith, you aim to make your life worth something.

Inevitably, death catches up, for he is the result of living. What eats you up and threatens to kill you before death has done his final deed is regret.

What could I have done differently? What did I do with the time I was given to live? You forage for answers. In those final moments, when you get into that empty space and invisible walls are caving in, what makes you strong is one greater than death and denser than life. Love. To live is to love—loving is living! There's a sequence to life, love, and death, and regardless of how hard one tries, no one can escape it!

PART I

Alessia – The Dawn of my Training

1. THE OCEAN IS YOU

essi! Dante's melodic and deep voice echoed fluidly inside my head, more refined than ever. *I can't quite make up my mind what's more spectacular, you in the ocean or the ocean in you?* Telepathy was a thing in Tuscania and even now, I was still trying to come to terms with the fact that this was real. It had been seven months since my arrival in my new world, and I still had no idea how to switch on or off the 'mind thing.' My mind just did its own thing. And I did mine.

Dante! I said with zest, albeit telepathically. *You're back!* I jerked up from the refreshing cool ocean water, whipped round, and gazed upon the guy who made my life a real every day fantasy. On his approach, four *gisbornias*—protectors dipped their heads in greeting.

Since the day I met him my life was like an unwritten story of something along the lines of *Jack and the Beanstalk*, except it read: *Alessia and Dante, the deepest depths of the oceans.* Being loved by him and loving him back, what I would have deemed as *fantasy* in my home world, and what I saw and lived as my *reality* were the same thing.

No distinction—no separation. Everyday was bliss.

Dante stood tall by the shoreline, fifty metres away, hands tucked deep into his beautifully tailored midnight-blue twilled cotton shorts, his vinous-red eyes drinking me in from a distance.

I wiped water off my face, breathed in the fragrant ocean-air, and smiled my heart out to him. He was millions of leagues out of my realm, yet when he regarded me unflaggingly with his luminous eyes, he suggested otherwise. Of everything else, it was something inside his eyes that always drew me to him. They were sensuous and exciting; they oozed freedom, strength, and hidden depths of mysteries I had yet to discover.

What are you doing here? I asked. A frisson of excitement flew through me. *I wasn't expecting you this week!*

He was meant to be discussing the kingdom's strategy with members of the highest council—the Dhareka—not standing in my line of view, looking like one of the gods of my new world. He chatted to the four gisbornia*s* who stood to his left, and then turned to me, a playful smile lingering on the corners of his mouth. *Are you intending to swim back to the shore, or shall I come and get you?*

I gazed at him for a prolonged moment, delighting in the way his olive-toned skin shimmered effortlessly in the midday sun. *To get to me you'll have to catch me first!* I dipped my head into the invigorating water and breast-stroked across the curvature of the ocean. Every time I dipped into the water, the jewel of the ocean that hung around my neck glimmered a rich cobalt. It was as though the longer I was in Zeneshia, the more colourful the pendant became.

Dante's light laughter bubbled free inside my head, bringing immense joy to my heart. Everything was just perfect!

The boundless deep-sea water was varnish clear, pleasing to the eye and untarnished by seaweed. The sand at the bottom of the sea looked lush and inviting, unspoilt by pebbles.

When I surfaced, I drew breath and sought Dante's gaze. Brows raised, a slight smile gracing his face, he carefully considered my proposal. He was a cautious guy, that I knew from the day I met him, at the banquet. Everything he did was well thought out. Even the occasional times that he broke the rules, rest assured, he would have weighed every option until he was certain the benefits outweighed the risks.

A second later, he took off one shoe, a dazzling smile lighting his face. "Don't make me come in, please," he pleaded, choosing to speak the normal way rather than the mind thing—telepathy. "I miss you!" He raised his voice just high enough so I could hear.

"And I miss you!" I called. "But I've missed the ocean, too." I raised my arms and swivelled around, loving the feel of water against my skin. My toes sunk into the sand, the texture fine and soft like puffy cushions. "If you truly and desperately want me, come and get me," I said playfully, my gaze locked onto him.

His laughter echoed inside my head. "I love it when you throw caution to the wind, but—"

"No buts, Dante Erajion! Dive in, or I'll drag you in," I warned to his added amusement. "The ocean is beautiful, but it'll be divine with you in it!"

From a distance, his red eyes twinkled, in competition with the golden-white sand glittering in the afternoon sun. The all-round view was incredible, like glitters had been sprinkled across the shoreline.

This was Tuscania, the land of my mother, the peaceable kingdom under the dual moons, the mystical world of moon-bows and myths under the sea. With the midday splendent sun at her peak, she blazed the land of the rising sun, emitting strokes of light that added to the radiance of the beach sand.

At peace, I glanced up to the sky, and my gaze settled on the azure dome. It was Tuscanian spring time, yet it looked like summer, felt like summer, and with Larize Charming, Dante Erajion of house Hantaria in my line of sight, it *was* summer!

Yet this beauty was untouched, untainted, and unspoilt. A soothing hush cloaked the land, the ocean creating an invisible mirage of peaceful sounding silence. Every so often, the hush was penetrated by the lulling whisper of the waves crawling gently to the shore. There were no inquisitive tourists, no hotels, and no form of commercialisation that I had become accustomed to in my home world. This was Shangrila, a hidden slice of paradise…private, pristine, and exotic.

A hundred metres from where Dante stood across the beach, towering sand dunes hid the bay from normal day-to-day life in Tuscania. Beyond was a massive parsley-green veld that led into the forests and a backdrop of heaven-kissing mountains looming mysteriously in the distance. Something about those jagged mountains gripped me. They had an enigmatic and secretive air around them that kept me absorbed every time I glanced in their direction.

My home, okay, my grandparent's enormous white house with contrasting mahogany-framed windows, sat to my left on higher ground. I could just about see my bedroom window from where I stood.

Down below, the refreshing vanish-clear water mirrored the sky! Taking it all in, there was no comparison to my usual coastline in my home world with grey waters and pebbled beaches. Here, the sand was soft, fine, and pure, like powder. Following my unexpected arrival, today was my first revisit to the same waters that had brought me to this kingdom. Early that morning, I had begged Zaira, my grandma, to allow me into the boundless ocean.

* * *

"Here." Grandma outstretched her arm towards me and placed a shiny diamond bracelet into my open palm. "Something I've wanted to give you for some time, now."

"Oh, Grandma!" I exclaimed, swivelling around on my bed. "It matches my necklace!" I flipped the multi-coloured white, blue, red, and silver glowing bracelet.

"The Larumia, jewel of the ocean, is a set of three, my velici," she said after a short thoughtful pause. "I gave Kaylinah the necklace and the diadem, so she could pass one to her daughter should the gods have blessed her with one and keep one for herself. I retained the bracelet." Her warm smile matched the sun-yellow chiffon dress she wore. "That way the three of us would forever be linked."

"It's beautiful," I said, lips parting.

"Not as beautiful as you are. You see beauty because you're made of beauty. It's impossible for you to see anything less."

Smiling, I rested my head on her shoulder. My mind drifted to my childhood days. "I never saw Mum wearing a diadem. Dad just gave me the necklace, n-nothing else." My voice cracked, and I cleared my throat.

"Perhaps she was buried with it, my dear." Grandma curved an arm around my shoulder. "The diadem is a heavy jewel. If she had it in her hair, you couldn't miss it."

A sad silence descended over us. Grandma settled her gaze on the jagged mountain tops that loomed in the distance. With the curtains drawn, my bedroom window was like a stunning picture of sun, sea, sand and mountains, a view people would pay for, yet thoughts of my mum's death tainted the beauty. Something was missing.

"The undertakers didn't allow anyone to view her body," I whispered through a constricted throat. "They said her body was too damaged." Tears formed in my eyes. I bit them back and drew in a sharp breath.

"There's a sequence to life, love, and death, my dear. Kaylinah completed hers remarkably well." She squeezed my shoulder. "Enough with the heavy. What would *you* like to do today?" With her free arm, she reached for her chalice on the bedside table and took a swallow of her *mamaira*, her breakfast soup.

"Swim," I said almost immediately. "Swim. I've missed the water."

"In the ocean?" Grandma's thin yet perfectly shaped eyebrows lifted. "That's too risky, velici."

"Please, please, please, Grandma!" I begged, coming shy of kneeling down on the floor. "Since I've been here, I've always watched the ocean from a distance."

She placed her chalice down. "Velici?" Her calm voice oozed

a pleasantly rich tone that was in parallel to the humming sound of flowing water cascading down the waterfall in the corner of my room. Bliss.

I held her hands in mine and gazed into her eyes. "I want to feel the sea again. I want to swim against the waves just like Mum and I used to do. I want to be at one with the water." I bit my lip. "Just once before I leave all of this for the birdhouse in the thick of the forest."

"Birdhouse?" Zaira raised her eyebrows, amusement dancing in her eyes.

"That's what Gradho said." Gradho was one of the twenty-four Dhareka councillors who relished in having the last word...everytime. After a short thoughtful pause, I went on. "He said Ralda likes to live a simplistic life and that he's always lived in a birdhouse in the middle of nowhere, away from the perks of modern living," I babbled. Ralda, on the other hand was one of the Seven Voices of Sequence, a wise and calm old man who had a lot of secrets cocooned inside him. "And—"

"You're worried about your training?" She gazed at me for a lengthy moment.

"A little." I dropped my gaze. It wasn't just my impending training that worried me. It was everything else: Leaving Dante! Being away from home. Saying goodbye to my family. "I'm more worried about leaving home...and the ocean behind."

"The ocean is you. You'll carry it with you inside your heart." She pressed the aglow moons pendant, the jewel of the ocean that hung around my neck gently against my chest.

"So, may I have a swim, Grandma, before I start my training, *please.*"

"I don't know about that, my dear. You're young and full of spirit, but Raldarinda will not be remotely amused," she said after a contemplative pause. "The ocean is you, but the water is not safe for you, velici."

"Grandma, I'll be fine. There's nothing lurking in the waters anymore. Even Ralda agrees the Nadeira are gone." My mind drifted to the time my utopia vanished and I was lured out of my room and woke up in the moving forest face to face with the most hideous creatures ever, the Nadeira. My heart skipped. I drew in a deep breath. *The Nadeira are just a memory.* "I was born to sail the Four Oceans of the Surging Tide. That's what you always say," I reminded her with a cheeky grin. "I'm in this world because of the wonders of the ocean. I'll swim close to the shoreline. I promise."

Through my bedroom window, Grandma and I gazed at the majestic waters at length. The mellow crash of the sea waves against the shore was like a dance of water and sand, inviting and alluring, calling to me.

"Please, Grandma!"

She gazed at me intently for a while and then smiled. "You'll wait until midday, and you'll have three, no, four protectors with you."

At her words, I let out a sudden yelp, threw my arms around her with eagerness, and pecked her cheek. "Thanks, Grandma! Oh! What do we use to swim around here?" I asked to her added amusement.

Her blue-green eyes sparkled. "I'll be right back." She left my room with haste, and in a few minutes, she returned and handed me a pair of wine-red shorts and a white tank top. "Don't ask," she said after my eyes widened. "Despite their elegance, these robes and dresses will drag you down to the bottom of the ocean." She held my head in her hands and shook her head. "We can't have that!"

* * *

I smiled, reminiscing as I paddled around in the water. The powdery sand slid through my toes like silk. Then I noticed that the gisbornias had vanished. I swung my gaze around the shoreline toward Dante. *Hey! What have you done with my protection detail?* I asked teasingly.

A warm and glowing smile lit up his face and spilled into his eyes. Unbuttoning his shirt slowly, he now stood barefoot under the Sun god of Light. My stomach fluttered.

I've given them some time off. I'm all the protection you need! His smile broadened, and he tossed his shirt to the ground.

I was dazzled to numbness. I'd never seen him without a shirt before. Every second he stood in my line of view with the sun's rays bouncing off him, my heart lurched toward him, like a candle that beamed to infinity. He lit up my world.

Oh my god! I'm staring. I'm totally staring! I gasped, struck by his enthralling athletic build, muscular yet not overbearing physique and well-formed abs. His blue shorts contrasted his russet skin tone effortlessly, like he'd been born in them.

My mind drifted to the first day I'd met him. He had swept me off my feet. The only complication was that he could read my thoughts, *all* my thoughts, of which ninety-nine percent were of him, how fascinating he was, how enticed and enchanted I'd been… Yeah, I still cringe with that knowledge. To my defence, I blamed the gene that our houses shared. The Sequence of First and Forever was inescapable. If someone had mentioned it on day one, I wouldn't have believed them, but that would have avoided a lot of death by embarrassment.

Auspiciously now, I could rely on my mind to reveal only what I wanted him to know…at times. I was still trying to work out the 'mind thing,' the range of telepathic communication and how to ensure that it was airtight.

Red is the colour for you, his low and smooth voice sounded inside my head.

A burst of heat rose in my face. I glanced down at my swim-suit, okay, my red shorts and tank top. It was the first time he was seeing me in minimal clothing too, considering every day was dress day in Tuscania.

Red is you! I said.

He favoured me with yet another dazzling smile. His red shock of hair glinted with the midday sun, creating an enthralling contrast to his skin. He seemed disinterested in the beauty around us, his complete focus rested on me. The cool breeze ruffled his hair, lifting the soft tendrils, and he ran his hands to try and manage them. Behind him were a scatter of coconut L-shaped trees, which reminded me of pictures of Caribbean paradise islands I'd only seen on screensavers in my home world.

I glanced back and looked at my starting point, a two-metre cliff into the ocean. I smiled. On earth, swimming was my thing from a very young age, and in my teenage years, it was my sanctuary. An invasion of voices inside my head had been part of my life since the age of fourteen. Torture. It was as though a crowded stadium continuously screamed inside my head. Without my water pouches or being in a body of water, every thought—every memory—every emotion from people within a three-hundred metre radius of me thronged my mind, piercing right through me. Death by voices.

Swimming hushed the voices, and underwater, it stopped the voices completely. Now I was in the world below the sea, swimming in the midday sun, and the voices that had made my life miserable were no longer a form of psychosis but a surreal gift from the East Star god of Peace. After months of not swimming, I doubted myself, so I stayed close to the shoreline, and enjoyed the cool-warm sensations of the ocean against the sun.

Dante paced into the waters slowly, leisurely, and slickly. His gaze never left mine. A thrill of elation bubbled inside me, a cool breeze touching the warmth of my cheeks. With each step, he took in my direction, my pulse raced. Any second, and I could see myself melting into the sea. Once the waters were waist deep, he dove forward effortlessly and swam toward me. My breath hitched.

Before I'd composed myself to breathe properly, a swirl of blue water lifted into the air from my left. A majestic bird leaped out of the ocean through the whirl. Astonished, I brought my hands to my mouth and caught my breath. In a hypnotic rhythm, the bird fluttered its watery wings in the air gliding over me.

Dante! I couldn't get any words out.

It wasn't a bird. It was shaped like a bird but looked like the ocean. It hovered over me, flitting and chirping like it was in a dance of some sort. I ducked, fascinated yet terrified by the surreal beauty of the creature.

In seconds, Dante surfaced inches from me and instantaneously swooped me into his warm arms.

"What species is that?" I breathed, mouth agape.

"*Larushia*—bird of the ocean," he said easily. "Larushias hardly venture above water."

He raised his hand towards the most stupendous bird I'd ever seen. At least two feet tall, the bird had wings as beautiful as a dove's and a serrated beak that beamed like glitters in the daylight. Magic. The bird gracefully glided towards us and nestled in Dante's free arm. Friendly, too.

"She couldn't resist your presence in the ocean," he said.

"You're a bird whisperer now?" I puffed a light laugh and stroked the bird's cool feathers.

Dante burst into a light chuckle. "I could be," he teased. "But not today. Today it's all about you." His voice was low.

At his words, the bird chirped and flitted its wings, and in seconds, she darted underwater as quickly as she had emerged. Dante wound both arms around me and drew me a fraction closer. A spark of delight went through me. For a long interval he held me close. I snuggled into him and curled my arms around his neck. I welcomed this haven. I embraced the feeling of rapturous excitement that he invoked in me every time he cuddled me this close.

His touch was like some stimuli that elicited a mix of sensations that kept me wondering whether I was hot, cold, warm, cool, or just right—I could never be sure, yet I was certain of one thing. Given the option, I would choose to nestle in his arms forever and never ask for anything else!

"Now that I've got you, what next?" he asked against my neck, his voice gentle and soothing, in perfect harmony with our surroundings.

I leaned back, met his wine-red sparkling eyes, and then bit my lip. "It depends," I whispered with a smile, my breath catching in my throat.

"On what?"

I paused before answering, "On whether you can hold onto me long enough!" I slipped free from his arms, swivelled around him, and before he could catch me, I breast-stroked away from him.

A burst of laughter escaped his lips. *Now you're making me work for your love, Lessi!*

It's only fair. You got me so easily from day one, I teased. *It's time you did some work, my Larize!*

I swam farther into the water, dancing to the rhythm of the waves and listening to the calm murmuring sounds of the ocean. Behind me, Dante swam close, chuckling inside my head. He was a good swimmer, something I didn't know until then.

You've got to stop, Lessi.

Not until you catch me! My heart beat unsteadily, working itself up into a frenzy, an every time thing when Dante was around, yet this time, it was in sync with the wave music of the ocean, too. I was having a blast in true oceanic sybaritic splendour. I did all my favourite strokes one after the other, spinning to my back and rolling to my front, always ensuring I stayed closer to the shoreline. Within minutes, I had swum much farther than I had intended.

After some time, fatigue got the better of me, and I stopped. Breathless, I whipped around. In a trickle, Dante rose from the blue watery wonderland, like a sea god. I tugged gently at the pendant dangling on my necklace, enthralled. A charming smile played at the corners of his lips. He blinked. His long dark lashes seemed thicker, his wet hair shimmering in the afternoon sun seemed longer, and he, well, he was simply captivating.

His eyes flashed brazier-red! My short breath shortened even further. Something strange yet stunning hung the air. He crossed towards me and halted inches from me. Unsure what I wanted to do next, I flicked water at him, trying to get his face. All I managed to do was arouse an amused chuckle that made my heart flip.

He returned the favour with a large volume of water that hit me right in the face. I shut my eyes.

"My moons! I'm so sorry," he said remorsefully sweeping me into his broad arms. "My big hands! I didn't think. I am so—"

I laid a hand over his lips. "I'm fine, Dante. I'm not made of soft cotton wool," I whispered. "Besides, I'm old enough to get hurt and still keep a straight face."

"I wouldn't want to be the one to hurt you," he said slowly in a honeyed tone, emphasising each syllable. I knew there was more to his words than he was letting on.

He gathered me close and drew me hard against his well-toned body such that I was pressed firmly to his bare chest. A burst of heat streaked through me in circular waves that intensified with each breath I took. I felt at home in his arms. Before I could soak in the embrace fully, he drew back, musing. That was his thing: death by cogitation!

Momentarily, he leaned a bit closer. A new surge of warmth pulsed through me like a charge of electricity. Suddenly, he curved both arms around my waist, and in one swift movement, he lifted me to him. I gasped. As my feet left the ground, gravity seemed to have given up total control, and aquatic microgravity took over. I curved my legs around his waist.

My pulse quickened. He drew one hand and cradled my jaw and cheek, telling me without words that he was ready. I was ready. I inhaled one last breath. My hands securely wrapped around his neck, and I didn't have to be a genius to know that this was it.

The moment was right. The timing was great. With my feet off the ocean floor and tightly curled around his waist, my heart thumped so hard against my ribs. Gravity ceased to exist. No ocean—no land; just me and him! The fresh scent of the ocean filled my lungs, yet now I couldn't breathe or even remember how to breathe. I couldn't afford to breathe. I couldn't blink. I couldn't risk missing out on this moment.

This was the moment I had awaited for a while now, so patiently, too. My very first kiss!

He edged his head forward, pausing a little, and then inched closer until I could feel the gentle caress of his breath on my lips. As my gaze soaked in the sparkle in his irises, I shut my eyes, unable to keep up with the dazzle.

I hate to spoil this sequence and all, but you've got to save that for another moon-day!

Our bliss, the beautiful sound of silence, and my almost first kiss was ruptured by Tan-tan's voice. My heart sank. I flung my eyes open and met Dante's unreadable gaze.

Tan, your timing! Leave! Dante's now frustrated voice echoed inside my head.

I let out my breath. Talk about breaking the moment. It was shattered. The kiss and everything else that mattered then flitted away like a wasp in the air.

I would leave, Tan-tan said, *but it's not me you should be worried about. If you hadn't been too engrossed, you'd have noticed. You've got company,"* he said with a short pause. *And not—*

They can wait, Dante said, still holding me. He had no intention of letting me go; his arm clasped tightly around my waist said it in more ways than one. "I'm sorry," he mouthed.

I smiled, feeling a bit flustered.

Not this company, Tan-tan went on to say. *Not everyone is here in peace.*

With the moment definitely lost, Dante and I spun round simultaneously and noticed Zaira, Gradho, and Ralda watching us from the shoreline.

Dante made a low grumble but kept his arm firmly around me. *What is Gradho doing here?* He seemed more annoyed than concerned.

I'm sorry to be the bearer of bad news, Tan-tan said. *Gradho is what he is. A sequence crasher!*

I drew in some breath. A telling off was imminent, I could sense it. Still everything I needed was right there with me. I could face anything as long as I had Dante. I flicked him a glance and flashed him a coy smile.

"What's that smile?" He lowered me gently into the water.

"I'll give you one guess. No cheating," I whispered, withdrawing reluctantly from his warm touch. I kept my eyes locked onto his for a drawn-out moment. "I'm your Delilah, and you're my kryptonite!" I laughed at my own jest. It didn't seem right at all.

"Delilah and Kryptonite?" A contemplative frown rolled over his forehead. For a lengthy moment, he wore a reflective expression on his face, smiling. His eyebrows rose. "My moons! Is that supposed to be good?"

"Hey, you breached my shield?"

He chuckled, smoothing his hair. "She opened up for me."

"She did it again! My mind is…is…" I feigned frustration as his eyes twinkled with subtle amusement. "She's something else."

I lifted my gaze to the immeasurable expanse of the Tuscanian skies then swung my gaze back to the shimmering ocean, musing. Streams of light danced over the ocean water, generating hypnotic illusions, like someone was constantly sprinkling diamonds into the sea.

I beamed, stood on my toes, and gave him a light kiss on the cheek. "Whatever she's up to, I want you to know that I love you more than she does," I whispered into his neck, and then brushed my lips lightly against his shoulder.

He smiled against my neck. "And I love you both!" he said.

2. THE SEQUENCE BECOMES YOU

"**D**id you enjoy your swim, velici?" Zaira, my lovely grandma, asked cheerfully as Dante and I strode out of the ocean. She handed me a radiant orchid towelling robe, her eyes glinting with controlled merriment.

Nodding, I beamed effortlessly. Zaira was Lake Placid on feet, the best grandma I could ever ask for. "Thank you. I'm sorry we hadn't realised you were waiting for us," I said in her direction before my remorseful smile froze at Gradho's piercing look.

"Was it worth it?" Gradho asked, unimpressed. He was one of the Dhareka councillors—a nightmare during the day! He caused trouble, and if there wasn't any trouble around, he hunted for it.

I curved my lips for politeness, tying the belt of my robe in silence.

"*Zera-pe-ladha*, flower of the water, was it worth the risk?" Gradho's loud and thick voice bounced over the sea. He was expecting me to snap or at least provide him with some form of reaction, but I knew my manners.

"Excuse me?" I asked.

"You are not excused! The entire land's survival is depended on the shield." His tone awoke an unwelcome feeling in me, and a frown crept up on my forehead. "The shield is you. Was it worth risking the entire kingdom's future for a dip in the Blue Ocean of Sequence?"

"Gradho, loosen up. It's just a swim," Dante dropped a hand to my waist. "You should try it sometime."

"No, Larize! This is reckless and unnecessary. The Dhareka are worried sick about—"

"Since when do you speak for the Dhareka?" Dante asked, his voice taking a frosty tone. "You are a constituent of the Dhareka, not the voice of the Dhareka!"

"If no one is speaking, I'm more than happy to be the voice of reason."

"Pick your arguments wisely. Frankly go and pick them somewhere else. This is one fight you will not win." Dante's hard and dark-red gaze roved over Gradho's face, and I knew then he had ended it. Gradho—the banquet crasher—was an every day crasher of anything good. He wouldn't remain quiet for long, that's for sure.

Gradho shrugged, offered a strange tight-lipped smile, and fixed his plush maroon robe around him, seemingly looking for a distraction. Squinting, he focused his gaze on my pendant. "If that precious jewel had fallen to the bottom of the ocean, what then?

"She would have swum to the deepest depths of the Four Oceans to bring it back up," Zaira said light-heartedly, her voice tinged with pride and maternal love. "The jewel and the bearer are inseparable."

"Zera-pe-ladha, your grandma can not answer for you." Gradho was relentless. "I'm waiting for *your* answer."

"Exactly like Grandma said," I replied easily. Bizarrely, a smile crept up his lower lip. "That's my answer, High Dhareka Councillor Gradho."

My addressing him formally invoked a loud bubble of laughter to erupt from Tan-Tan and Dante.

"Give it a rest, Gradho," Tan-tan said. "There's no way you can penetrate the calm in Aless."

I swung Tan-tan a surprised look that said, *Me, calm? There's a first.*

"Chosen one, despite the grace of the guardians who safe-guard these waters, the ocean is much deeper than you think," Ralda, one of the Tuscanian elders, a humble old man with an art for riddles, said in a low voice. He had a few titles, but one that was used most times was Voice of Sequence, only that title was way too orthodox. He was a 'riddler.' *Riddle of Sequence.* Yes, that was more fitting. "And no place for you."

I smiled remorsefully and bit my lip before swinging an apologetic look in Zaira's direction. "I'm sorry—"

"I had my eye on her the whole time, Ralda," Dante has-tened to say, casually wrapping a towel around my shoulders to help soak in some of the dripping water from my hair. "She's an exceptional swimmer!"

His eyes glinted. *You're the heart of the Four Oceans.* His voice sounded inside my head, and I leaned into him, smiling.

Gradho puffed out a laugh. "If you ask me, I'd tell you that you had more than just your Southern red-eye on her!"

"That's why I'm not asking for your opinion," Dante snapped, his jaw tightening.

"And a sharp eye that you have, young Larize." Ralda patted Dante's hand. "I do not doubt your instincts or your intellect, yet there are hidden entanglements in the deepest depths of the ocean that cannot be viewed by eyes alone." He gazed into the distance, seeming preoccupied.

As one of the seven Dhareka elders, otherwise known as the Seven Voices of Sequence, and the sole custodian of the shield that protected Tuscania, he had a huge responsibility to the land.

His gaze settled on me. "Chosen one, the time for healing is over." He took a moment to catch a breath. "There are three phases to your scheduled training: external strength, internal strength, and absolute strength. We leave for the first phase tomorrow at the crack of dawn."

My world came crashing down on me, and my breath caught in my throat. How could my period of respite be over already? "I thought I had another week."

* * *

A month had gone past since my encounter with the most mystical and hideous creatures ever! Even after I'd had a whole month to think, relax, and accept that there was more to me than I originally thought, it remained difficult to comprehend. Faced with the torment of losing Dante to death by the Nadeira's claws, I, okay, my mind had managed to control one of nature's greatest elements: water.

As if that wasn't creepy enough, I built an ice dorm, a real smoking-ice gigantic curved ball made of real ice. I even created a name for that happening. *The Rise of the Red Ice Smoke!* Weird? Yes, I hit the highest level of creepiness in my new world.

* * *

"Swimming with the *Maurola* guardians of the water, are we?" Gradho's orotund voice brought me back to reality with a thud. "Like I was saying, I hope you soaked in enough of the Sun god of Light. Ralda's bird house will not be as accommodating or warm. The Dhareka agree that we hasten your training for the greater good. You are too *precious* to be spending valuable time in a reckless swim in the ocean." He had his hands behind his back.

"I wouldn't call it reckless," Tan-tan countered with a playful wink in my direction. He was Dante's best friend, and loyal, too. Even if I had been an ogre with two heads, I was sure Tan-tan would have cared for me regardless. The fact that Dante loved me was enough for him to love me, too, in a brotherly way, of course. "Aless is bold. Daring is the word I'd prefer to use. She has proven beyond doubt that she's capable of taking care of herself."

"At what expense?" Gradho voiced. "At the expense of the land! The shield is on its knees, and yet she's swimming the seas like an absconding fish from the walled city of Felradia." He threw his hands into the air.

"I stayed close to the shoreline," I said.

"She's young and full of spirit," Zaira added, wearing a fond smile. *Don't mind Gradho! He likes to find a crisis even if there isn't one!* "The ocean is she!" She made me sound so special, yet I felt so normal. Surreal.

"Well said, house Serenius." Ralda turned to Gradho. "House Merinda, here's my counsel to you, despite you not seeking it. It is indisputable that the chosen one carries the gene to save the land," he said with a heavy inflection in his voice, "however it does not follow that she has to cease being young and joyful." He took a breather, wheezing. "The gift of youth is priceless but not timeless. It does not redeploy. It never returns. Happiness is non-committal. When you have it, you will be a fool not to embrace it." He swivelled round, looked me in the eye, and swung me a warm smile. "Be sure to take note that this gene is not a curse but a blessing, a true gift from the East Star god of Peace. The gods chose you because they knew you were capable. They do not make mistakes. The land will allow you the free will to enjoy the fruits of youth—"

"Within reason, my Honourable Voice of Sequence!" Gradho cut in, eyebrows raised.

"Within reason," Ralda agreed in a low and agreeable voice. "The gods have given you the gift of youth in parallel to the gift of saving a nation. No man can deny you of either. You will live, love, and be loved whilst carrying the future of the entire land in the palm of your hands." His voice trembled a little. "Our responsibility is to nurture that happiness, guide your emotions, and find the central core of the most stable, solid and unfaltering mother of the shield in you." He watched me studiously to ensure I was attentive. "Walk with me, chosen one." Ralda outstretched his hand.

I reached for it. We strode leisurely along the beach. The fresh ocean breeze brushed against us, refreshing.

"We are on a journey—you, me, and the land of your mother," he said after a short pause, which was necessary because his words were wreathed in artistic riddles. He was what you'd call the Da Vinci of riddles. Any second he could break into a brainteaser song or start speaking in Ursprache.

We both gazed into the distance. The sand stretched for miles, and gigantic pinnate coconut tree leaves danced merrily to the midday ocean-breeze.

"Once you get to my age you will realise that a journey—any journey—is a succession of events as are our footprints in the sand."

I glanced back. My footprints followed me faithfully like my shadow. A cool and strong wind swept around us, lifting the damp hair off my temples. Ralda halted to steady himself and held on tightly to my arm. He was getting weaker every day. His eyes were drooped with fatigue, face creased with worry or sadness, I could never tell.

"With the Felradian halkateiy relentlessly spinning the wheels of the future and redesigning sequences, what begins as a short journey soon becomes a peregrination. It is filled with ups and downs, lows and highs, tears and laughter," he said with a heavy drawl. "What distinguishes the ones who reach their destination to the ones who do not…is tenacity, wit, courage, and heart." He took a long and deep breath, visibly relishing the fresh air.

Then he broke into a song. Yes, out of the blue, but that was Ralda's thing.

* * *

When the Sun god of Light rises,
She rises in her heart and with her rays.
When the Sun god of Light shines,
She shines in her heart and with her rays.
When the Sun god of Light sets...

* * *

He paused and gazed at me studiously, expecting me to do something. When he was met with a blank face, he nudged me. "Sing, chosen-one," he edged.

I cleared my throat in surprise. "I'm not a good singer."

"Humour the old man," he said tiredly. "Sing with me.... When the Sun god of Light sets…"

"She sets in her heart?" I said the words.

"No! Your heart," he corrected, his gaze roving across the endless gown of jewel-blue to our right. For a second, he seemed distracted.

"She sets in *my* heart and with her rays," I said.

He beamed in acknowledgement. Then he spun around and watched Dante and Zaira for a drawn-out moment before staring at the cocktail-blue sky. "Follow my gaze," he summoned, and I stared into the midday sky. "What do you see?"

"Am I now in training?" I had to ask. Ralda was stranger than strange.

"What do you think?" He dearly clutched his walking stick.

I smiled, squinting and shading my eyes from the bright sun. "I don't know what to think," I answered honestly. I never knew if there was a right or wrong answer when it came to Ralda.

"What do you see right above you?"

I hesitated. *The blue sky? The flock of vociferous birds? The yellow sun? Air? Empty space? Nothing?*

"We don't have all moon-day, chosen one," Ralda said. "At this rate, I'll meet the gods before you have answered me." He gazed at me, his face pale and drawn. "You need to learn all you can from me before my time is up."

"The sky," I hastened to answer.

"What else?"

"The Sun…god of Light?"

"Precisely." He smiled then tottered forward, and I matched his strides. "You don't believe in the gods, chosen one."

"Well, I—"

"You're an intellect." He watched me with a grin. "You believe in what you see. The *Sequence of Particles*—physical science. It is not by any way right or wrong. It confirms that you have an active mind. Now, here is a question for you. How many sunrises have you seen?"

"A lot?" I wasn't sure of the answer he was expecting from me.

"Very well." His face was a roadmap of time, each wrinkle seeming to tell an unwritten story of his life. "How many times have you taken a moment to thank the Sun for the gift of light?"

"I am thankful every day," I said easily, unsure where he was going with this.

He squeezed my hand and resumed his doddle forward. "Yes, you are…inside your heart, yet the Sun god of Light does not know that. Hence why our people take a knee to show our thanks—if not for light, for love; if not for love, for life. The Sun god of Light should become your inspiration. She works with precision, timing, and a carefully aligned sequence." He smiled like he knew something I didn't. "She rises with her rays, beams with her rays, and sets with her rays in a faultless sequence that will take us a lifetime to understand." His voice trembled. With his free hand, he gripped my arm. "Are you with me?"

I nodded, wondering exactly where this conversation was leading. His expression gave no clue as to what he was alluding to.

"What we all see is a seamless sunrise, a flawless midday sun, and a spectacular sunset, yet what we do not see is what transpires after sunset behind the veil of darkness, when she's all alone, without anyone to lean on." He strode for a while, and I followed suit. Our slow movements sounded like soft whispers in the sand.

The sun has to be my inspiration? Okay, I got that, but why?

"An astute mind should constantly be asking questions that are beyond questionable." He squinted in deep contemplation. "How does the Sun god of Light continue to fight for her sequence? How does she maintain her alignment? How does she ensure that the land is alight every single moon-day without fail?" He paused to catch a breath. "Is her sequence aligned entirely to love of the land, or is she keeping a promise to life?"

"If I ask, will I be expecting an answer?" I asked in a low voice.

Musing, he ran his hand across his grey lengthy hair. "I know young ones find me exhausting." He patted my hand lightly.

"Er, not really—"

"The morale of my words is all about tenacity. The answer should come from within. If the Sun god of Light has fought for millions of moon-years for her sequence and still managed to keep the land alight...so can you, chosen one. You will fight for your sequence until the sequence becomes you. And when the sequence becomes you, only then will you keep it in a seamless alignment."

Really? Okay! What sequence, now? What alignment? Ralda was a man of great sagacity, but some of the words he said didn't make sense whatsoever.

"Sequence is used every day in this land, I get that, but I still can't work out exactly what you as the Voice of Sequence mean by sequence?" I should have asked him this long back, but now was a good time as any. He had a deeper way of thinking, and as the Voice of Sequence, perhaps he could explain fully what I had been trying to figure out on my own. Whether I'd get an answer that made sense was something else entirely.

"Sequence is your great ancestor's legacy. From the teachings of one great halkateiy, sequence is as complex as a pyramid and as simplistic as a triangle." He looked to the distance where jagged mountain peaks pierced the sky. "Beyond the mountains lies the answer to your heritage." He smoothed his hand over his forehead. "Sequence is a natural order of elements, thoughts, and beliefs that brings about a nation. It is a journey from birth to death, a path from genesis to exodus, a number from one to infinity. A sequence never ends. It rejuvenates, refreshes, and rekindles with time. It adapts to new players, observers, and spectators."

I was even more lost than I had been before.

"Chosen one, this is all you need to know. There's a sequence to life, love, and death, yet the winds of destiny are not team players." He took a breather, staring at length at the endless blue ocean. "There are rules to an aligned sequence, yet the hand of destiny does not play by the rules. With the Felradian halkateiy continuously churning the wheels of the future, today you could be swimming blissfully in the ocean. Tomorrow you could be dragging your feet in the heart of the desert." He stood still and appeared to be reminiscing about something.

His eyes seemed a shade darker today. Something was eating at him; that was evident.

"A walk in fine sand is better suited to those with longer strides, chosen one," he said, rubbing his left temple gently. "But if you have short legs, you must improvise."

For a short while, we strode across the moons' glow-white beach at a leisurely pace. Ralda's full-length ivory robe left a trail as it scooped some sand into the air. The salty tang fused with the sweet fragrance of sunshine hung in the air. Every so often, I swung my gaze to him. He was a man of a very small build, but his wisdom and profundity was enormous.

"Your training will not be as undemanding as a walk along the beach, chosen one," Ralda started with an intonation in his voice. "Your gifts are immense. As such, your responsibilities are colossal. Time to ease you gently into your new role is time we do not have. I want you to be fully prepared for the task at hand. The shield of our ancestors is a complex mass of energy that is powerful enough to protect and destroy. That energy is in you! You have the power to give life, and take life."

That doesn't sound good! My heart grew heavy.

"In the moving forest of the Nadeira, you discovered the power of your mind and witnessed with your own eyes what you are capable of. The energy in you is an unrivalled mass of unstable and fizzing air that needs to be carefully controlled." He took a short breather. "So are your human emotions, for they both go hand in hand."

With a wavering gait, he turned around and glanced back at Dante, Zaira, and Tan-tan. Gradho seemed to have made an early exit.

"I have a good eye for a Sequence of Hearts, and I have asked the young Larize to accompany you for this training."

A frisson of excitement slithered down my spine. I almost let out a whoop of elation. Control my emotions—yeah, like that was easy! Dante brought out every emotion in me, including some emotions I never knew I had.

"I do not wish to rob you of your youth, your happiness, or your Sequence of First and Forever. That is not the way of our people. I want your mind fully at peace when we unleash the power in you. Do you understand?"

I nodded, perhaps a bit too eagerly, and smiled. *Dante's coming with me!* All my earlier nerves and worries vanished in an instant.

"However," Ralda said. There was always a but somewhere; I knew that now. "Should the young Larize become a distraction, I will have no choice but to ask him to leave."

"He won't be a distraction. I promise!" But I didn't think it was entirely true. I tore my gaze away from Ralda and settled on Dante's twinkling eyes. He was smiling at Zaira. With his red shock of hair glinting to the midday rays and creating a beguiling contrast to his sun-kissed skin, he was a constant and persistent distraction. *Distraction? Maybe not. Focus? Yes. He's my focus!*

"Are you still in my world, chosen one?"

I nodded, realising how easy it was to drift away from the present issue of the weakening shield and the untamed energy in me. I had been sceptical about the whole thing of being the "chosen one" at first, but now I had to face facts. I wasn't crazy. I wasn't normal either. There was something inside me that was more powerful and stranger than crazy or normal. Yes, I had seen it, so there was my proof, but what I didn't know was its trigger—its depth—its profundity—its limits.

"Now heed my words. The future of this land is shaky. Without the shield, there is no future for our people. Your priority is the land." He took a breather, leaning into his walking stick. "Every action you take from now on should be in the best interest of many! You will say your farewells to your family." His tone hung somewhere between fatigue, perseverance, and thoughtful contemplation. "At dawn, you will leave house Serenius as a girl and will return as the mother of the land and the Custodian of the Ocean Crown!"

My stomach knotted. That sounded a bit too heavy for me. *I'm seventeen!* But I merely settled my gaze into the distance where the ocean and the sky fused and melted into one. Such was the staggering beauty of the kingdom under the moons meshed with the uncertainty of what lay ahead.

3. POWER OF MIND

The next morning, the majestic Tuscanian dawn carved the horizon in an enchanting yellow-red that kept me enticed and enchanted for an interval. Dressed in a long sky-blue dress, red cloak, and matching cowl, I stood in the sun room, hands crossed in front of me. The fresh scent of morning flowers fused with salted ocean air filled my nostrils, refreshing and calming, yet my mind was troubled. *How do I say farewell to my family...my home?*

"Goodbyes are never easy, velici." Zaira's velvet voice sounded from behind.

I spun around, gazed at my grandma, tears brimming my eyes. "They get harder every t-time." My voice cracked.

She opened her arms wide, a warm smile gracing her face. I took a few loping steps towards her and threw my arms around her. Her ivory satin gown brushed against my cheek, soft and lulling.

"You're a Serenian," she whispered. "This is your sequence. You'll make the best of what the gods have given you."

"I'll m-miss you, Grandma."

She held me for a fraction longer in silence. "You're a living flower of our house—a bloom of our Sequence." She stroked my back, her words lulling. "The beauty of your exceptional fragrance is immense; it will linger in our house, in our hearts, and in our lives until you return to us." We embraced for a moment longer, and she drew back. "Your grandfather is much more emotional than you are this morning," she said as the

33

sound of footsteps echoed beyond the double-glazed doors that led into the sun room. "You'll have to stay strong for him."

There was an edge to her voice, something you didn't hear every day from Grandma. Despite her composure, she was a tad more nervous than I was. The knowledge that Dante was coming with me was enough to keep my nerves at bay, yet it couldn't quell the pain of saying goodbye.

"Velici!" Blamorey made firm and brisk steps towards me. "Are you ready for your destiny?" he joshed, his voice tinged with paternal humour.

"No." I shook my head, smiling. "Not really."

"Great answer." He curved his arms around me and hugged me close, serious now. "Learn all you can. Live all you can. Love all you can." His voice cracked. "Return to us wiser, stronger… just return to us." He drew back and gazed into my eyes. "May the winds of Sequence guide you through the right path."

"Thank you, Granddad." I threw my arms around him and embraced him tighter.

Looking back, this was the first time that I had said good-bye to my loved ones. My parents' deaths had hit me hard. One moment we were celebrating my greatest achievement, winning the Young Violinist of the year, the next, Mum was dead and Dad was in intensive care, fighting for his life. Even though Dad had said goodbye to me on his deathbed, it was not the same. That wasn't farewell. That hurt. Then Isle Speranza happened, and even then, I couldn't say goodbye to Aunt Kate or my cousins. Now, they'd forever wonder what happened to me. As the thoughts flooded into my mind, my stomach churned.

After we said our goodbyes to my family, at first light, Ralda, Dante, and I left house Serenius. I had packed a decent-sized bag of essentials, which had proved difficult. I didn't know when I'd be coming back. Worryingly, Zaira held back tears when I bid her final farewell.

At the gate, three snow-white ewies and a wagon were

already in position. With the sun beaming through the morning skies, the ewies looked spectacular, their white coat gleaming gently in the sun's rays. Dante swung his arms around me and placed me on the smaller winter-white ewie before assisting Ralda onto his. One *dreyri*—helper—loaded our bags into the wagon in silence. I glanced at the dragon-shaped gate with admiration. There was something enchanting about the gate design against the heavenly white walls. I nodded my goodbyes to four protectors, who bowed their heads in return. My heart skipped at the prospect of what lay ahead. *How will I ever know that I'm ready—*

"Chosen one," Ralda startled me. "When you can tame the Rindigas of Sequence, only then will you know you're ready to fulfil your Sequence." He stared at the dragon gate, keeping his gaze steady.

"Oh. Oh!" I exclaimed, finally catching up to Ralda's statement. "Rindigas of Sequence!" I puffed out a laugh, realising exactly what he was alluding to. Forget that he'd just been inside my head. "You mean dragons?" I avidly turned to Dante, risking tumbling off the ewie. My eyebrows rose, forehead crinkled. "There are dragons in Zeneshia?"

"If I were you, I would not be too excitable, chosen one." Ralda stroked his ewie. "These are not dragons."

"They look like dragons," I said with zest.

"Myth suggest they're the same family, Lessi," Dante said in a calm voice, mounting his ewie. "They're not quite the dragons you're thinking about. Perhaps a crossbreed between dragons and dinosaurs." He slid into the saddle with ease.

"Well said, Larize." Ralda turned to me. "Rindigas are notorious, flesh-eating, mind harvesters and the most feared predator of our world." He held onto the reins, getting ready to motion his ewie forwards. "They are the original 'dragonsaurs' of your world."

"Dragons are not real, Voice of Sequence." I beamed. "Dinosaurs, yes, but not dragons. They never were."

Ralda gazed at me with piercing hazel eyes. "You have a multitude to learn, chosen one. Now heed my words. All life began in the deepest depths of the Four Oceans of the Surging Tide. The world beneath the ocean is not real to your fellow earthians, but here we are." He grinned.

Like always, I appreciated that he had a point. But 'dragon-saurs'? No. Not that point.

"If you had spent some time with the favoured house from Felradia, house Regai-Rallias, you'd soon have been enlightened."

"They're not ones for small talk, Voice of Sequence." My mind drifted back to Lavia's family. House Regai-Rallias disliked me. In Gradho's words; Lavia and her family had every right in the Four Kingdoms to detest me because I had unknowingly thieved their seven moon-year agreement from them by falling in love with their Foretold Sequence to the Ocean Crown. Absurd? Yes, sad but true. "Certainly not with me." I swung Dante a look, but I couldn't read anything from his face.

"House Regai-Rallias are not ones to give up on their foretold sequence. Your paths will cross again."

"If rindigas are feared this much, why are they designed into the—"

"All generations of house Serenius have been known for their fearless courage, hence why Rindigas of Sequence mark the entrance to your home. A reminder that all Serenians are born of bold and noble blood."

All along, I thought the dragon-shaped gate was simply an imaginative design. Now I stood corrected. "They live in the wilderness?" My voice was barely above a whisper. "Is it wise to be going out into the forest?"

"Face your fears, chosen one. Your first lesson of the moon-day." He scratched his forehead. "Settle your mind. Within the boundaries of our ancestors' shield, we're safe."

For the first part of the day, we journeyed on ewieback

until we reached a mountainous terrain. A cold burst of wind rose and circled around us like a whirlpool. We dismounted and prepared to continue the journey on foot. Ewies were not ideal for the hilly region. I wrapped my cloak around me more tightly. A sharp gust of howling wind swept through, tousling my hair and ruffling my cloak. I shivered, inhaling the freezing air.

"Here." Dante outstretched his hand towards me.

"You brought me some gloves?" I asked, surprised.

"The young Larize is not one to take any chances," Ralda said. Bizarrely, neither Dante nor Ralda were affected by the cold. "Not when it comes to you, chosen one." He beamed and broke into a forest song that echoed around the terrain bringing the hills to life.

I smiled at Ralda's take and followed closely behind him. It was strange. For someone who didn't walk that fast, he insisted on being in front, his back hunched against the chilly wind. A journey that should have taken three or four hours at most—my time—took at least double that. Trekking behind Ralda and Dante, I kept expecting a clearing in the forest.

"Welcome to my home, chosen one," Ralda said.

I glanced around. *How can anyone live in the heart of such a dense forest?* The rustle of exotic trees against each other made my heart leap. Layers of lush greenery, fronds of forest-green plants, and bountiful vegetation meandered around us. Thick leaves dangled overhead like cloaks of green in the sky. The trees had huge trunks, like nothing that I'd ever seen before. They were humongous, and the only comparison I could think of was a double-decker bus in London. We were midgets alongside them. *This is like something out of Lord of the Rings; surely it can't be real.*

A path formed as we trooped deeper and deeper into Ralda's forest home infused with a delicious fragrant of wood, pine and vanilla. Suddenly Ralda, and Dante halted, and I bumped into the back of Dante, to his amusement. From the corner of my eye, I noticed some stairs disguised by the forest foliage. Perched among the umbrella trees, it looked like the stairs led to a magnificent nest.

The birdhouse? I smiled, drinking in the unusual yet alluring environment. Gradho's words had some element of truth in them. *Is this a home or a dragon's nest?*

We climbed the spiral wooden stairs that wrapped around the thickest part of the tree until we reached a platform formed out of wooden planks. The timber had weathered over the years, had a dark, mouldy look, but seemed in good shape. The deck was surrounded by a seasoned timber balustrade. Above the decking stood a thatched house with lovely brown doors and window shutters.

I let out a sigh of appreciation. Gradho, the epic, unreliable exaggerator! This wasn't a birdhouse at all but a charming, little, cosy cottage in the trees. The walls, formed from overlapping timber planks, were bonded together to perfection. The planks colour had altered over time to a distinct dark mahogany colour, with moss protecting the wood. A curvy, thick thatched roof completed the awe-inspiring look. It was admirable—oozing character, delicacy, and a soft cuteness that invoked a sense of pride in my people's sense of style.

The dwelling was well hidden. There was no way of expecting a house in the middle of such an expanse of forestry with branches that extended forever. I smiled as the thought of *Tarzan* and *George of the Jungle* came to my mind. *Maybe Dante and I can try and swing from tree to tree…* I suppressed a light laugh.

The house was small, neatly built, and just the right size for a man who lived on his own. *It's a lonely existence, though.* As much as the scenery was postcard-perfect, I wondered how Ralda managed to get all the supplies he needed to survive. Going up and down those stairs was a chore. He had to catch a breath after every two or three stairs.

I stood on the decking. We were part of the forest's majesty, nestled deep in the trees; I loved everything about it. It was a constant reminder of the Tuscanians' pride in their possessions. The basic set-up resonated inside my heart, simple yet sophisticated.

As Ralda opened the door, an unpleasant squeak sounded; the hinges needed oiling. Dante had to bow his head slightly to get in. The door was smaller than average. He seemed so big for this little house. It must have made him uneasy. I stepped in and was struck by overwhelming heat that sent my body into acute thawing. My eyes were drawn to the orange lit fire. The flames danced merrily to their own tune.

"The kitchen is through that door," Ralda pointed out. The tiny kitchen was towards the rear of the house. Inside was a simple solid fuel stove that had seen years of burning. "And, chosen one, you can have that room to yourself. I may be old, but I know young ones like their own space. Larize, you can share the other room with Hyperian."

"You didn't mention there was someone here with you," Dante furrowed his brow with concern.

"He's my helper. He lit the fire…. He can't be far…" Ralda said, gripping his walking stick more tightly. His energy was draining away. "At my age, I couldn't possibly manage to run about fetching supplies and cooking. Hyperian does that for me." Ralda took in Dante's strained expression. "You can lift your guard, Larize. I trust him."

"How long has he been with you?" Dante asked, keeping his cautious hat on.

"For as long as I can remember. He's sworn to secrecy."

I strode towards Ralda and touched his arm. "Can I get you anything?"

"A new set of legs." He smiled, patting my arm. "I need to lie down. Rest is all I need. My home is your home."

The lounge had a small green couch, two walnut wooden chairs in front of the fire, a hard-wearing brown rug, a wooden cabinet and a small table. The fully reticulated wooden chairs caught my attention. The back rests were intricately hand carved into a figural shape, depicting two boys, each holding the moon in the palm of their hands. Curvy tree branch armrests embellished with a dash of green and silver added charm and a vintage look that mesmerised me. The save-the-environment activists—or tree huggers, as my shrink, Mr Tate used to call them—would love this place.

When Ralda left, Dante carried my bag into the small bedroom allocated to me. It had a tiny, single bed in the middle and a little window overlooking the forest.

"It's tidy but small," Dante said.

"It's fit for purpose," I said with a smile.

I sat on a small chair adjacent to the window. The petite dresser looked like it hadn't been used in ages. As I took off my *Red Riding Hood* cloak and my shoes, Dante eased onto the bed opposite me, his gaze fixed on the wooden floor.

"What's bothering you?" I asked.

He took a deep breath, gave a slight smile, and then shook his head. "I don't know." He shrugged, which was so out of character for him. "I have no idea why I feel this edgy, and it worries me. I've just got a bad feeling about it all."

"Like a premonition?"

His lips curved. "I think we have enough of Ralda's foretelling's to keep us occupied for a lifetime."

"Are you uncomfortable being here?" I was slowly turning into my shrink—if you ask more questions in different ways, eventually you'll get the answer you're looking for.

"No, on the contrary. I'm uncomfortable having you here," he said simply. "We're too close to the shield, and we're a long way from home. On my own, I wouldn't care less, but you being here scares the Tregtarian life out of me."

I was silent for some time. "They wouldn't let us come here if we were in any danger," I tried to reassure him.

"I know." He threw me a warm smile and held my hand. "You matter too much for me not to worry. If you had come here without me, I would have lurked in the woods to ensure your safety. I feel like…it's my destiny to protect you, and this milieu makes it pretty difficult." He scanned the room again, his gaze settling on the lengthy branches that hung across the window.

"You're the Larize. You're destined to protect this land—not me."

He gazed into my eyes and stroked my palm for a while, like he was mulling over my words. "You're the Larizon of my heart. You'll always come first, every time." He leaned forward, bent his head, and dropped a light kiss on my forehead. "There will be no Larizon without you. I don't know what I would do if something—"

"I'll be fine. Nothing will happen." I rose up and sat next to him on the bed. "And even if it does, it's the moons' wishes."

A light laugh tore free from his lips and his eyes twinkled. "Since when did you become an advocate for our highest power?"

"From the day I fell in love with you," I said truthfully. "We'll soon be home." I smiled at him.

In return, he dazzled me with his sparkling eyes and a gentle peck on the cheek.

That evening, just before sunset, a middle-aged man entered the living room where Dante and I lounged playing a game of *tso*. Blamorey had taught me to play. It was similar to chess but with slightly different rules.

When he flung the door open, we both swivelled around to look at him. The firewood he was carrying fell with a loud thud onto the floor. His jaw dropped, and he gripped onto the door. His already pale face grew even paler as he stood there, motionless.

"Hello," I said in Zenesh, hoping to break the silence.

"Hello," a nervous voice said, as he knelt to pick up the firewood. He had a quiet, soft, warm tone to his voice.

"I'm assuming Ralda didn't alert you to our visit," I said, and he nodded. "I'm Alessia, and this is Dante, of house Hantaria."

"My Larize," he said, with a slight bow of his head.

Dante rose to his feet. "You must be Hyperian."

"Yes." He nodded, meeting Dante's gaze.

Dante looked at him intensely. "Have we met before?"

"No, I don't believe so, my Larize." His voice was now edgy.

"Call me Dante. Please. Your face seems familiar to me." Dante strode toward him, grabbed the firewood from the floor, and then straightened. "Where do you want this?"

"In the kitchen. Thank you." He was polite, too.

Hyperian was of medium build, probably in his mid-forties. He had a few wrinkles and a short beard on his chin. I kept my smile steady. There was just a hint of warmth about him, or maybe it was the cosy nest-house which made me feel placid inside.

That evening, the four of us had a light dinner in the lounge. Nothing too heavy; just a tasteful bowl of vegetable soup, and a few slices of bread. After dinner, I bid Dante goodnight, and like always, he kissed me on the forehead. He'd decided to sleep in the lounge instead of sharing Hyperian's room. Ralda had not made any objections. Dante felt he could protect me better if he slept in the only room that had a direct door leading to my bedroom.

I didn't know what I could do to assure him that everything would be all right. Clearly, the warrior trait of his Tregtarian side and the self-composed trait of his Tuscanian genes were in conflict. He was placing too much responsibility on his shoulders, and there was no way of convincing him otherwise.

Instead of getting enough sleep, I twisted and turned, unable to get him out of my mind. Whilst he worried about my safety, I worried about his happiness. He was my Zeneshian sunrise. In the gloomiest of places, I knew he would always shine. To my heart, he was like the dual moons' glow on a dark and lonely night.

He was my own personal sunlight in a storm. Although I

couldn't always see him, I knew now that he was everything to me. I could never love anyone else the way I loved him, and I vowed to keep myself safe, if not for me—for him!

* * *

A pounding knock woke me up the next morning. *Ralda is up too early. It's not even daylight yet.* I yawned and forced myself to sit up in bed.

"Tuscanians are never late, chosen one!" Ralda called out.

Immediately, I threw the covers off and scrambled to my feet. "I'll be out in a minute," I answered in a croaky voice.

I had a responsibility to my family, and being late was not a good start. "Sorry, Mum," I murmured. She'd given up her world—her home—to save her people, and now I had to finish the job she'd started. I just didn't know how.

I had planned to wake up earlier, before everyone else, but obviously that hadn't gone to plan, and now I was rushing through combing my hair. I grabbed the warmest clothes I could find—two thick robes—and got dressed in layers in less than five minutes. From the mist on the window, it looked like Siberia outside.

In the lounge, I was met by an eager Ralda and a patient Dante, both ready to go.

"I'm sorry I'm late," I apologised, shivering. Dante opened the outside door bringing the sub-zero air inside.

"Very soon, your mind will wake you, even when you don't want to." Ralda picked up his walking stick. "Your mind is the most important aspect of your being. If you can control it to your benefit, and to the benefit of the majority, you will become the master of the Game of Sequence."

We left the warmth of the house and headed outside into the arctic chill. The decking was white with snow. The spiral stairs were like soft, white cushions as we made our way through the morning mist.

"Snow again!" I exclaimed. Tiny flakes brushed my hair. "It's not winter."

"This location is winter all around, Lessi," Dante said.

"And perfect conditions for your training," Ralda said.

I disagreed but knew better than to say anything.

A blanket of snow had covered the land overnight. The sharp breeze pierced through me within seconds. Pulling my robe around my shoulders, teeth chattering, I kept a brave face. Dante and Ralda strolled comfortably, as if the conditions were normal. But it was so bitterly cold!

As much as I tried to endure, I trembled. *Why do we have to do the training now?* I couldn't grasp why we couldn't wait until later, but I knew my manners—I wouldn't ask until it was necessary. Dante kept throwing me the look that suggested, I'm-with-you-on-this-but-stay-strong.

We trooped for a short while, going uphill until we reached the top of a hill.

"Sit," Ralda said authoritatively, easing himself to my left.

I kept a straight face out of respect for Ralda and then forced my body into the wet ground. Dante sat on the other side, wearing a serious look. He was inscrutable; I didn't know what was now going through his head.

"Let's be thankful to the gods." Ralda reached for my left hand, and Dante held my right hand. "We're thankful to the moons for constantly beaming on us. You lit the path for the chosen one into our world. May you guide us through this sequence of discovery and save our land so we can forever enjoy peace, love, harvest, and fertility. Amen."

The prayer was short but softening. My eyes watery, the brittle frost penetrated my bone marrow. I was sure of it.

"Your training begins now, and it will end…when you're at one with nature. You're feeling the glacial winds, Alessia. Your mind has the power to keep you warm," he said.

He'd called me by my birth-given name. It would have been great if I wasn't in acute mental and physical pain. Finally, we could at least drop my new unwanted name. *Chosen one.* It was starting to sort of freak me out.

Ralda glanced sideways. "Focus on the horizon. Find that part of you that's controlling you, and control it," he said to my befuddlement.

Surely it was a windup. Staring at him and then at Dante, I opened my mouth to speak, but no words came out. My mind was its own person, I knew that, but I just didn't see how it would keep me warm, or it would have done it already. It was impossible. My mind was frozen. I sat there, waiting for something to happen—but nothing. Minutes felt like centuries. The brittle chill rose inside my body like a tornado. A strange, gelid force of energy whirled inside me.

"I-I-I'm c-cold…" I managed to say. My muscles weakened, and my lips trembled. As for my teeth, I couldn't feel them anymore.

"Concentrate, Alessia. If you don't find that spot in your mind that will release you from the frost…you'll freeze."

With difficulty, I glanced at Dante, and the pain I saw across his face was unbearable. He was worried for me; his fists clenched, and his eyes narrowed. He couldn't disrupt Ralda's bizarre training—that much I knew. Respect and traditions were a big thing in Tuscania. But from the drab look in his eyes, I knew it wouldn't take him long to break his silence.

Tuscanian ethos or not, I was dying a slow death here. *Death by frost,* now that was a plausible possibility! After a few minutes, I could barely feel my hands, and yet my trainer appeared normal—still as a dead dodo. *How are they not feeling the cold?* The brittle chill escaped my trembling mouth. *How can he justify this? It's torture.*

My face numb, my toes were burning from frost. I could hardly speak. As much as I tried to focus on the horizon and find 'the invisible thing', I couldn't. I just couldn't do it anymore. Groaning in agony, I tried to move, but that was equally difficult.

Help me, I wanted to say, but the words never reached my lips.

Tears pierced through my cheeks. Inevitably, I leaned towards Dante.

It must have triggered his cautious side. "Voice of Sequence, enough for today! She can't take it anymore," he commanded, holding me in his arms effortlessly.

"We've just got here. This is necessary, Larize. Her mind will be her saviour long before nature inflicts any harm on her," Ralda reassured.

"And if you're wrong?" Dante countered, wrapping his arms more tightly around me.

"The Voice of Sequence is never wrong."

"She's not ready," Dante pleaded, his eyes on me.

"You have to let her do this on her own. The chosen one was born ready, and the time is now."

Reluctantly, Dante unwrapped his arms from me. My tears had stopped falling by now—probably frozen inside, like the rest of me. Both Ralda and a hesitant Dante helped me sit up on my own again. Without Dante's body heat, the piercing cold was ten times more intense. Their discussing me as if I wasn't there made me more determined to get through this.

Dante was in agony, and if my pain was not enough to help me get through this, then his would be the absolute ignition. I couldn't let something happen to me; he would be devastated. *I can't do that to him. I have to try...*

As I thought through my limited options, a surge of energy wrapped around me. It was the most bizarre experience I'd ever had, and that was saying a lot. At first I thought I must have been hallucinating. I didn't understand what was happening. The hot energy engulfed my body—lifting me up from the ground, literally hoisting me up into the air like a levitating monk.

This energy was new and different. In the forest of the Nadeira, I hadn't felt anything at all. The water had merely mimicked my movements, swirled around, and rippled high and low into the air. Even though it was my doing, I was as much a spectator as the instigator. But now, the energy was doing something inside me.

I was burning from the inside out. Transforming from freezing to almost boiling in an instant, an excruciating pain stabbed my head. I couldn't think straight. I could see Ralda beaming and nodding with much vigour. Dante, shocked to silence, the colour had drained from his face. Wide-eyed, mouth agape, he stared at me like he'd just seen an apparition of some sort.

"Control the energy, Alessia!" Ralda said. "Now that you've found it—hold it—control it. Keep calm. Collect yourself, and regulate your thoughts. Control that part that currently has a hold over you."

I tried to do what he was saying, only I didn't know how.

"I'm really hot," I said, automatically removing my double-layered robes, leaving just my tunic. As I kicked them off above ground, I felt like I was burning from the inside.

"The more reason to control your mind, Alessia. Find that trigger. You must concentrate. You're shifting from one extreme to the other. The end of the beginning is the beginning of the end."

"What?" I wanted to say.

Ralda crossed his palms. "Find it—grasp it—keep it. Regain that equilibrium. It's there somewhere. Find it."

"How can I possibly find it if I don't know what I'm searching for?" I muttered for my own benefit. I was seconds away from screaming—growling—howling in agony. I closed my eyes and searched for the invisible trigger. I told myself that I could do it but no luck. *I can do this. I must do this.* Still no luck. I was getting hotter as the minutes passed.

How much hotter can I get before I die? Again, unbearable agony enveloped me. Hot threads of tears dripped down, scorching my cheeks. Groaning and screaming in anguish, I fell to the ground. Writhing in pain, I saw Dante's horror-struck face from the ground.

His nostrils flaring—eyes blood-red—he voiced his anger in Zenesh. "Enough! You're hurting her!"

"You have to calm down, Larize. She'll make it through!" Ralda's voice was composed.

"You can't expect me to sit here and watch her suffer!"

"You went through a similar training yourself, and yet you're still here—alive and well."

"I was younger. This isn't right," Dante said, his anger building even more.

"You have to trust me. You need to trust the power of her mind."

Their voices seemed distant now, fading away little by little, but now it made sense. Dante had gone through the same training. Willing myself to try harder, I focused on getting through this. I had to try. I had to survive this. I could not let the pain control me.

Closing my eyes, I searched for the invisible. I concentrated. I thought of nothing but that I'd get through this. Gradually, the burning begun to emanate from my body like a passing heat wave. It was surreal.

Ralda's words kept ringing in my head. I knew if I couldn't control this quickly, Dante would end up doing something we'd both regret. I didn't want to start freezing again. I wasn't even sure which one was worse—excessive heat or intensive cold. I couldn't bear seeing Dante suffer because of me.

No, I won't allow it!

Suddenly, an instant release of energy engulfed me, pushing my body against the ground. It was like gravity, pulling me down below—except that there was nowhere to go as I was already on the ground. I lay down taking short, raspy breaths.

And then it was over. I was free of the cold, liberated from the heat—I was free. A minute later, I sat up and then smiled. I felt normal again. I was exactly how I wanted to feel:

warm—calm—happy! I'd done it. Somehow, I reached my ideal temperature.

But deep down, I didn't know how long it would last.

Ralda and Dante just stared at me, lost for words. I didn't say anything for a while either—I couldn't risk losing my focus and going back to either extreme. The old man was wise. He knew what I was capable of. I knew there was something inside me. I couldn't dispute it. This was double confirmation that I was something like Superman or Wonder Woman, except I felt completely normal, like Lois from *Lois and Clark*.

"You're doing well," Ralda encouraged. "If you can hold it for longer, you won't have to concentrate that much. By the time we're finished today, it should become as natural as breathing." He smiled.

I didn't respond, continuing to focus until my muscles unwound, and my whole body relaxed in return. I glanced sideways at Dante. "Are you okay?" I asked.

He took a deep breath, followed by a hint of a smile. "You're asking me? I'm not the one having a near-death experience."

"If you're able to speak and continue to hold it, you're almost there," Ralda said.

"How're you feeling?" Dante asked.

"Better than before," I replied, casting another quick look at him. "You?"

"Better than before."

We both laughed. It was a surreal experience. I could see the frozen leaves, hear the brittle wind churning…but what I felt was warmth, peace, and calm. This was Zeneshia—where the impossible was possible.

We sat there as the sun began to rise. The brilliant rays beamed above us, a stunning display of red, yellow, and orange hues over the snow-picked mountains. Ralda had asked me to maintain my temperature until he said otherwise. It was now easier to do it without trying too hard. His patience was incredible.

It didn't bother him that they were sitting there, waiting for God knew how long. Dante, on the other hand, was calmer now, which made me feel tonnes better. I was thankful that he was there. He was my inspiration, and being able to do this now was not just for me but for him, and hopefully for Tuscania.

After spending almost half the day waiting for Ralda's words, he finally spoke. "You've far surpassed my expectations, chosen one. You can release the energy now."

I stared at him vacantly. "I don't know how to."

"Release your mind from the task at hand," he said wearily. "You'll soon find that the hold is broken."

My mind drifted back to my childhood days and the fourteen good years that I'd spent with my parents. As if by magic, I felt in total control of my body and mind.

"It's time you went back home." Ralda lethargically rose to his feet. "Training is over for today," he said, staggering towards the opposite direction to where we had come from. "You two can find your own way. I'll see you at dinner."

"Where are you going?" Dante asked.

Ralda didn't answer. He just began humming his favourite song again and didn't look back. He was as strange as they came.

Around us were cobalt-blue leafed trees sprinkled with flakes of snow. The brown tree trunks were smooth and pleasing to the eye. The contrasting hues of blue, white, and brown created an enchanting beauty that made all the pain of training worthwhile. Crystals of snow sprinkled over Dante's hair, which heightened the colour of his eyes to an arresting shade of burgundy.

After some time of walking back home, every step became more than a chore. Burned out, my legs heavy, I dragged them across the blue-and-white forest wonderland, fatigue finally settling in.

"I can carry you if it'll help," Dante said.

"Is it that bad?"

"I feel so helpless, Lessi. I'm here for you…with you." He bit his lip. "But I'm not really able to help or make this any better for you."

"It's over now." I tucked my hand into his. "You don't need to help me every time. I must help myself. Hopefully, something good will come out of it," I said as we continued trudging through the forest.

Because of the excruciating pain, a tiny part of me wanted to give up, but another part didn't want to be a failure, especially when the consequences of my failure would be felt by thousands of people.

When we reached the spiral wooden stairs, I sighed. *What an exhausting day. If this is only the beginning, what's next?*

Dante stopped and held my face in his hands. "For the second time, you gave me a fright, Lessi. Honestly, I don't know how I can cope with the rest of your training." He glanced up towards Ralda's nest as if planning an escape.

With me, I hoped. We could run away like star-crossed lovers. I gazed into his glinting eyes. "It was hard trying to find something I couldn't see."

"You did great." He dropped a soft peck on my forehead. "I'm glad today is over, but I fear what tomorrow will bring."

"I fear what the day *after* tomorrow will bring if I fail."

"You won't fail. Today assured me of that. It's the pain you'll go through that bothers me. He drew in a deep breath. "It takes people moon-years of training to master that amount of energy, it took me the best part of a moon-year to master it and yet, it took you half a moon-day. That's profound."

"That scares the life out of me." I bit my lip. "If I can do it that quickly, that only confirms there's something wrong with me."

He shook his head. "There's something inside you that's strong, precious and right. I always knew you were special from the moon-night I met you, and in the forest of the Nadeira you proved it, but today…you smashed all the levels of special."

"I'm glad you were there with me," I said tiredly.

"I wish I could say the same. I was ready to pick you up and carry you back home. As stupid as it sounds, I just couldn't sit there and watch you suffer. But the moons were looking down on us. Before I did something that I'd end up regretting, you surprised me." He stroked my cheek with his right hand, his touch leaving a warm tingly trail on my face.

The sensation was beautiful, and I never wanted it to end. I laid my hand on top of his and tilted my head so I could soak in more of his warmth. For a moment, we stood still, listening to the quiet sounds of the bewitching forest.

"Of all the gifts I've witnessed in this land, I've never seen anything like what you're able to do," he said. "First you swept into our lives, *my life,* like the goddess of light. Then the Rise of the Red Ice Smoke. Now this. What you've accomplished today is amazing." His vinous-red eyes held me captive, bathing me in a sea of his love for me.

I flashed him a smile. I was one blissful captive, a captive to him, his love, and his world.

He smiled warmly and dropped a light kiss on my nose. Seconds later, he drew me towards him and cuddled me close. His lips brushed my neck, his voice silky and smooth. "You're a girl of astounding substance and one of a kind, Lessi. I am honoured to be loved by you. Don't you ever forget that!"

"When I'm old and wrinkly and my mind has since ceased to function, I might just forget." I teased.

He tightened his arms around me and enveloped me snuggly in a warm hug, his breath caressing my neck. "Then I'll make it my lifetime quest to remind you of my love, every moon-day, every moon-night, and every moon-week of our lives."

I returned his hug and buried my head in his chest. His heartbeat reverberated against my cheek. I didn't know if it was fatigue or something about the 'birdhouse' in the magical forest, but this embrace felt so precious I didn't want it to end. Three things were certain: I had a destiny, I had a sequence, and I had him. I could stomach losing everything else. I just couldn't bear the thought of losing him.

So I held onto him, my body moulding effortlessly against his, absorbing all of him. A torrent emotion consumed me, and my eyes misted. I pulled him towards me just a fraction closer. The flavourful forest breeze whistled a symphony around us, as if in cheer to our Sequence of First and Forever.

"What in the moons' name could be the matter, Lessi?" he whispered against my neck.

I swallowed back my tears. "I just need you to hold me forever and never let go."

It was a simple enough request, yet something inside me told me to cherish every second of our time together.

He puffed a light laugh and tightened his hold. "I think I can just about manage that, Lessi."

4. Death by flying door

Following an exhausting day, I retired to bed early. By the time the sun dropped below the horizon, I was shattered—drained of any form of energy I still possessed. Dante stayed with me until I fell asleep.

With fatigue kicking in, I didn't hear him leave my room. I slipped into oblivion, but my dreams were troubled.

In a forest, a starless black curtain blanketed the heavens in an eerie mask. Dazed, I twirled around multiple times. Ethereal mountains loomed in all directions a mere few hundred metres away from where I stood. Nothing seemed familiar. *Where am I?* My heart lurched and threatened to burst out of my chest.

My eyes flickered back and forth. A loud noise screeched. I ran, but my legs were not cooperating. I kept looking back, but I couldn't see who or what was coming. I ducked under the low-hanging branches. A hissing sound lacerated through the air. I plodded along. *Run!* I quickened my pace but tripped and fell hard onto the ground, hitting my head. Blood gushed out of my forehead. I lay in a pool of blood, unable to move.

From a distance, Dante rushed towards me. When I tried to reach out to him, he vanished. The trees crackled, and tree branches swayed like wind-snakes in the night. A thick branch fell and missed my head by an inch.

Startled, I woke up with a jerk, drenched in cold sweat!

Just a dream. I drew in a heavy breath. A piercing pain shot through my eyes. *Please let it not be a migraine.* I touched my pulsating head and exhaled. Eyes wide, a tinge of relief washed through me before a stringent noise inside the house made my heart almost pop out of my chest. Heavy footsteps and the screeching sounds of furniture being dragged on the floor rose into the air. My breath caught.

Thud. Thud. Thud! The noises emerging from the lounge were loud. I leaped out of bed. Bloodcurdling shouting and screaming echoed inside the small house. "Hurry! Hurry! Tie him up!" a menacing voice bellowed. My insides turned. I didn't recognise the voice. "Bring the human."

For a second, I numbly stared at the door, clutching my blanket tightly to my heaving chest. Droplets of sweat accumulated on my forehead. The thundering sound of furniture hitting the wooden floor filled the air. Fear gripped me. My insides froze. Panic-stricken and terrified, I managed to shift my rigid body and hid underneath the small bed, shaking.

"Where is she?" an angry voice shouted.

"Have you checked all of the rooms?" another one bellowed.

My heart skipped. My legs turned into jelly. My breath rasped in my throat. I waited. Waiting for what? These people were searching for me. *Who are they? How did they find us? Where are Dante and Ralda?*

The sound of the bedroom door opening rendered me motionless, frozen. A numbing chill trickled across my back. My palms sweating, I prayed for this nightmare to end. Sadly, this wasn't a dream anymore.

Three men garbed in heavy grey cloaks stomped in. In a trickle they had found me. Tremors consumed my body as if death had caught up with me except I could still hear my palpitating heart.

"She's here!" one of them shouted, his face mere inches from mine.

"Fear is worse than death, human girl?" another man drawled, bending to look under the bed. "Much worse." His grating voice made my limbs shake. He was middle aged, and his eyes were a shade of dark-hazel.

They pulled me out, lugged me forward, and carried me like a sack of potatoes. One man held my upper body, and another supported my legs. Tears trickled down my somber face. They brought me into the lounge. Four men gritted their teeth, struggling to lift Dante. My stomach knotted. His eyes were closed; he wasn't conscious.

"Dante!" I cried, but there was no answer. "Dante! No. No. No!" My arms and legs flew in all sorts of directions. "Dante... Dante...What have you done to him!"

"Don't waste your breath. If I were you, I'd stop being hysterical and consider my own fate," one of the men, older than the others, tall and average-built, harshly commanded. He was obviously in charge. "Maybe this will help." He roughly tied a cloth across my mouth. My hands were tied behind me, legs, too.

They shoved my head into a dark hood. Gloom covered my eyes. I lost my fight. Tears falling, I was forcibly dragged out of the house into the cold, silent night. The last thing I remembered was being thrown onto a frigid metal surface before I blanked out.

* * *

When I woke up, darkness blanketed my vision. Motionless, I lay on the floor, hands and legs untied. My head throbbed. The pounding felt like my brain was trying to make its way out. I cringed and tried to sit up. No luck. My rigid body seemed foreign. I darted a glance around, shivering. More darkness.

"Dante," I called, hoping I wasn't alone.

No one answered.

"Dante!" My whispers echoed in the silent room. "Dante." Again there was no answer.

I turned my head sideways. Eerie gloom enveloped the dwelling. An unnerving hush cloaked over me. Night sounds were non-existent. A stale stench filled my nostrils. My throat tightened. A cold chill ran through me. It dawned on me that I was alone. My breath hitched. I didn't know what time it was, nor even how long I had been unconscious. My abduction played up in my mind. I remembered being taken from Ralda's house and Dante lying down. I didn't know whether he was dead or alive. My heart shattered.

"He's got to be all right," I murmured. My voice scared the life out of me. The room was so quiet. *He has to be okay.*

A ball of fear formed in the pit of my stomach and rose to my chest. I was now at the mercy of god knows whom. The warring Tregtarians—the dreamers of Felradia—the sleeping ones? I couldn't believe the people I'd come to love—the Tuscanians—could be that brutal. Why would they?

I sat up. My hands shook as I crawled towards the edge of the room. Once my palm touched the surface, I tried to work out what it was. It was rough—ragged and cold.

A sharp object slit my palm. "Ouch!" I cried and leaped back. Raw, trickling blood dripped onto the ground. Gritting my teeth, I clenched my fist, hoping to stop the blood from seeping through.

More carefully this time, I ran my hands over the wall again, taking in the texture until I felt a smooth wooden surface.

A door. I reached for the handle and tried to open it. No luck. It must have been locked from the outside. I leaned against the door, my loose curls drenched in my tears that still trickled down. I didn't know how long it would take before they dried out.

"L-Let me out, please! P-Please let me out!" I cried, pounding the door with my fist—my good fist. Still, silence. "C-Can you at least tell me what you want?" My voice wavered. "Someone, p-please tell me what you want from me!" I blurted, tears gushing down like raindrops falling off a leaf.

My eyes stung. I squinted and used the back of my hand to wipe them. The situation was hopeless. I shut my eyes in frustration. When I opened them, I turned around and tried to see through the darkness. Shadows swirled around my feet. I gazed up. The tiniest of windows sat at the top, well out of reach. It was night time. A faint burst of light gleamed through from the silent moons.

"Thank you," I muttered, and sighed. It wasn't as dark now. The East Star god of peace was somewhere up there—just watching.

There was no bed or chair. The room was claustrophobic. *What do I do now?* I tapped my feet on the floor. *How do I get out of here?* After agonizing about what I should do and realizing that there was nothing I could possibly do, I decided to sit it out until someone came for me.

I lay down next to the door but couldn't settle enough to get an ounce of sleep. The bumpy and cold floor chilled my skin and pierced through my resolve. The night dragged, prolonged by my troubled thoughts. I was finally happy in Tuscania—totally at peace with myself and everyone around me. Until now!

I can't do this anymore... How many times do I have to go through uncertainty and distress?

The only thing that kept me going through the night was the thought that it would be daylight soon. Hopefully, I could plan my escape when I could see a bit more clearly. I just had to wait. The next morning, the silvery daylight shone through the round little window, cutting askew on the ragged walls. At least I could see more of the room, thanks to the rays of light shining across the empty space. The walls were made of stone, like someone had dug into a cave and welded a door onto the opening.

A much more pronounced musty stench wafted through the confined space. The wait was unbearable. The entire agonizingly longest day of my life I expected someone to come, but no one did. I sat dejectedly, my head resting on my knees. Hungry, thirsty, and suffering from complete mental and physical fatigue, I curled into tiny ball, tears cascading down my cheeks.

After the sun had escaped into the heavens, a glimmer of hope shone through as the sound of footsteps emerged from beyond the door. Rays of light gleamed through the door threshold. I listened attentively, hoping to learn the identity of my captors—but I couldn't read their thoughts.

I staggered to the door, formed a cup-shaped opening out of my palm before leaning against the door, but all I could hear was my racing pulse. I took my hand off and placed my ear directly in between the joints in the door. Then there were soft whispers. I tried to focus my mind to make sense of their thoughts again, but I kept hitting a brick wall.

I heard the shuffling of keys and I waited anxiously for the door to be opened. Instead, a key went through a flap door at the bottom side of the door, and a wooden plate of food was shoved through it, followed by a chalice of water.

I slumped to the floor and outstretched my hand. Before I could grab my captor's arm, the small opening closed shut vigorously. Frustrated, I kicked the plate with so much force I screamed in agony.

"Ouch!" I held my foot and limped towards the edge of the room then plunged to the ground. It was clear; I was a prisoner, and for whatever reason, they needed me alive—for now.

Surely I couldn't be in captivity in my alternate reality, too. Punished in both worlds. First, it was the mental asylum at Isle Speranza and now, here. *What have I done to deserve this burden in both lives?*

I reached for the plate and tasted the remainder of the thick substance that was meant to be food. The awful taste made my stomach turn; it was like eating rubber. After taking a couple of spoonfuls, I gave up and drank the water instead.

The second night in my newest prison, I struggled, cycling in emotional turbulence. Was Dante still alive? Just the thought made me shudder. The heart-wrenching feeling of being let down by the people I had begun to trust and love in a very short space of time threatened to overwhelm me. It was like a sharp knife had been shoved into my brain.

The pain in my throat made it impossible to swallow. I needed to escape. I *had* to escape. Through the night, I engineered a plan to free myself. I intended to grab onto my captor's hand through the flap door and fight him until he yielded and handed the keys to me. It wasn't a great plan, but I was out of options. The next day came and went, and by the time my plate was shoved through the door, I was too weak to move.

My ability to maintain emotional balance diminished by the day. I cycled between tears—depression—disbelief—anger—denial. I had lost control of my life; my life was controlling me. I spent agonizing hours gazing at the damp, forbidding, hard walls.

This experience was just too ghastly. There was not enough lighting. The walls were caving in on me. No toilet. Just a creepy hole dug into the ground. The next couple of days were the worst. A hollowness had settled deep inside my chest. I went through various emotions without any ability to control how I was feeling. One minute I was crying, the next I was staring vacantly at the ground until my eyes were sore. My body ached. My physical discomfort added to my torture.

Sometimes I used the little energy I had to hit the stone walls with my hands, but I only hurt myself in the process. Using a piece of broken stone, I wrote on the walls to keep count of the days. I thought of my thirty-one days at the mental institution on earth and how I had managed to escape. My fate had been leading to this, from one prison to another. Just like *Final Destination*, there was no escaping fate.

On day five, the door squeaked and opened for the first time. A masked man emerged from the dark corridor. The sound of his boots echoed with each step he took. He was short, average built and dressed in a deep-green robe. *Who are you?* I couldn't get the words out. His gaze caught mine as I lay on the ragged ground. My energy reserves had wilted away. Worn out, I could hardly bring myself to move or speak to him. My tears had dried up; I had accepted my fate. It was time to say good-bye to this life.

I tried to keep my eyes open, but they were shutting down. As I waited for him to drag me out, he hauled an old man through the door instead. Throwing him vigorously onto the ground, he showed no care or humanity. The old man's clothes were in tatters, and he had bruises all over his face and arms. He looked like he had been dragged through the dust for a long time. My captor left him lying helplessly on the stone-cold floor next to me and marched right out before shutting the door.

The next sound was of two bowls of food and water being shoved through the small opening at the bottom of the door.

The old man grimaced in pain, and it looked like he could hardly move. *I have to help him.* I wriggled on the floor, but it was a struggle to get up. I took a deep breath and scrambled to my feet. Halfway up, my knees shuddered. A surge of hot energy engulfed me. My pulse jumped. Inevitably gravity dragged me down. I hit the floor and lost consciousness.

When I woke up, I was still imprisoned. Nothing much had changed except that my companion sat next to me, dabbing a small, wet cloth across my forehead.

"How are you?" he asked, lips pressed.

A throbbing pain roared through my head, excruciating. "M-My head." I touched my forehead. The air was much more condensed now. The smell of smoke wafted through the air. A small fire was burning next to us. *How did he manage to light a fire?*

"You took quite a nasty fall. You could have died."

My slight frown doubled up the pain inside my head. "It seems a better option than being here," I muttered under my breath.

"Wrong!" he bellowed like I had wronged him. "Death only comes once. When it does, it doesn't give you a warning. Even when you're thrown into the pit of fire, you have to refuse to burn!"

I stared at him with confusion. "Do you know who I am?"

"Even if you were my daughter, I would tell you the same. If you're still alive, you should yearn to live." He dabbed the fabric into the water on his lap before placing the cloth on my forehead.

"Thank you," I said. "Where did you get the water from?"

He didn't answer. I swallowed a thick lump in my throat. "How did you manage to light a fire?"

"Being in captivity is a path of your sequence. It's not your death. Even the most unmerciful of captors can be bargained with. Now we have water and a fire." He nodded and then wiped his own brow. "There's nothing more final than death. Being here is not final. There are always opportunities to better your life, if you believe."

He was quite the preacher, except I wasn't in a believing mood.

"If I believe," I said slowly. "I've tried that already. It doesn't work."

"Try harder!" he snapped.

"There's no point! It's not as if either of us is getting out of this alive." My voice wavered.

"You don't know that. Your life is your own—you choose your own destiny. Don't let anyone choose it for you."

Despite my fatigue and depression, I smiled. Zaira had told me something similar.

"Drink this." He handed me a chalice of water.

"Thank you." I appreciated that he wasn't my enemy. "How long have I been asleep?"

"Two moon-days." He turned his thoughtful hazel eyes on me.

"May I ask who you are?" My throat tightened.

"Sianze of house Prandroni is the name." He bowed his head slightly.

"Alessia Appleton." I bit my lip. Maybe I should have said Alessia of house Serenius. Perhaps that would mean something to him. Glad to have someone to talk to, I cleared my sore throat, and grimaced. An acute and burning pain pierced through me. "H-How did you get here?"

"I was captured from my home three moon-nights ago," he said.

"I'm sorry." I paused. "Do you know who's holding us?"

"I'm sure we'll find out one moon-day." He smoothed his long, white beard.

So much for preaching; he was now providing some very brief answers.

"Do you think they'll let us go?"

"You ask a lot of questions." He took another short pause. His eyes narrowed. "If we can bargain with them, perhaps. Every sequence has a price."

"I don't understand."

"How could you?" He startled me with his authoritative voice. "Do you know the fundamental mistake you made?"

"I suppose you're about to tell me." I lifted my eyebrows.

"You gave up. You can hardly fend for yourself. I want you to learn something..." He poured some more water into the chalice and then pointed at me. "You should always fight to the end. Never give up just because you're in a situation you can't control. This world might look peaceful, but there's darkness lurking on the horizon." He took a deep breath. "Now, you'll finish this food and regain your strength—your hope—your courage—your faith." His hands shook as he brought the spoon to my mouth.

"Have you had any food for yourself?" I asked after taking a couple of mouthfuls. I didn't want him to starve for my sake.

"I've had my portion for today," he said. "You'll eat and find your strength."

After I finished eating, I felt terribly guilty for letting this fragile man help me through something I could have avoided. To escape, I needed strength, and to gain strength, I needed food. It wasn't rocket science...but he was right. I had given up.

"Thank you," I said again.

* * *

The next few days were easier. With Sianze's help, I learnt to accept where I was—what I was—who I was. I regained my energy, hope, and faith day by day. Why he was helping me was a mystery. I had asked him countless times if he knew who I was and why he felt the need to help me. His answer was the same every time; "Focus first. Questions later."

Every evening after our meal of porridge—surprise—we would sit together and meditate. We would face the east and close our eyes for hours. It's not like we had anything else to do, but still; if anyone had asked me if I possessed that tremendous willpower and self-discipline, I would have said a huge, resounding no! Sianze helped me see the world in a different light. He taught me to focus on my emotions.

He had described me as a 'bag of emotion' that had never been packed neatly. He intended to 'tidy me up' for as long as we were imprisoned. He was comical but wise—courageous, too. A true Tuscanian. My emotions had gone from one end to the other.

When I meditated, Sianze would ask me to focus on the time I had spent in the prison and all the feelings that had gone through me. Each day, he made me explore those emotions and how to control them. His teachings were effortless. He was clear sighted. He reminded me of Ralda. Even now, I didn't know whether I should have trusted Ralda or not. Everything had happened so fast I felt cheated of happiness.

Despite my newest composed self, thanks to Sianze, one person I couldn't shake from my mind was Dante. To keep the pain of missing him away, I tried to block him out of my mind but failed. I didn't want to think of him lying helplessly on the floor. I couldn't contemplate any harm coming to him. If he were alive, I knew he'd be searching for me. He would not rest until he found me. And if he were dead—no, I couldn't think of that. I might as well be dead, too.

By the end of the third week, I could control my emotions with ease. It became like second nature. It was natural, as if I had done it for years. Sianze would ask me to cry, and I would, *totally Hollywood style*.

He would ask me to stop, and automatically I would, at just the right time. He would hurt my feelings by bringing back some painful memories of my parents' death and my time at Isle Speranza. As much as it hurt, I could now control whether I got depressed or not.

It was just like magic or a miracle...I was reborn!

* * *

"You've come a long way, young one," Sianze said, reaching for the doorknob. Strange? Lines formed on my forehead. "Controlling your emotions is the only way to have an advantage in any world. Peace of mind is greater than physical peace."

I smiled, heartened by his relentless energy. Not once had he faltered. I thought I had seen self-control, but from him, I had seen something far deeper than that. I couldn't put a name to it.

"If your mind is at peace—you are at peace—your sequence is at peace." He wiped some sweat from his forehead. "What you're now able to do will pave the path for your future. I'm proud of you, young one..." He jiggled the doorknob.

The door is locked, Sianze. I smiled. *They're hardly going to leave it open for us to just waltz right out.*

He smiled, too, and then stared at me for a while. "The second session of your training is complete!"

My stomach squirmed. With a total look of calm, contrary to the surge brewing inside of me, I looked into his eyes. "What do you mean my training is over?" I gritted my teeth.

"Exactly like I said. The second phase of your training is over, Alessia. Your mind can now protect you from yourself.

You're your own worst enemy. This was the most dangerous and excruciating part of your sequenced training," he said, smiling, shaking the knob. When he realised that it was locked, he knocked on the door. "Ralda! It's time!"

My breath caught in my throat before exploding in an out unevenly. "All this torture and heartache was just some form of…training?" I yelled, my eyes almost popping out in anger. My mouth quivering, I crouched back and sank to the ground.

I stared at the markings on the walls. *Twenty-one days! Twenty-one moon-days! All for some form of training.* I shuddered as I clenched my stomach tightly. *That's not fair… It's not fair.*

I swallowed a gulp of air and instantly felt like I was about to choke on it. A trapped bubble of broiling energy whirled inside of me, looking for a way out. I was angry—fuming—but what was happening inside of me was something else, entirely.

I didn't have control over it. I tried to suppress *it*—whatever *it* was—but my body convulsed irrepressibly. I gripped my neck. My throat scorched the life out of me, like someone had started a fire and I couldn't put it out.

My eyes fixed at the door, my body cemented to the floor, I watched thunderstruck as the door unhinged from the walls and flew towards me with vigorous force. I shut my eyes.

I'm so dead. Suppressing a scream, I raised my arms to shield my face from the blow that would end my life and waited for the inevitable *death by flying door.*

But a surreal silence descended instead. In the quiet chaos, I heard the tinkling sound of bolts and hinges dropping onto the floor. I opened my eyes and saw the door floating inches from my face.

Scared to breathe, let alone move, I froze in time. A second later, the door plummeted to the floor with a thundering thud, which sent me flying in the other direction. I gasped for air, trembling. I glanced at Sianze, and he was motionless, unreadable.

Mouth agape, I stared at the entrance and noticed Ralda

standing there stock-still, shock-struck. His arm was raised mid-air. The keys dangled in his hand like he was just about to unlock the now non-existent door.

"I suppose I don't need these anymore..." Ralda rattled the keys. "You were chosen to defend, not to destroy, chosen one." His voice was calm and comical. He smiled.

Out of breath, I struggled to fill my lungs with air. "Did I do that?" My voice wobbled.

Who else but the chosen one can do that? Ralda's voice echoed inside my head. He nodded.

Shivering, I accepted fully why strange things kept happening around me. Death by fish—death by glass—the Rise of the Red Ice Smoke—and now, death by flying door.

"C-Can I do that anytime—all the time?" I felt numb inside.

Ralda didn't answer right away. "Only in the land of the ancestors...on the right side of the shield, your powers are limitless but perilous. Beyond the shield, you're as good as an ewie that falls at the weight of its own fur. You could have easily died by your own hand. You unwittingly created a situation in a flash but solved it in a trice. That's why *you* are the chosen one," Ralda said.

"But..."

Forget the fish, the glass, the ice dorm, and the door; I was imprisoned for twenty-one days! I held my head in my hands, failing once again to accept my new life. I just couldn't believe they were capable of that amount of deception. My eyes glistened, and tears cascaded down my cheeks.

Burned out, I stared vacantly at the walls. My anger had been replaced by desolation. The irony was unreal. I'd spent twenty-one days mastering the craft of self-composure, and at the first opportunity to contain myself, I wavered and almost killed myself in the process.

Ralda staggered towards me and then held my hand comfortingly. "It's over now. You endured; you sailed through," he said, his voice breaking. "Now is the time to control those emotions."

I wiped my tears with the back of my free hand, memories of my twenty-one days in hell still fresh in my mind. I took a deep breath to calm myself. "Surely, there must have been an easier way!" My voice broke, too. "Why didn't you tell me?"

"If you knew, you wouldn't have come this far this quickly. The final stage of your preparation will ensure *that*…" he said, pointing at the shattered door, "never happens again unless you want it to. You will learn when and how to control and release the energy within you."

I nodded and then swallowed a thick lump in my throat.

"A person of your gifts requires strength of mind and emotional stability at all times." He helped me rise to my feet. "It's time to go home."

I heaved a sigh of relief. At least it was over.

"Thank you." I bit my lip. A thought that was now bugging me came to my mind. "Was Dante in on your plans?" It was one thing having Ralda toy with my emotions, for love of the land, but quite another knowing that Dante was in on it, too.

"I knew from early on he would not partake in anything that had the slightest potential of hurting you. We had to improvise," Ralda said after a moment.

I beamed. Dante's steadfast love would never falter.

"A tiny component of the Jajaja tree made him drift into a comfortable sleep whilst we executed our plans," he said simply.

My smile vanished, replaced by concern, worry, and confusion. "Is he okay?"

"He wasn't harmed."

I breathed another sigh of relief.

"When we tap into the energy that makes up your power, you'll become the most powerful person in this land and beyond. You have the capability of hurting yourself and the people around you. Only you can prevent that."

"Just training," I muttered under my breath.

At least I'll get to see Dante again. A jolt of excitement went through me. Was he waiting for me at Ralda's birdhouse in the trees? With a slight smile, I traipsed out of the emotional prison, glancing back once and then ahead towards a bright light. *If the Sun god of Light can fight for her sequence, so can I. It's over! There's a light at the end of the tunnel, after all.*

5. THE HEART TO HEART NOTELET

The journey back to Ralda's home in the trees took forever. Welcoming me on the small wooden deck, an aged woman introduced herself as Snodia of house Prandroni, Sianze's wife. I sighed; Ralda had certainly pulled one over on me. He had my abduction all planned and executed meticulously, too. I had been none the wiser.

"You're in need of a hot bath, child," Snodia said, guiding me into the small lounge.

"Sure." I took one whiff of my hair and wished I hadn't. It smelt awful—a bizarre mix of smoke, dirt, and something else I'd rather not know about. I silently scanned the room for Dante—I didn't want him to see me like this. I was a mess.

"Come this way. I have hot water ready for you," she said, holding my hand.

"Thank you."

Following my much-needed bath, I felt fresh but exhausted. Taking a deep breath, I tried to relax, but how could I? The person I wanted to see most of all was not here. It had been at least six hours since being back at the Ralda's house, and I hadn't seen or heard of him.

"Ralda, where is Dante?" I asked as we sat for a light dinner in the small yet cosy lounge.

He raised his head slowly, placing his spoon on the table. "The question is long overdue."

"Is he okay?" I laced my fingers together, bracing myself.

After a moment's pause, he said, "Physically I suppose, yes. Emotionally, perhaps not quite." He pushed the water flagon towards me.

"I can barely grasp what you mean," I said slowly and deliberately.

"After he awoke from his forced sleep, his anger at the severity of your training threatened our cause. We had no choice but to send him away." He picked his spoon up and dug into his *mpunga*—rice mixed with something that tasted like peanut butter.

I furrowed my brow and tugged on my ear. "So he just took off?" *It doesn't make sense.*

"He couldn't bear to watch you deteriorate." His voice was low.

"And he left…just like that?" I muttered. *He wouldn't leave me. Not like that.*

"The Seven Voices of Sequence made him leave." Ralda held his gaze. "It was the right thing to do."

"You sent the Larize away?"

Ralda placed his spoon down and grinned. "He's not Larizon yet. Once the Ocean Crown is on his head, he will do as he pleases. For now, our cause is the priority. If he'd stayed, he would have broken you out before the training was over. That was not an option!"

"So he left me," I said again. I couldn't help myself. When it came to Dante, all bets were off.

"You do understand that his instincts are to destroy anything that has the slightest potential of hurting you." He rested his arms on the small table. "We gave him no choice. It took the Seven Voices of Sequence and a congregation of elders—some who had not left their houses in decades—to force him away."

"Is he coming back?" I shifted my gaze to Hyperian, who was just entering the house carrying some firewood.

"I'm sure he will. A Sequence of Hearts always follows

through." He dished some more mpunga into my plate. "Get plenty of rest for the next few moon-days. We won't begin the next session of your training until you're fully recovered."

* * *

The next few days were quiet. The nights were long and peaceful but also lonely and soothing—and unbearable. The days were better. I spent time perched by the deck, watching the forest foliage. I felt like I was at the very edge of Zeneshia, and beyond that was my previous home, earth. Watching the tree line from above was like looking at a postcard—only this was for my eyes only.

The night sounds from the creepy-crawlies were more pronounced. I stared wide awake into the dark night, and a few tears found their way down my cheeks.

Dante. I missed him—too much. Each day I waited for him to return, but every day was a disappointment. Ralda was reluctant to talk about him despite his assurances that he would come back. My heart slowly crept and sunk into a wormhole.

The pain wouldn't go away. I just wanted to know that he was all right and for him to know I was fine, too. As patient as I tried to be, when it came to him—I wavered.

On the third day, I sat in the lounge, my head in my hands. The birds chirping away in the trees were the only sound inside my head. I blocked everything else out. The front door creaked and swung open. A sound of footsteps echoed, the tread slow. I raised my head briefly and sighed. One look from Ralda, and he eased himself next to me.

"Alessia, I know you're hurting." Ralda waited, and I reluctantly sat up, only out of respect for him. "The reason you can't control that part of your mind is because love is an abstruse phenomenon."

"You're aware of my love for Dante?" I asked, my voice

almost choked. I'm not even sure why I asked. I knew he knew. What I wasn't sure of was whether he fully grasped the extent of my love for him.

"I may be old, but my vision is good." He grinned and took a swallow of his water. "Foretold love is a sequence that can't be broken—not by magic, not by any form of training, not by anyone." He reached from my hand and held it in a tight grip. "As much as you can control your emotions, chosen one—love is one emotion you can never control. Once it's unleashed, there's no stopping it. That's why mind training works best when you're young. Your predecessors were barely ten moon-years old. By the time they reached adulthood, their emotions were so intact, they never found the trigger for love."

A momentary silence descended. The strong breeze flung the door open. I automatically swung round to see if someone was coming—but no one was. Snodia was in the small kitchen cooking some honey-glazed vegetables. The scent wafted through the air as I breathed in the exotic scent.

Shifting my gaze back to Ralda, I murmured, "You notice my pain?"

He flashed a gentle smile. "As clear as if it's my pain, too. Love is an emotion that will either make, mould, or break you. Your heritage means you harness the best of both worlds... and the worst. This love you feel is a part of you, and it's part of your destiny—your path in the world of your mother. Some people go through their entire lives without finding it. Some are unable to find it because their hearts are filled with hatred. You found it in its most wholesome form." His voice shook. "I've sent Hyperian to ask the Larize to return before we begin the third and final part of your training."

My pulse hitched, and I came short of jumping up and down with elation. "Thank you, Voice of Sequence. It means a lot to me!" Truthfully, it meant everything to me.

"I need your mind at peace before we unleash the power that will save our land," he said. "Peace of Mind gives birth to

Peace of Heart that gives birth to Peace of Blood and results in the ultimate Peace of Soul. A complete Sequence of Peace."

"Absolutely," I said, a bit too eagerly. I would make sense of it another time. His words cheered me up for the rest of the day.

* * *

Like a child anticipating Santa's arrival, I paced about anxiously, waiting for Hyperian to return. My hands were clammy with sweat, and my lips quivered. The day had dragged like a snail creeping uphill. Just after sunset, Hyperian returned—by himself. When he shut the front door behind him, my stomach knotted. "Where's Dante?"

"Where's everyone else?" he countered, scanning the small lounge.

I inhaled deeply. "Ralda never says where he's going. Snodia has gone to meditate. Why?" I tapped my feet on the floor.

He didn't answer right away. "So I can tell you the truth about the Larize."

I furrowed my brow. *Is lying even an option?* "What are you implying?"

"He's not well." He rested his legs on the chair.

"What's wrong with him?" My voice broke, and my sunken heart shattered. In seconds, my life flipped over.

"He caught a fever." He paused. "He doesn't look too well, Alessia. He can't travel, but he gave me this for you." He slid his hand into his pocket, extended his arm, and handed me a piece of paper, neatly folded. A notelet with a *litapra*—chocolate design on top.

A numbing chill trickled across my back. Hands shaking, my throat was suddenly dry. I shut my eyes, and a single tear dropped from my left eye. I used my shawl to wipe it off and then swallowed a thick lump in my throat. I opened the notelet and recognized Dante's crisp, precise writing. Leaning against the wall, I took in a deep breath to steady myself.

Lessi,

I'm sorry I can't be with you right now. My body has decided to take its hold over me, but I'll fight through this for us—for you, for me. I hear your training is going well. I'm sorry I left when you needed me most.

I couldn't stand by knowing you were suffering and in agony whilst I did nothing. I failed you—I vowed to protect you, and I'll keep that promise—I'll make it right. Don't worry about me. I'll overcome this setback and will be with you in a few moon-days.

I love you. Heart to heart. Mind to mind. Till the end of time!

Dante

By the time I finished reading the note, my eyes had glistened. In tears, I plunged onto the couch. So much for three weeks of learning to control my emotions. Hyperian repositioned himself to sit next to me on the couch. My heart shattered like glass. I re-read the letter a dozen times, hoping for a better message. My vision blurred from tears. I scanned the notelet again, as if Dante would pop out like a genie in a bottle, and noticed the writing changed partway through the note.

"This is not all Dante's writing." I stared at Hyperian, mouth quivering.

His lips tightened. "He couldn't complete it…He had to dictate the rest. Lariana wrote for him."

A single tear dropped. I had always imagined Dante as

strong, bold, and fearless. There was simply no room for illness. With a heavy heart, I rose to my feet and then strode out onto the decking. The shadows of the dark branches were bigger, stranger. The moons silently watched me but didn't speak. This place wasn't the same without him. I was a lost bird pacing the nest in loneliness. I was lonely—but not alone.

Clearing his voice, Hyperian joined me on the decking. "I can take you to him if you like," he offered.

"Are you sure?" I exclaimed, spinning around to look at him. I was free to follow my heart. And I knew where my heart was.

"Yes."

My mind already working overtime, I asked, "What about Ralda?"

"I'll leave a note. We'll come back tomorrow at first light." He scratched his beard. "He wants you to be happy, Alessia. He'll understand," he said with determination, strolling back into the house.

I followed him through the door. My world suddenly became brighter at this turn of events. I would see Dante again. "Is it far from here?"

"It's a fair distance…but we'll be there in no time—if we leave now."

"If it's not too much trouble for you," I said, and he smiled amicably. "Can I have something to write on? I'd prefer to explain to Ralda myself. I don't want him worrying about me, too."

"Sure." He flipped the lounge cabinet open and grabbed a handful of sheets of paper and a quill pen.

Dear Ralda,

Dante is ill. Hyperian has kindly offered to escort me to see him just so I can put my mind at rest. Peace of mind, peace of heart, peace of blood, and peace of soul. That's my sequence. I'll be back tomorrow at first light.

I can't go through another night without seeing him for myself. He needs me. I hope you'll understand.

Thank you.

Alessia

Once I had written it, I placed it on the table, hopefully in his line of sight when he eventually returned. I gripped my pendant and pressed it against my chest. *I'm following my heart. I'm seeking my Sequence of Hearts. I'm fulfilling my promise to him.* My heart to his heart. My mind to his mind. Me to him. He needed me. I needed him, too. Without fail, I had to answer to the calling of our Sequence of First and Forever.

* * *

Armed with the thought of seeing Dante again, Hyperian and I headed towards house Hantaria. In the middle of the night, only the soft midnight glow of the moonlight guided us. Monstrous silhouettes danced a creepy dance of darkness and light, yet the jewel of the ocean that hung around my neck swung merrily in the light breeze, swaying to its own tune. Storming through the forest like men on a mission, I was bursting with adrenaline rush. My earlier exhaustion and scrapes and pains seemed a distant memory.

Nothing would slow me down. The eerie silence of the mushroom-shaped tree forest didn't bother me. *My love for Dante will protect me.* The gushing sound of water stunned me. Like a vampire at the smell of blood, I noted the fresh scent of water wafting through the air.

"We are close to the sea," I said, taken aback.

"Yes," he said, increasing his pace.

I became anxious and halted. "Hyperian, we've been walking most of the night. Are we lost?"

"Not lost…we may have missed our turnoff. We're taking the longer route, I'm afraid." His voice was undeniably shaky.

"How far do we have to go?"

"Not long," he said abruptly. "Do you see the trees ahead of us, just after the huge clearing?" He pointed to the south.

"Sort of," I answered, trying to gauge the distance from where we were.

"Beyond that is the Hantaria's residence."

"We'll get there at daylight then." I sighed. In a world with light generated by the moons, where were cars when you needed them?

"I-I'll go back to Ralda as soon as I get you there, to stop him worrying."

"Oh, thank you, Hyperian. That would put my mind at ease."

He didn't respond.

When we approached the vast clearing, I took in the beauty of nature. Tiny white daisies grew neatly over the short grass, shreds of mist creeping like cobwebs in the rain. With a smile of contentment, I looked up to the heavens and noticed that the Sun god of Light—my inspiration—was beginning to come out of the horizon. In Ralda's sequence, the stunning display of orange and golden rays peeked out of the horizon like they were in a daring game of hide and seek. The night wind-chill was beginning to soften.

I trekked through the clearing slowly, exhaustion finally catching up with me. But I was determined to see Dante again. *Death by fatigue.* When I reached the middle of the clearing, a surge of hot energy went through me like a shot. My heart lurched and slid into a frenzied gallop. I was on fire.

"Ouch!" I cried. The sensation was nothing like I had ever felt before. I was burning alive, like my body had been submerged into hot charcoal. I plunged down in agony. My hands sweating, I shook like a leaf.

Focus…just focus. What is it with energy in this world? I fought through my newest affliction. From the corner of my eye, I noticed Hyperian was motionless. He was like a zombie, his skin cold and pearly.

Something was not right, but I had to get through this. I had to survive this, whatever *this* was. After agonizing minutes, I found the beginning of the end, or the end of the beginning, and somehow I reached my equilibrium and managed to regulate my body temperature.

Thank you, Ralda. I rose up with Hyperian's help and trotted to the environs of the clearing. I couldn't get away fast enough.

Awe-inspiring brown-barked trees formed a dome above us. The woody incense invoked an inching sensation in my nose as the rustling sound of the tree leaves made the forest seem enchanted. I shivered, my senses on high alert.

I don't remember being here before. "Something is wrong." I halted. The hair at the back of my neck stood up.

"W-What do you mean?" he asked, his gaze focused on the way ahead.

I spun around. "There was something weird about that clearing and now this forest!" My breath hitched.

His lips trembled, like he was trying to say something but couldn't. His eyes looked feverish, full of terror; there was no hiding it.

"Are you all right?" I placed my hand on his shoulder. "You look like you've walked through hell."

Before he could attempt to answer, a jangling, stringent noise startled us. From a distance, it sounded like a stampede of large animals trotting towards us. Within seconds, the stampede came to an absolute halt. Then a dead man's silence descended.

I glanced back at Hyperian, and by now, he looked cold and pale. Drifting, he took three steps back, and by the fourth step, he stumbled and plunged to the ground. Whatever it was—it scared him so much he couldn't stand. Before I'd asked him what it was, I saw it for myself.

A gigantic group of well-built men stomped in unison through the mist in our direction. Six men led the way, marching with confidence, perhaps arrogance; I couldn't be sure. Heads held high, they were tall, huge, and powerful.

Every tiny fragment of their bodies was naturally engineered for battle. Looking a lot bigger than the average Tuscanians, they were like tigers prowling the jungle in the early hours of the morning. Just staring at them made me have an inclination of swallowing my tongue in awe. The crunching of their armoury sent shivers through my body. I trembled in the knees, my pulse beating in all my veins.

Hyperian threw me a terror-filled gaze and managed to form two choked words. "I'm sorry!"

My eyes widened. "Tregtarians!" I whispered, not expecting a response. I already knew. He had led me to the notorious and vicious Tregtarians. There was no question about it. Even the stories in Zeneshian books didn't do them justice. They were a force unlike anything I'd ever seen.

"The shield?" I asked, finally realizing that I had stupidly, so stupidly, crossed the shield without the slightest inclination about it. The hot energy was *pointless* if it didn't speak to me.

"The clearing…Forgive me!"

I glanced back towards the invisible shield, seething. *What good are you if you let me out of your protection and into the mouth of the enemy?*

But it was too late. I was now on the wrong side of the shield, and we couldn't run fast enough to save ourselves.

I have to be strong now, or this will be the end of me. Ralda's words flashed into my mind. *Beyond the shield you're as good as an ewie that falls at the weight of its own fur.*

I placed my hand on my chest, my palm grazing my pendant, steadying my pounding heart.

They stared at us with blood-rimmed eyes, their red shocks of hair shimmering to the morning sun. There was nothing alluring about them; Dante was one of a kind. He had his own air around him, a warm glow, yet these men in my line of view had something menacing and fearsome tagging around them. Their clay-red amour sat perfectly on their bodies, swords placed in their left pouches, knives peeking through from the right.

"Is this petite thing the human?" one of the men bellowed. His deep voice echoed in the trees.

I shivered inside, but I kept still. I had to look brave…but I didn't know how long I could keep it up.

"Yes, High-Commander Jizu," Hyperian said, still sitting on the ground, paralyzed with fear. "P-Please don't hurt her!"

One of the men strode menacingly towards me.

"It's not for you to decide," High-Commander Jizu—undoubtedly the leader, thundered. "Now you feel it's appropriate to beg for the human's life? You should have considered that before spying on your own people…traitor!" His red eyes flashed continuously. "There's no greater coward than one who betrays his own kind."

Hyperian turned to look at me. "I'm sorry."

I willed myself to keep still. This time there was nowhere to run.

"It's too late for apologies. You'll never, ever betray your own kind again. Slit his throat, and be done with him!" High-Commander Jizu said in a gruff, no-nonsense voice.

I slumped to my knees. "Please, please, please spare his life. He doesn't deserve to die," I begged.

"The little creature with a shiny jewel talks!" one of the men said.

"Lord De-Deganon will be impressed!" another answered.

"If you value your life, you'll zip it." High-commander Jizu ogled me, brought his huge hand to my throat, and hastily tugged my pendant off. "Traitors don't get second chances."

I shuddered at his lack of pity. With my necklace off my neck, a hole formed inside my chest. I glanced up to the gods.

What did they have planned for me now? Ralda's riddles seeped through into my consciousness, but sadly they lacked solutions. I watched the Sun god of Light in her seamless sunrise sequence as she took her first glimpse into the land of the warriors. With each ray of light, I knew my life would never be the same again.

Fight for my sequence until the sequence becomes me.

"Please forgive him," I pleaded again. "Let him go back home. Take me! Just, please let him go."

They stared at me, their eyebrows raised. "Why do you care for a traitor's life? He's not only betrayed his own people; he betrayed you, too. Who is to know when he'll stop? Once a betrayer—always a betrayer."

The smaller of the men pulled out a shiny silver sword and handed it to High-Commander Jizu. When Hyperian and I realized that it was the end of the road, Hyperian grabbed me by the shoulders. "I failed you—Tuscania," he whispered into my ear. "My death will free me. Stay strong. Dante will move all four lands until he finds—"

"It's okay. I forgive you." I even managed a smile. He was a dying man—the least I could do was allow him to die in peace. He was the cause of my problems from now on, but I was to blame, too. I wasn't thinking straight.

"Enough! Get it done, Gidron!" High-Commander Jizu bellowed. His austerity and authoritarianism were unrivalled. He viciously threw the sword to Gidron—the man with a daunting scar that ran through the right side of his face.

With ease, Gidron lifted the sword up, and in one hasty movement, he sliced Hyperian's body in half. I leaped back, squinting my eyes, my teeth chattering. Hyperian's blood splattered across the tree leaves, and as I shut my eyes, the smell of blood wafted through the morning breeze. When I flung my eyes open, a wave of nausea engulfed me. Blood filled the ground, the grass soaking to a deep-red colour. They didn't show any mercy—there was no compassion. Ruthless and unforgiving, remorse was foreign to them.

Thunderstruck, I stared into the horizon. My short life had come full circle. I was a hostage to the dreaded Tregtarians. If there was ever any hope of seeing my loved ones again, I had to use everything I knew and had learnt to survive Tregtaria.

Gidron used one hand to pick me up and put me on his shoulders. "She's as light as a feather."

"Haha haha haha." They laughed in unison, as Gidron carried me through the trees to a cart. Gidron threw me recklessly into the blood-stained cart, and I had to share my ride with headless animals undoubtedly meant for food.

He harshly cuffed my hands and legs in chains. I was now a prisoner—slave—hostage. "Don't shut your eyes, feather girl. If you do, the Jungle of Voices will eat you from the inside out." His voice drawled, his breath vile as his words. "Tonight, we shall feast!" he raised his head to the men and bellowed out each word slowly.

"Yeah!" they roared in unison.

We rode south, leaving the Tuscanian lands behind. We were heading towards Tregnika—the capital of Tregtaria. The land I had come to love said its silent good-bye as we blasted through the terrain. I crossed my chained hands over my chest, as if to protect my wilting heart. My jewel was gone. My life was no longer my own. My love… Tears cascaded down my cheeks.

With Dante, I had begun to dream of a happy-ever-after for me—for us. I had read enough fairy tales to know that this wasn't one of them despite my finding my prince charming. There was no *Cinderella* story for someone like me. Not even close to *Snow White and the Seven Dwarfs*—my favourite.

Only the number rang true. I had seven captors, however they were not dwarves, but huge ogres without a shred of humanity. And I wasn't Snow White, but a girl who yearned for a normal and happy life.

Cruel and cunning, they left Hyperian's body halves on the edge of the forest with no burial or dignity. To them, they had their prize. Finally, they had captured a human. The road to earth was just a stone's throw away!

PART II

Jadherey – Through the Eyes of a Servant:

A Taste of Tregtaria

6. Jadherey - The Life of a Tregtarian Servant

Tregtaria! The land of the ill-tempered goons—excuse my lack of etiquette—*warriors*. My land—the only home I knew. On a bad moon-day, I called them worse, which was every moon-day in this damned land. Deemed a coward at birth, shunned by my house at first sight, the land of the injudicious, supposed *warriors* was not for the faint-hearted.

This gigantic slice of doom had never been sympathetic, to me *or* my people. Born to a heartless Tregtarian high-commander, my first cry at birth had sealed my fate. A newborn's squeal rendered one a coward. Unworthy, filthy, and tagged. To them, I was unworthy of the name. As if I needed the inefficacious name! I intended to inscribe my future and make my own destiny.

My path wouldn't be set by the Tregs but by *Jadherey*, of house…who cares. They never told us. All I knew was my father is a ruthless—cunning—cold-blooded high commander of the most merciless and bloodthirsty army in all the Four Kingdoms.

I needed an opportunity to come knocking, softly, subtly—loudly—and I'd ungrudgingly open the door. How I imagined the moon-day when Tregtaria would tumble to its mighty knees. I would watch the pillars plummet to the ground.

Tyranny was the order of the moon-day. What the ill-tempered De-Deganon said was word. The high command's ruling to unworthy Tarians—myself included, was word. Total totalitarian, with no reform or reprise.

Perhaps I should count myself fortunate; I wasn't sliced in half at birth. Coward babies were sentenced to death by the sword. A few survived…but only through their father's—scrap that—*breeder's* word.

Why those deluded breeders bothered to stand up for the life of their coward babies was a mystery I could never work out. Our lives were not any better because we survived when others didn't. Death at birth was a better option.

The survivors were marked on the wrist—the fallen sword imprint of cowardice. Every man, woman, and child, and even the annoying *tonzos* had to know we weren't worth the ground we stood on. Tarians were forbidden to live in the inner part of the city. Division of power, land, and beliefs was chiselled into society with the sharpest of swords—Tregtarian steel. My tiny all-in-one red-bricked hut in Taria, at the outskirts of Tregnika, wasn't luxurious, nor was the village.

Insects and tonzos had made a comfortable home for themselves as the population grew. The little hut served its purpose, I reckoned. My sanctuary. A place to be the true me. Not a servant. Not a slave. Just Jadherey. My insignificance would be the fall of Tregtaria. Tarians' ordained destiny was to serve the warriors, the high command, or the lord himself. But I had a different dream. My time would come!

* * *

"Jadherey, moon-daydreaming again?" Ezra, another Tarian servant, called out as he thundered into the kitchen. "This isn't the walled city of Felradia. Lord De-Deganon demands his—"

"Calm down, Ezra. The lord's morning feast is almost ready." I threw more firewood into the stove before flipping the *njiri* steak onto the tender side. I was a servant, a chef, a cleaner, an all-in-one drudge. You named it; I was it.

"Your hair is loose again." Ezra quickly weaved a knot in my shoulder-length hair and tied it back.

I glanced at him with appreciation. "It's blistering in here. The knot won't hold." Sweat trickled down my forehead, and I wiped my brow. "Those goons were late with De-Deganon's menu choices again."

Not that there was much variety of food to choose from. Every meal—meat, meat, and more meat. But De-Deganon was specific in his choices. If I got it wrong, he made sure I felt the full wrath of his temper.

"I may be the best servant he's ever had, but I'm not a mind reader. You of all people should know I'm not the cause of this delay." I dragged the breakfast tray towards me.

With a nod, he dodged out of the way. "That doesn't change anything, my friend. Lord De-Deganon wants things done yesterday. Remember." His lips tightened.

He outstretched his arm, revealing his burgundy fallen sword mark to me. The imprint of cowardice. Mine had scribbles inside the sword that I had no clue what they meant.

"Tarians don't have the privilege or the pleasure of doing the right thing—let alone the wrong one. Go. Go before he cuts off your other finger. I'll bring the tray to you."

"You're sure?" I asked, my gaze fixed on what was left of my left index finger.

"I'm right behind you." He took over preparing the final touches to De-Deganon's breakfast.

Arms swaying, I forced my feet to tread onward until I reached De-Deganon's chambers located on the sixth floor of his castle. I didn't have the tray but I had to show my face to buy some time, whilst hoping I wouldn't end up with my head on the tray instead. De-Deganon stood tall, by the high-glazed window, arms held behind his back, staring at the capital—Tregnika. He relished his power—his dominance—his authority. He was a proud and powerful man, an irascible and difficult man. Tarians feared him, Tregtarians adored him, and the high command worshipped him.

To his admirers, he was a heroic, moon-chosen, larger-than-the-Four-Oceans commander, but all of that was for nothing. He was a lonely, crestfallen man, who could have any woman he chose, but his ego, the size of the Four Kingdoms, got the better of him.

Rumour had it he'd been jilted by a Tuscanian beauty, the daughter of Sequence, when he was still a boy. He'd been scarred for life and never found love again. Any other woman would always be a replacement of the one he apparently fell in love with.

Love. Could he feel it? I supposed he must have felt it once in his lifetime, but now I was sure he didn't have a heart. But still, I wished I'd been old enough to see the beauteous Tuscanian that had fragmented his once-beating heart. Her grace, charm, and beauty were beyond words. Yeah, that's what they said! The word around was De-Deganon had only met her once, immediately agreed to an alliance with Tuscania, and vowed to make her his wife.

Love at first sight—surely that was a myth! If it was love, which I seriously *doubted* it was, it was too bad. It was a one-way path to doom and depression!

Apparently this Tuscanian beauty would have created a *new* Tregtaria. A land of peace, harvest, fertility, and love, where everyone had a life emulated by the Star gods. Her heavenly eyes were meant to end all wars. Her alluring charm would calm the ruthless, dreaded warriors into submission, and her enchanting smile was said to miraculously heal the sick. *Yeah, right, as if that would happen! Not in the world I grew up in!*

It was just a bunch of bedtime stories that had gone a bit too far, if you asked me. But if any of it were true, it was unfortunate she chose *death* over De-Deganon. Death was a better option for her. Now I had to contend with serving the most irritable, cantankerous man nursing a splintered heart.

"You are late," De-Deganon said sombrely.

"Good morning, my lord." I bowed, keeping my head down. "I apologize for the delay."

"Save it." He scowled at me. His mood was not any better today. "If it were not for your father, you'd be rotting in the dirt." He inhaled deeply, glancing around. "My feast?" He frowned, his piercing eyes torching me.

It didn't take much for him to lose his temper.

"Your meal is just coming, my lord." I rushed through the words.

"How can you be both a coward and stupid? The world doesn't stop for Tarians. Get a move on!" he vented out like he did every moon-day.

Nothing was ever good enough, especially if it came to my *kind*. We were named Tarians, because the word *Treg* was not meant for *cowards*.

I rushed out backwards, my head lowered as was the law. *No one gives their back to the Tregtarian lord* was one of the first teachings from the Tarian School of Discipline.

Thank the Star gods, Ezra was already waiting outside De-Deganon's door. "Thank you!" I heaved a sigh of relief, patting him on the shoulder.

I lugged the tray into De-Deganon's chamber, carefully ensuring my back was not to him. I dropped to one knee and poured water into the bowl. He towered over me, his gleaming armour jingling as he washed his hands.

"Bring my feast to the *mzinda*," he commanded, splattering and showering me with water from his wet hands. "There are matters to discuss."

Where's the love? One thing he revelled in was a good meal. He constantly foraged for food and grazed to destruction. But not once had he said a simple, *thank you.*

"Certainly, my lord." I rose to my feet, wiping my brow.

I staggered backward, the heavy tray sipping my energy. De-Deganon sauntered proudly after ensuring his sword and dagger were suitably in place. His armour caught the sun's rays and shone like Tuscanian diamonds. I squinted and strode anxiously, carefully, across the large cream-and-gold hallway and down the spiral stairs.

On approach, Tradhu, the guard-warrior, bowed his head and swung the creaking door for De-Deganon. Slightly out of breath, I knelt by the humongous pine door, feeling much smaller than the threatening guard-warrior who eyeballed me relentlessly.

I wondered which of the egotistical goons would carry the tray into the mzinda. Thank the Star gods, Tarians were forbidden to enter. My drudgery was done…for now.

"My feast, Tarian!" De-Deganon gestured for me to cross the threshold, his red eyes flashing menacingly towards me.

"Yes, my lord." I fumbled, scrambling to my feet, unsure of his motives.

I trod as lightly as I could. For the first time in my twenty-one moon-years of living, I stepped into the mzinda—where no other Tarian had set foot before. The large, oval room was menacingly dull, despite the freshly painted white-and-red stone walls. My arms ached with the weight of the tray.

The suffocating scent of wet paint wafted through the air. There were no windows and no proper air circulation. I smiled inwardly. *Maybe they will be the end of themselves…*

"Put my feast on my table, and take your place." His guttural voice, thick and dominating, rose into the air.

My place? "Yes, my lord." I obliged, unsure if the mad lord had, for a heartbeat, forgotten who I was. I laughed internally for even considering that thought.

Tregtarians were known for their draconian laws. Change didn't come easily to them. The law was the law. Justice—reasonableness—righteousness weren't in the equation. Their pride made them stick to their ruthless laws to the death.

I sat on the floor with the lord's throne to my right. Lack of direct sunlight slightly darkened the chamber. Fortunately, a few oil lamps gave a bit of light. Nine members of the high command and nine goons—okay, *warriors*—who attended to them were already seated in their high seats. I crossed my legs in the shadows of De-Deganon's throne as he rummaged through the tray.

The interior setup isn't that bad. I suppose, something should be tolerable in a place where discussions are always the opposite. A balance must be kept. Every positive requires a negative. This I'd learnt from books I'd devoured since I was a child.

Tregtarians didn't read. They believed reading was for the weak, for people who couldn't think for themselves. Logic and intelligence were so far away from their minds it was sad. No, not even that. They were a bunch of bibliophobes who thought they knew it all.

The high command sat proudly in the arched seats, their heads held erect. On the right side of De-Deganon was the ferocious Jizu Haurilio, the highest commander of the Tregtarian warriors. He'd never uttered a word to me. He made sure I knew he despised me. Well, the feeling was mutual! De-Deganon had so much respect for him, though. He was a lonely man, having had his Tuscanian wife and son run away from him. He was an *embarrassment* on feet!

Next to Jizu was Scarface Gidron, a ruthless and heartless commander, whose scar reminded everyone of the battles he'd started and won. Then there were Gandu and Ragha. They served Jizu and Scarface Gidron. Ferocious but *stupid* warriors—and that's putting it nicely.

Behind them were the protectors of the reign, whose sole purpose was to ensure the safety of De-Deganon and the high command. As if they needed protection. They were the *cause* of distraction across the Four Kingdoms.

"Commanders! Shall we begin?" De-Deganon said.

I knelt next to him and poured some wine into his goblet.

"May we dispose of this Tarian, my lord?" Jizu scowled with utter disgust. "He grins like he deserves a place in your chambers."

As if the arid, fruitless Tregtarian land was special. It was the worst in Zeneshia.

"Let him be, Jizu," De-Deganon said simply, to my added amazement. I almost frowned as I took my seat on the cold floor. "What is the order of the moon-day?" His voice jarred the senses.

"Your unconquered regiment have annihilated the Legtaria tribe," Scarface Gidron voiced, his red eyes glancing at me with revulsion.

"Did they put up a fight?" De-Deganon asked.

Scarface grinned, his scar wreathing in collaboration. "They surrendered before our warriors had a chance to showcase their new weapons."

De-Deganon took a bite of his steak and looked up. "What a shame," he said slowly with a shake of his head. "I'm itching for a good fight…"

"The women have been brought back to Tregnika, my lord," Scarface continued.

"Share them among yourselves," De-Deganon roared, uninterested.

Jizu cleared his voice. "There's a beauty among them, my lord. Perhaps you may prefer to have first refusal?"

"No!" De-Deganon's voice was harsh. "I don't need those filthy, cowardly women in my bed!" He stabbed the fork down so hard that it broke. Immediately I grabbed the broken pieces from the table and quickly handed him another fork.

"Yes, my lord," Jizu agreed, dipping his head. A while later, he cleared his throat again. "There's a small matter of the *hearts*, my lord…"

"Continue."

"Gagan and Dreya have marched ahead to seek your council." Jizu gestured to the entrance.

My moons! Gagan and Dreya were the worst of the bunch. They were first and second in command of the nastiest regiment—the unconquered. The world was a better place without them.

"Summon them in," De-Deganon commanded.

Gagan and Dreya tramped in, each with a grin the size of the Tuscanian shield. Both carried misguided notions about being victorious through tyranny and torture. Their armour pasted in dry blood, they ambled forward and then halted in the middle of the chamber of gloom and doom.

"My fearsome conquerors!" De-Deganon welcomed them with pride. "My due congratulations on your latest conquest." He wiped his mouth with a napkin, his gaze shifting from his feast to his generals—a proud moment, no doubt.

"My lord," they said simultaneously, bowing.

De-Deganon threw them a victorious smile. He raised his wine goblet before bringing it down with a bang. "Tonight, we shall feast in your honour." His chest protruded with each word.

"The honour is all yours, my lord," Gagan, the first-in-command, said.

That much power was surely suffocating! I remained still, wishing the time away.

De-Deganon rubbed his hands together. "What matter requires your lordship's council?" His voice dragged, like he was taking in his own address; the arrogance!

There was prolonged silence. "There's a dispute over a woman, my lord," Jizu finally said. "Both seem to have a valid claim on her."

"A squabble over a woman?" De-Deganon said in a cynical voice.

"S-She's more than a woman, my lord," Gagan said hesitantly.

"Hmm." De-Deganon placed his fork on the table and gazed up. "Now you have me intrigued."

"She's a contender for your bed, my lord," Dreya said.

"First you squabble over her, now you offer her to me?" De-Deganon was right for once. It was the most hasty and ill-thought-out suggestion I'd ever heard.

"Anything for you, my good lord," they both answered. *Crazy!*

De-Deganon smiled crookedly, raising his hands towards the not-so-clever warriors. "My conquerors, your generosity touches me." In a moment, he replaced his grin with a frown. "But women have no abode in my bed." His tone was vicious, the smile he'd held earlier completely non-existent now.

Quit whilst you're still ahead. De-Deganon was unstable, and asking him for any decision was dangerous—let alone if it involved a woman. He could flip any moment.

De-Deganon held his chin, stroking it in silence. "What to do…what to do…"

Inside I was wishing to be anywhere else but there. *My moons, let it pass.* I knew De-Deganon. Any time he attempted to use his mind this much, a calamity awaited.

"Shall we settle this dispute the traditional way?" He pointed to the rear of the chamber.

I looked up and held my breath. The arena of death… *I thought that was a myth.* My eyes settled at the inscription. *Death Square.*

"We'll fight to the death, my lord," Gagan said.

They both drew their swords out and waited for De-Deganon's go-ahead.

De-Deganon watched them intensely. "What good is a fight if it ends in the death of one of my most victorious warriors? We'll settle this another way. Gagan!" he called out. "How many wives do you bed?"

"Seven, my lord."

"Dreya?"

"Six, my lord."

De-Deganon grinned whilst gazing at both. "If I were to rule in Dreya's favour that would make it even. Yes?"

"We'll accept your ruling, my lord…" Gagan's voice faltered.

It was quite comical, really. The warriors terrorised every Tarian for being a coward, but in the presence of De-Deganon, they were worse than shrimps.

"Only that, this woman is worth thirty women in one."

De-Deganon lifted his gaze, placing a half-eaten piece of bread back onto his plate before rising to his feet. "I shall have to lay my eyes on this woman. Where is she?"

"She's in the antechamber, my lord," Dreya answered, bowing his head.

"Bring her to me," he said in a thick and threatening voice.

All gazes darted towards the door. A moment later, Gagan and Dreya marched a petite woman in. Shivering, she clutched her hands to her sides, her hazel eyes seeming as if death had visited her.

When the warriors let go of her, she wobbled forward, raising her gaze upon the chamber of gloom, searching—hoping—wishing for an escape. Her legs collapsed underneath her, her shaky hands now clenching her stomach.

Tear-stained cheeks, hair doused in sweat and blood, she'd suffered enough. Mouth quivering, she dropped her head to her knees, tears dripping down.

De-Deganon took a swallow of his wine before edging towards the fragile woman. "This is the cause of your tiff?" He scrutinised her.

"Yes, my lord," they both answered like stooges.

De-Deganon bent down and held the woman's chin so she could look up to him. Military silence followed as he regarded her with absolute concentration. He didn't blink, he didn't speak, and his chest heaved up and down, eyes glued onto her.

Precipitously, and so unexpectedly, he drew his sword out and aimed it at her throat. For a moment, I thought he wouldn't, but I knew he would. In a heartbeat, he raised his sword high, collapsed one knee, and struck the doomed woman's waist in one hasty movement that split her in two.

In the chaos of De-Deganon's actions, she let out a whimper as her upper body jerked viciously before death came to her. The sight was horrific, but I dared not shut my eyes for I knew I could easily be next.

I blinked a few times and remembered I had a job to do. A splatter of blood splashed across the immediate area, dousing De-Deganon's face, hair, and armour.

I staggered to my knees, grabbed a napkin from the tray, but dropped it in a trice. It was already soiled. I jumped to my feet and rushed forward, hastily taking off my cloak midway before kneeling down next to De-Deganon.

"My lord?" I asked.

He nodded.

With controlled hands, I used my cloak to wipe the blood from his face first then his hair and armour. I was careful as I resisted and hid the trembling I felt inside.

"Enough," he bellowed out, rising to his feet.

I kept still in a pool of blood.

He directed his gaze towards the two fools who were the cause of the innocent woman's death. "You wanted my council. There you have it." He sauntered across to his throne, wearing *De-Deganon's* unmerciful smile.

A moment later, he glanced back at the high command, who were as stoic as they came, no doubt to assess if anyone was in defiance of his actions. This was not a first; De-Deganon was known for worse.

"She was nothing but a measly coward." De-Deganon scowled at the dead. "You don't need her tainting your beds." He placed his blood-soaked hands on his chest. "But I'm a just lord. Gagan, you can take the top half, and, Dreya, the bottom half is yours."

He was a mad lord, as mad as one could possibly be.

"My lord." Gagan and Dreya dipped their heads. They hauled the remains of the woman out of the mzinda, leaving a trail of blood.

De-Deganon gestured me to sit in my previous spot to his left. I edged forward, the poor woman's blood now dripping from my tunic.

Prolonged silence followed before De-Deganon spoke. "Anything else?"

"Yes, my lord," Jizu said, rising to his feet. "A human has been spotted in Tuscania."

Shock-filled eyes lifted. I, too, stared at Jizu. *Someone has a serious death wish.* My heart pounded—this wasn't something one heard every moon-day. Humans were a *myth.* In books, there were stories of humans, but they were just *stories.*

"Human? Impossible!" De-Deganon rose like a volcano to his feet. His eyes almost popped out of their sockets.

Jizu had to be absolutely sure before bringing such news to De-Deganon's attention. Mistakes were not tolerated in Tregtaria—he was digging his own grave.

De-Deganon smiled smugly. "My good commander Jizu of house Haurilio, are you watching your tongue?"

"With both eyes, my good lord," Jizu said, beaming. This was one of their personal jokes, which I didn't think was funny. "Impossible we thought at first." Jizu's voice was oddly calm. "But my spy has informed me he's now laid eyes on the creature."

"How does this creature fare?" De-Deganon asked after a moment.

"The details are still shady, my lord, but she's young."

"A woman?"

"Indeed, my lord. A girl, to be precise. Just reached child-bearing age."

"When? What? How did she reach Tuscania's shores?" De-Deganon threw the questions at Jizu. The rest of the high command was silent but fidgety, perhaps contemplating Jizu's fate if he were wrong.

"We don't have concrete details in that respect, my lord."

"Hmm." De-Deganon swaggered about the mzinda, the sound of his boots echoing in the quiet room.

I kept still but felt uncomfortably awkward. I was surrounded by the wrong people for one, and totally underdressed in a short, bloody tunic for two. I stared at my best cloak that was now blood-soaked. How was I going to rid it of the stain?

"How far are we from collapsing the coward's shield?" I heard De-Deganon ask.

Jizu looked up with haughty self-assurance. "The minders are close, my lord. We're moon-months away."

"I'm assuming you have a plan for the human?"

"Indeed. My spy is searching for an opportunity to coerce her to the coward's shield. Once she crosses over...we'll be waiting," Jizu confirmed, blinking with pride.

"Timescales?" De-Deganon's voice burst with smugness.

"A few moon-days. Seven at the most, my lord."

De-Deganon grinned. "Fantastic news, Jizu. I want this human brought straight to my castle. Our promised fertile land is almost upon us." He sat down. "Take the best warriors with you when you transport the creature. I don't wish for any surprises."

"Yes, my lord."

"And keep me informed of your progress."

"As always, my lord!"

"And, Jizu, the *human* takes priority over any grudges you hold...that includes your boy, Dante. From now on, all efforts must be directed to bringing the human to Tregtaria." His mouth slanted to one side. "Is that understood?"

"Very clearly, my lord."

7. TWO SIDES TO DE-DEGANON

For the first time in my twenty-one moon-years of living, I woke feeling a wave of buoyancy and optimism about the future, but I didn't know why. Everything in my line of sight was revolting. I dared not yawn; the sickening stench inside my hut threatened my sanity. The tonzos had taken it upon themselves to relieve their stomachs all over my floor!

"Damn it," I said, kicking off the sorry excuse of a blanket that had tangled around me. Spraining my ankle in the process, I snatched the tattered blanket and forcefully flung it to the ragged door.

Consequently, the swarming tonzos awoke from their sleep, screeching and scuttling about my already tiny dwelling.

"Come on!" I vented out in frustration, kicking myself for forgetting to tuck the threadbare cloth underneath the door's threshold to keep the annoying creatures out.

This is not living! I forced my aching leg muscles to support me. With difficulty, I rose to my feet.

"One moon-day, it only takes one moon-day for my life to change," I muttered as I prepared for yet another moon-day of being a servant—a punching bag—a slave to the ill-tempered, mad lord. "One moon-day, I'll have my sweet revenge. One moon-day, I'll stop living in the shadows of Tregtarian warriors," I muttered again, like I did every moon-day.

With a drag, I swung the door open and forced my feet to follow each other to the castle.

Since the news of the human, the last week had been different, though. De-Deganon had held a puzzling sort of normality, and at times, he'd even called me by my birth name, Jadherey—not coward, Tarian, or bastard. A change was so near; I could feel it.

* * *

That afternoon as I attended to De-Deganon, the news he'd been waiting for finally arrived. The human had landed on Tregtarian soil. As expected, De-Deganon called in a long-awaited meeting with the high command. Fortunately for me, De-Deganon now expected my presence in the mzinda. Why? In case he needed a punching bag to vent out his anger on, a tramp to stamp on, a servant to lick his boots…

An overwhelming silence engulfed the chamber. The high command waited anxiously for Jizu and the human to arrive. Scarface and the unconquered five responsible for bringing the human had already taken their seats. Heads held high, hands resting on their knees, they were wallowing in their triumph.

I sat in my spot, quietly ensuring my head was lowered. I didn't know how much lower it could go. It was as low as it possibly could be—my seat on the floor ensured that. Servants weren't allowed to raise their heads higher than the lord or the warriors. To my right was De-Deganon's polished iron throne, and to his right were the notorious seventeen—and that was putting it mildly—the eight warriors and nine protectors of the reign.

For some time, there was silence, and when the impatient De-Deganon gave up on the wait, he stood. He swaggered about the mzinda, his hands behind his back. The clogging sound of his boots was the only distinct sound in the chamber.

In a jiff, the heavy tread of Jizu's boots echoed from the antechamber. My heart skipped. The stomping echo of his footsteps were unmistakable. He had a strutting walk that was more like a parade. A moment later, he booted open the pine door and marched into the mzinda, displaying a huge grin on his olive-toned face.

He halted by the door. The seventeen thugs—err, warriors—and I stared back at him. He strode forward, carrying the *supposed* human over his shoulder. His puffed-up movement sickened me, but that was Jizu—the most pompous of them all. Once he reached the diamond sculpture in the centre, he waited to present De-Deganon with his newest conquest.

I shifted my gaze to De-Deganon, who had his back to Jizu. He was still pacing about, mumbling something to himself like he was in a debate of some sort—but only he knew what the debate was. He'd been acting strangely again that morning. Sometimes, I thought he was losing his mind, or his mind was losing him, or maybe they had lost each other many moon-years ago.

"The human, my lord," Jizu boasted with an over-exaggerated bow before dragging the human down from his shoulders.

Moving swiftly, De-Deganon pivoted and settled his gaze on the human.

I noticed her shoes first; they were muddy but appeared comfortable. The red cloak she wore was torn and blood-stained, but the threading and the weaving seemed of good quality. Her head was covered, and I was sure she had no idea what awaited her.

De-Deganon grinned for a moment and then pressed his lips. He strolled forward and stood in front of both Jizu and the human. He patted Jizu on the shoulder lightly and gestured him to take a seat, which he proudly did. Profound hush enveloped us. All eyes were on the De-Deganon. I didn't know what to expect. All I knew was we were making history, and I was a part of it.

Hastily, De-Deganon removed the sack covering the human's head. He tossed it towards the door and stared right into the eyes of the human. Parting his lips, he staggered back three steps before halting in shock. He breathed raggedly.

My heart thumping steadily, I faced the human and blinked a few times at least. She was eye-catching. Her sun-kissed, light olive-toned complexion brightened the dim-lit room.

In a jiff, De-Deganon staggered back again, five more steps, only to collapse into his throne. Catching his breath, he stared at her without blinking. It was as if he'd seen an apparition.

A tiny moment, and he rose to his feet. His eyes flashed. He marched towards the human, ferociously grabbed her by the shoulders, and immediately moved his hands to her neck, encircling her in a stranglehold.

No, please, no! My heart leapt. I kept my eyes on De-Deganon.

In a flash, he loosened his grip and slid his hands to her shoulders again, gripping them for a while like he was of two minds. Quickly, he withdrew and strode back before taking another step forward. His mouth slightly open, speechless.

His reaction would live in my memory forever. Shock, bewilderment, and disbelief mixed with anxiety clouded the chamber of goons. To all, this was the only time De-Deganon had shown any form of mixed emotion or confused feeling towards anything.

The mad lord's actions were bewildering. *Is this anger? Is this hate? Is this some sort of confused love? Which way is it going to swing?*

De-Deganon's power, pride, and glory seemed to have been dragged out of him, and for now, everything was about the human with her waist-length, raven-black hair that flowed in waves over her slender shoulders. Flawless, she was quite mesmerizing. Strangely, she didn't look terrified, despite De-Deganon's actions or the ordeal she was in. I didn't think she'd fully grasped how each breath could be her last.

Gaping at her, I subtly gasped for air. For a moment, I thought she held her gaze on me. Being the only one sitting on the damned floor, she couldn't miss me.

She was just like us--shaped like us and breathed like us. She was much smaller than the average Tregtarian woman. Her beauty shone through the dirt, mud, and bloodstains. I glanced back at the mad lord again. His actions were caused by something far greater than the human's looks, I was sure. I just couldn't pinpoint what it was.

As if De-Deganon's voice had been obscured by something in his throat, he said, "H-Human?" He gripped her neck and immediately thrust his hands onto her shoulders, which sent her tumbling to the floor.

I clenched my fists, my pulse racing. My first reaction was to protect her...which was odd. I'd never protected or even attempted to protect anyone other than myself. So I sat there, like the coward I was proving to be, suppressing the urge to rush to her aid.

De-Deganon watched her menacingly, glanced at the high command, and traipsed back to his throne. This was a strange side to De-Deganon. His usually unruffled stance had vanished. Jizu and Scarface exchanged glances, and I knew they would exploit that situation soon enough. The silence in the chamber was mind-boggling.

A moment later, the human collected herself. She sat on the floor, her gaze fixed at the diamond sculpture. Her dark hair covering most of her face, she kept still. The mad lord sat in silence for a very long time, visibly gathering himself, too.

With a jerk, he bared his teeth, chest heaving up and down. "Your name, human."

She raised her head, slowly fixed her curls behind her ears, and flashed a smile. "Alessia Appleton, my lord," she answered in the sweetest of voices with a lingering, soft tone. You'd think she was whispering.

De-Deganon's eyes flashed red, brow furrowed. "Age?"

She hesitated. "S-Seventeen...my lord." Thick, dark eyelashes fluttered above her beautifully crafted nose.

De-Deganon paused, holding his silence. His facial features

tightened with each beat of his boot against the wooden floor. He was brooding over something.

"The name of your world?" he finally asked.

She kept her gaze on De-Deganon. "Earth, my lord." She paused. "I'm sorry for my address to you. What shall I call you?" she asked, tilting her head down with respect, to the amazement of the high command. She seemed so vulnerable, and yet she possessed this unbelievable courage in a chamber brimming with the most merciless people in the Four Kingdoms.

"On your feet," De-Deganon commanded, gesturing her to stand up.

Swiftly she stood and crossed her palms, without losing her gaze on De-Deganon.

De-Deganon rose to his feet, too. He strode towards the human, his hands behind his back. "I am the Land-Lord De-Deganon, Lord of Tregtaria." He circled her, bellowing out each word as if he wanted the whole world to hear. "Everything in Tregtaria is at my bidding. Everything behind these walls says 'Lord De-Deganon.' Everything outside sings 'Lord De-Deganon.' All creatures great and small abide by my rule." De-Deganon was like a loose cannon. He halted inches from her before taking one step back. "You can address me in any way you feel fits my station."

"Thank you…Your Grace," she said, bowing and curtsying all at once. "I've heard nothing but the greatness of your name."

Why is she gracious to such a tyrant?

De-Deganon was taken aback. "H-How did you address me?"

"Y-Your Grace," she whispered hesitantly.

"So, you've heard of me?" De-Deganon savoured this little charade. His ego had been boosted tenfold; he didn't know what to do with himself.

"Yes, Your Grace. I'm honoured to finally be in your presence." She smiled with a slight dip of her head, making me wish the graciousness was directed at me.

I sighed subtly, remembering I was a servant and I had to act like one. I kept my eyes on the human. She knew exactly what to say and how to say it. The fact that she was the smallest in the mzinda didn't seem to bother her. If it did, she hid it too well.

"Have my warriors treated you well during your travel to Tregtaria?" De-Deganon asked.

Now, Jizu flinched, and Scarface, too. None of the kidnappers had expected that question, which had serious consequences depending on the human's answer. De-Deganon had taken to this girl. This was slowly edging towards a new Tregtaria. The dawn of a new era. The beginning of divisions across the high command.

"Yes, Your Grace, they treated me with caution. I expected nothing less. One can never be too salient in these times. I'm still a stranger. I hope in time you'll consider me a friend," she said.

It's an act. The best act I've ever seen. Someone who could silence a chamber of Tregtarian warriors at first sight was a force to be reckoned with. She was intelligent; that was clear. The power of her beauty knocked De-Deganon senseless, but the words that came out of her mouth made him forget who he was.

I wondered what De-Deganon had in store for her. Judging by his silence as he paced around the mzinda, I doubted he knew, either. His mind was floating in space right now. I doubted he'd ever used it this much in his lifetime. It was amusing. This little charmer had made history in Tregtaria. It was as if she had practiced for this moon-day all her life.

Finally, he stopped pacing, his chest heaving through his armour. With his back to the human, he bellowed, "Take her to the gallows!"

My heart raced, and I held my breath. The darkness of the mad lord's shattered heart had won over.

Jizu lifted his gaze. "For immediate e-execution, my lord?"

His voice wavered with a hint of uncertainty. His eyebrows raised; he hadn't expected this, either.

"You heard me!" he thundered, keeping his menacing eyes fixed at the walls.

I shifted my gaze to the human. *It's time to drop the act and beg for your life.* I anticipated a scream, wail, cry, yelp…any sound at least. Some sort of pleading or begging or grovelling, just like a normal person would do.

Instead, she lowered her head, curtsying, as if she was accepting her untimely death as just. "Your Grace," she whispered.

At her words, De-Deganon spun around to face her. I clenched my fists again, willing myself to keep still. The gallows meant hanging, and hanging meant death. The fermenting good against evil battle inside of De-Deganon was tipping towards evil.

Her death would be no ordinary death. It would be the death of a beautiful creation, the death of my ticket to freedom. There was just something about her that gave me hope of a different Tregtaria.

Jizu gestured to Scarface to grab her. Scarface swiftly rose to his feet and leapt towards her before carelessly gripping her arm and forcing her towards the door.

"Stop!" De-Deganon bawled. "The dungeon!"

I let my breath out slowly so it wasn't noticeable. The dungeons were a kind offer. *If you believe in the gods, now is the time to offer thanks to them for sparing your life.* Dungeons were preferable to an early death. It was evident that De-Deganon was only buying time to sort out the conflicting emotions inside of him. Regardless, he let her live.

He couldn't afford to show weakness in the presence of his high command, but it had been obvious to me. I knew him well, like a father. This human was his weakness, and his weakness was my passage to revenge and a ticket to freedom. Be it in this life or the next.

* * *

When the doors shut, the chamber echoed with the sound. De-Deganon held a serious look. "Tomorrow, at the crack of dawn, we leave for Felradia," he said.

"W-We, my lord?" Jizu raised his eyebrows.

De-Deganon looked up slowly, smiling. "I have this insatiable thirst for battle. It's been far too long." His thick voice dragged the words out.

Jizu rose to his feet, bowing slightly. "If I may, my lord…the Felradian halkateiy will see us coming. Perhaps we should head east instead?" Jizu's voice was careful.

"My good commander Jizu, when have you ever shied away from a fight? We attack Felradia. I itch for the chase. Gather two hundred of your best men from the unconquered." His gaze darted across the chamber. "Sharpen your armour. Bed your women tonight. At first light, I'll lead you into battle!"

Jizu and Scarface exchanged conspicuous glances again. That was the second time that moon-day. They were up to something; I was absolutely certain of it.

"T-The protectors of the reign, my lord?" Jizu asked. Now, that almost made me laugh. The protectors of the reign were cowards dressed in armour. They had never seen the battlefield. They preferred to cause havoc closer to home.

"We all leave at first light. The reign is on its feet, and the protectors are to be on their feet, too. It's time you witness your lord in battle…De-warrior Dranisha will hold the fort in my absence."

Boom! Boom! Boom! The sound of their swords hitting against their armour echoed inside the walls of the mzinda. For now, they were in agreement.

"And the human, my lord?"

"Let the human delight in Tregtarian hospitality from the comfort of our *dungeons*." De-Deganon lingered on the last word. He picked up his wine goblet and eased it to his mouth.

A burst of laughter emerged from the high command.

"On our return, we'll have a much willing and cooperating pawn," De-Deganon said. "Time doesn't wait for anyone. Go. Go make your preparations."

In a jiff, the high command swaggered their way out of the mzinda, leaving me with De-Deganon, awaiting my next set of instructions.

He watched me for an agonizingly long time without saying a word. "Sit," he finally said.

I looked around, puzzled by his words. I was already sitting next to him. I crossed my palms and dipped my head slightly.

"I said take a seat." He shook his head and gestured to Jizu's chair on his right.

My heart thumped. I rose to my feet, hands clasped in front of me, before steadily lowering myself into the high seat next to him. I sat at the very edge—complacency and self-indulgence in a reverie of Tregtarian comfort was plain right stupid.

He held his chin, his other hand resting on the arm of his throne. For now, silence reigned in peace and harmony. With a sharp jerk, he pounded his fist on the armrest. "To what lengths would you go for your freedom?"

"My lord?" I asked. Momentarily, I half-smiled, cautiously. I couldn't be sure if this was a trick question.

"The question is simple, *son*," he said. "What would you do for your freedom?"

PART III

Alessia's Fortitude:
A Test of Strength

8. In my Mum's Footsteps

To my captors, death was justice. There was nothing precious about a man's life. Tregtarian warriors had no sympathy or empathy. Hyperian's body would rot by the edge of the forest like an animal. The look in his eyes as he succumbed to his death was blinding. It was as vivid in my mind as if it was happening repeatedly.

As they dragged me into the six-wheeled cart, I had no chance or hope of escaping. The tight chain on my wrists cut into my skin. The four brown-toned animals hauling the cart were hitched side by side. With spiral horns at least two-feet long, they were fierce creatures, way bigger than the ewies of Tuscania.

My captors trudged through the wilderness, content with the day's events so far. I couldn't fault their physiques—body builders would be put to shame. I was at a total disadvantage. Only my mind could save me from this ordeal.

As I watched the forest melt away, I appeared relatively calm, considering the danger I was in. I didn't want my captors to smell my fear. I had to accept my fate and mould it to my best interest. I had make a mistake. A huge one. It was all on me.

I planned to play my captors to my benefit, and when the opportunity came, I'd find a way to escape. I doubted they'd kill me without using me to their advantage first. I had a few days, at least, so I told myself.

The dense Tregtarian jungle reminded me that I was a long

way from home. Tall, nut-brown trees with thick, hanging branches darkened the jungle. There was barely enough sunlight to outline the forestry in its entirety. The ground was bare, no grass or plants, the soil black and ashy. The beautiful flowers from the clearing were now a distant memory.

The ground had been starved of sunlight due to the thick canopy above. The sound of distant animals haunted my ears. The air around me was foul and putrid. The stench of dry blood wafted through the cart, making it impossible to get comfortable. After hours of feeling every bump of my unpleasant mode of transport, the jungle came to an end.

Ahead was barren, dry land. The sweltering heat blasted over me like an oven. The scorched land had seen weeks, if not months, of little to no rainfall. In my line of sight was the infamous Tregtaria.

As we descended down the hill, I saw enormous, Corinthian-style buildings. It was a city built in a semi-desert except there was no sand. A few trees were scattered across the city, but from the viewpoint at this higher level, it was hard, solid, torched ground.

A handsome cream-colored castle—the tallest of the buildings—stood in the middle, surrounded by red-bricked columns. From a distance, I could see small crowds roaming from street to street. The architecture was impressive; if nothing else, the buildings weren't too bad. Again, no cars, buses, or even bicycles. Nothing but a filthy cart. How they'd managed to build such handsome buildings and lack things like cars would always be a mystery to me.

This world and earth had never met, but the similarities would confuse even the most educated humans. If I ever went back to earth…no, I couldn't think that. *What about Dante?* If I ever went back to my home world, I'd have to leave him behind. That, I couldn't do. He was *everything* to me.

I would survive Tregtaria for him, and I knew he'd pull through his illness, too. *He has to. How long will it take them to find me? They won't risk a war with Tregtaria.* But Dante would. He'd keep his promise, or die trying. I couldn't risk it. I needed to find a way out before he put himself in harm's way.

Without the powers of my mind, my plan was simple—play to their egos and see where it would land me. Their pride was bigger than Europe; that I could see for myself. All I had to do was nurse that pride until I found my way back home.

When we reached the winding streets of the city, they were quiet, *really* quiet. People had been forced out of the way pending our arrival. The man in charge had alerted me to that fact. I glanced from side to side and up and down, taking in the high, lavish, red-stained columns with armour-decorated imprints along the sides.

My eyes caught sight of a little boy peeking through from behind one of the grooved shafts. His eyes were glued to us— he reminded me of Dante. It could have been him at that age, unaware of another life he'd end up leading.

And then the castle was in my line of sight. Large and dominating, it stood high and proud—like my captors. Ahead was an arched entrance engraved with armour and vines. My gaze went to the prepossessing and gigantic statue of two warriors sat on four-legged animals that was erected at the ingress. It was enormous—threatening—bound to leave a footprint inside my mind. My breath caught at the thirty-foot gloss-black marble sculpture proudly depicting war-hungry warriors wielding their swords into the air.

My captors halted; so did the cart. One of the warriors with a daunting scar on his face dragged me out, and I fell with a thud onto the hard ground. My hands still in chains, I used my elbows to support my legs and scrambled to my feet.

Intense heat flashed across my face. I squinted and staggered through the arched entrance into a massive open space to the bloodcurdling sound of the most daunting chanting I'd ever heard. Yanking my head to my left, I was met by hundreds of armoured men in formation, and to my right were hundreds of armoured women, squatting, arms against their chest.

"Zigara-zigara ragum, ragum—lahuuuum—lahuuuuum…" The ferocious voices of the male warriors echoed inside the enclosure. Like an open-air theatre, stone seats on the left side were carved onto a semi-circular hill.

"Zigara-zigara ragum, ragum—lahuuuuum—lahuuuum…" the women warriors chanted, stamping their feet on the ground. They were humongous, their red, bulging eyes wide open. Their muscular chests beat visibly like drums. Now I understood why they couldn't be mothers.

A taut knot tightened inside my stomach, and a feeling of dread welled up inside of me. To make it worse, my captors decided to stand still with me, in the middle of this war cry. My gaze darted from one side to the other. I shivered in the blazing heat. My earlier calmness had been replaced by plain and complete fear.

A thundering noise echoed from the male warriors as they chanted in unison. Their rhythmic, vigorous movements were unlike anything I could ever have imagined. The passion in each movement overwhelmed me. It was surreal. With each distinct step, each shout—every grunt—they edged closer and closer to us. This undoubtedly traditional war ritual sent shivers to the core of my heart.

And it clicked. It reminded me of the *Haka* from the New Zealand rugby team, in my home world. Back then, it was supposed to be fun, but this was meant to cause death by fear, scaring the life out of any opponent.

"Rangande, rangande ragora—ragoraaaaaa!" The warrior men leaped up. They poked out their tongues as far as they could go, and their neck veins looked like they were about to burst. They were menacing, ferocious and merciless. They cocooned us in the middle, edging towards us in spectacular fashion.

In comparison, my captors were as still as a river on a calm day. Heads held high, they seemed to relish every second of the ritual. The women and men warriors halted from both directions mere inches away. I dropped my gaze. I couldn't look directly into their faces.

"Lahummmmmmmmm!" the female warriors chanted, waving their swords in the air.

"Ragoraaaaaaaaaaa!" the male warriors responded, dropping to one knee with their swords raised above their heads. A grave silence descended, and I just stood there, silently calling out to all the Star gods to guide me—protect me—pity me.

A moment later, we were trotting towards the deep-red castle doors, the women warriors towering over us. I took subtle, deep breaths to keep my feet moving. I kept my head straight, avoiding all eye contact with the scary-as-hell women warriors. I heaved a sigh of brief relief when we reached the castle doors. Marble, bell-shaped columns towered over us from both sides. I was set free of my chains.

We strode into a square reception room. I squinted a few times. The high ceiling sparkled with various colourful gems that emitted twinkles of light in the shadowy room. "Cover her head!" High-Commander Jizu's voice echoed through the spacious, dim-lit room.

"Yes, High-Commander Jizu," one of the younger warriors said, and within seconds, a dark hessian sack covered my head.

Deep, lonely darkness blanketed my vision. Choked gasps escaped my quivering mouth. All my earlier smothered nerves, fear, and desolation broke free as burning tears cascaded freely down my cheeks, now that it was just me and gloom. Sadly, my life was one prison after another. There was nothing normal about my short life, and even in a distant world, I found myself plotting an escape again.

"I'll bring her into the mzinda. Lord De-Deganon awaits," High-Commander Jizu said.

He effortlessly lugged me onto his shoulders, ensuring I was secure. My stomach hardened. He gripped my legs too tightly for comfort. A moment later, the sound of doors opening and shutting behind us echoed as he marched through a couple of rooms.

We went down a set of stairs, and another, before he swung open a few more doors; by that time, I had lost count. The hurried sound of his footsteps echoed inside my ears. *Just breathe. Compose yourself. Fight for your sequence. The end of the beginning is the beginning of the end...* I tried to remember Ralda's teachings.

A minute later, he halted. For a short while, he didn't move, and I knew this was it. The final door squeaked. A few steps followed by hush indicated we were inside the *mzinda*—the council chambers—if we hadn't taken a detour. When my feet touched the ground, I stood motionless. I took short, deep breaths to compose myself fully before facing my newest adversaries.

"The human, my lord!" High-Commander Jizu said, his voice brimming with pride.

His words were met by silence bar a set of distinct footsteps advancing towards me. A second later, I felt someone's presence. Someone else stood next to me, towering over me. *Just breathe, keep breathing,* I told myself—Dante would tell me the same.

High-Commander Jizu's footsteps faded away into the distance. I managed to swallow one gulp of air at which point a hand vigorously snatched the sack off my head. Darkness persisted, but not for long as I forced my eyes to open.

Robust, shiny armour struck my vision first, and when I raised my gaze, I was met by a man's chilling, dark-red eyes as he staggered back, to my befuddlement. I kept still, immobile, and unable to look away. He was huge, like *really* huge.

He must be the lord.

His clean amour hung to his body like a glove. His veins looked like they were near bursting point. He staggered back again and then plunged into his chair.

Gobsmacked, I wondered if I hadn't met his expectation. His reaction was mind-bending. What did he see in me?

Quickly, I dropped my gaze and subtly glanced across the room. *Just men!* A slight tinge of relief washed over me—the women scared me more!

A young man sat on the floor. He was dressed differently, in a pale-purplish tunic. *He must be a servant or a slave.*

I squinted. His striking resemblance to Dante made me question whether I was too fatigued to see clearly. Dante was physically bigger than him, but the soft features of their faces held some sort of similarity.

Abruptly, the huge man with a short, well-groomed beard sprang to his feet and swooped towards me at incredible speed, like he was about to pounce on his prey. *I'm so dead.* I kept still, suppressing my nerves, but inwardly, I was shivering to destruction.

He gripped my shoulders and then grasped my neck instead, not losing his gaze on me. Immediately, he loosened his clutch, holding my neck lightly before clenching my shoulders again.

Baffled, I held his gaze. His masculine face was battle-hardened. His eyes flashed like a traffic light except there was no green or amber, only a sea of red. When his hands were clasped against my shoulders, his eyes were a lighter shade. When he moved his grip to my neck, they were blood-red. I'd spent enough time with Dante to know that this man had conflicting feelings going through him.

Acute anger and another emotion rose and fell, as his features contorted with emotional commotion. He was feeling something; that was clear. *Why?* I subtly gritted my teeth. I thought of Zaira and what she would do in such a situation. *I have to be strong. I'm a Tuscanian, I'll ride the storm. I'll ride the storm.*

Suddenly, the man shoved me back with so much force I tumbled before hitting the floor. I smothered a scream and suppressed my tears. *Now is not the time to be scared.* I sat up, practicing a smile behind my hair, and subtly glanced at the man who now sat in dejection, visibly planning his next move.

If Ralda's words were anything to go by, my life was proving to be similar to a game of chess, except this pawn was planning its own move, too. *Cowardice or bravery isn't going to save me this time. Graciousness is the key.*

If water could turn into wine, and if beauty could tame the beast, I intended to try and charm my way to save my life. Tregtarians were people, after all, with feelings. If Dante could love with a passion, I was sure my captors could feel something with a passion, too. It just had to be the *right* something for *me*.

When the man with the lengthy, glossy hair revealed his name to me, his reaction made sense. Lord De-Deganon—my mum's betrothed. I was a spitting image of my mum, and he'd seen her in me. I'd walked right into my mum's footsteps. Rewind nineteen moon-years, and he'd been staring into my mum's eyes.

His reaction when he first laid eyes on me was baffling. I didn't know whether it was acute hatred concocted with a tinge of love for my mum or something else.

As I responded to his questions, totally Anne Boleyn style, I was as calm as my grandma. I'd played the part of Anne Boleyn in a school play of *The Six Wives of Henry VIII* when I was twelve. It all flashed back; I surprised myself.

Even when I thought the end was near, and the gallows awaited, I somehow kept my composure. I would probably scream the life out of my lungs before I met my death, but before then, I accepted the gallows with grace. "Your Grace," I whispered.

"Stop! The dungeons!" Lord De-Deganon's bellowing voice was welcome to my ears.

Perhaps my Anne Boleyn role-playing had bought me a few precious days, at least. I wasn't about to give up. Not now, not ever.

* * *

Two warriors hauled me down through the eeriest, spookiest staircase ever. The claustrophobic, blood-stained walls were ragged, marked with scratches of my predecessor's fingernails that had dug into them over the years. I shut my eyes to save my mind from such a ghastly sight.

When I reached the dungeon a stench of death, torture, and despair engulfed me. I opened my eyes to the creepiest and nastiest cell I could ever imagine. Dark mould plastered the walls like a thick coating of grime. A cold chill slithered down my spine. I darted a gaze around. Twisted vines and dandelions pierced through the cracks in the walls invoking a sensation of dread within me. When the cell doors were slammed shut and locked, I stood still, my arms wrapped around me. *What's next?*

A lit candle was set at a stone table, wavering in the draught of the dungeon. It was almost burning out.

"What moon-day is it?" a voice echoed from the darkness of the cell next to mine.

"Loveday," I answered, peering into the shadows of our cells separated by rusty railings.

I sighed, recollecting Dante when he had taught me the names of the Zeneshian days of the week. The third night we'd spent together at his home was incomparable. We'd had an amazing and most quintessential day in the snow; the sun had finally graced us with lustrous, golden rays of warmth beaming through the cirrus clouds. On the horizon, the snow-capped canopy of trees had shimmered like tiny diamonds, whilst light snowflakes floated about like mini cotton cushions.

We'd spent part of the afternoon with Sigenta and Lariana. They were attempting some unusual form of snowboarding down the hilly slopes of the Hantaria's estate. Dante had surprised me with a board my size. Instead of trying his cousin's version of snowboarding, he'd sat on the board and straddled his legs before reaching for my hand. "You trust me?" he'd asked, his arm still raised.

I'd nodded. A frisson of excitement had slithered down my

spine, as he sat me in between his legs, his arms curling around my waist. We both stared at nature's stupendous landscape of white wonderland.

"Are you ready?" he'd whispered.

Before I'd formed an answer, he'd propelled us forward. Gliding down at incredible speed had been thoroughly exhilarating but also incredibly nerve-racking. I remembered shutting my eyes, my hands tightening against his arms, screaming my lungs out. It was like gravity was pulling us down, and yet he kept us above ground.

Once we were at the bottom of the hill, we'd rolled in snow and laughter before he'd scooped me up, placed a light kiss on my cheek, and called it a moon-day.

"Shall we give thanks to the gods?" he'd said that night as we prepared for bed. He'd lowered onto one knee whilst I sat on the bed.

I'd nodded with a smile, and he'd reached for my hand, stroking it gently. It didn't bother him that I was still learning to crawl when it came to their gods and traditions; nonetheless, he didn't impose or force his beliefs on me.

"Today we give thanks to the West Star god of Fertility in a special way." He'd squeezed my hand gently. "We dedicate this moon-day to you from the deepest parts of our hearts. Flood us with your never-ending blessings. Most of all, I ask that you shower Lessi with every grain of fertility in everything she holds and everything she is. Amen."

"Amen." I'd bitten my lip for a second. "Of all the Star gods, you chose to give thanks to the West Star god of Fertility, and you just had to throw my name in there. Is there something you need to tell me?"

He'd laughed lightly before bringing my hand to his lips. He held it there for a while with both his hands then planted a soft kiss. His ruby eyes had held a sensual warmth that was so genuine I could still picture it now.

"Do you believe in foretellings?" he'd asked.

"Not really...maybe just the Foretold Sequence of First and Forever," I'd said truthfully. "But I'm willing to listen. That counts for something, right?"

A knowing and secretive smile had played on his lips. "What about Foretold Curses of First and Forever Love?"

"Hey! Are you saying it was foretold that *I'm* not fertile?"

"No," he'd said light-heartedly, an expectant look settling on his face.

"That *you're* not fertile?"

He shook his head.

"That together *we* are not fertile?"

He'd hadn't answered, as though I had hit the correct spot. A little frown had crept up my forehead but was soon replaced by a beam when I noticed that he was stifling a laugh.

"Perhaps, but that's not the reason for our prayer." He'd taken a deep breath, eyes shimmering a tranquil red. "It's Fertilityday today, and as it's the end of a beautiful moon-day, we give thanks to the Star god of Fertility. Tomorrow we'll pray to the moons, because it's Moonsday. And the moon-day after that, we'll praise all the Star gods because it'll be Starsday," he'd said simply.

"Is every day named after the gods?"

"Every moon-day of the moon-week, yes. Each moon-week is seven moon-days, just like in your home world." He'd kept his hands on mine, weaving delicate, gentle patterns. "The first moon-day of the week is Peaceday. In peace, everything good is always possible. Moon-day two is Harvestday, and the one after is Fertilityday, followed by Moonsday—Starsday—Sunday, and lastly, but more importantly, Loveday." His velvet voice lingered on Loveday.

I'd raised my eyebrows, stroking the back of his hand. "Does it mean you love me more on Loveday?" I'd teased.

He'd chuckled softly and cupped my face lightly with both hands. "That would be unattainable," he'd said after a moment, his voice growing quieter. "Loving you more than I already do...is beyond the bounds of possibility."

"Are you still here, little angel?"

The shrill voice from the shadows of the cell next to mine brought me back to reality too soon. I had no idea how long he'd been speaking to me. For a minute, I'd shut the pain out of my heart and drifted back to a time when every day was Loveday!

"De-Deganon wants you alive, for now," he said.

"I believe so," I answered softly, minimising the eerie bounce of my voice against the walls.

Two stained wooden stools were placed behind the stone table, but I didn't sit on either of them. In the dimness of the cell, I couldn't work out what the stain was, and I didn't want to speculate. I stood uncomfortably in one spot, wondering how I would make it through the night and however long I'd be in captivity. This was a test of strength. I just wasn't sure I had enough of it to last a day...let alone forever.

A faint shadow cropped out from behind the cell next to mine. "You will want to make yourself comfortable, little angel. De-De can be as patient as an ewie." His hoarse voice was strained but high pitched.

"De-De?" I whispered for confirmation.

"T-That wretched boy who calls himself lord." He limped towards the rails.

I flashed him a light smile. He obviously wasn't Lord De-Deganon's fan.

He was just an old man with a whole lifetime behind him. Days of solitude and hardship had chiselled by each wrinkle on his aged face. His tattered tunic had seen better days. With slumped shoulders, he watched me silently.

"Hello," I said.

"Good moon-day to you too, my little angel." He grinned. "Today is a good moon-day to die. Do you concur?"

I inched closer to him, reached out for his hand, and gently placed my hand on his. He was as cold as ice. I shuddered. Staring into his tired eyes, I instantly realised he preferred death to captivity. *How long have you been held in here?* I wanted to ask, but I held back.

"Fly me home, my little angel...fly me home," he said in a raspy voice.

I wish I could. But I need wings, and for that, I need Tuscania. I'm on the wrong side of the shield!

I removed my cloak and pushed it through the gap in the rails. It wasn't much, but it was something. "Here, take this," I offered.

As he reached for the cloak with trembling hands, my eyes brimmed with tears. In some ways, I could see myself in him. Fast-forward sixty years from now and he could be me, stuck in a dungeon for years on end.

"Moon-nights are long my little angel. You'll need this."

"No. You need it now," I said, shaking my head and patting him on his hand.

Suddenly, a shuffle of feet and the rattling sound of keys echoed from the corridor. I swivelled round towards the light beaming from the entrance and shrank back. The guard hastily unlocked my cell. *What now?*

"Lord in the dungeon!" he said before taking one huge step out of the way.

My first reaction was to run, but that was the old me. This new Alessia had to stay strong. I took a deep breath, bracing myself.

"De-De, De-De, is that you?" the old man voiced in a piercing tone. "I can smell the whiff of you from here."

"Sintirion, testing my patience on such a moon-day is unwise," Lord De-Deganon thundered as he marched into my cell.

"Your Grace." I curtsied, catching a glimpse of the servant or slave. He set the oil lamp on the floor and immediately curled on the ragged floor next to the entrance. *That's not right.*

The extra lighting revealed cobblestone walls with intertwined moss and vines growing from the fissures.

The lord halted a few metres away before pivoting towards the guard. "Leave us."

The guard left hastily. The servant kept still, head lowered, eyes fixed at the ground.

"I see the moons are tainted with blood today, De-De," the old man said from the confines of his cell. "A sign that blood will be spilt. Is it going to be my blood?" His voice was shrill.

"Keep yapping, and you'll soon find out," Lord De-Deganon replied simply, his gaze steadily on me. I couldn't work out his age. His features were robust and well groomed.

"Now you threaten me? You threaten me with death many times over, De-De. It has since lost its value. You're not lord to me. I earned my freedom long before you were spat out of your mother's womb, you ungrateful—"

"And yet you're still under my roof," he said. He seemed strangely tolerant towards the old man with quite a sharp tongue.

"What are you going to do about it? Ha!" He scowled at Lord De-Deganon. The wrinkles on his face seemed deeper than earlier. "Are you going to kill me? Send me to the gallows... Get me chewed up by the jingwes... Take my word, De-De. You'll be chewed up by your people the moment I start singing like a firebird as I'm led to the gallows."

Oh, no, no, no. Don't make him angry. The old man had serious issues with the lord, but this wasn't the right time... for either of us. I bit my lip subtly, watching the lord who was bizarrely pacing about my small cell.

"You wish for death?" Lord De-Deganon vented out, storming towards the old man. With one arm, he gripped the old man's neck through the rails, lifting him off the floor. I smothered a scream, my hand covering my mouth. Within seconds, he thrust him backwards and strode back to his spot in the middle of my cell, breathing heavily. Certainly, he was fuming internally.

"Much blood has been spilt before my time, De-De." The

old man grimaced, his voice almost choked. "The ground is already stained. My blood will not soil the blemished ground you stand on," he said, picking up the cloak and wrapping it around him.

"Grant him his wish!" Lord De-Deganon thundered towards the servant, who immediately called out to the guards. Within minutes, two guards emerged and briskly hoisted the old man up with their massive arms. It was as if they were picking up a twig from the ground.

"When I die, I'll die happy knowing you're in trouble and my *sequence* is complete!" the old man shouted as the guards restrained him. "There are tremors on your seat, De-De. Y-You're on shaky ground. One of these moons shall collapse over you. The pillars of your throne will give way to your dead weight, and your dead weight shall plummet to the ground with the head going west!" A glower of resentment lingered on his face as the guards dragged him out of his cell.

Sequence is complete? Who in their right mind would be crazy enough to get into a fight with Tregtarian warriors? I watched the old man with sadness. It was suicide. The poor old man was like a little toddler among adults in comparison to the warrior's size. They reminded me of the expression *the bigger they are, the harder they fall.*

But how do you get them to fall?

"Take my word, De-De," the old man said from the corridor, his voice fading away into the darkness. "This word shall only be spoken once… To the gallows it shall be… where I shall gladly meet my fate. I'll whisk up to the creators, who will take me in as I casually walk through the gates. Judgment be upon you, De-De, as Tregtaria will pass its judg—"

Silence followed the old man's departure. The lord huffed and puffed in my tiny cell, planning his next move. Numbed to stillness by the old man's untimely departure, I was out of moves. I crossed my palms, took a deep breath, and waited.

"What parentage are you?" Lord De-Deganon asked after prolonged silence.

"Your Grace?"

"I said…" He raised his voice. "What parentage are you?"

"My father is human, Your Grace, and my mother is Tuscanian." I hurried the words, hoping he'd catch just some of them.

"Which house?"

"Your Grace?" I was buying time, unconvincingly, too. Would the truth set me free or send me to the gallows?

He threw me a sharp stare. "The house of your mother's birth."

I took a deep breath and glanced at the servant, who quickly dropped his gaze when our eyes met. "Serenius, Your Grace," I answered.

He kept his features steady and stroked his well-manicured beard gently. A minute later, he strode towards me and held the side of my face lightly. "My crown jewel," he said.

I stood still, unsure if he was referring to my mum or me.

"My commanders deceived me! They told me…she chose death over me…death over dishonour…death over *my* love." His eyes flashed; he'd worked out exactly who I was. He stroked my cheek lightly before gripping my chin. "No one defies me. I am the lord!"

A moment later, he withdrew his hand before easing himself on the stool a few metres from me. I let out my breath as he held his head in his hands in deep concentration.

Although I felt inclined to sit down, too, it was much more respectful that way, the only other stool was too close to him.

He lifted his gaze, his eyes not opening up fully. "They told me she was dead…" He stared into my eyes like he was searching for an answer. His voice was so low, like he meant every word.

Oh, my word, he's hurting. My brow furrowed. *But she's gone. She wasn't dead nineteen moon-years ago, but now…she is.* My heart shattered.

"I loved Kaylinah with a passion that haunts me every moon-day…"

I bit my lip. Everything that had happened this day was bizarre, but this was beyond strange. *Yes, it's Loveday, but you can't have loved her. You only met her once.*

"Her image haunted my sleep for moon-months before I laid eyes on her."

My eyes opened wider. "A dream, Your Grace?"

He shook his head. "A sequence of images of Kaylinah."

"You dreamt of my mother before you met her?" I murmured, trying to work it out myself. Zaira and Ralda hadn't mentioned any of this. If they knew, I'm sure they would have said.

"Tregtarians don't dream," he answered, after prolonged soul-searching. "Dreaming is the Felradian's curse. What I saw were visions. She was part of me long before I pledged my love to her."

My gaze strayed towards the slave who kept raising his gaze towards Lord De-Deganon every now and again like he was listening in on a bit of gossip. His red eyes held a constant deepness that was too familiar. There was a sadness about him I couldn't shake.

"She was taken from me, along with the images, until you." His features hardened. "Last moon-night, her image returned, and today, you appear. Why do you torture me with these visions?" He said the words slowly, but with such strength in his voice it was surreal.

It's just a dream, I wanted to say, but deep down, I knew this was too freaky to be a mere dream. There were always two sides to every story—I knew that—but still, this was too puzzling.

The ferocious and callous lord of the most cold-hearted warriors in all of Zeneshia possessed some form of humanity within him. He was capable of loving, and yet everything I'd been told suggested he couldn't see past his ego, power, and callousness. *What about the slave on the floor?* I couldn't answer that one.

Lord De-Deganon held his head in his arms again.

"Your Grace," I whispered, not sure what I wanted to say, or what I could say to lessen the pain. Against my better judgement, I felt sorry for him and the slave, too.

He lifted his gaze, silver streaks of his otherwise black beard catching the light. His features softened. "She is the only one who addressed me as such…and now you."

Oh, dear, I didn't realise. I raised my eyebrows. Whilst I was busy playing the gracious side of Anne Boleyn from my acting class, I was actually playing my mum. I just didn't know it. That was a *really* spooky coincidence.

My thoughts were thrown into disarray. What I thought I knew wasn't as it now seemed. Unless he was playing me… *Oh my God, is this just a ploy to deceive the gullible side of me? But why? It doesn't make sense.* Or, going by Ralda's words, this was his gambit—the next move was mine!

"You will take me to her?" He rose up.

To her tomb in Wroxham? "On earth, Your Grace?" I asked.

"I'll journey through the Four Oceans and bring her home." He paused, studying me for a while. "You could have been my daughter," he said. Slowly he edged forward, reaching for my hand. He scrutinised it for a minute before spinning me around. "You're courageous, but you lack the sturdiness of Tregtarian blood!"

Okay…. Not sure if it's a compliment or insult.

"This is how it's going to play out. Tonight," he said, his gaze darting around the cell, "you'll find a way to get comfortable. There's a stench of disloyalty among my commanders. Tomorrow I'll lead them into battle at first light. In my absence, you'll be treated to Tregtarian cordiality and kindness, the same way I would have coddled your mother if she'd allowed me."

My stomach knotted. I couldn't tell him that Mum was dead for fear of what he might do to me. Keeping the lie was as risky as telling the truth. My choices were limited and I chose the former. Perhaps I had bought some time for a few days, at least.

"When I return, you'll repay my kindness by putting your charm to virtuous use. You'll take me to your world and restore honour to my house. Together we'll bring Kaylinah home. She belongs with me."

* * *

The old man had been dead-on. The night hauntingly dragged. Alone in the darkness of Tregtaria, I curled over the stone table, my trembling hands encircled around my legs. Dante's velvet voice, beautiful and melodic, was now a distant reverie of what might have been. By now, my family would have found out that I had been taken. I couldn't begin to comprehend how much my grandparents were hurting. Ralda and Sianze had prepared me for this possibility, but it didn't soften the pain inside my heart.

All the pain, fear, and confusion I'd held back most of the day escaped in the form of tears cascading down my cheeks. With everything going on, I'd tried with difficulty to keep Dante away from my thoughts, but he *was* my mind. Sadly, he wasn't speaking to me. I needed the voices back, yearning for the chaos inside my head if it meant hearing him one more time.

I was a confused piece in a set of massive puzzles. Blind. Deaf. Voiceless. The moons were watching—the Star gods were gazing—but none of them were feeling or seeing the bleeding of my heart.

How could I win a losing battle? I didn't know the rules of the fight. I wasn't ready. I didn't have the armour. My sequence was out of alignment. But I would do whatever was necessary to realign it. I would fight hand, tooth and nail until I realigned my sequence. Now I was surrounded by a sea of red, the same *red* that was just a colour until I met Dante. Now everything red reminded me of him. I shut my eyes and cried myself into a prayer. My better half believed there was a higher power. I had to believe, too.

"T-To the East Star god of Peace, please bring back the voices inside my head…please bring them back," I whispered into the night. "Please show me the way home. Please get me back to my Sequence. To the South Star god of Love…please bring back my love. Return me to him. I know you have a plan for me. I wish you'd let me in on it." I wiped my tears with the back of my hand. "Now I ask that you give me the strength to fight. My life has meaning. My sequence has meaning. Please make my fight mean something, too. If I stumble or plummet, please help me up. I must fight…for myself—for my family—for my love, and for my people. Please stand with me. Please fight with me. Please show me the way home," I said into the darkness. "Amen."

9. THE CURSES
OF THE STAR GODS

"My lady." The calm but deep voice woke me, and I opened my eyes to a pair of venetian-red eyes gazing right into mine.

A glint of daylight streamed through a crack in the ragged walls. I squinted, shading my sore eyes. "You're safe with me, my lady." The low voice made my heart thump. I jerked sideways, only to almost topple over the stone table in true Alessia fashion. Strong arms held me up, stopping me from hitting the floor headfirst.

My breath hitched. I held onto him, wondering how I'd managed to sleep on a stone table without tumbling to the ground. All parts of my body ached. I took short deep breaths for composure and caught his fresh masculine scent of peach infused with lime, a welcome haven to the filthy, damp, and horrid smell that had filled my nostrils all night.

"The lord would never forgive me if you were harmed, my lady, even if it's by your own hand." His sotto voice was tinged with a silvery tone that was more Tuscanian than Tregtarian. I was clearly fatigued.

The servant from last night.

"Thank you," I pulled away from him and created some distance between us.

He lowered onto one knee. "I'm Jadherey…the lord's servant." His lips curved into a contagious smile.

"Alessia of house Serenius...the lord's captive," I said.

His smile widened. By the glint in his red eyes, it was evident he hadn't expected a full introduction from me. His skin had a natural glow that kept me enthused for a second longer than I should. He didn't dress like the warriors, but he was physically strong, well built.

Dante! My heart sank. The kneeling servant reminded me of the man I loved: his deep-red eyes, his flawless skin...his shoulder-length hair. Looking at him was torture. I edged back and averted my gaze.

"Come with me, my lady," he said simply, his arm stretched towards me. When he noticed my reluctance, he moved closer, still on his knee. "The guards are changing shifts. This is the only time I can get you across the castle without being seen."

I was quiet for some time, ruminating over if all was as it seemed. "When they realise that I'm not in my cell, what then?"

"My good lord has cordoned off the dungeon, my lady," he said easily. "The guards have been instructed not to enter."

I considered his proposal and then shook my head. I took three backwards strides and rested my back against the filthy walls. "Please leave me. I'm quite happy staying right here. Thank you."

He drew in a deep breath and inched a couple of paces towards me, palm up. "My lady, this is not a negotiation. Forgive me for being blunt. Your happiness is not under consultation. Your comfort is."

"I beg your pardon?"

He edged forward again, determined. "The good lord has tasked me with the responsibility of ensuring your comfort. With all due respect, my lady, happiness is not something that I can provide for you." A flash of something that resembled humour lit up his red eyes. The richness of his deep-blue tunic brought a burst of colour to the dim-lit surroundings. "Neither is it something that you'll get within the confines of this dungeon."

"If my comfort is all you seek, what's in it for you?" The quiet murmur was out before I'd even considered exactly why I was asking.

"Take my hand, and I'll make it worth your while." He kept his hand steady. When he took in my added reluctance, he quirked his brows. "I insist."

"You demand," I said instead, my back pressed hard against the cold cobblestone walls. I couldn't afford to trust anyone but myself.

"No, my lady. I wouldn't dare speak out of turn." He sounded sincere. His voice was smooth without an ounce of harshness in it. "I am but a servant, my lady."

What if it's all an act? "You're not *my* servant."

"I am, my lady." He flashed another one of his contagious smiles. "The lord has relinquished my duties to him so I may serve you fully, my lady." He dipped his head. His hair was tidily tied at the back, and a rich-red shock of hair ran along the left side. "With or without your permission I am serving you."

I couldn't help but smile at the rather charming and quite unusual servant.

A glimmer of amusement and recognition of my yield to his request shone in his eyes. He ran a hand through his hair and swallowed hard. "My lady, every moment that you're debating whether to take my hand or not is a moment closer to you spending another long and uncomfortable moon-day and moon-night in here." The muscles in his sturdy jawline contracted with each word.

My throat ached with sympathy for him. He seemed kind; his voice was toned in a melodical way. *Unless he's Lord De-Deganon's Trojan horse*, a little voice inside my head warned me. *You can't trust anyone!*

"The dungeon is no place for a lady," he said. "A few more moon-days in here and you'll lose yourself."

"And it concerns you?" I asked, trying to assess his reaction.

"More than I'll care to admit, my lady." He startled me with the frankness in his tone. For a servant, he was well spoken and well dressed, yet he knelt for me subserviently as though I deserved it.

"But you're admitting it?" I surveyed him intently.

"Only because my first duty as your humble servant is not to lie to you. I'm here to serve you profusely, and I intend to do good by you."

His words invoked a strange sensation in me. For a few seconds, I was rooted to my spot.

"My lady, either you take my humble hand, or I sling you over my shoulder. Either way, I'm taking you to your comfort." He watched me for a quiet moment, thoughtful. "Which do you prefer, my lady?"

"The less extreme of the extremely limited options," I said in surrender, my voice low as a whisper.

"Good choice." He outstretched his arm even farther towards me. When he noticed that I wasn't too eager to accept his strange kindness, he rose to his feet and asked, "Would you rather follow me instead?"

My back still pressed hard against the rocky walls. I was too numb to move.

"There's nowhere to run, my lady," he said, seeming concerned. "If you attempt to run, I'll simply run after you. The only way to your well-being is through me."

I breathed and swallowed back my tears so I wouldn't look weak in front of him. I looked at my hands and squirmed at the dirt, filth, and grime that attached to me. "Lead and I'll follow," I said in a voice just above a whisper, hands clasped together.

* * *

Jadherey escorted me fluidly out of the dungeon to my new *prison*—a large, wooden-floored room with sliding glazed doors that covered one side of the wall. Lord De-Deganon was true to his word. I gazed in awe at the prodigious view of Tregtaria from at least four floors up.

The servant busied himself, laying towels and a melange of cloth on the bed in silence.

"W-Why is the lord doing this for me?" I hesitated, unsure if I was right to ask.

He stared at me for a prolonged moment, expressionless, like he was thinking of the most perfect response. "What would you have him do, my lady?"

Okay, this was pointless. "Please call me Alessia. I don't think I've earned the word *lady* yet."

His eyebrows arched—well manicured, I observed. "If my good lord says you've earned it, then you have." He held his gaze. "You need a bath," he pointed out with a slight grin.

"Thanks," I muttered, smiling.

"It's that way," he said, gesturing towards a wooden door to my left. He strode closer. His deep-blue tunic contrasted his eyes, but it worked. When he reached me, he dropped to one knee and handed me a set of towels.

I stumbled towards the bathroom, feeling the weight of my legs. As I placed my hand on the brass door handle, I turned round to notice him watching me, a thoughtful expression on his face.

"You can put your mind at ease, my lady. Lady De-Deganon's court is sealed off from leering eyes. There are only two guards beyond the corridor, and they don't venture this far in. You'll be safe." He ran his hand over his mass of hair and dipped his head slightly before pivoting to leave. "I'll see to your breakfast."

"Thank you," I said, failing to shake off the quiver in my voice.

Maybe the Star gods are watching over me, after all. I looked up to the wooden ceiling as I strode into the rather quaint bathroom. *Thank you. Thank you.*

I took my time in the bath to rid my body of all the filth

from my travel. Once I was certain I'd scrubbed and buffed everywhere, I tiptoed back into the spacious bedroom. After drying my hair, I quickly braided it into a side knot to make it more manageable.

The dress on the bed drew my attention, and I picked it up and flipped it a few times. I couldn't work out which was the front or the back. It was just a mishmash of red and blue cloth. *What kind of a dress is this?* There were eight belt buckles, six fasteners, and loose material sewn into it here and there. The farrago of cloth confused the life out of me. Giving up, I wrapped a towel around me and sat on the four-poster bed in silent dejection.

Now what? I sprang up and swooped to the closet in the corner of the room to find something else to wear, but it was empty, and my clothes were missing, too. I shut the doors, crossed to the bed, and eased myself onto it.

The bed cover was made of animal hide. "This is Tregtaria," I muttered, reminding myself. I was a long way from home. My mind floated in a sea of what might have been.

A pounding knock at the door made my heart gallop. I jumped to my feet, wrapping my towel more tightly.

"Y-Yes?" I hesitantly called out.

The door swung open, and a woman swept in. Her dark gaze wandered over me for a second. Suddenly, I felt way too under-dressed—well, *undressed*—now that she glared at me with something between disapproval and dissatisfaction.

Her black leather armour fit her to perfection. It was as if I was standing face-to-face with *Xena: Warrior Princess*. "My brother's secret obsession," she said slowly in an orotund yet modulated voice.

Charming. I dipped my head.

"If your intention is to remain undraped for the duration of your stay, it could easily be arranged."

A surge of heat rose inside my chest, and I grabbed the dress from the bed. "I'm so sorry. I've tried everything I could think of...but I'm not sure how to put this on."

She raised her thick eyebrows then narrowed her eyes. She used her boot to slam the door shut, strode towards me, and drew her sword out.

I smothered a frown. *Is the sword really necessary?* She aimed her sword at me before pointing it towards the dress, effortlessly lifting the dress off my hands. She threw the dress into the air and caught it with her left arm.

I gazed in awe at her fluidity and quick hand. She was much taller than me, muscular, too, but not too overbearing. She slid the sword back into its sheath before doing a 360-degree walk around me.

"This frock is for the weak," she said from behind, her tone scathing. She stood behind me, too close for comfort, for a prolonged time. Swiftly, she slid the dress over my head. The towel dropped to the floor. "I'll set the boundaries now." She spun me around effortlessly to face her. She glared at me, her hand on my chin. "I'm not here to hold your hand. My due is to keep you safe until De-De returns."

In silence, she tied the belts and loose fabric across my body so quickly that I wondered how I would manage to take it off later.

"There." She placed her hands on my shoulders. "Now you look like the Honourable Tregtarian lady of house De-Deganon."

I looked up to meet her eyes. "Thank you."

She half-smiled, raising one eyebrow. "I'm De-warrior Dranisha, the lord's sister." Her voice rose in pitch, pride bordering on arrogance evident in each syllable.

Younger, I discerned. "I'm honoured to meet you."

"For the first time, *De-De* has trusted me with the realm, thanks to you." She circled me a few times, observing me like I was for show. "In which case, I should love you…but how can I love a pebble in my brother's shoe?" Her light-red eyes maintained their colour. "He asked that I behave myself around you. Not sure why he was at all concerned. You're as weak as a new-born ewie." She halted. "Breakfast?"

I nodded out of obligation, slightly nervous now, and followed her through the sliding doors to the enclosed glazed parapet balcony. The air beyond the glazed shutters was thick with dust; I could hardly see the city clearly now.

"The land of our ancestors," she said cynically. "A sand storm is just one of our many curses."

She perched herself at the edge of the table with one leg resting on the chair. I blinked several times. She stared at me again. Now I was even more uncomfortable.

Thankfully, Jadherey emerged from the bedroom lugging a food tray. "My De-warrior," he addressed Dranisha, bending down on one knee.

She nodded, and he stood and transferred some gleaming silver food flasks and sparkling trays onto the octagon-shaped table. Dranisha eased herself onto the chair opposite me, her gaze remaining on me.

With a quick hand, Jadherey placed a water pitcher and a couple of goblets on the table. Next he laid a handful of napkins on the side before setting a wooden bowl next to me. Meticulously, he lifted the lids off the trays.

"Oh my God!" I gasped in horror.

My stomach squirmed. I leaned back, tilting my head backwards with a sudden movement. Dranisha lifted her left eyebrow. If I were anywhere else but there, I would have bolted in the other direction. Breakfast was a ghastly horror show. Two harrowing animal heads with painful expressions etched on their faces faced each other on two silver trays. Various cuts of brown and reddish rancid meat were set around the heads, and in the third tray were at least a dozen skewered rat-looking creatures that appeared to have been flame-roasted.

Absolutely not. No, no. I'm not touching any of it.

Jadherey dished a large portion into Dranisha's bowl, filling it to the brim. Next he strode to my side of the table. He placed a couple of smaller cuts of meat into my bowl, stealing a glance at me like he could sense that I wasn't intending to eat any of it.

"Tarian, that's not the way to treat our guest," Dranisha said in a quiet voice. "De-De wants her fed, and that's exactly what we'll do."

"My De-warrior," he answered. He ladled my bowl with extra humongous portions that topped an already large-sized bowl. Once he was done, he dipped his head, edged backwards, lowered himself onto the floor, and crossed his legs and arms.

It's so wrong.

For a while, I fought off nausea. I watched my plate like it would suddenly grow feet and move away from me. I kept my hands under the table, clutching my thighs, unable to find the courage to touch or feel the texture of the meat. At some point, my plate had to look empty. Dranisha, the strange, uneasy lady of house De-Deganon, sat contentedly, enjoying her meal, which was more than I could say for me.

My gaze strayed towards the balcony walls. They had been canvassed over. An oil-painted portrait of Zeneshia's map glimmered in the dim light. It was an exact replica of the one Zaira had given me, but seeing it on a larger scale made it much more grand.

"Do you know much about my people?" Dranisha asked, obviously noting my interest in the painting.

I shook my head out of respect. Inside I knew enough. All I wanted was to return home, to *my* people—my family—to Dante. To a land of peace, tranquillity, and serenity, to the kingdom under the moons.

She ripped a piece of meat in half and took a bite. "All the four kingdoms are wreathed in curses. We're all cursed," she said in a toneless voice. "Those good-for-nothing Star gods that hover over our lands...are nothing but a nuisance." Abruptly she drew a pocketknife out of her holster and flung it towards the canvas.

Jadherey ducked sideways. The knife missed his eye, only just!

I caught my breath. Wide-eyed and open-mouthed, I placed

my hands on my chest, steadying my racing heart. She could have easily injured him or worse, but she didn't even flutter an eyelid.

She took another bite of her meat before eying me intently, and I dropped my gaze. "The Curse of The Triple P's is Tregtaria's very own gift from the gods—passion, pride, persistence." She picked up a napkin and dabbed it over her mouth. "And the whole raft of curses that comes with it—desire, hunger, thirst, obsession, and the resilience and tenacity that makes us unstoppable once we set our sights on our target."

Okay. From everything I'd been told, it rang true.

I looked up to the map and noted that the knife was pointing right at Tregtaria. Her aim was incredibly precise but careless.

A second later, she drew another knife before tossing it towards the painting. It landed on Tuscania. "As for your people...they are under the Curse of the Triple C's—calm, conviction, and cowardice, all under the dreamers' deceptive cloak of Sequence. There's no greater coward than one who hides behind an invisible force, too afraid to fight." She glanced at Jadherey and threw a bone at him. "They are worse than Tarian mongrels," she said, her voice filled with disgust.

What does that make me?

Jadherey picked up the bone and set it to one side. "My De-warrior."

We exchanged glances, only briefly.

Dranisha drew her sword out and flung it towards Felradia. "The original gamers of Sequence, Felradians are cursed with the Triple D's—dreams, deceit, and distrust." She glanced at me, and I smiled halfway, to assure her I was attuned to her words. "As for Njuzathians—the silent sleepers, they pulled the shortest straw. Now, how can one defend himself when one's asleep?" She laughed.

I didn't answer. I hoped it was a rhetorical question. I stared at my still full plate and immediately felt like the animal heads were staring back at me. Their eyes seemed to tell a story of torture, agony, and death. I'd spent the best part of the previous day in the company of those dead animals; now I had to eat them? I was famished but not that famished.

Abruptly, Dranisha grabbed a fork from the table and stabbed it into my plate. "Your meal is not to your taste?"

I swallowed before I could speak. "N-No, my De-warrior. I'm just not that hungry," I lied.

"In Tregtaria, if you don't lick your plate, it is an insult," she said in a stern voice, her face creased with frustration. "I trust you will not disrespect me in my house."

"I would never do anything to offend you, my De-warrior."

"Good." Her magenta-red eyes drank me in.

I picked up a slice, the smallest I could see, and forced my teeth into taking the first bite. The taste—oh, the tang! It was awful, the smell even more revolting. I don't know how I managed to keep a straight face. My teeth chattered. I tried to chew but the vile taste just didn't do it for me. The texture was a confused substance between rubber and plastic. I gulped!

For minutes, I shoved the meat into my mouth, cringing inside, swallowing without chewing. By the time I could see the bottom of my bowl, my eyes had brimmed with tears. Sweat accumulated on my forehead. My body temperature spiralled. *I'm sick. I need to retch.* My stomach couldn't process the invasion of indigestible meat, so it was driving it back up. With difficulty, I forced it down; in the end, it just got stuck inside my throat.

"That wasn't too difficult, now, was it?" she asked, a triumphant smile lingering on her face.

I shook my head, unable to speak. The agony of what was going through me threatened to end my life. *Death by meat... is that even possible?*

"I have a land to command," she said, leaning across the table towards me.

No, no, no. Stay away from me. The last thing I wanted was to throw up all over her shiny armour.

Abruptly, she perched herself onto the table, knocking all the trays and flasks onto the floor. She slithered towards me and stopped when her legs were straddled wide, too close for comfort.

I tried to pull back, but the chair seemed like it had been nailed to the floor. I leaned backwards as far as I could manage. Before I could consider her intentions fully, she hauled me forward with both arms. I gripped the edges of the table, my nails digging into the wood, breathing heavily. She held my chin for a second then slanted forward and pressed her lips tightly against mine! Afraid to move and scared to draw back any farther, I shuddered as I fought the vomit that was already brewing inside my throat and shut my eyes.

She drew back almost immediately. "You have so much to learn, human."

I opened my eyes.

She subjected me to a piercing assessment for a few heartbeats before sliding off the table. "The Tarian mongrel will attend to you." She half-smiled, pivoted, and swept away from the balcony through the sliding doors. In seconds, she vanished from view.

My hands came to my face, my breathing uneven. By then, my legs were shaking. Thick sheets of sweat dripped down my face. I gasped for air.

Jadherey rushed towards me. "You need to breathe. Slow, deep breaths."

I met his gaze, my eyes stinging. *I'm trying to!* I wanted to say but couldn't. Something putrid was stuck inside my throat, suffocating me. Air was suddenly in short supply. My stomach turned, and my throat burned. I jumped to my feet and blitzed to the bathroom with Jadherey following quickly behind.

I grabbed a bucket and shoved my head into it. Inevitably, a forceful expulsion of my stomach contents spouted out of my mouth. Every piece, shred, and grain of food I had consumed found its way into the bucket. At one point, I felt like my gut was on its way out, too. My stomach tensed, my muscles flexed, and my body spasmed violently. My energy reserves sucked out of me, I collapsed to the floor.

Jadherey grabbed a towel from the wooden rail and handed it to me.

"P-Please leave," I said with difficulty.

He knelt next to me but didn't answer.

"Y-You don't need to be here." It was bad enough for me to see my own bile and undigested food, and it had to be even worse for him, I was sure.

"Let me help you, my lady," he said, slowly hauling the bucket from my shaking hands. His eyes held a sincerity that made me even more tearful. "I'll tip it out. You need to lie down on the bed and regain your strength."

"Thank you."

He smiled earnestly and moved the bucket away from me.

I staggered into the bedroom, my head in a whirl. Seconds later, I plunged on top of the covers and shut my eyes. When I woke up, darkness met my eyes. A faint light flashed from the bedside table. I tried to sit up, but a hesitant hand held me back. I jerked my head to my left to find Jadherey kneeling next to the bed.

"You have to take it easy, my lady," he said in a low voice.

"What time is it?" I whispered.

"Just gone midnight."

My brow creased. I'd slept all day! "H-How long have you been here?"

"Not all moon-day, if that's what you mean." He rose to his feet and grabbed a goblet from the side table. "Water." He gently passed the goblet into my trembling hand. "May I?" He helped me to sit up.

I took a sip and handed the goblet back to him. "Thank you." My voice was barely above a whisper. "Why are you not asleep?"

He flashed a knowing smile. "I'm working."

"Kneeling next to my bed…is working?" I smiled, too, just for a second. My lips were dry, and I didn't want them to crack.

"I'm not kneeling now," he pointed out with a grin that implied he took in my subtle joke. "I didn't realise my cooking was that bad until today. Now I'm not sure what to offer you other than water." He raised his tidy eyebrows and held out the goblet again.

I felt a pang of guilt. "I'm so sorry—"

"Don't be. It's meant to be a joke."

"Oh! Okay." I blinked a few times, stretching my arm towards him. "Water is just fine." I took a couple of sips as my stomach rumbled.

He seemed kind but sad. Still, there was something about his striking eyes that made me feel a bizarre kind of calm.

* * *

The next day, I woke up early—by my standards. Astonishingly, a set of fresh towels and a couple of tunics were laid out at the foot of my bed, and, for once, I was alone. After my bath, I slipped into a chartreuse-green over-sized tunic that transformed into a robe once I put it on.

I strode to the balcony and leaned on the rail. Today, the air beyond the glass was clearer, but there was no change in relation to the intense heat that met me. I opened the glass shutters to try and get some fresh air. Instead a gust of warm wind blew in. The clip-clop of hooves from the street called out to me.

I stood on my toes and peered into the vast Tregtarian city. Hundreds of colourful Corinthian-style buildings complete with eye-catching columns coupled with a scatter of trees sat in my line of sight. My escape was next to impossible…alone. I needed someone who knew the land; an ally.

The sound of distinct and unhurried footsteps came from behind. I spun round and was face to face with Jadherey.

"My lady." He carried a silver bowl and bent down on one knee.

"Alessia," I insisted.

He grinned, showing a sturdy set of white teeth. "I'm sorry, my lady. I have to address you appropriately."

I found myself smiling, too. *I have to make you my ally. You are my way home. You just don't know it yet.* "Okay," I said after a moment. I strode closer to him. "Could you at least stop kneeling down for me?"

"I'm here to serve you, my lady." He held out the bowl.

I placed it on the table and then shook my head. "Not like this, Jadherey."

"I don't know any other way, my lady." He raised his gaze and smiled again, earnestly. "You're a guest in Lord De-Deganon's house."

"You're wrong." I eased myself into the chair, tweaking at the sleeves of my oversized tunic. "I'm a captive, not a guest," I murmured.

"Tregtarians don't treat their captives like guests, my lady," he said quietly, sitting down on the floor like it was his rightful place. He cleared his voice. "I took the liberty of keeping meat off your menu today, my lady." He hesitated. "I'm afraid it's just *hichesa*—bread and honey." He seemed kind, considerate even, and I was a stranger.

"Thank you. Will you eat with me?" I tried my luck. If he was to become my passage to freedom, I needed him to feel comfortable around me.

His jaw tightened. "My place is right here, my lady," he said unconvincingly. I was sure, inside, he knew it wasn't his place.

Okay, this isn't working.

Just then, a thought came to me. With the bowl in one hand, I stood and strode towards him. His forehead creasing, he kept still. Once I reached him, I smiled and eased myself onto the floor next to him.

He edged back slightly, eyes wide open. "M-My lady…this is not my lady's seat!"

I gave him an upward glance to acknowledge his words, took a slice of bread, and handed it to him. He accepted it hesitantly. I picked the knife from the bowl and spread some honey onto my slice.

"My lady, this is highly inappropriate behaviour!" He edged away backwards like I was a plague, only stopping once his back was pressed against the mapped balcony wall.

I moved closer, trailing him until I sat right next to him. "In whose eyes?"

"In the all-seeing eyes that matter." His furrowed brow deepened farther. He darted a glance towards the door that led into the balcony like he was ensuring we were alone. "Lord De-Deganon—the high command—DeWarrior Dranisha."

"Honey?" I offered.

He nodded, puzzlement etched on his face. I held his hand. It was strong and warm, but a tiny bit of his index finger was missing. What happened? An accident? He kept his hand steady as I spread some honey onto his slice.

"Thank you," he said in a low voice, clearly still unsure of my motives. "Ladies should not get attached to their servants, my lady. I'm nothing but a subject to you."

"I don't see any lady, servant, or subject here." I swept my gaze around to make a point. "All I see is you, me, and some bread and honey."

He took a moment of thought, his chest heaving up and down through his tunic like he was trying to compose himself. "If I may be frank, this is highly abnormal behaviour for some-one of your station. It's strange, my lady."

Not as strange as it is to me. I smiled and caught a glimpse of warmth in his eyes. There was a softness to them, yet there seemed to be a story behind the face he revealed to me. *You're my way home, and I'll do anything to return home.*

"You'll get us both into serious trouble," he said in a strained voice.

I looked up at him. "Are you afraid?"

"Not for me, my lady. For you. For what they might do to you." He drew in a deep breath, his bread still untouched. "I'd hate it if you were hurt for something we could have avoided, my lady."

"Your concern is admirable." I touched his hand briefly, inciting a shivery reaction from him. I jerked back. *I'm so sorry.* He gazed into my eyes, an unfathomable expression settling on his face. "But I can take care of myself."

He lowered his voice. "Not in Tregtaria, you can't."

I smiled, pleased that we were getting somewhere. "That's why I have you."

"You have a servant, my lady. A subject. That's all you have," he lamented in a low and slow voice. "I'm not your guardian. I can't protect you from them."

Not wanting to admit that he had a point, I took a bite of my bread in silence.

He did, too, eyeing me every so often as if he was trying to read me like a book. "If this were a Game of Sequence, I would tell you that you're making a bad move aligning yourself to a worthless servant."

I jerked up, suddenly extra-attentive. "What do you know of a Game of Sequence?"

"Not an awful lot, just that everything that the minders and the dreamers do is done in perfect sequence; it's their way of life."

"Tuscanians and Felradians—minders and dreamers?" I enthused. Perhaps he could explain to me more about what I had tried to work out on my own.

He nodded. "Right now, you should be protecting your sequence and aligning yourself to a fruitful cause. I'm not that cause. I'm a lost cause. Look elsewhere, and you've got yourself a smart move, my lady."

"This is my move," I said with great resolve. "Two people sharing food, that's my move."

"My De-warrior will object to this, m-my lady," he stuttered.

"I'm pretty sure she'll object to a few things." I took a bite of my slice of bread.

His eyes twinkled, mine, too…I was certain. A sparkle of conspiracy, perhaps?

"I won't say if you won't." I beamed, and in return, he flashed a genuine smile that made me so hopeful. He *was* my way back home. For a short while, we ate in silence. Every so often, I intercepted a glance in my direction.

"My lady, the lord demands your comfort," he restated. "Sitting on the floor and dining with a servant is not a good start."

"Do you do everything that the lord asks you to do?"

"I'm a servant. My choices are limited."

"Now you serve me?"

He nodded and lowered his head.

"So if I were to ask you to do something for me, would you?" I looked him in the eye.

"Within reason, my lady."

"If I were to ask you to let me go back home, would you?"

He took a moment of thought. "That would be going against my reason for being here. Out there in the wilderness, you're not safe or comfortable. The Sands of the Dead is no place for you. If the blustering furnace doesn't get to you first, the sand snakes will."

My breath hitched. "Sand snakes?" I had an acute fear of snakes. Anything else, I could face, but snakes would be the death of me.

"If you manage to survive both, the warriors will get to you, and what they'll choose to do with you is brutal. They won't show any mercy."

"So you're saying I'm safer in De-Warrior Dranisha's arms?" I raised my brows.

"And lips," he said in a quiet voice. "If you can work your way to her heart, you'll have the game safely in the palm of your hands!"

My pulse raced. I shot Jadherey a look, my stomach squirming.

"A joke," he said with a short chuckle and a smile. "Not a good one. All I'm saying is she's a much better option than what's out there." He sighed. "Trust me on that one."

"Does she have a thing for women?" I asked after some time. I had to know what I was dealing with early on. I couldn't speculate.

"And men," Jadherey said easily.

"So she's like that with everyone?" I had to ask. The vision of her hurtling towards me before placing her cold lips on mine presented itself to my mind.

Jadherey watched me for a moment, eyes shimmering. "Not everyone, my lady," he said in a low tone that made my stomach dance. "She has impeccable taste in her mates." He took a short reflective pause. "This time she's struck the Rindinga of Sequence right between the eyes."

10. BLOODLINE

The days that followed were agonizingly slow. There was nothing for me to do except eat; not eat; drink; sleep; take a stroll around my bedroom, the balcony, and the long corridor, taking in displays of armour, family history, marble warrior statuettes, and back to my bedroom, like a prisoner without chains. It was surreal, but preferable to being in a dungeon under the castle.

Every day at noon, I was allowed time in the castle gardens for some fresh air. I had worked out that I was permitted outside for thirty minutes only, which was the time when the guards changed shifts.

An escape was constantly on my mind, but as the days went by, my faith in finding a way out was beginning to crumble. It had been two weeks since my arrival, and the only people I spoke to were Jadherey and, on occasion, De-warrior Dranisha.

The huge doors on both sides of the corridor were a deterrent. Regardless of the amount of time I'd spent taking in the bolts and the hinges, I couldn't figure out the locking mechanism.

Jadherey, the endearing servant, and I had become better acquainted. He reminded me of my teenage years on earth, how I'd tried to fit in and failed. But my plight was nowhere near his. While I had a home with Aunt Kate, even though she didn't understand me or the voices, Jadherey was all alone. I didn't know what was worse: having experienced love and losing it, or not having experienced it at all.

* * *

My third week in the land of the burning sun, I sat in the enclosure of the castle gardens underneath a sessile fig tree. My scheduled thirty minutes of fresh air was really thirty minutes of increased calefaction. The unbearable scorching heat blazed the land—it was one of those things you could never get used to. Fortunately, the setting was pleasing to the eye. Various marble pillars and fig trees adorned the huge garden. In the middle, a water fountain sprayed continuous water into the air. The downside being that the water wasn't cool.

The sun beat down like a furnace—with no breeze to soften the air—no clouds holding a promise of rain. Tregtaria, a slice of hell in Zeneshia. I'm glad I didn't have to worry about sun cream. I'd never needed it in my home world, and fortunately, I didn't need it now. Thanks to my Mauritian grandma on my dad's side of the family, I had inherited a shade of her Mediterranean skin tone. My skin was adapting better than I could say for myself. As for radiation from the sun, that was an unknown.

Jadherey, on the other hand, seemed in a brooding frame of mind. He stood by the wooden bench next to me wearing a wistful look.

"If you share your troubles, it won't take them away, but it'll make you feel ten times better," I said, knowing full well that even though we were almost like friends, now—I hoped—still, he wouldn't tell me the deepest of his inner problems. Maybe not yet, anyway.

"Apologies. I didn't think anyone would notice."

"Of course I did, and without even trying."

"You're very observant." He eased himself closer to me.

"Only to the people who are worth being observed," I comforted him. He was like a brother I wish I had.

I smiled with satisfaction, liking the idea of claiming him as my brother. It was all so surreal, though. The idea that humans were alone in our universe was nothing more than a popular fallacy on earth. In my new world, I had found a family, a love, and now a brother—in Tregtaria of all places! The gods were smiling down on me.

His shoulder-length dark hair was neatly tied at the back, and his red shock of hair gleamed in the afternoon sun. Not a strand was astray. His well-ironed wine-red tunic fit him to perfection, highlighting his broad shoulders and a well-toned body. If you didn't know better, you'd assume he was Lord De-Deganon's son, not a servant.

"What is it, my lady?" he asked.

"Are you really a servant?" I threw the question at him. As absurd as it sounded, that question had played up on my mind and kept me awake for nights on end.

He smiled breezily, rose to his feet, and stood a couple of metres from me, adjacent to the sprinkling water fountain. "What? Don't I tick all the boxes for a servant, my lady?" He slanted me a playful look, dipping his head slightly.

"Not even one box," I said honestly. For a few heart-beats, I watched in admiration at how his eyes twinkled and his russet skin seemed to glow beautifully despite the unbearable heat. "There's something about you. You take an enormous amount of abuse from the warriors, which sug-gests you're indeed a servant or a slave, yet you're thoroughly kempt—well-spoken—astute—etiquette…"

"For a servant?" he asked, stepping to the other side of the spraying fountain.

"Well, yes. All this time, it's been troubling me. And today it's still occupying my mind. I can't quite figure you out."

He paced around the marble floor of the gardens, hands behind his back. Every so often he glanced in my direction. He looked trendy in his dark-red tunic with black trim, just as though he had stepped out of a storybook. "Lord De-Deganon takes pride in his hygiene and sanitation." He swung me a charming look. "He considers it unhygienic to have a servant who looks like a dust mop serving him."

"Perhaps, but you're too kempt for that role...as if you are his son."

He flashed me a knowing smile. It was as though he was thinking of the most perfect response. I merely watched him and realised I enjoyed looking at him. Perhaps he was Lord De-Deganon's Trojan horse, maybe not, but the fact was he made each day bearable for me, and for that, he was *my* Trojan horse and *my* way back home.

Suddenly, he spun round, amusement dawdling on his lips. "Servants in your world don't bathe?" He raised a quizzical eyebrow, his tone somewhere between a jest and a dare.

I smiled. "Of course they do."

A teasing smile lingered, summoning a twinkle in his red eyes. "They don't bathe as well as I do?"

I managed a short laugh. "No, I didn't mean that."

"Are they mutes?" he continued with his rather funny charade of questions, leaning against the trunk of the tree.

I shook my head. "Again, I didn't mean that."

He loped to the other side of the fountain. "Do they lack some impeccable manners?" He flashed a casual smile, his red eyes dancing with subtle amusement.

"For the last time, Jadherey," I raised my voice playfully, "I didn't mean that either!" I laughed. He was a banterer. It was as though I was watching a beautifully choreographed one-man theatre production.

Effortlessly, he sidestepped, and in less than a heartbeat, he eased himself next to me. "So what exactly did you mean, my lady?" He lowered his voice, his masculine scent of lime, peach, and cucumber wafting into the air.

We stared at each other for a while until we both broke into a peal of laughter.

"You're insufferable," I jested in between bursts of laughter. "Do you know that?" I gathered myself, accepting fully that I would never figure him out completely. He was one of those mysteries that would always remain unsolved.

He took a moment of thought, gaze fixed on me. "Anything to put a smile on my lady's face is worth my time and effort." The words slid off his tongue so slickly like he had practiced that line for decades.

My smile broadened into a grin. "So all that stunning production was just to make me smile?" I had to ask.

He didn't answer right away. "There isn't much in the way of entertainment, my lady. I had to improvise."

Heartened, I patted his hand lightly. "Thank you."

"Anytime," he said in such a joshing way I bubbled in laughter. "You're happy." A curious smile flickered across his face.

"You remind me of someone," I blurted out with a grin. His deep-red tunic matched the colour of his eyes, too familiar.

"Care to share who that someone is?" he asked, a grin travelling across his face. He ran his hand over his hair—just like Dante used to do.

I held my breath. "You wouldn't know him—his name is Dante." I halted when I felt a flutter inside my stomach.

Mouth agape, he stared at me. "You've met Dante the runner?" he asked urgently.

"Well, I suppose, if that's what you call him." My brow crinkled at his enthusiasm.

"He's Tregtarian, right?"

I nodded, even more curious. "You know him?"

"I met him once, only briefly, the moon-night he ran away." He looked away, reflecting. "High-Commander Jizu Haurilio's only son."

My heart skipped and went into a gallop. "High-Commander Jizu is his dad?" I repeated, taking it by the chin.

I knew his father was the highest commander of the Tregtarian warriors, but I just didn't think it was *him*. Having it confirmed was a bit difficult to bear. High-Commander Jizu was my captor, a ruthless warrior. He'd ordered Hyperian's death by the shield. He'd stolen my pendant—the jewel of the ocean—from my neck. He was the most unforgiving man I'd ever met.

"You're in shock?"

I nodded my head, slowly. "I-I just hadn't processed that."

His gaze darted about before he stared back at me as if he was looking to ensure we were alone. "Dante's defiance is a sore point for Jizu. He's never quite recovered from his son's betrayal. If Dante is anything like his father…" He left the words hanging in the air before leaning back on the bench.

"He's *nothing* like him." I swallowed hard.

Jadherey leaned towards me and whispered, "He means something to you? Thank the moons he's under the protection of the shield. The high command is unpredictable, and Jizu even more so. And one thing he doesn't do is suffer betrayal gladly."

My mind sifted through his words. I knew the high command would get their wish soon—for I was certain Dante would pull through his illness and would come for me. I could feel it!

* * *

A month went past at a snail's pace, and I was dwindling. The heat drained all the energy from me. I shrivelled inside and out. Lord De-Deganon was still at war. I was glad I had Jadherey. I supposed it would have been worse if he weren't there.

But there was something bizarre about his whereabouts, too. Some days he was there, and others he was gone. I'd noticed a trend: three days around, two days away. With the abuse *they* inflicted on him, I didn't think he was allowed a moment off, let alone a couple of days off. On some days, I'd watched discreetly from the balcony as the guards in the courtyard poured insults at him, lashing at him whenever they wanted. For some peculiar reason, he chatted about everything else except where he went when he wasn't there. And then every time Jadherey was away, there was a mysterious someone who slipped in at the crack of dawn and left my daily rations in the hallway. He'd disappear before I awoke. The guards beyond the corridor were stealth-quiet. Not once had I heard a sound from them.

Fortunately, De-warrior Dranisha had since vanished, too. She hardly ventured to my room, thank the gods. Any time she was close, she kept me on my toes, and I didn't like it. I could never work out any of her moves, or whether she had any moves at all. She did as she pleased.

The bedroom door squeaked. I twirled round, beaming. "Jadherey!" I enthused. "You're back!"

Jadherey returned my smile. In silence, he mulled over something again. It was becoming a habit. His eyes sung a different song to what he let on. I hadn't seen him in two days. He was the highlight of my day—someone to talk to—someone to relate to—someone who was as much a prisoner as I was.

"You're dressed in deep purple today, yet, it still seems to work with the red of your eyes," I teased, striding towards him. "What's the secret?"

"If I didn't know better," he said, keeping his gaze steady, "I would say my choice of wardrobe seems to appeal to you more than I do to you."

I threw my arms around him, and he gave me a warm hug. "Well, I'm not hugging a walking wardrobe right now. I'm hugging you," I said with a short chuckle. "That must mean something."

"Since my wardrobe doesn't bother you," he whispered, amusement in his tone, "if I were to disrobe, would you still hug me?"

"Oh my god!" I drew back, and pressed my palms lightly against my cheeks. "I don't want that image inside my head."

He broke into a peal of laughter. "A joke," he hastened to

say, his expression remorseful. "A really stupid joke. I don't even know why I said it."

"You just look so stunning in tunics," I said truthfully. "Every time I see you, it's as if you've stepped out of my history book."

He quirked an amused brow. "I remind you of your ancestors? Now, that hurts, my lady." He dipped his head.

"Hey!" I punched him lightly on his arm. "You know exactly what I mean."

"My lady." He bowed theatrically, his voice low and melodic. We were way past the formalities.

"My servant," I responded, feigning seriousness only I ended up laughing.

"Your humble servant is making an effort to impress you with his limited variety of tunics, and yet he reminds you of your ancestors?" He dramatically brought his strong hands to his chest. "Please tell me they died young and still in their prime."

I slumped onto the four-poster bed in laughter. I treasured these few moments of bliss. Jadherey made me laugh. In his own unique way, he made me forget that I was a prisoner. With him, I had moments of freedom—I had moments of happiness…incomplete joy for nothing could fill the hole inside my heart at missing Dante—my family—Tuscania.

Still, he made my time in Lord De-Deganon's castle bearable. He made the days shorter, the nights endurable. He made me believe in the Voice of Sequence's words: *there's a sequence to life, love, and death.* My sequence, my life in my new world had to be aligned to his in a perfect, seamless alignment that was mindboggling. Yet there was one thing I could never work out. Why?

"I have something for you." He slid his hands into his tunic pockets, strode towards me, and handed me a couple of narisha fruits.

I raised my eyebrows appreciatively. "Oh, Jadherey, you remembered!"

A few days before, as we'd sat on the floor having lunch, he'd asked me what I missed most of all. Naturally my first answer had been Dante, followed by my family, Tuscania, Aunt Kate, and my cousins.

"What about the food?" he'd asked.

"Narishas," I'd said without even thinking. "Because they remind me of Dante." My mind had wandered off to the day I first had the narisha fruit, and I'd relived every second we were together; his striking ruby eyes—his flawless smile—his touch…everything about him was perfect to me.

Jadherey had laughed lightly before his features tightened. "So we can safely conclude that the only son of the most callous and notorious high commander Jizu of house Haurilio and the man who instigated your abduction…is your life?" His voice had grown quieter.

"And everything in it," I'd said. "Dante's not like him, Jadherey. He's more like you."

He'd paused. "He was brought up a warrior, I a coward." He swallowed. "There's a huge difference."

"Not to me. You have a good heart. You're more than a warrior…you're you!"

He'd smiled handsomely, his red eyes searing into mine. "W-Would you ever go back to your home world without him?"

We both knew that my returning to earth was Lord De-Deganon's plan, only he and his commanders would be in tow. I'd imaged how the human world would stand still at the sight of red-eyed Tregtarian warriors emerging from the waters. The last thing I wanted was to appear on Sky News leading an invasion of aliens into my home world.

"Over his or my dead body," I'd said truthfully. There was no way I would return to earth without Dante.

I threw Jadherey an avid glance. "Where did you get these?"

Dante had mentioned that narishas only grew in the Forestland of Felradia. "I took the liberty of picking them from the warrior's kitchen…Scarface and his entourage have returned early from Felradia."

"No, no, no. You have to take them back!" I passed them urgently back into his hands. "If you're caught—"

"Don't worry about me," he reassured. "You should be worrying about *you*. You're not eating much. I've tried all I can to cook to your liking, but all there really is is meat."

"I know." I smiled.

In one month, we had come a long way. I didn't see him as my passage to freedom anymore. I wanted him to find his freedom, too. I knew now he deserved it more than I did. He didn't kneel for me, either, except in the presence of Dranisha. He even called me by my birth-given name. Knowing him was a true blessing.

A playful smile lingered on the corners of his lips "I may be the best cook in all of Tregtaria, but I can't miraculously transmogrify meat into vegetables. This diet you're on will kill you faster than Dranisha's sword. You need the strength," he whispered. He placed the narishas back into my hands, his fingers tightening around mine.

Something bothered him. His cheerfulness was too controlled, his eyes too wistful.

"What's the matter?" I asked.

He released my hands and paced about the room in silence. A while later, he strode towards me. "I c-can't let them turn you into one of them. Y-You need to go." He gritted his teeth.

"What do you mean I need to go? Where?" He wasn't making sense.

He held my hands again. "Home, Alessia. Home!"

A flood of cold water drenched through me. "You're scaring me."

He took a deep, hurried breath. "The guards will change shifts soon. Grab your shoes." He looked around the bedroom and at the door. "Take nothing else. Wait for me to come for you," he whispered, edging quickly towards the door.

"Jadherey, stop!" I rushed towards him and pushed myself in front of him. "Is there something you're not telling me?"

He bit his lip and raked his hand through his hair. "I don't know where to start. Y-Your bloodline is a threat to Tregtaria."

"You know about my bloodline?" I demanded, my tone higher than I'd anticipated.

He held my right hand in both of his, like he needed my full concentration. "Six hundred moon-years ago, Alessia the warrior slayer—your ancestor—drove an army of Tregtarian warriors out of Tuscania using the power of her mind. She made them all turn on each other, slaughtering thousands of men and injuring many others."

"She had my name?" I mumbled, flummoxed.

"Your name sealed your fate long before De-Deganon knew you were a descendant of house Serenius. Since the great battle, house De-Deganon were tasked with finding your bloodline and have been seeking to control or destroy any traces of it."

My brow furrowed. *Is that why Lord De-Deganon is after my mum?*

Blood rushed to my head. A migraine was seconds away. My hand shook in his as I tried to piece the information together. I needed to understand my place in this world, but this information tripled my confusion.

"H-How do you know all of this?"

"I can't explain it now. As long as you're in this land, you're not safe."

"I was never safe, Jadherey, but neither are you!" I cried. "If I'm going, you're coming with me."

"My fate was sealed long before my birth. I accept that now. You were born for far greater things. Staying here is not right for you—"

"It's quite droll what you two have going on there," a voice echoed from the doorway.

Jadherey instantly let go of my hand and dropped to one knee.

I swung my arms back, curtsying, my heart pounding in all my veins. I stared at De-warrior Dranisha's chilling eyes, praying she hadn't heard us.

"What's not right?" She strode closer, ogling us.

"My De-warrior," Jadherey whispered, head lower than low.

"Carry on." She perched her leg on top of the bed. "You can't stop now."

Her gaze darted from me, to Jadherey, and back to me. Although I kept a straight face, I trembled inside. She appeared calm, but I now knew she could flip any second. Jadherey kept still, head dipped.

"If your tongues are of no use to you, I can easily find a new home for them," she said flatly. She drew her whip out of her belt and pulled her bludgeon out, keeping her eyes at us. I didn't know if she intended to use the weapons, or it was just to scare us.

She half-smiled, like she was inside my head. Her angular face wasn't giving much away.

I cleared my voice, nervous. "My De-warrior, we—"

"Time's up!" bawled Dranisha, cutting me off.

Like a cheetah about to pounce on its prey, she lurched towards Jadherey. Before I'd taken another breath, she thwacked the side of his head with the bludgeon. I screamed and then froze! Ice splinters cut through my body vein by vein. My eyes grew misty, my breath came sharp and choppy, and my stomach squirmed.

Jadherey tumbled to the floor, hitting his head yet again. A moment of silence followed; he wasn't moving. He just lay still—helpless—eyes shut. My hands came to my face, and my gaze followed Dranisha's arm as she raised her leather whip into the air.

"No!" I cried.

I streaked towards Jadherey, the corner of my eye catching sight of Dranisha's whip on its way down. I was too late. She struck his back, and before she could thrash him again, I threw myself on top of him. Inevitably, Dranisha lashed me twice across my back.

"Ahhh!" I cried.

She halted, her heavy breathing sounding louder with each breath. In acute physical and mental pain, my tears didn't need an invitation this time. I remained still, laying over Jadherey, unsure of Dranisha's next move. My mouth quivered. I cautiously got up to my knees, avoiding eye contact with Dranisha. I held Jadherey's head carefully. Blood oozed from his left temple.

The numbness, subsequent itch and searing pain from my back were the least of my worries. "S-Stay still, you'll be fine," I whispered into his ear. I didn't know what else to say. He was as motionless as death. Jadherey needed help. I checked his pulse; it was faint. My dad had taught me the basics of first aid, but it was of no use now. He needed a doctor, a healer...someone.

"Touching!" Dranisha's cold voice burst with cruel sarcasm.

My mouth still trembling, I looked up at her. "H-Help him, please...h-help him," I begged.

She glowered at me, her upper lip curled in disdain. "You exhaust your tears on a Tarian mongrel, an inferior being who was shunned by the Star gods, the moons and the devil himself. You disgust me!" She charged out of the bedroom, slamming the door shut behind her.

"Jadherey," I whispered. "Can you hear me?" My voice wavered, my tears in free-flow.

He didn't answer.

I rushed towards the bed, grabbed a pillow, loped to the bathroom for a wet towel, and dashed back to him. Taking short, raspy breaths, I cautiously turned him round so he could face upwards, ensuring as minimal movement of his head as I could manage. I laid his head on the pillow and dabbed his temple with the towel. He remained motionless.

"You'll pull through," I whispered helplessly. "You have to... your life will not end like this. You have to live. You've yet to live." A single tear dropped from my eye and onto his cheek. I wiped it off. "T-To the South Star god of love...p-please love him enough to spare his life. He needs you...he needs someone...he needs you, please—"

The door creaked and swung open. Three warriors stormed in. I fled back towards the balcony, but one grabbed me by the neck. A numbing chill trickled across my back. I held onto the warrior's hand, kicking vigorously, trying to scream, but I was too choked to find my voice.

One of the warriors jabbed a syringe into my neck. I wailed in agony. The corner of my eye caught sight of the scar-faced warrior smiling cunningly. Moments later, the man shoved a sack over my head. Darkness triumphed, and as a matter of course, I lost consciousness.

11. THREE-PINNED MEN

From the depths of oblivion to the strange reality of a chilling douse of water, I opened my eyes in terror. My breath came short and raspy. A continuous ringing and the sound of my heartbeat thrashed in my ears. My head pounded as a pulsating pain engulfed the back of it. I trembled, a cold chill cascading down my spine. My teeth chattered; I rolled over and realised I was lying on soggy ground. Twisting tensely in the muddy, two-foot-deep waters, I prayed for some warmth. I hugged my knees between my arms before an orotund voice made me look up in panic.

Three peculiar-looking men in pale-blue robes loomed over me. "*Titambire ze*—welcome to...*Sanchuri atunya*—the house that thunders," the tallest of the men said in Zenesh, the one in the middle interpreting in English. I curled into a tiny ball.

Their eyes flashed a strange yellow colour.

I shut my eyes, and a surreal vision of me flashed across my vision. I squinted. I lay on some sort of altar whilst the three men hovered over me. *Protect the womb!* A drawling voice inside my head made my heart lurch. *That's your sequence. Protect the womb!* I opened my eyes with a jerk.

I'm dreaming. I'm awake. The three men? Dizziness engulfed me. I blinked. Fear clutched at my stomach, freezing my insides, and I gulped down breaths to stay quiet.

"About time you graced us with consciousness," the one in the middle, sporting a broken lip, said. "We were beginning to lose the will to keep awake."

Unable to quell the tremor within me, I shuddered at his feverish look. Their skin was pale white, so pale you'd think there was no blood running through their veins. *Who are you? What are you?* Terror kept the words inside of me. I shivered.

"Rise," the broken-lipped man said, gesturing with his hand. His voice sounded so distant, emotionless.

I took a deep breath and used my hands to help me to my feet. My legs shook. I struggled to keep myself upright. The long, ivory silk dress I wore had since lost its richness of colour and weightlessness. It dragged heavily over my shoulders. A throbbing pain shot through my legs. Coupled with the excruciating pain inside my head, it was a matter of time before I sank into the waters.

What have you done to me? Slowly an awareness of my captivity sank in. My gaze darted about. I wasn't in Lord De-Deganon's castle. *Where am I? How did I get here? Could it be days, weeks, months?*

I was in a swampy courtyard. Dark-tea water ruled the terrain. I couldn't work out if it was a man-made swamp or just one of nature's wonders. Three trees with twining vines rambling over their trunks dominated the water-logged area. The smell of composting leaves suffused the air.

I vividly searched for an escape, any escape, but surrounding us was a maze of identical doors. I looked around for any sign of Tregtarian guards or warriors, but it seemed to be just me, the three men, and an unusually wet terrain.

Set in a droke, a marvel of architecture set the scene of a triangulated cloister, except there was nothing marvellous about it. Dark waters made the courtyard inhabitable. The brown brick building with pillars and at least a dozen, arched doors carried a rusty but solid air. A panorama of snowy peaks surrounded us in all directions; an escape was totally fruitless.

The three men led me west. I staggered behind the them, my legs heavy through the muddy waters. They would give way any second. I brought my hands to my head as an unusual ringing sound buzzed continuously, like I'd been submerged in water for a long time.

Suddenly, a roaring and rumbling sound echoed. I halted, my hands on my mouth. The ground shook, and the water swirled haphazardly. *Earthquake!* I lost my footing and slid into the waters with a splash. My heart hammered at the vibration.

The quaking lessened. I wiped the mud off my face and settled my gaze at the towering mountains surrounding us. I blinked a few times. I couldn't believe my eyes. *Oh my God! We're in a volcanic crater!* I quickly shifted my gaze to the three men. They had halted, too, now kneeling, facing the north. They appeared to be in a meditative state.

What are you doing? I wanted to scream out, but the pounding inside my head seemed louder than the rumbling coming from the mountains. I clenched my head. I wasn't sure if the strange men grasped that we were sitting ducks.

Panicking, I tried to stand up, slipped, and tumbled into the water again. *The volcano can erupt any minute!* Death by burning ash was not how I'd envisaged my demise.

Minutes later, the tremors and thundering noise subsided. I rose to my feet, and so did the three men. Hands behind their backs, they strolled forward slowly, as if time stood still for them. Their lengthy robes with long trains floated behind them. There was an eeriness about them—an unnatural aura— spooky, even.

They didn't look Tregtarian; neither did they appear to be Tuscanian, but they could speak my native language, which until now, I thought only Tuscanians could do. There was just something about them that made them less human, more creature…

I shuddered, shivered, and took a very deep breath to calm my nerves. With slow, hesitant movements, I toddled behind them, squelching my way through the water. A moment later, they all stood by one of the doors, staring back at me.

The tallest man swung the door open and beckoned me towards them. "Enter!"

I watched in disbelief as the water channelled around the door despite the room being on slightly higher ground. I took three steps up before stopping. Summoning all the courage I could find, I took four more steps and halted by the uninviting entrance.

My captors ambled in, and I edged in, too, suppressing the shiver inside of me. The door slammed shut. Darkness followed. A rush of cold, chilling air enveloped me. *How can it be so cold if we are in a volcanic crater?*

I inched back, but there was nowhere to go. A spine-chilling gloom met my eyes. My feet trembled in the waters that now reached just above my ankles. I smothered a scream. We were secluded and isolated from the reality of the world. I braced my back against the door, shivering. All I could now see were the three men's glowing eyes in the dark.

"The house that thunders is not kind to strangers…" a voice said. I couldn't tell whose voice it was.

An eerie bounce chorused in return. I jumped, my eyes darting around the darkness. I leaned against the wall, my heart pounding inside my chest. My spine felt like a block of ice had replaced it.

"Your elusive human mind continuously seeks to defy us," the same voice as before drawled and a chorus of whispers echoed.

What? Are you for real?

"In your sleep state, you denied us passage into your mind—into your precious womb." The echo was so loud I placed my hands on my ears. "Now you force our hand to use our ancestors' way."

"W-What do you want with my womb?" I somehow managed to get the words out through a burning throat. It didn't make sense. "W-What do you want from me?" My voice shook.

"The sequence of your womb is what we need," another voice drawled and a reverberation followed. I couldn't tell who was speaking.

Surrounded by pitch-darkness and six flashing eyes, I huddled against the wall whimpering to destruction. There were no shadows or anything that resembled a whisper of hope. I shut my eyes to try and keep my sanity, but strangely, my earlier vision returned. I was laying on a wooden altar, water dripping to the floor, with the three strange men looming over me. Despite my exhausted mind, I tried to work out if it was a mere dream, a surreal vision, or maybe a weird hallucination, or a glimpse into some bizarre future or past.

Before I could comprehend an answer, an excruciating pain shot through my head, as if three daggers had been shoved into my brain. I collapsed to the waterlogged ground, groaning and writhing in agony. This was a hundred times worse than a migraine.

"The sooner you let us in, the earlier we can all go back to sleep." The creepy voice got creepier.

I realised then that the three men were the reason for my newest affliction.

"P-Please s-stop!" I cried, but my plea was barely audible. "H-Help me!" The three-pronged piercing pain continuously shot through my head. Clenching my head with both hands, I curled into a tight ball, doused in water.

"Let us in!" the eerie voice bounced back against the walls. "Let us into the womb!" The sound magnified tenfold.

My breath came in in choppy gasps. My throat ached. I couldn't swallow. I couldn't scream. I couldn't let them into my mind or my womb, but I couldn't block them, either. Whatever my mind was doing, I had no control over it. I didn't know how to do what they were asking of me, or I'd have done it already, just so I could get rid of the pain. *I just want to go home.* A blinding pain pierced the sides of my head. I pressed my fists to my temples, wishing the pain away.

"H-Help me!" I cried again, tears streaming down.

"Let us in!" The eerie voice was drawn out.

There was no one to save me but myself. Through the agony,

fear, and confusion, I recalled Ralda's teachings: "Maintain your mindfulness. Your life is precious! Be aware of the sequence to life, love, and death. The path to death is through life and love. Life ends, and death comes for everyone! Recall that everything you do, whether righteous or not, whether courageous or not, whether willingly or not has an outcome, complete Sequence. Focus on your strengths. Fight for your sequence. You are your own destiny!"

"I'm my own destiny... Fight for my sequence... I'm my own destiny," I recited into the darkness.

In my moment of despair, Dante flashed across my eyes. From the throes of pitch-darkness to the deepness of Dante's red eyes, I saw him in front of me. He seemed so real, so inviting—expecting—wanting—waiting. His strong arms rose towards me. I was a few steps away from my safe haven. My arms stretched towards him, reaching out.

"Dante!" I called out. "Dante!" I knew he wasn't real, but I had to take a chance. Maybe he could hear me.

"Your mind can run...but it can't hide." The whispering voices threatened to drive me mad.

I focused on the one thing that made my heart continue to beat. Yes, I knew he was just a hallucination, but still, I held onto his image for as long as I could. "Dante," I whispered. His lips moved, but I couldn't hear what he was saying. "I'm not okay... I'll never be okay! I need you!"

"Time is our forte, human." The chilling voice was colder than the murky waters I lay in. "You will yield—you will break—you will succumb."

Jets of strong, pulsing pain shot through me. I kept my eyes shut, holding onto the image of Dante, but inevitably, the vision began to fade away.

"No! No! No!" I tried to get the image back. Replacing it was the strange image of my body lying on the altar again.

"You will let go."

"Don't go, Dante. Don't go…" I whispered, my mouth quivering.

"You will unlock those memories!"

"No, no, no." I shook uncontrollably, the cold water splashing around me.

"You will accept new memories!"

"Don't leave. P-Please don't leave."

"You will reveal the path to your womb!" they chanted continuously. "You will reveal the gateway to your world!"

A sudden pounding knock at the door broke the three-pinned men's hold over me. The pain vanished. Replacing it was overwhelming mental and physical exhaustion like I'd been running a marathon. I flung my eyes open. A streak of light emerged from the partly ajar door. Breathing heavily, I nestled against something that felt like a log. The creaking door opened and shut almost immediately. I searched around for the glowing eyes. Nothing. I was now alone.

Soft rustling sounds resounded from beyond the walls. The voices were muted. We weren't alone I gathered with a slight tinge of relief. I listened intently, but I couldn't make out any of the words.

A while later, the door squeaked and flew open. The broken-lipped man strode in. He hooked an oil lamp into the wall, and a flash of light zapped across the room.

You're giving me a lamp so I can see my demise? I was thankful for the light but I didn't understand their intentions.

He stared at me for a second before tossing a bowl of something that resembled food towards me. The wooden bowl floated about in my direction. "Regain your strength, human. Death is not an option for you. We will resume our game, and you will reveal the path to your womb long before death has met you." His feverish eyes tightened. "Eat."

When the man left, I noted that the room was like a bare eggshell. No windows, no colour, the floor submerged by dark-tea-coloured water. A few logs were scattered across the room, guiding the water in a peculiar spiral way. My breathing evened out. My shadow seemed much bigger and daunting, too.

Where is the water coming from? The babble and gurgle of water suggested there was a brook or a river nearby. Strangely, the continuous circulation indicated there was an outlet and an inlet of water. I was slowly getting hypnotised.

* * *

Throughout my life, water had played an unsurpassed part. When the voices on earth had threatened my sanity, crystal-clear water had been my sanctuary. When I thought my life was ending, deep-blue ocean water had provided a passage to a new life in Zeneshia. When my true love was faced with death, I had discovered the power of my mind through water in the forest of the Nadeira.

Sadly, I was now on the wrong side of the shield, yet, somehow, this murky water would have to lead me home, too.

"If you're ever in doubt, or you're unsure of your place in this world, always follow the water…" my mum had told me on our last adventure holiday in Africa. Unfortunately, a car crash had claimed her life three months later.

Every year, en route to Mauritius for my parents' anniversary, we always took a detour to Africa. Mum had an unabated fascination with the caves dotting the vastness of Southern Africa.

On our last ever trip when I was thirteen years old, we visited the Chinhoyi Caves in Zimbabwe. When she'd laid eyes on a calm pool of cobalt-blue water, something changed in her. She appeared as though she'd seen her destined serendipity—a fated encounter—a magical karma—like she'd found whatever she was looking for.

Her eyes had brimmed with tears at the sight of the Sleeping Pool. If only I'd read the signs, if only I'd carried the faith to visualise what my eyes couldn't see.

"It's really quiet here," I'd whispered as I clung onto my dad's arm.

He'd laughed lightly. "That's why it's called the Sleeping Pool, Lessi."

I had swivelled around to seek confirmation from my mum, but her tears were already in free-flow. "Mum, you're crying?" I'd asked, concerned, edging closer to her.

"I could never cry at such divine beauty. These are happy tears, Alessia," she'd answered, hugging me tightly. "This pool reminds me of a life full of endless possibilities." She'd thrown a quick glance at my dad, and he'd returned a warm smile.

I remember gazing at the pool, wowing at the colour of the water; it was a blue wonder. Strangely, it wasn't a reflection of the sky, for it was a cloudy day. But still, the deepness of the hue was simply majestic.

"The locals believe that these caves are shrouded in myths and mystery," she had said excitedly. "And to this day, no one has yet reached the bottom of this pool."

"It doesn't look that deep to me." I was young and happy, unaware of how my life would be turned upside down a few months later.

"Looks are not everything, my dear." She'd planted a soft kiss on my forehead. "It's possible that this pool could be a portal to another land."

I didn't realize she was being serious. I was young. A few years before then, I believed in Santa Claus and the Tooth Fairy, too. Now I knew she meant something much more phenomenal; Zeneshia—the world with many faces!

* * *

Whilst I floated in a reverie of my previous life, my eyes caught sight of an opening, a stone vent that appeared to be leading outside. A flicker of hope passed through me. To my right was a smaller vent channelling the water in, but that led back into the courtyard, so that wasn't any good.

Immediately, I crawled towards the vent to my left. With my head partly in the water, I stretched my hand towards the opening. I felt my hand being pulled out and realised there was some form of suction. I ran my hand over a vertical rail made from metal. I held my breath before dipping the side of my head into the water so I could try to see clearly.

"Alessia…"

A whisper made my heart skip a beat. Fear spiralled through me. I froze, unable to think, feel, or see anything.

"Alessia," came another whisper.

That was it for my nerves! With a splash, I recoiled and crawled backwards at incredible speed, gasping for breath. I'd seen a lot of bizarre happenings in my life, but a *talking vent* was just too freaky.

As if I didn't have enough problems, my knees got caught up in the strange dress as I tried to distance myself from the whispering vent. I held onto a log for comfort—security—sanity.

"Alessia!" The whisper was much louder now, the voice somehow familiar.

I retreated even farther into the wall. *They're playing with my mind.* I tried to calm myself. *They are Gaslighting me.* There was no other logical explanation. They were trying to break me.

"Go away!" I said with a shudder. If there was ever a time I was a second away from complete insanity, it was now.

"Alessia…it's me."

"You're not real. P-Please, just go away," I said again, quailing in the corner of the room.

There was silence for a while.

"It's Jadherey, Alessia. Jadherey."

"Jadherey?" I called out, rising slowly to my feet. I stepped over my dress and lurched sideways. *Is this real? Is this really you? You're alive?*

"Are you harmed?" he asked.

A shudder of hope went through me. Staggering slightly, I lifted my dress and plodded towards the vent, only to swivel round and troop sideways towards the lamp. My hands shaking, I grabbed the lamp from the hook and rushed towards the vent; I couldn't get there fast enough. Without any more deliberation, I threw myself onto the wet floor and peered into the vent.

It was Jadherey—alive—peeking inside. His head was levelled lower than mine due to the sloping vent. I never thought I would ever see him again. His friendly face, his calm demeanour...if I didn't know better, I'd say he was more Tuscanian than Tregtarian or Tarian. But again, what's in a name? A sudden spasm of hope went through me.

"You're here?" My voice wobbled. "You're alive." I breathed, hoping my eyes were not deceiving me. I stretched my right arm in between the vertical rails.

I used my left arm to keep my head above water. An overwhelming sense of relief washed over me. Through the rails on his side of the wall, he extended one hand, too. His other hand clung tightly to the rails like he was suspended in air.

The thickness of the wall was mind-boggling. Several layers of stone separated us. The stonemason's patience was second to none; that was evident. Fortunately, the lamp emitted a little burst of light through the lopsided vent. Our fingers brushed against each other, but that was as far as we could reach.

"What are you doing here?" I asked, whispering.

He didn't answer right away. "I can't stay long. There are two Custodians of the Secret B Code manning the exterior."

My forehead creased. "What B code? Why...H-How are *you* here?"

"I'm on De-Deganon's errand." He squeezed the bit of my fingers that he could touch. "But I have an errand of my own."

"I don't understand," I whispered. "I thought you were dead."

"Maybe soon, but not yet, my lady...not quite yet." He

smiled playfully, just like he used to do. He knew it bugged me when he called me my lady.

"Don't say that." Some water went into my ear, and I shook my head.

"Dranisha is unpredictable, but she'd never kill De-Deganon's servant," he said slowly. "It was just a small retribution for forgetting my place." Suddenly he twitched and drew his hand back. He held the rails tightly with both hands for a second. "They're coming. I have a plan to free you. I'll be back in two moon-days." He retreated, his face pulling farther back. His words were rushed. "Unlock your powers, Alessia. Don't lose—"

In a twinkle, he vanished into the silent night. That night was the longest ever. The three men returned four more times during the night to torture me. They demanded answers to the same questions repeatedly, inflicting excruciating and piercing pain that thronged through my head until my head was reeling. I cried until my tears had dried up. My hope was Jadherey. His promise resonated inside my head. He had a plan to free me. I just had to be strong enough to survive a couple of days, and after that, I'd go home. I didn't know how, but I trusted Jadherey's word.

12. The River of Lost Dreams

Time in the wet room was abundantly sufficient to propel the most strong-willed individual to an untimely and premature demise. How I managed to endure the three-pinned men's sixteen, hour-long torturous sessions—the three-point excruciating pain—the quiet loneliness when I was finally left on my own—is one of my life's mysteries.

One thing had kept me hopeful: Dante. Every second I was down, the thought of him lifted me up. I held onto him, every day, hoping—praying—wishing to be in his arms again. With him, I had a destiny to fulfil; without him, I had an abyss that could never be filled.

It had been just over two hours since the three-pinned men had left me to my own devices. In a world with no watches, I'd taught myself to predict the time. Nothing scientific—just a constant tapping of my fingers against my palm until I got bored and got the time wrong anyway.

But that night I was attentive. Jadherey had promised he'd be back in two days' time and that he had a plan, so I waited, my gaze glued at the vent like I was afraid it would grow feet and run away. It was my only shred of hope. In my two days in captivity, I had worked out that if I could get rid of the metal bars, I could swim my way to freedom through the vent.

Whilst I deliberated on how I could dispose of the bars, a splish-splash of water beyond the walls sounded. The hair at the back of my neck rose. I jumped to my feet, holding my breath. I grabbed the lamp and clutched it against my chest. Another noise, and I sploshed my way towards the vent. *It's got to be him.* I plunged to the floor, peeking into the vent. I couldn't see him.

"Jadherey," I whispered. "Is that you?"

Silence followed, bar the gurgle of water flowing across the vent. I repositioned the lamp so I could see a little bit better. Another splosh, and there he was.

"Alessia," he whispered, gasping for air. His hands clutched the rails.

My heart racing, I stretched my arm, and he reached for it. His fingers were cold, but they were all I had that resembled hope.

"You came back for me!" A brief thrill of excitement cascaded down my spine.

In the poor lighting, his eyes had lost their bright rufescent tint, but even more worrying was his jitters. Every now and again, he looked over his shoulder.

He squeezed my fingers, breathing heavily. "If what they say is true, and you have some powers within you... now is the time to unlock them... like, *really* unleash them." He was still panting.

"I don't know the full extent of my abilities, Jadherey. Whatever *they* think I can do, it only works within the Tuscanian shield. Not here."

He took a deep drag of air and almost swallowed a gulp of water in the process. He swivelled his head again like he was trying to see if he'd been followed or watched.

"I thought you had a plan," I said impatiently.

"I do... I did... but I think it's been rambled," he stuttered.

"You're not giving me much confidence, Jadherey."

He turned his head again, and all I could see was his shoulder-length hair that was weltering in the water. A while later, he looked back at me. "I know. I'm sorry. Something went wrong." He pressed his head against the bars on his side of the wall. "There were only supposed to be six Custodians of the B Code."

"Now there are more?" I couldn't hide the panic in my voice.

"At least a few dozen…maybe more. There's too much activity in the valley." He paused, breathing. "I don't have enough *ahwira* potion to knock them all out."

"What about the three-pinned men?"

It was some time before he spoke. "They are in deep sleep… they won't be waking anytime soon."

I crinkled my forehead in bewilderment.

"It's the Custodians—"

A sudden explosion of noise erupted from outside. A loud war cry followed by adrenaline-fuelled uproar emerged from beyond the wall. I could hear people racketing around for a minute before it became more like a stampede.

Jadherey jerked his head, his fingers tightening around mine. Commotion pursued.

"Grab your armour!" a voice bellowed from outside.

The quiet silence of my time in the wet room had vanished. Replacing it was a clamour of voices. "Fire! Fire! Fire!"

Panic shot through me. "W-What's happening?"

A loud chiming sound of metal accompanied by a babel of voices rose into the air.

Jadherey hastily withdrew his hand from mine. "I'm so sorry…I'll come back. I'll come back for you. I don't—" He slid back, his words lost in the night. Like he was never there, he vanished into the darkness with a heavy splash, leaving me alone and calling out to him.

"No! No! No! Jadherey! Come back!" I cried, my arm still stretched across the vent. "Come back!"

My freedom was flying away in front of my eyes.

With every breath I had, I screamed. "Jadhere-e-e-ey! Come back!"

A blood-curdling wail tore free from my lips. I curled up

into a tiny ball, a tight knot racking havoc with my insides. My cry rang inside my head like a shrill and haunting screech.

Consumed by an overpowering desire for freedom, I held my breath. Something rose inside of me, fizzed and bubbled like it was seconds from coming out. The water beneath me heated up. Surreal energy whirled inside my stomach. It surged up into my chest and throat. My eyes stung, and a burning, tingling sensation cascaded down my arm.

The din from beyond the walls seemed a distance away now. Inside my head, an ear-splitting and sudden dinging noise engulfed me. I flipped my eyes open in panic, clenching the sides of my head. What transpired next made me question whether I was human or alien. My mind had done it again. It was its own person!

Mystified, I watched as the vertical bars on both sides of the vent moved, like *really* flexed, as if they were made of a pliable substance. I scurried backwards. Confused. Terrified. Powerless! *I'm on the wrong side of the shield.*

My mind was paving the path for my escape. It was at that juncture that I truly and unequivocally believed there was something in me that was much grander—greater—superior than I!

Jadherey! My heart skipped. I scuttled towards the vent. Just like I'd envisaged it for forty-eight hours, I quickly crept into the tiny vent. I bruised my arms and legs, but I didn't flinch or stop. Sliding through the dark tunnel, I shut my eyes, and prayed for safety. I had no idea where I was headed. One word resounded inside my head. Home!

As the cold water cascaded freely underneath me, I trusted it would steer me towards my freedom. I had two objectives— find Jadherey and run for our lives.

I reached the outer wall, still reeling from the shock of the power of my mind. I didn't have time to process it all before unsettling screams and the crunching of armoury intensified from a distance. I glanced around, my hands holding onto the edges of the wall. The texture was smooth but in the darkness of the night, I couldn't tell what it was made of. I tried to balance my legs, but they ended up dangling across the slanted, slippery wall.

I noticed with astonishment that I was at the top of at least a six-foot man-made waterfall that sloped into a meandering river. I took a deep breath to steady myself. Now I could see where the water was flowing into. *Who in their right mind would build a house across a river, and in a volcanic crater?*

I turned my gaze around several times and tried to get my bearing. The uneven sound of my breathing echoed loudly inside my head. Ethereal mountains loomed in both directions a mere few hundred metres away. The harvest moons glowed like silver disks watching over us in silence.

With one deep breath, I slid gently down the lopsided wall, climbed down and halted once I reached the bottom. My legs wobbled. I had no idea of the depth or what would meet me once I leapt into the river.

A storm of arrows flew through the sky, buzzing and fizzing inches above me. I ducked, willing myself not to scream. My spine tingled. A hissing sound lacerated through the air. I wasn't spoilt for choices. I jumped into the river.

A thundering noise emerged from my right. My heart thumped. Quietly I swam left and slithered across the river. A few metres in and the water reached just below my shoulders, so I dipped into the warm water and swam for my life. When I surfaced, I took short and shallow breaths, legs wobbling.

I wasn't sure what shook me more: the ongoing battle across the river, not too far away from me; the fact that I had controlled matter with my mind; or that I had done it outside the boundaries of the shield. Or worse, the depressing fact that it had taken me weeks of pain, torture, heartache, and desperation to discover that I *could* save myself after all. Ralda had said the powers of our minds were non-existent outside the shield, so I hadn't attempted to use my mind to save myself. *How did I do it?*

By the time I reached the riverbank, I was breathless. My pulse beat in my ears, and my head throbbed in my temples. Teeth chattering, I knelt down, resting for a second. A light scatter of trees stood in my line of sight. Dominating, mountainous terrain loomed in all directions.

I picked up a scramble of hurried feet headed in my direction. Hairs rose at the back of my neck. I sprang up with a jolt, catching a glimpse of shadows across the other side of the river. The subsequent crunch of weapons against armour sent me flying along the river. I sped off in a flash, robbed of time to decide on the best route. My soaked dress threatened to slow me down, so I heaved it up and crested my way along the river.

The silent glow of the moons' light guided me as I wove through the shrubs and saplings. The trees crackled, and the wind whipped at my face unmercifully. I didn't know whether it was my fear or paranoia but someone was trailing me. Adrenaline flew threw me.

The hisses of swords slashing through the air a few hundred metres away on the other side of the river perplexed me. *Who's fighting whom?*

Amid my flight to safety, a hand grabbed me from behind and whisked me off my feet. Before I had a chance to scream, a pair of strong arms hauled me back. A hand covered my mouth. Unable to let out a sound, I kicked and booted to no avail.

"Shhh," an urgent voice said into my ear. I didn't recognise the voice.

My breath dragged out of me, and I submitted. My shoulders drooped, and my legs collapsed under me. Sturdy arms held me up. Slowly and cautiously, a pair of strong hands spun me around, only for me to almost squeal with elation when I stared into Jadherey's berry-red eyes.

"Don't make a sound," he whispered, loosening his grip from my mouth.

His other hand held my back firmly against him. Meticulously he inched us left until my back was resting against the trunk of a tree. He gestured for me to remain motionless. It was impossible; my whole body convulsed with adrenaline rush. I took in a deep breath, my wide eyes fixed at him. He raised his hand to signal four guards were close by. I nodded, still breathing heavily.

For minutes, we stood there, my back against the trunk of a cedar tree, my front pressed up against him. His rippling and athletic muscles helped calm my frenzied heartbeat. I was safe with him. The aromatic, sweet fragrance of wet cedar wood wafted through the air—too familiar. My mum used to burn cedar wood every year to celebrate New Year's Eve.

Jadherey shifted his gaze from right to left. Too stumped to get my brain working again and too terrified to look around myself, I drew in a shaky breath for composure. Skirling fire arrows broke out from the horizon and blazed the night sky. The heavy tread of marching feet yards away resounded in the night. Moments later, the rippling sound of flowing water alerted me to someone making their way through the river.

After seconds of taking short, shallow breaths, I caught a glimpse of a group of at least a dozen Tregtarian warriors moving stealthily through the waters towards us. *They're coming!*

As if he was waiting for the right time to run, Jadherey gestured for me to remain still. I did just that but with difficulty. My heart pounded inside my head. A continuous shudder went through my back.

"We need to run!" he mouthed slowly.

I nodded.

Suddenly, he crouched. He swiftly balanced the rucksack he carried on his back and without giving me time to think or react, he ripped the hemline off my dress in one rapid movement. Fortunately, the noise of fireballs blazing the night sky drowned the sound. He gazed up at me apologetically, like he wanted to make sure I understood why he'd done it. I nodded again. This was no time for pleasantries! The long dress was dragging me down, anyway.

He rose up slowly. His gaze shifted from me to the river and back to my eyes.

"On three," he whispered, extending his hand towards me.

I reached for it hesitantly, wondering if we would make it, after all. Trying to outrun Tregtarian warriors was impossible, and we both knew it. Tregtarians had a natural ability to run faster than any other people in Zeneshia. The warriors more so because they enhanced their talents through training.

"One. Two—"

"The human is gone!" a guard shouted from across the river,

My heart thumped. In the chaos of the night, I hadn't grasped that the guards were only just picking up on my escape.

The warriors halted and swivelled round, the water swirling around their armour.

"Escaped?" one with a stringent voice bellowed out. "Retreat! Retreat!" They edged back, their red, bulging eyes scanning the immediate area.

"She can't have crossed the main river yet. Find her! She's within the boundary!"

At that moment, whilst the warriors tried to work out how I'd escaped from the wet room, Jadherey and I bolted. Weaving through the terrain, I lost all sense of direction. Jadherey led the way, and I followed blindly.

Running was never my pastime, but I had done it enough times now, I could easily mistake it for a hobby that I wasn't very good at. On that chaotic night, my heart was pounding to the beat of my feet against the ground. My feet were soaking wet and slogged in boots that were a size too big. A bead of sweat trickled down my face. I held onto Jadherey's hand like my life depended on it.

As I saw the forest fade away behind me, I was taken back to my escape from Isle Speranza. I had run with hope—fortitude—conviction for a future defined by me. Now, in a world surrounded by mystery, I was still trying to shape my destiny, only I wasn't on my own anymore.

As we ploughed along the edges of a craggy, mountainous terrain, the shrill sound of fire arrows from the battle began to fade into the distance. Jadherey was a sprinter, while I was more of a jogger, but even more so, he was a patient runner. I struggled to keep up. Instead of letting go of my hand, he reduced his pace to accommodate me.

Fortunately, the chaos of the battle had given us a much-needed advantage. Ahead a surging river bubbled with roaring energy. We skidded to a halt. As I caught my breath, I glanced around. The droke was more vale than valley, and it wasn't a stream; but a massive river. The sound of gushing waters filled the air. The only way out was to run along the edges or go across it.

Going across is far too risky.

He gave me the look that suggested he knew exactly what I was thinking. "It's the quickest way and the only viable option to be at least a moon-day ahead. The Custodians and the warriors won't risk crossing the river, nor will they think we're bold enough to weather the surge."

"If the rocks don't get to us first, we'll drown, or we'll be swept away." I gazed at the glimmering rocks winding across the surging waters. This wasn't one of the adventures from *Indiana Jones* films. This was happening.

He deliberated for a second. "So says the *princess* of mind control who, by the way, flexed matter with her mind…" A smile of amusement dawdled on his face. His jawline was perfect, sturdy. The wound left by Dranisha's bludgeon on his left temple was almost healed. His blue shorts suited him. He didn't look like an ill-treated slave now. He stood tall, athletic, determined, his blue rucksack balanced perfectly on his back.

"You saw that?" I flashed a smile. He was like a friend I never knew I truly needed, a brother I never had but wished for!

"Right now, I'm more scared of you than I am of the *River of Lost Dreams*!" Jadherey said.

You and me both!

"Why is it called the River of Lost Dreams?" I asked.

He glanced at the night sky. A heap of clouds were starting to form, the stars fading like stardust into the clouds. "A fair number of unfortunate souls have lost their lives along with any dreams they might have had."

"You're telling me this now?" My voice was higher than I expected.

He chuckled. "Do you think you could use that clever mind of yours to open a passage for us?"

I raised my eyebrows with a halfway smile. "Divide *those* waters just like Moses did for the Israelites?"

He stared at me vacantly. When he was met by more silence, he asked, "Well, can you?"

"I don't know," I said honestly. "The last time I played around with water, it wasn't me; my mind just did its own thing."

"Played?" He quirked his brows.

"Well, the water mimicked my movements like it was in a game of some sort." I sighed. "It's hard to explain, Jadherey."

"You and the water engaged into a game of…flow and—"

"Don't even try and insert logic into it." I smiled. "It doesn't make sense, does it?"

He shook his head. "Nothing ever does. Could you resume the game and get us across the river unharmed?"

"Even if it's possible, I don't know how to."

He was quiet for some time seeming to be in deep contemplation. "You're out of sequence?" His words startled me.

"What?"

"Your game is out of alignment," he said again.

"I've heard a lot about Sequence, but right now, I honestly have no idea what you're saying."

"Every game ends with a result. To get to the result, a sequence is required. That's the way of *your* people, and even more so the way of the dreamers of Felradia. And since you can't seem to resume your game, that can only mean that your sequence is out of alignment. I read that from one of the Tuscanian books, and I'm still trying to work it out," he whispered, poking me playfully on my arm, smiling breezily.

"Oh! Okay," I said.

"Go for it…my lady," he urged. "I'll stand back in case you miss your target."

I swung him a look, then took a deep breath. "But I can't use my powers outside of the shield."

"You just did. The vent proves you can," he reassured. "Now you need to find the strength and do it again."

"Ralda said it was impossible," I murmured more to myself than to him.

"You were misinformed." His voice was tinged with a joshing tone. "It happens all the time."

Ralda is the Voice of Sequence. He's never wrong. I didn't voice my thoughts. *I must try.* On that thought I drew in a deep breath. *How do I do this?* I stared at the churning river and exhaled. *Do I raise my hands? No that's silly. Do I command the water to just move? What do I do?* My chest heaved. Talking to myself was as absurd as trying to part the gushing river with my mind. I brought my hands to my head and concentrated. *Open! Move! Create a passage for us!* I commanded from inside my head. *The end of the beginning is the beginning of the end.* I recited Ralda's teachings. Sadly, the menacing river didn't twitch. *Please just do something…anything…*My eyes misted.

"It's not working?" Jad finally said.

"I don't know how to do it." My voice broke. "I'm sorry. I just don't know h—"

"Hey. Don't be sorry. We'll go for it the traditional way."

I nodded, tearfully, drained of my resolve. *What good is a clever mind if I can't use it?* It was as though, there was someone else inside me who chose to do as she pleased when she wanted to. I wasn't in control. I was never in control.

"We jump, on three!" He strode towards the riverbank, his eyes fixed on me.

"Now?"

"Yes. Every moment is precious. We can't delay any longer."

I nodded, took in a steadying breath, and then edged forward cautiously. The rocks under my feet were a tad slippery. Any mishap on my part and I'd land on all fours, in true Alessia fashion.

He tied a knot on his rucksack and flung it on his back, the strap going across his chest. "See you on the other side." He squeezed my hand, his grip firm, yet his touch light.

I took a deep breath as he counted. On three, we dove deep into the shimmering crystal moonlit waters and allowed nature to take its own course. A thrumming sound emanated from the river as the mountains stood silently in the background. I fought to stay afloat. Out of control, I gulped a few litres of water, but that was nothing. Chasing our freedom, and hopefully heading home was everything. The experience was unbelievably terrifying yet thoroughly exhilarating as the roaring waters heaved us up and down the meandering river. It was the longest and most liberating roller coaster-like cruise of my life.

13. THE RUINS OF
THE WATER WALKERS

Following our daring slide and spin in the River of Lost Dreams, we ended up on the other side of the burbling river in yet another valley. I took the liberty of renaming the river; the River of Renewed Dreams. Serrated mountains loomed all around us. I gazed to the east and beamed. Spikes of the Sun god of light penetrated through the jagged mountain peaks as if she was reaching out to us. The early morning stars shone like silver diamonds in the sky. Soaked to the bone, Jadherey and I lay on the riverbank out of breath. The beauty of the moment was in the knowledge that we had taken a risk and somehow came out unscathed.

Throughout the day and night, we endured hours of trekking and trooping up and down the hilly terrain. My protector, Jadherey, was painstakingly meticulous in every action, every move, like he was born to defend and protect. By midnight, the second night, I could hardly feel my feet, but I kept going across the rocky landscape, staggering—running—breathing, for I knew I was going home and Jadherey was coming with me.

Exhaustion finally got the better of me near twilight. I lumbered behind Jadherey for a long time until I could barely lift my feet off the ground. Jadherey started running again, his hand holding mine. I tried to keep up, but he ended up dragging me instead. In submission, I stopped at the foot of yet another mountain. He skidded to a halt, too.

The ancient ruins before us would have been spectacular if we were in a much more favourable situation. The stone structure oozed culture and great importance, yet it appeared to have been deserted.

"What's this place?" I asked, gasping for breath.

"The Ancient Ruins of the Water Walkers." He sounded equally fatigued. "History suggests, it was once a royal city. The Water Walkers could walk and breathe underwater as they did on land. I'm afraid there's no time for a tour." He laughed, his kind eyes twinkling.

I smiled. Jadherey was a constant reminder that, even when surrounded by darkness, if you looked carefully, you'd most certainly find a light.

The mist and fog had stuck in the air like a veil of thick smoke, reducing visibility had to about a hundred meters. The partly visible ruins were suspended between two mountains. Enshrouded in mist, they exhibited a multitude of mystery and richness. This was *Zeneshia*! I thought I had seen it all, but now, I was sure, it was just the tip of the iceberg.

"I-I can't keep up." I hunched over, my hands resting on my knees.

He surveyed the path behind. Throughout our *great escape* he'd been cautious, not leaving anything to chance.

I caught my breath and held onto a stone-coned tower that stood next to me. "I'm so s-sorry. I'm slowing you down." My legs gave in, and I crumpled to my knees.

He gazed back at me, breathing heavily, too. "I'm not running *with* you, Alessia. I'm running *for* you." When he noticed my vacant and bushed look, he sighed. "You're the one running for your freedom…not me. There's no way you could be slowing me down. My end is set," he said, his eyes tightening.

Whilst my actions were driven by an intense desire to go home—*complete nostomania*, as my shrink would have said—Jadherey's actions were driven by something else that I was failing to work out. He took a huge risk helping me.

We stared at each other for a while until my knees gave way. I repositioned myself and sat on the ground. The night dew clung to the soil effortlessly. I felt the texture of the fine soil for a moment before a spell of dizziness creeped in.

I held my throbbing head. "Are you not coming with me?"

He shook his head, his arms resting on his knees. "I'm taking you as far as the shield." He gestured north-east, where the ruins were receding into a dense forest. "Once you're home, you'll be safe." His face was bleak, bereft of all hope.

"What about you?" I asked, my voice a mere whisper.

I hadn't considered his intentions fully. I'd just assumed we were going home, together. He would be safe in Tuscania; I knew he would.

"I'm not sure yet." His face clouded over. "I'll probably spend the remainder of my time dodging De-Deganon for a while." He allowed himself a little smile, moving closer. "Until I tire of running." He paused, squatting next to me. "Or maybe... I'll just wait for the high command to do as they please with me."

My nails dug into my palms, my throat tightening. My brow crinkled. "You're giving up?" The quiet silence of the sounds of early dawn rang inside my ears.

He shook his head again and then swept his arm at me. "We need to keep going." He let out a huge, shuddering breath.

I blinked a couple of times. "Why give up now?" I demanded, strangely seething, my hands still resting on my knees. It just didn't make sense.

"I'm not giving up, Alessia." His teeth ground together. "Could you take my hand, please? It's not safe here!" he pleaded.

"No, Jadherey. I'm done!" I snapped.

I was never one to throw a tantrum, but that early morning, I flew into a rage. If I'd had an ounce of sleep at all, then I would have said I woke up on the wrong side of the bed. Sadly, it had been too long a night!

All the swelling emotion that had been brewing inside of me for days on end came up to the surface. "I'm not running anymore!" I vented out, my throat dry.

"Now, who's losing heart?" His normally calm voice turned a corner.

"You are!" I raged, my lips quivering. "I-I thought you were coming with me to Tuscania! Now you're bailing out!" Steamed up, I couldn't control my voice. "Freedom is all you ever talked about...yet you're giving it all—"

"Why do you keep mistaking me for *your* people?" He stopped me dead in my tracks, kneeling down next to me. He smiled ruefully. "Do you even know what your shield does to my people?"

I didn't answer, and I couldn't hold his gaze, either. My eyes glistened like morning frost, and I stared out to the misty ruins, the early morning breeze whipping me.

"The shield isn't just going to open up for me. No one is ever going to welcome me!" He held my chin and tilted my head so I could face him. "I'll be dead before I can say a word.... I am Tregtaria—"

"Tarian! Jadherey...Tarian. You are nothing like *them*!" I pointed sideways, my voice wobbling. I had lost all sense of direction, but I had to make my point.

"Same difference!" He sprung up. "Your ancestors' shield was built to keep *my* people out of your land. If any of us try to walk through, it obliterates us without mercy."

"No!" I yelled. "You've got it wrong. The shield is there to protect, Jadherey, to keep the peace between our lands. Never to destroy! Tuscanians are not killers. They live in peace. They would never build something that ends people's lives. It's not in them."

"It's not their style? It burns, Alessia. It burns us to ashes."

"It's not true!"

"It exterminates us to nothing but a mound of cinders."

"It can't be true."

The truth was, I had never asked how the shield deterred non-Tuscanians from entry. I'd just assumed the shield was an invisible wall, and if one couldn't get in, they would just bounce off it. Simple! *Oh My God! The ice dorm?* My heart thudded. Now it was beginning to make sense. My mind had built an ice dorm that froze the Nadeiras to their death.

But they were creatures not people.

"I've seen it with my own eyes." He slumped to his knees again, reaching for my trembling hands. "The high command have used the shield to execute hundreds of *my* people."

I shook my head, frozen in shock.

His hands closed around mine. "It doesn't distinguish the good from the bad—Tarians from Tregtarians—saints from thugs…. It brands us all as *the enemy!*" He paused. "You can't take me *home* with you. Helping you was never about coming with you. This is my land…my home. Soon enough, I'll get what's coming my way."

There was prolonged silence after that.

My chest grew tight and hot. My anger turned to guilt, sorrow, and self-condemnation. "I'm sorry…so sorry."

There was always a tinge of sadness behind his eyes, and now that he'd conceded defeat, the light that always shone somewhere inside was gone, too.

"I-I-I didn't know. They never told me." My heart froze inside me. *I never asked.*

His eyebrows arched, his hands still closed around mine. "If you want me to cross the shield with you, you might as well shove a dagger into my heart first. I'm already dead anyway!" He squeezed my hands lightly before he let them go. He paced around in circles, his lengthy hair covering the side of his face.

I held my head, a sudden feeling of dizziness racking me. Then a sudden thought came to me. "There's still time for you to turn back." My words were rushed, my voice hopeful. "No one saw us together, and even if they did, you can say I tricked you or something… anything. Jadherey, save your life. Don't give up."

He threw a *wishful thinking* glance at me, shaking his head.

I wished I had the energy to stand and propel him towards

Tregnika, but sadly, I was so worn out that my legs felt like they were someone else's.

"I'm coming to terms with reality...not giving up."

"Don't sugar-coat it, Jadherey!" I snapped, exasperated. I was fatigued, upset, and confused about the whole thing. *He* may have accepted his fate, but I wasn't about to. "This is you giving up on your life...your future...your destiny. Why would you do that? Why give up something so priceless, something you hold dear—"

"For you, Alessia!" His voice wobbled, and he collapsed to his knees again. "For you..." He reached for the side of my face but immediately pulled his hand away.

I was thrown back. My already-racing heart virtually exploded at his words. I was left agog, not quite understanding what I'd just heard. We stared at each other for an endless moment, just listening to the sound of our breathing.

"I defied De-Deganon," he said after the prolonged silence. "I was going to be a free man." He gritted his teeth. "The mad lord promised me my freedom, Alessia. My freedom! The only thing that meant something to me. But I let it go. When I was given the chance...I ch-chose you over my freedom."

The raw pain in his voice left me too hurt to find my voice. Not only that, something else was happening to me. My body was shutting down, my insides turning. I breathed.

"My task was to get close to you. You were supposed to trust me, to share with me everything you knew, and my job was to relay everything to De-Deganon. Failing that, I had to lure you to the gateway to your world.... But you didn't know where that was, so that was of no use. De-Deganon knew your mind was superior from early on. He knew you were your mother's daughter." His jaw tightened. "You were more special than his high command realised. That's why he took them to war and left you hidden in De-warrior Dranisha's court. To him, you are a spectre of your ancestors, who built the shield by bloodshed. The house De-Deganon guard the secret code to your bloodline, and the three men in the valley are their weapon... the Custodians of the Bloodline Code. The high command was not privy to this secret. If they had caught wind of your bloodline, there was no telling what they would do."

I shook my head, stumped. All this information, and he'd never said a word about it. He had been asked to betray my trust yet found it in himself to save my life. My throat ached. The ruins caved in. My toes tingled for a few seconds before my legs went numb. *What's happening to me?* My vision blurred and grew dark for a few seconds before I could see again. Drained of all energy, I sat still, huddled against a stone sculpture, my stomach hardening.

Jadherey's eyes hazed over. "De-Deganon couldn't risk your death at the High command's hands without knowledge of how it affected the shield, but he couldn't stop them, either. You pose too great a threat..." He swallowed hard and sat on the ground. "But I was just an insignificant servant. I couldn't pose a threat to anyone, so De-Deganon put me to work, and I accepted. He promised me the only thing that meant the world to me: my freedom. But when I failed to get him the information he needed, he summoned the Custodians of the B Code. And you were brought to the house that thunders—"

"You spied on me?" I whispered, hurt, too exhausted to raise my voice.

"I relayed information," he said in his even, cool voice.

"Same difference!" I said his words exactly. Somehow, I managed a smile. Instead of being angry, I was saddened by it all. At the time, I was a stranger, and he did exactly what everyone else would have done in that situation. My fingers tingled.

He smiled in return. "I stopped when I got to know the real you. I couldn't do it." His eyes were warm.

My heart frosting, I sighed. He'd gambled his life for me. It wasn't right!

"I sold my ticket to freedom the moment I set my plan to rescue you in motion."

"I didn't ask you to give up your life for me."

"You think I don't know that?"

"So why? Why let go of your dream…your future, Jadherey?" I was slouching now, my back against a half-standing stone sculpture.

He watched me for a second in deliberation. "Does it really matter?"

I nodded, eyes closing on me. My body was counting down to an acute collapse. "Should anything happen to either of us, I would like to know," I said honestly, fighting through my body's shutdown mode.

"Because for the first time…" He took a breather. "I realised that *freedom* was just a rug to keep me warm at moon-night. What I needed was something worth more—something priceless; happiness. Something that lasts—moon-day and moon-night." He touched his chest, and with his free hand, he held mine.

My heart went out to him. Tears misted my eyes.

"You gave that to me. I didn't know what was inside of me until you. You are the only one who makes me feel like I matter…like my life matters." He averted his gaze for a second. "You seek to see only the best in people, Alessia. You even saw the goodness in De-Deganon." He chuckled lightly. "You bring out the best in everyone!"

By then, I was drifting slowly into unconsciousness. My eyes must have been shut. Something was happening to me. I just didn't know what it was. I was in irreversible shutdown mode.

"I am sorry, Alessia." He hovered over me before placing a soft peck on my forehead.

I forced my wan eyes to open. "For what? F-for choosing me over your freedom?" My voice faded into the skies, too.

"You know exactly what I mean," he said calmly, lifting my chin up so I could face him. "I'm truly sorry."

A single tear dropped to his hand that was encircled over mine.

He let go of my chin and wiped it with his free arm. His eyes were sad. "Don't waste your tears on me. I don't deserve them!"

"I have more than enough tears, Jadherey. I'm sure they won't be missed!"

A light chuckle escaped from his lips.

"You've given me a burden that I can't shake off," I said, resisting the urge to drift into oblivion. "The honest truth is, you made the wrong choice. You should have protected your own interests first, not mine."

In silence, he swept his arms around me and embraced me so tightly it brought out a surge of emotion rising from inside. My tears cascaded freely down his shirt. The realisation of this moment and the impending doom hung over us like a cloud of smoke. I was powerless—vulnerable—incapable of shaping his destiny or my own.

He held me snugly against his chest, making gentle, circular strokes across my back. In some ways, this was a subtle farewell—an untimely end to a journey that had not yet begun. This was too sad. After witnessing the inhumane and brutal treatment of Jadherey at the hands of the high command, if there was anyone who deserved a second chance—a divine intervention—a rebirth, it was he.

"You're paying a debt you never owed," I said, my voice betraying me.

"It was my choice. One I'll never regret!"

"Now I'll always have a debt I can never repay. How am I supposed to live after this, without knowing what happened to you? How will I forget everything…forget you?"

"You need not worry about any of that," he whispered into my ear. "I won't be alive long enough to warranty any sleepless moon-nights." He pulled back and wiped my tears off with the back of his hand.

"Don't say that," I whispered, lips quivering.

He held me tightly once more as I grasped now that I'd killed him!

Falling short of pointing a gun at him, I was most certainly going to be the reason for his premature death. When Lord De-Deganon finally caught up with him, he wouldn't show any clemency; we both knew it.

Either that, or the shield of my ancestors—the same shield I was deeply connected to—would end the precious life of the one who risked his to save me.

Death by Alessia! That silenced me!

My vision blurred from stinging tears. A deep hollowness settled inside my chest. My energy drained away—my mind drifted off—my consciousness floated into the dawn of the morning.

"You're not sleeping yet, are you?" Jadherey's calming voice replaced the sound of chirping birds ringing inside my ears.

I flung my eyes open.

He was smiling warmly, but he couldn't conceal the pain in his eyes. "We've spent too much time here. We need to go." He rose to his feet.

I remained motionless. I couldn't feel my legs anymore. They had since frozen over the ground. It was the end of my fight. But Jadherey could still try and save himself.

"Leave me here," I whispered. "Don't give up your dreams for me. Find your freedom. Survive. Live. Eventually you'll be happy."

"I'm not doing any of that," he said firmly. "If you don't get up now, I'll have no choice but to force you." He extended his arm.

"I can't, Jad."

"Why? You called me Jad…. What do you mean, you can't?"

"You don't want me to call you Jad?" I asked listlessly, forcing my eyes open.

"No…well, yes…I mean, I like it." He dropped to his knees, and his arms constricted around my shoulders. He began to panic. "Why can't—"

"I-It has a nice ring to it…J-Jad," I stuttered. Sweating and starting to judder, I was in my own world now, disoriented. I was sort of gone, and sort of here; floating between sleep-world and reality. I trembled. It's as if a cold chill had gone through me yet my body temperature spiralled. I rubbed my forehead. A haze of sleep blanketed over me, my chest tightening. Mental fatigue soon followed.

He checked me over. "What's wrong?" he demanded.

"My legs...I can't feel my l-legs. I r-really want to s-sleep," I stuttered, shivering.

Promptly and hurriedly, he untied the laces of my boots, pulling them off before drawing in one deep breath and letting it out almost immediately.

I squinted, unsure whether to scream or cry. Everything was just falling apart; now, my legs were no longer my own. My ankles had swollen beyond belief. I gasped.

"It looks worse than it actually is," he said. "The *zeze* sand-fly is notorious for causing deliria. The swelling is just your body trying to fight off the venom." He took in a deep drag of air. "It's a tiny bite; you'll sleep it off."

He modulated it for my sake, but I could see it was the end of the road for me.

He edged closer and held my shoulders lightly. "Don't move."

"It's not like I'm going anywhere."

He smiled earnestly before blitzing out of sight, and in seconds. he'd disappeared. I fought the urge to drift to sleep. The ruins appeared to be turning upside down. The sun was beginning to take over from the moons, but there was nothing bright and sunny about how I was feeling inside.

In a flash, Jad was back. My eyes partly open, I watched him stick wet leaves over my feet, only he seemed upside down!

My head in a whirl, the world appeared to be spinning. "Why are you standing on your head, Jad?" I asked as I took in the rotational shift of gravity.

He laughed lightly before holding me upright; at least I *thought* I was upright. "Lessi, get some sleep."

My heart thudded. "You called me Lessi?" I whispered, thoughts of Dante flooding my mind. My Dante!

"You called me Jad."

"My father called me Lessi," I said. "Dante calls me Lessi. Now you?"

"Granted. Lessi is already taken," he hastened to say. "How about I call you Alee instead?"

I puffed a laugh. "Alee and Jad," I mumbled. "I like it."

"Now get some sleep." His voice was firm. "When you wake up, I promise, you'll be just fine."

A flying light above us caught my eye. I gasped. "Am I seeing things or is that a bird on fire?" Mouth agape, I watched in stunned silence as a large gold and red bird winged its way swiftly through the air. Fluidly it fluttered its wings over us, twittering a strange yet adorable musical in the night skies. *I'm seeing things.* I squinted.

"It's a firebird, Alee." Jad's words brought a surge of relief through me. The bird was real. "It's one of a kind. Friendly yet very rare. It gives the illusion of a fire but it's not alight. It never burns. Not many people have seen it. My guess is it's simply lighting our path and guiding us home…to *your* home."

"You don't know that," I whispered in awe at the whirring bird with gold glowing eyes. "You don't know if we'll ma—"

"I know about hope and courage even when everything is pointing the other way," he said. "I'll get you home."

The last thing I remembered was being scooped up into his arms. I must have been heavy for him yet he seemed at ease carrying me across the ruins. His calm breathing sounded inside my ears, cracking my fragmented heart. He was taking me to safety, yet he'd thrown away his life. *I'm sorry,* I wanted to say but my head was spinning and I couldn't get any words out. As we made our way across the forest, every so often I forced my eyes to open. The sight that met my eyes was surreal. The trees were upside down, as if they were growing from the sky. Sand particles hovered in the air like gravity was non-existent.

I held onto Jad as tightly as I could manage yet I felt as though I was dangling, and any second I'd tumble to the ground. At one point, I cried, "I'm falling! I'm falling."

"You're not falling, Alee," came Jad's answer. "I'd never let you fall. I'll hit the ground first…I promise."

Before long, I floated into the depths of unconsciousness, where things made a lot more sense—no dancing ruins, no floating sand particles, no images of the sun rising from the ground…nothing like that!

14. Home shield Home

A dome of bark-brown trees was the first thing I noticed when I awoke. The mystic canopy of forestry enchantingly graced the skies. I lay on my back on the hard ground. A lesion of colour escaped from the west. *It's sunset.* My heart thudded. Woody incense wafted through the air. The air was laden with the aroma of fresh pine and garden-fresh daisies.

A refreshing and cool easterly breeze brushed against my face, lifting the torn hem of my dress. I beamed. Everything was going to be all right.

I rose up with a jerk. "Jad!" I called out. I swivelled around, realising that I could feel my legs again. Thank the gods, my legs were as good as new.

My heart bubbling with a thrilling sensation, I glanced around with enthusiasm. The clearing and the shield of my ancestors lay in undisturbed tranquillity in my line of sight. *Eureka, I'm almost home!*

"Jad!"

He didn't answer.

He wouldn't. My heart missed a beat. I gasped and turned slowly, the breeze tossing my curls in my face. *He wouldn't just leave.*

"Jadherey!" I called again, panicking. I spun round endlessly. A sudden haze of tears filled my eyes.

"You didn't think I'd go without saying goodbye, now did you?" he asked from behind, his voice low and melodic.

I pivoted and looked into his eyes. "Don't ever do that again!" I warned.

He laughed softly. "The shield may span for miles on end, but it's just a matter of time before the high command edge this way." He stepped forward and placed his hands on my shoulders lightly. For a prolonged moment, he simply gazed into my eyes, drawing me in.

"What's that look?" I asked when his dark-red gaze became too piercing.

He didn't answer right away. "I'm trying to figure out how to say goodbye." The honesty in his tone made my throat tighten. "I don't know how."

My heart sank, my throat constricting. I took a swallow of air. I didn't know how to say goodbye either. *How do I say farewell to one who has thrown away his freedom and his life for me?* My mind in turmoil, I gazed at length into the depth of his eyes until the red seemed to be moulding and blending inside me. His hands were warm against my bare shoulders, a warmth I'd soon be bereft of. In a heartbeat, hot scorching tears formed in the nadirs of my eyes.

With a surreal wave of courage, I tried to see beyond the red irises—beneath the sad gaze. All I found was a guy with a huge heart, someone born a servant yet exuded strength of character, courage—etiquette—heart—mind—soul and the intellect befitting a prince—a Larize. He had traded his freedom for mine, and he had brought me home. *I'll be damned if I let you return to a life of misery and slavery!* But I didn't say the words out loud.

"It's time to part ways." His mellifluous voice made my heart lurch. A single tear escaped from my left eye. He brought his strong palm to cup my cheek and brushed his thumb across my cheek, wiping the tear away before letting go. In a heartbeat, he curved a strong arm around my back, drew me closer, and planted a soft and lingering kiss on my forehead. I breathed. This was his silent way of saying goodbye. For me, it wasn't anywhere near enough.

"I'll miss you," he whispered into my hair. "You know that, right?"

I nodded, leaning farther into his lean, hard frame not wanting to let him go.

"If happiness could be bought, I would have sold everything I could get my hands on, just so I could *forever* feel the happiness you gave to me so freely," he whispered raggedly. "I'll cherish that till my death."

"Jad?" His name was all I managed to say through a burning throat.

"Take care of yourself. Be safe."

I'm safe with you, something inside me wanted to say. With a heavy heart, I realised that I wasn't ready to say goodbye. I would never be ready. I couldn't leave him behind.

On that thought, I drew back, took his hand, and held it gently between mine. "When Lord De-Deganon asked you to spy on me under the pretence of providing some bizarre form of comfort, did you ever anticipate this?" I asked in a low voice.

He shook his head, his skin glowing a warm russet in the dying sun. "Not in a million moon-years, my lady." He flashed one of his whimsical and sincere smiles that incited a torrent of emotion to flood my eyes.

I was quiet for a while. Jad's freedom and mine were aligned side by side. Either we were going home together, or neither of us was going home at all.

I moved away from him and took a few steps towards the clearing. "I'm not saying goodbye just yet. With or without your permission, you're coming home with me."

His eyes twinkled, and I knew he had registered that I had used his words against him. "With or without your permission, I'm serving you," he had said to me a while back. Now it felt like it was a whole lifetime ago. How far we had come.

I breathed, looked up to the sky, and watched the remaining hues of mauve, red, and yellow that graced the heavens. *Thank you*, I said to whoever was up there.

At that moment, I grasped fully that the gods loved me. In all my time in Tregtaria, it's as if they knew I needed someone to survive captivity. They gave Jad to me—all of him. They had dished him out to me on a full silver platter of everything that summed him up: compassion—love—humour—courage—determination—perseverance. He had made the days shorter and the nights endurable. At night, we'd sit by the balcony, chatting about everything and anything up until the early hours of the morning. Every moment we'd spent together—every spoken word—every laugh was healing my broken heart.

Yes, I'd missed home. With all my heart, I'd missed my family—the love of my life—*Dante*—and yet I knew that if I were to return home without Jad, I would miss him to the moons and back. He was my family, too, and wherever I would end up, I wouldn't leave him behind.

I swept my gaze around the landscape. The flourishing white daisies whispered merrily to the silent breeze. I spun round to him. "Walk with me." I raised my hand towards him with determination.

"Go home, Alee." His face was a mask of sadness.

"Just walk with me, please."

He edged back three strides, one hand clutching his rucksack.

"Don't even think about running!" I said. I was determined to get him through the shield. Nothing would stand in my way...not even him!

Three more steps, a silent smile, and a little swivel.

"Jad! Don't you dare!" I warned, taking a frosty edge. I even managed to scare myself. This was a new Alessia, swelling with complete conviction of making things right. "If you run, I'm running after you!" I raised my voice high, giving him no choice but to yield.

He halted, smiling just a little and loosened the straps of his rucksack before letting it slip to the ground. His eyes sparkled, but I wasn't sure if it was the sinking sun's rays, fatigue, or despondency that added the shimmer.

I sighed and scrutinized the shield for a moment, well, the daisies, really…the shield was there somewhere! The toughest challenge yet awaited: how to defy my ancestors' ways and get a Tregtarian to cross the shield unharmed?

"Do you see the shield in its true form?" I asked.

His brow furrowed. "I don't need to see it to know it's there." His voice was detached. "Your ancestors made it pretty obvious where it is. It's hard to miss."

I was silent for a heartbeat.

The tree line and the distinct clearing bursting with sprouting white daisies was an all-year, all-round phenomenon; I knew that now. On the Tuscanian side, mushroom-shaped trees guarded the land of my ancestors, and on the Tregtarian side, dark-brown pine trees towered along the environs of the clearing, about a hundred metres in width of grassland dotted with white and pinkish-white daisies in bloom.

"Answer the question, Jad. Do you see the shield's true form?"

"No, of course not," he said.

"Neither do I."

He stared at me vacantly like he was saying *and your point?* I smiled, noting how the breeze kept sweeping by and lifting his black and red shock of hair.

"The point, *Jad*, is…if we can't see it, but we both know it's there, then we believe in the impossible!" I glanced to the reddening sky. The sun god of Light was now sinking into the horizon.

He raised his eyebrows and raked his fingers through his hair in silence.

"Now, take my hand please," I said.

"We're not discussing this again, Alee."

"I wasn't planning to," I said with absolute resolve. There was something about him that brought out a different side to me—strength, courage, and confidence. "All I want is your hand."

He finally reached out hesitantly, his face clouded by befuddlement.

I held his hand. "Your dagger, please," I said with urgency.

A frown crept up his forehead. He waited, his gaze wandering between my eyes and my hands. With my free hand, I smacked his shoulder, not taking no for an answer.

He cringed in mock pain. "I must rub you the wrong way, or you've gone a little berserk!" He freed the dagger with an ivory handle from its holster and held it, flipping it a few times.

I grabbed the dagger hastily and aimed it at him. His gaze followed mine cautiously…to his chest…towards my hands… and back into my eyes.

He caught my hand and guided it towards him, pointing the dagger to his chest. "If you were to stop my heart beating right now…it would be a much preferred option, one I'd cherish forever in the afterlife," he whispered, his eyebrows pulling down over his eyes.

I tugged my hands away and swayed. He put his hands in his pockets, watching me.

"If I'm connected to the shield, I *am* the shield, right?" I said slowly, emphasising each word.

He let it sink in for a bit. "I don't think it works *quite* like that."

"Humour me." I glanced up to the sky. The last remaining rays of the fiery-red westerly sun filtered through the Tregtarian forest.

"It's too big a risk."

"Now you're worried! A second ago, didn't you just say you were at peace with death?" I teased.

"By your hand, yes. By your ancestors' freaky magic, no! Death by burning doesn't appeal to me at all."

I laughed. It was like he was inside my head and took the words right out of my mouth. I strode towards him, serious now. "I'd never be reckless with your life, Jad." I pointed the dagger at him. "You have to trust me." Before he'd contemplated my intentions, I grazed him on the arm.

"Ouch! Alee! What in the moons' name was that for?" He held his wounded arm with his other hand.

"Science," I said, stretching my arm to his cut and using my free arm to squeeze his blood out so it could drip into my palm.

"Didn't your science masters teach you about care?"

"My tutor was on point, Jad, and my dad was a fine physician. I could never ask for more." I took a breather. "You think I don't care," I said, my voice low.

"I know you do, but not right this moment!" Jad stared at me with a confused mix of shock, disbelief, and anxiety.

With his blood in my palm, I twirled round and started towards the blossom of daisies. I wasn't sure of the consequences of my actions, but I had to try.

"Alee, stop!" he called after me. "What are you doing?"

"Exactly what you think I'm doing!" I strode forward, the daisies in full bloom reaching my knees where my hemline ended.

"No! What if you get hurt?"

I turned round to look at him. "The shield would never hurt me. Now stop speaking…I need to concentrate."

"You know what this means, yes? If by some miracle your little experiment actually works, and the shield lets me through, what if it collapses? Have you thought about that? The *thugs from next door* will be on your doorstep by dawn! And when that happens, you might as well kiss your fruitful land goodbye."

I was about twenty metres away from him now. "*If* that happens, I'll just have to rebuild the shield now, won't I?"

"Are you confident?"

"No!"

"You're willing to take that chance, anyway—one that could end thousands of lives for me?"

"Every life is important." I turned round and kept my gaze on him, walking backwards. "The Voice of Sequence's words, not mine. I'm standing by them!"

The breeze billowed his hair, mine, too. "Tell me again. What are you trying to do?"

I strode backwards slowly. "I need to know if my genes can protect you through the shield."

"And?" He was getting more anxious, and so impatient.

"If your blood burns, so will my hand. Then we'll know."

"Are you listening to yourself?"

Smiling, I kept edging back.

"That's crazy, Alee. You have to turn back!" he called out, but I was halfway through the clearing. "Come back!"

He didn't know there was nothing crazy or impetuous about my actions. I had thought through every scenario—every plausible possibility—each likely consequence imaginable, and now I was acting on it. As he'd carried me from the ruins of the Water Walkers, I'd been drifting in and out of sleep. Every time I was awake, I was searching and rummaging through my mind for an answer that would save him, too.

I had prayed to all the Star gods for this not to be our farewell, for them to grant him the happiness that he'd been robbed of all his life. His sacrifice for me was too immense to disregard. Like they say...where there's a will, there's a way. If I was truly the mother of the shield, then I had a say in who entered the land of my mother.

A step at a time, I took the longest walk of my life. His blood safely in my palm, my heart was not even racing. I didn't allow myself to feel nauseated, either. Something inside made me feel certain I'd come out unscathed and together we were going home. I could sense it.

Just like I'd pictured it for endless moments, my feet touched Tuscanian ground. I looked back with a smile; the shield didn't even flicker an eyelid. There was no electric shock—no surging energy bar the calming soft breeze at sunset.

"Hang out the flags, I'm home!" I had to mark the moment somehow, so I knelt down and planted a heartfelt kiss to *my* motherland. For a few heartbeats, I remained still, cherishing every second. A moment later, I sprang up and waved at Jad. He waved back.

"It worked, Jad. It worked!" I called. I allowed his blood to drip to the ground, tainting a couple of daisies with a dash of red. "I'm coming to get you!"

For a moment, I basked in the afterglow of victory... I had done it!

But a paroxysm of hot energy swelled inside me, and I hurled hard onto the ground. At that moment, my eyes were no longer my own!

I saw a vision, a vivid, haunting occurrence, as if it was happening right then, at that precise moment. Lord De-Deganon sat high and proud, his eyes bulging out. My eyes steadily gazed at the high command, my father.

Compelling words from one who's about to meet his makers. Lord De-Deganon's voice invaded the hushed silence inside my head. *Tell your lord what brings you to Tregtaria after all these moon-years?*

I was inside Dante's head, seeing through his eyes, feeling his heart beating against mine. At that time, I was him, heartbroken—desolate—fuming.

In a trice, the vision disappeared, and the voices vanished. All that remained were the daisies dancing lackadaisically to the evening breeze.

I gasped in horror at fate's laughter in my face. "No!" I cried. "No! No! No!" I wailed until I couldn't hear my voice. "I've just come back!" I curled on the ground, shaking. "I've just come back!" My heart dropped. "Why!"

The gods couldn't answer that one!

Then I jumped to my feet and bolted across the clearing towards Jad. As I ran towards him at full throttle, so did he towards me. That threw me back, but I didn't stop. He'd acted on impulse. So carelessly, he sprinted towards me, weaving his way through the daisies, unthinking, not caring that he was seconds away from *death by my ancestors' shield.*

I didn't want to worry about him, too, but I couldn't help it! "Stop, Jad! Stop running!" I called tearfully. "I-I can't protect you from here!"

With each stride, his face contorted with emotional chaos. I quickened my pace, my strides longer. Around halfway into the prairie of daisies, I thrust myself in front of him with so much force we both heaved to the ground.

He picked himself up and held me upright. "Are you hurt?" he asked, panicking and out of breath.

"W-Why are you running!" I almost screamed my lungs out.

He abruptly gave me a vice-like hug, like I'd risen from the dead. "You were running!"

I pulled back, my hand in the air. "S-So you blitz towards the shield!"

"When you run, I run!" His voice boomed over us.

"Even if it means running to your death!" Breathless, I fixed my gaze on him. "Why would you do that? You don't value your life?"

"Are you hurt?" He ignored my words, checking me over just like he'd done at the ruins of the Water Walkers. "Just tell me, please."

I shook my head. A momentary pause, stress—adrenaline—anxiety—Dante!

"Why were you screaming and running like a—"

"I have to go back!" The lump in my throat threatened to suffocate me. "I need to go back!"

He took a deep breath, his eyes tightening. "Go back where?"

"To the capitol. Tregnika."

"Tregtaria," he repeated, a rueful smile playing at the corner of his lips whilst he allowed my words to sink in fully. "You want to journey through the *Jungle of Voices* and across the *Sands of the Dead,* and somehow survive both, just so you can return to captivity?" His lips compressed. He glared at me, seething. The veins in his neck bulged, his jaw tightening. "Have you lost your mind?"

I wished I had. That would have made everything a little easier. "They have Dante!"

He sat down, still breathless. "How do you know this?" he finally asked, his voice calm. His self-control was baffling.

"I just know." I wiped my tears with the back of my hand and let out a huge breath. *I have to be strong, I need to be strong.*

"That's not good enough!" he fumed, his voice taking a new tone. "We've come all this way. Now you want to go back? By the moons, I won't let you!"

"I saw h-him." My voice broke. Despite more tears blurring my vision, I took in his expression and the look that suggested I was hovering around the boundaries of insanity. "A vision of him, okay?"

"You're seeing visions now?"

"It was more than a vision, Jad. I was seeing what Dante was seeing…through his eyes! I felt him…inside." My hand came to my heart, but he stared at me blankly. "I feel him, right now. He needs me." I allowed myself a moment of weeping. "The high command are holding my *life* hostage. I'm going back for him!" I hastily rose to my feet, with him in tow.

"Spare me the drama, Alee!" His lips pursed. "Your life is within your grasp. Your home is on the other side of this clearing. Go home!" He gestured grandly towards the daisies in bloom glistening in the evening sun.

"No!" I started off backwards.

"You'll not survive Tregtaria this time round." He followed me. "You are home. Why won't you save yourself?" he pleaded, the glow from the setting sun making his eyes shimmer. He drew me towards him. "Listen to me. I'll go back for him if you agree to go—"

"He's not your responsibility, Jad. I'm not leaving him."

His eyebrows pulled together. "Do you see what you're doing? Do you?" He tried to shake some sense into me. "You're being stubborn. And that will get you—"

"No! Y-You listen to me! I'll take you through the shield.

And I'm coming straight out. Find house Serenius…my grandma, Zaira, tell her everything—"

"Stop it! Stop it right n-now!" His voice broke, his hands gripping my shoulders more tightly. "I brought you here. I'll damn well take you back!"

"I won't let you risk your life for me *again*."

He sighed. "And you're not doing the same for your *precious* Dante?"

"It's different!"

"Same difference, Alee. Remember! Same difference!" He gave in. "I sure hope he's worthy of your love! I really hope that he is."

At that point, I was on my last tether. I tapped my foot on the ground to keep from pulling my hair out. My heart had sunk into a hole I couldn't reach. *Why now? Why me? Why us?*

"This is so reckless," Jad said. "You know that, right?" He leaned down and dropped a light kiss on top of my head. "Stubbornness and recklessness are a lethal combination!" His brow creased over his troubled red eyes. "We can't go back across the River of Lost Dreams. The only way to Tregnika is through rough terrain, Alee. The Jungle of Voices and the Sands of the Dead are no place for you, me, or anyone who still value their life." He held out his hand. "No regrets!"

"No regrets!" I wasn't sure I said the words out loud or they got stuck inside.

* * *

As the sun faded into the night skies and the pale moons' peeked at us from the glittering stars, Jad and I trekked through the terrain into the land of the warriors. Destination: Tregnika. After coming to terms with the devastating turn of events, I channelled my anguish to courage.

We were walking a perilous path, but I was armed with

strength bordering on tenacity and resolve coupled with a self-confidence that could only be beaming from the moons! I'd known from early on that Dante was my all, my soul, and his life was worth a million times more than mine! He was my *home*, and I would never leave my home behind.

PART IV

*Dante – A Glimpse into my
Quest for my Lost Heart*

15. YOUR HEART WILL BREAK AND SHATTER BUT IN TIME...

"My moons! Look who's returned from the dead!" Gradho stood haughtily in the doorway of the Dhareka hall. Garbed in an embroidered crimson robe and a matching cowl, he took his time to move out of the way for me. Strike one!

I gave him a piercing stare. Today wasn't a good moon-day to pick a fight! I kept a cool head, for now, stepped sideways, and shifted my focus to the Dhareka councillors, my soon-to-be Larizon council. They met my gaze. If there was one voice I couldn't tolerate right then, it was his. Someone had to shut him up, for all our sakes, or by my father's blood, I'd send him to an early grave.

"Good sleep, Larize?" he asked in his usual pompous voice.

Ignoring him as best I could, I marched towards the outer councillors table. They sat in cow-horn formation; matters of utmost gravity required all twenty-four provincial leaders to be in attendance. I hurried towards Uncle Gabe and Aunt Zabi.

Tan, my best friend and voice of reason, saw me enter, sprung up and hurried closely behind me. He forced himself inside my head. *Take no notice of him.*

"Has the *jingwe* got your tongue, Larize?" Gradho emitted a throaty laugh. "I must say, you're in contrast to the moon-day of the gods!" That was strike two! He'd always made it blatantly clear that I wasn't the gods' choice for Larize. I set my rucksack

219

on the wooden floor and somehow refrained from punching the life out of Gradho's smug face. *How dare he chooses today, of all moon-days, to goad me into a fight!* I'd just heard the *worst* news of my existence, and yet he had the audacity to make snide remarks to me! I breathed.

The Dhareka councillors watched me cautiously. They knew how quickly my blood's curse could take control of me, but most of them were too acquiescent to pick sides, so they kept quiet and waited for the inevitable.

"Gradho, not now!" Tan warned.

"How can I forget Tan-tan, the perfect sidekick with the hair to match!" Gradho's mockery bounced off the glazed louvered ceilings. "He's just found out then?"

I pivoted towards him, clutching the chair I was about to sit in, willing myself not to smash his brains out. Aunt Zabi placed her hand over mine, calming me.

Gradho brought his chalice to his mouth and drank from it slowly. "As I was saying before you barged in here like you own this demesne, whilst *you* were sleeping…*we* have been working tirelessly on a strategy to rescue *our* Alessia—"

On the umpteenth strike, his words died! I leapt over the table, and my hands gripped his neck. *Say her name again!* With ease, I pinned him to the wall, daring him to speak again! Any word, a whisper, a cough, anything to give me an excuse to smash his head into the wall. My Tregtarian curse…I drew in some air, steadying myself. I was close to silencing the scorn out of him but not close enough. At least I was in control.

"Dan!" Tan was at my side in a jiff. "This isn't helping. Let him go." He patted my shoulder.

I glanced at him, seething, and back at Gradho. The light penetrating from the louvered windows made Gradho squint.

"This won't bring her back," Tan said.

I kept my hands firmly on Gradho anyway. My intention wasn't to hurt him. I needed him to learn to never pick a fight he couldn't win.

"Aless won't want to see you like this."

That brought me back. Immediately I loosened my grip, edged away, and slumped into my seat at one end of the horn-shaped table. Lessi was my ray of light, but even she could not extinguish the flame passed down through the darkness of my father's blood.

For eleven moon-years, I'd endured intense training to suppress my Tregtarian instincts, learning the Tuscanian art of self-composure, yet at times like these, it seemed fruitless.

"This is the man you want as your Larizon?" Gradho asked gruffly.

"Enough, Gradho!" Gabe sprung up. "We've put up with your insults for too long! He's the rightful heir."

"Heir! He's a Tregtarian—"

"He's Tuscanian first, my cousin's blood. *My* blood!" Gabe broke in.

"Not with that temper, he's not!" Gradho waved his plump hands. He was one to talk.

My breathing seemed louder inside my head. I was beginning to regret my decision to seek the Dhareka's counsel. If I'd just followed my instincts, I'd have been in Tregtaria by sundown, but in the depths of my heart, I'd hoped Sig and Lariana were mistaken, that I'd find Lessi at home...waiting for me!

Following two moon-months of being in a semi-comatose state, I'd begun to regain my strength, a couple of moon-days ago. You'd have thought my family would tell me then that Lessi was gone, but no! Finding out by chance had crushed me in ways I couldn't begin to tell!

I had been walking towards my bedroom when I overheard Sig, my cousin, the one I shared everything with—almost everything. He was whispering, and I couldn't help eavesdropping.

"This isn't the right time to bring him this news," he had whispered.

I'd halted at my door, hand resting on the knob.

"It's not ideal. I agree," Lariana had whispered crisply. "He needs to know."

Their muted voices had made me more attentive.

"It'll break him and only prolong his recovery," Sig had said. "We'll wait."

"We've waited enough! Any longer—there'll be consequences. You know his temper. She could be dead!"

My eyes had felt as though they were burning in their sockets as I'd shuddered at my sister-in-law's words.

"If they wanted her dead, we would have found her body halves next to Hyperian's."

Falling backward, I'd felt like a dagger had stabbed me... before my heart plunged into a dark hole. Inside my head, I'd taken a loping stride. In reality, I'd staggered, and sank to my knees. I'd clutched the door and inhaled deeply. My eyes shut, I'd prayed for Lessi, for us, for our sequence. A fuelling and burning sensation had rippled through me. The pain was just too real.

*Hyperian is dead...Lessi...*I dared not think about this. Not *my* Lessi. *How many times do I have to lose her?* She was all I had, all I longed for. On my knees, I'd thrust the door forward; it squeaked.

Sig and Lariana had jerked.

"D-Dante! Why are you not in bed?" Lariana had stuttered and then rushed to my side.

"Tell me what you're keeping from me," I'd demanded coldly, rising to my feet.

"What did you hear, cousin?"

I'd shot Sig a frustrated gaze.

"It's Alessia," Lariana finally said. She'd sighed heavily.

I'd given no acknowledgement, just waited for the inevitable words that would fragment my sunken heart.

"You may want to sit down," Lariana had offered, before lowering herself into the chaise lounge along with Sig. I'd remained still, as they'd exchanged conspicuous glances.

She'd cleared her throat. "Now is not the time to freak out… okay?" She was biding time, trying to soften me for something that was impossible to prepare for. "She was abducted…by Tregtarians."

My greatest fear realized! In choked desolation, my jaw had tightened, my hands naturally clenching into fists. I'd felt the urge to hit something—anything—and I still felt that same urge. The burning sensation in my bloody eyes had blinded me to a sea of red.

It's my fault. I let her down. I had to struggle to fight through my Tregtarian blood. *I should have never left her.* "How long…h-how long has she been gone?"

Sig had shot me a forlorn, apologetic gaze. "Two moon-months—"

"Two moon-months!" If he'd been anyone other than family… "And you're telling me—"

"You were fighting for your life, cousin!" he'd thrown back. "There's nothing you could have done."

"That's not your decision!"

"I'm sorry, Dante." Lariana had been sincere, tearful. "We all are…"

Trying to force some calmness into me would have meant going against nature; my family knew the full wrath of my father's curse. I'd succumbed to silence. With each breath I'd drawn in, ice splinters pierced through me, cutting deeper and deeper into my heart.

I'd grabbed my rucksack from the closet, located a few essentials, and charged out of my uncle's home. The journey to the land of my birth had been long overdue. I'd always known I would return to Tregtaria. What I hadn't envisaged was going back to claim something they'd stolen from me!

I was breathing heavily, shoving away the memories, trying to focus on the here and now. I studied the map in front of me, planning my route.

Zaira's light touch on my shoulders reached out to the core

of my heart. "We're all worried about Alessia, Dante more so." Her normally calm voice sounded strained. She squeezed my shoulders and dropped a kiss on top of my head. "The Dhareka will allow him the courtesy to deal with this in his own way."

"By storming in here and pretending he's the only one affected…" Gradho swung his hands in the air and then sank into his chair at the other end of the table. "She means…s-something to all of us, but we're not threatening to kill each other!"

"Not *something*, Gradho. She's everything to me," Zaira said firmly.

"Exactly my point, Zaira. I'm with you on this!" Gradho voiced. "Dante should be thanking the Star gods he's only had half a moon-day to live with this blow. *We've* had two moon-months to come to terms with such a calamity!"

I tore my gaze from the map laid on the table and stared piercingly at Gradho. "And yet you've done nothing!" I lowered my gaze back at the map, planning my route.

"You call this nothing?" Gradho sprang up, his booming voice reverberated across the room. "Whilst you were delight-ing in your nap, Larize, we've been discussing strategy."

"Two moon-months of fruitless discussions when Lessi could be dead!" My jaw tightened.

"At least we were doing something." Gradho bellowed. "What were *you* doing?"

I shot him an unamused look. "Are you blaming me for something I wasn't aware of?"

Gradho's lips moved into a wry smile. "Yes, I hold you accountable!" He wasn't one to beat about the bush. "You left her, didn't you? *Unprotected!*"

That silenced me. He was right. I'd devoted my life to her, and yet I'd allowed the Seven Voices of Sequence to force me away.

I shifted my gaze to the council of elders, the Seven Voices of Sequence who sat at the inner round table, seemingly oblivious to the exchange happening around them. Respect went a long way in my world. It was times like these when I realised I should have asserted my authority.

Despite their assurances, the onus was on me to keep her safe. I had succumbed to the elders' cause—the land's cause—and left mine to dwindle away into the shadows. Now I'd been robbed of my future, a future I thought I had lost eleven moon-years ago but had only just found in Lessi.

My mind drifted to the past, to when I'd lost the will to live or love—the moon-day that my mother died in my arms when I was ten moon-years old.

"You're home," Mother had said with a faint smile. She had regained consciousness for a short interval; just long enough to allow her to say her farewell. "But my time is up, Dante. Your heart will break and shatter, but remember this, in time and in sequence, it will mend again." She'd squeezed my trembling hand.

Even now, I still remembered her soothing voice, her soft touch.

"A time will come when you will lay your eyes on your *Larusia*...only then will you begin to feel like you're home." She'd forced the words out through quivering lips, tears coursing down her cheeks.

Helpless tears had spilled out of my eyes and streamed down my cheeks uncontrollably. It was then that I vowed never to shed another tear ever again.

"Learn about your gods, my son. Have faith in their beauty. Live with the expectation that the moon-day will come when you'll stop mourning my death and begin to celebrate my life." She'd beckoned me to lower my head so she could wipe away my tears. "House Hantaria are favoured by the Moon gods of the night skies, and so are you." She'd paused, catching her breath. "You're not alone, and you'll never walk alone. You have a home in every household in this land. Do you understand?"

"Yes, Mother."

"Have courage, faith, and love. You're heir to the Ocean Crown, and in time, you will live, lead, love, and be loved as the Larizon of the kingdom favoured by the moons." Her voice had been strained.

A shuffle of feet had emerged from the doorway. Zaira had walked in and knelt next to me.

My mother had nodded to Zaira before taking her hand and placing it over mine. "You're as much a Hantarian as you are a Serenian," she'd said in a whisper. "Your future is aligned to both houses, and one moon-day you will understand what I'm saying."

Anguished, I could barely speak.

She'd turned to Zaira, her tears seeping freely. "This is my gift to you." She'd swallowed hard. "Take care of Dante Erajion for me."

"Erajion?" A single tear had escaped Zaira's eye. "You named him Erajion."

"Our houses have lost enough. By the grace of the moon gods, we will gain more than we've lost," she'd whispered.

"You have given me a grandson, Raquel. A grandson whom I'll cherish for as long as I will live," Zaira had said. "I'll take care of him as I would my own blood."

Following my mother's passing, Zaira had stayed faithful to her word. She'd taken me into her house, and for two moon-years, I lived under her roof as a Serenian. In her house, I was home. At that time, none of us knew that my heart would indeed be forever aligned to house Serenius. Zaira taught me to persevere. She taught me to live. She taught me that it was possible to love again. Little did I know, and unbeknownst to her, she was preparing me for her granddaughter.

As my mother had said, everything became as clear as water when I first saw Lessi at the banquet. Immediately, she'd filled my heart with completeness and warmth, something I had searched for since my mother's death.

Everything about her had pointed to the heart of the ocean.

She came through the Four Oceans of the Surging Tide like an unexpected tidal wave, mellowing everything she touched, drenching my heart in ways I never thought were possible. Her blue eyes were the soul of the ocean, and one look from her was enough to make me forget the past and want to build a future I could share with her. And when she smiled, her heart of hearts shone in her eyes. There was no doubt in my heart or mind, Lessi was my *Larusia*—the heart of the ocean.

I loved her unsparingly. I would fight for us. I would fight for our sequence. I would live for her until my last breath. And now I was faced with the reality that she wasn't just mine. She was every kingdom's pawn in a sequencing game of life, love, and death. My love for her was an infinite element in that game, yet every time that she was taken from me, I was ripped apart. I had a fight on my hands. *Save her...save us!*

16. FATHER TURNS MURDERER...

Don't let *Gradho get to you.* Zaira's mind found mine.

I floated back to reality, and the anguish inside my chest. I had no idea how long I'd been distracted. I remember being vaguely aware of Zaira dragging her chair and positioning it next to me. Gradho must have been mumbling more disdainful statements, but the gods had spared me his derogatory utterance somewhat briefly, considering the vapour he was now billowing out.

"That's precisely what happens when you leave the zera-pe-ladha under the misguided guardianship of a protector for hire!" Gradho's effrontery was unequalled. Tact was not one of his strengths. "He wasn't sworn in! He *may* be Larize, but he didn't take a vow to protect her; now look where we are!"

Again, I didn't respond. I ruffled my fingers through my hair. My people breathed peace before war. No one had silenced Gradho, yet. Tuscanians had lived under the protection of the shield for centuries, fighting was foreign to them. They believed in the power of words...constructive words. Only that Gradho was a different breed. But this time we had a crisis that words could not solve. "Enough, house Merinda!" I snapped. "All this talk is not accomplishing anything. I'm here to seek the Dhareka's counsel, not to listen to your finger pointing expedition. It stops now, or I'll throw you out!"

To be fair, I endured his ill-placed chutzpa more than I

should. He couldn't see past my Tregtarian roots. For a long time following my mother's death, I couldn't, either. Not until the moon-day I found my *soul* in the depths of sea-blue eyes, my offering from the South Star god of love.

Dispirited murmurings emerged from the council of elders.

"The blame does not lie with the Larize." Ralda, the Voice of Sequence, lifted his head listlessly. The unfortunate events had taken a toll him. His ivory robe drooped over his shoulders as he staggered to the centre, gripping his walking stick. "My fiery Gradho, you've had your say, a right in this council. I don't dispute your ardent zeal for this cause or how much you're willing to sacrifice for our chosen one."

Ralda was quiet for some time, catching his breath. The six Voices of Sequence at the round table nodded in consensus. Finally, they seemed in the same room as the councillors.

Gradho smiled, self-satisfied.

"Demeaning the Larize lacks forethought and tact." Ralda swung me a look of concern. "Contrary to your misconceptions on the Larize's upbringing…he's more patient than you credit him for."

"Him!" Gradho's features froze, and he slashed his hand through the air. "The patient one! He almost choked the life—"

Ralda raised his hand, and Gradho stiffened, his jaw visibly tightening. "When a man is pushed to the summit of a cliff… he only has two options—to jump or plummet. Regardless of *you* being the perpetrator or an innocent bystander…*you* do not want to be in close proximity to that cliff, and certainly not at the bottom." Ralda shook his head. "In the future, you will want to select your words with due care. It's only prudent—my gift to you. The young Larize will, without a doubt, become Larizon. It's the moons' wishes." Ralda paused as though he was expecting an objection. "He will choose to rule as he desires. You will not want to make an enemy of him." His words dragged, his eyes dark with unfathomable emotion.

Gradho's impudent rudeness appeared to have left him for

a minuscule span. He looked at Ralda, scandalized. He merely lifted his chin and narrowed his eyes.

Ralda turned his attention to me. "Larize of everyone here, you carry the right to feel great anger at this turn of events. We, the Voices of Sequence, were wrong to send you away." He cast a quick glance at the table of six elders.

Nods and grunts echoed around the room.

"As history is inscribed, what you will do next will define how this will end. You need to channel that anger towards me…if it helps your cause. *I* am at fault." His voice sounded strained. "I failed to see the ripple effect of my decisions, and the domino slide that pursued. The component of the Jajaja tree *I* used on you…to hasten the chosen one's training… almost robbed us of our only Larize."

"A poison?" I puzzled over it.

In the little time I was conscious and aware of my surroundings, I had pondered over why I'd been consumed by an illness unknown to Tuscanians, and yet here Ralda had the answer! Every moon-day, the physicians sang the same tune over and over again.

"Your Tuscanian and Tregtarian genes are in conflict… you're your own healer," they had said, and I'd been too weak to press the point.

"A miasma of Jajaja leaves is lethal to your Tregtarian gene." Ralda's expression was one of remorse. "We're aware of that now. The potion was intended to send you into a deep sleep for one moon-night, so we could execute our plan. It's been used on Tuscanians for centuries. There haven't been any side effects, until you…for that I apologise, my Larize."

A tight knot twisted inside my stomach. I clenched my fists, and swallowed a thick lump in my throat. *Now is not the time to lose control.* I inhaled deeply and nodded out of respect. *I need a clear head.* I'd made my fair share of mistakes…it wasn't my place to judge. Especially not now. My only focus was Lessi.

Ralda scratched his forehead. "Sending you away for the

cause was a miscalculated risk. I underestimated the entire conundrum. The chosen one was under *my* protection, yet a snake was slithering inside my house. Hyperian was *my* trustworthy and honourable apprentice. I misjudged the whole quandary, but from great mistakes come substantial results…if we open our hearts to a favourable outcome. The chosen one's life lies in the balance. She means something to all of us…"

Not to me she doesn't! Lavia of house Regai-Rallias decided, against all logic, that now was the time to barge inside my head. Her nagging voice was so loud she demanded my full attention. Lavia and I had been set to marry for political reasons, but I had called it off. Since then, she had never got over the fact that I cancelled a seven moon-year agreement by choosing Lessi over her, and now she made sure I felt her frustration.

She'd been unusually quiet. She always found her voice one way or another…her Felradian curse. I thought she may have turned over a new leaf, but sadly *a bird that sings the same way never changes its tune.* My ancestors got that saying spot on.

Telepathy had its sway, but one thing it didn't do was separate emotion from voice. Every word that echoed inside your head was distinctly attached to every grain of emotion in such a way that it felt louder than spoken words. And having your mind invaded by a disagreeable voice was an unwelcome intrusion into your domain.

I hated that she was doing this to me, especially now, today.

I'm sick of this chosen one issue! She's an overrated alien, an elusive new toy for the fools of this land—

Lavia! Keep your thoughts to yourself! I warned.

Or what? she yelled inside my head. *And no! Why should I—*

Just stay out of my head!

Don't tell me what to do, Dan!

I leaned forward in my seat and shot her a silencing gaze across a dozen or so heads between us. She frowned.

I don't have the time or the patience to deal with you, too, today.… Don't let me force you out! I don't want to hurt you.

She laughed a cynical laugh. It echoed inside my head like a loud cackle. *So the Larize has a conscience! Hurt me? Like you haven't done that already. You can't hurt me anymore, Dan. The damage is done! That shiny new toy you're all obsessed with, one of these moon-days, it will bite—*

What am I...in preschool! Grow up, Lavi—

Shhh. To top it off, I'm not allowed to speak. Why? Because we're in the almighty presence of the honourable Voices of Sequence. Half of them are dozing off anyway.

Get out of my head!

No! She regarded me above the rim of her chalice.

Get out, Lavia, or by the moons, I'll block you out.

I don't care. I stopped caring a long time ago!

"...she is to us, as a collective, is what we need to protect," Ralda said as I focused on him and not Lavia. "We will not go down in history as the generation that put us back into Tregtarian slavery. The chosen one is gone, and yet the shield still stands."

"On wobbly feet!" Gradho had to add.

"Still, it stands!" Ralda reiterated with authority. "That assures us our chosen one is alive, and the moons are in our favour..."

Don't they tire of calling her the—

Why can't you just zip it, Lavia! I brought my hands to my head. My patience was just about worn out at this point.

Why? Because you can't handle the truth? Here's the truth, Larize! Whilst you're busy strategizing with the wise council... some are asleep, by the way...your precious, troubled toy is more likely than not tirelessly worming her way into some Tregtarian fool's heart right now!

The sting from Lavia's words propelled me into a deep surreal silence. I breathed. I tried to keep calm. It wasn't easy. *Lavia. I'm asking that you stop, please.*

I'm just warming up! That fool could easily be of your own blood, after all, she seems taken by your kind! By the time you pick up your rucksack and get to Tregtaria, your little princess could be living in your childhood home, married off to your father, and carrying his child! She smiled to triple the sting in her words.

Lavia, shut up! She was disturbed, even more than I realised—bordering on neurosis.

How's that for some truths! The man you call Papa, that same man who raised you and murdered your mother in cold blood, takes your new toy for a wife! She gave a harsh, derisive laugh.

I stiffened, my eyes burning into hers.

That would make quite a headline, an interesting read for the Tuscanian Sunrise. *'Father turns murderer...' No. 'Husband murders wife before claiming son's new toy as bride!' Not even a creative genius could engineer that one, Dan! Ha! Now that makes me wonder, if they did have a child, what would you call it? Brother? Or—*

My forbearance ran out. I sprang up, fuming.

In return, she flicked her dark curls and smiled, obviously delighted she'd caught my attention once and for all.

Dozens of eyes turned to me. My head was spinning. Lavia's sick humour had some hard, incomprehensible truths in it. Tregtarians were capable of anything.... I feared the worst, and the worst ranged from a tiny leaf grazing her to...I couldn't contemplate.

My gaze swung to the council. "With all due respect, what we're all failing to grasp is time. Every moment we're debating this is a moment we don't have."

"The chosen one is equipped to survive this, Larize," Ralda said. "Her training wasn't in vain. She's strong...but we shall not tempt the gods." He strained his eyes to look up at me. "It's settled. The delegate of five councillors of the Dhareka will leave for the south tonight."

Tregtaria! My brow furrowed. "For negotiations?"

"Yes, young Larize!"

Silence pursued as I pondered over the probability of success. Tregtarians didn't sit at the table and talk. They breathed death before words.

"Did you miss that, Larize?" Gradho pitched in, rising from his seat and positioning himself next to Ralda in the centre. "I'm leading the party that's bringing Alessia home. Sit back and watch me work." A smug grin cut across his mouth. His arrogance was troubling.

With a desperate sadness enveloping me, I appealed to the one person who devotedly had Lessi's best interests at heart. *Zaira, you're allowing Gradho to lead the delegation.*

She looked up to me, her eyes sparkling with tears she'd been holding back. *We're at a crossroads with limited options. Blamorey and Gabe were part of Kaylinah's delegation. Lord De-Deganon will have their heads on the chopping block at first sight. Gradho is a lot of things, but if there's someone who'll talk his way into any situation, it's him. On this cause, he wants her home as much as we all do.*

I took a deep breath to fill my lungs. "Respectfully, a negotiation with Lord De-Deganon is a fruitless strategy that won't yield results."

Gradho threw me an opposing smile, cleared his voice, and dipped his head for show. "Larize...since you seem savvy with the ways of the *Wicked South*, perhaps you should let us in on what *you* think the council should do."

"The Dhareka should do what it deems right. I'm not arguing with you. I'm merely offering an opinion." I picked up my rucksack and strapped it across my chest. "I'm leaving for Tregtaria."

"You're not joining my delegation." Gradho shot me a look. "I can't have prior bad feelings tainting our talks before we've begun."

"I wasn't intending to. I'm doing this alone. I'll not interfere with your talks, rest assured."

"My Larize, take a seat," Ralda said, and when I didn't act on his words, he continued, "The Voices of Sequence concur; we can't allow you to go."

My gaze swung sideways. "I'm sorry. I don't follow."

"You're heir to this land. Allow the delegates to bring the chosen one back. The land can't afford to lose its Larize."

I smiled tight-lipped. "With all due respect, the land is fine without a Larizon. I'm not asking for your permission. I would sooner give up my life for her before I'm crowned Larizon."

"Well, now. Some honest truth…at last." Gradho raised his chalice. "Are you denouncing your throne, for her?"

I threw him a sharp stare, gulped in a breath, and didn't grace his flippant remark with a response.

"Frankly, Larize…is there something more than the obvious between you and Alessia we should all know?" he continued.

"Gradho!" Blamorey, Lessi's grandfather straightened, his eyes haunted. His face was drawn with worry. "Focus on the task at hand. Let Dante do what he must. Being Larizon is his birthright. He can't denounce his throne, even if he wanted to. What we all need is Alessia back home…it doesn't matter how."

Thank you, Blamorey. Those were all the words I could manage. He was a thoughtful man, level-headed, a true Tuscanian. Throughout this meeting, he hadn't said a word. With him, silence spoke louder than speech.

Bring my granddaughter home. His expression was shadowed.

I won't return without her.

"May the winds of Sequence guide you in the right path, Larize," Ralda said.

The elders looked up and nodded.

I dipped my head, gazed at the council, and said my farewells.

Tan rose to his feet and was beside me in a trice.

You can't come with me, I said.

I know. You made your point clear, Dan. I'll ride with you to the shield. We always ride together, you and I. Don't ask me to stay back now. He hardly grinned.

I patted his shoulder. With Tan, I never had to look behind because he always had my back, but Tregtaria was no place for him. I had to have my own back.

I pivoted and strode towards the door with haste.

"Larize, stop!" Gradho's loud and abrupt voice came from behind.

I spun round, confused. *What now?*

He gave a little shrug, took a deep breath, and brought his hands to his back. "I suppose now is a good time to ask you to be extra cautious," he said with care.

Something was amiss… He didn't care whether I lived or died, so this muddled blend of concern was disturbing.

"The scouts I sent across the shield have returned word that Alessia is held in one of two places." He paused, taking a breather. "De-Deganon's castle—"

"That's the obvious place—" I said, a bit too bluntly.

"Wait for it…" He strode to the map and pointed to the southeastern land between Tregtaria and Tuscania. "Or the deserted lands of the Water Walkers."

Heads lifted at this somewhat unexpected statement.

"That land is uninhabitable. Why would they take her there?"

"That's what we need to find out. Tregtarian warriors have been spotted manning the area. There's definitely an operation going on there. Just this morning, I sent an army to the Lands of the Water—"

"An army of what?" I interjected.

"Try and keep up, Larize. Troops—soldiers—an infantry of a hundred-strong men. If she's there, they'll bring her home. Meanwhile, my delegation will head south—"

"Hold on, Gradho!" Gabe recoiled in horror. "You have a private army?"

Gradho rubbed his temples. "That's not important. What—"

"Stop right there!" Blamorey raised his voice. "Explain why you have a personal army undisclosed to the Dhareka!"

"For times like these." Gradho arched his brows. "Surely you didn't expect me to storm into the land of the warriors with *just* my mouth for protection!"

"The East Star god of peace will protect you," Ralda said. "Tregtarian warriors are no match for the gods."

"The gods are for all, not for one. They watch over Tregtaria, too!" Gradho voiced. "We need a diversion and auxiliary security. As it stands, I have a second card to play."

"This is not a simple game, my fiery Gradho, but a complex one," Ralda countered in a strained, stricken voice. He'd been standing for longer than he should, and his legs were beginning to jiggle. "The life of our chosen one is at stake...the land of our ancestors is at risk. All future generations are depending on the shield...and the shield is *she*."

"With respect to all," Gradho said, "if each land brings a set of gauntlets, and an extra pair of gloves to a game of flapdragon, it would be unwise to turn up with a pocket full of nothing! I'm not getting my fingers burnt!"

The Dhareka lapsed into deafening silence.

"Did you know she'd be taken?" Gabe asked, a question I had held back.

"No!" Gradho's puzzled expression seemed genuine enough. "I'm livid you'd ask," he muttered under his breath.

"So building an army, and deploying it exactly when we need it, is coincidental...not forgetting that you did that in secret!" Gabe said.

Gradho's face went pale for a minuscule moment. "With the shield on its knees, I'm not one to sit back and wait for the inevitable collapse. I had to do what no one else was willing to do."

A nerve throbbed in my temple. I frowned, wishing the pain away. "Are they trained?"

"Of course. I'm not mindless, Larize. I wouldn't send men to certain death. They're an advanced infantry, with five moon-years' combat training, and armoured with the latest and most advanced weaponry to date."

"All of that under the council's nose," I bellowed. "If it was a righteous act, why keep it from the Dhareka?"

"*This* peace-loving Dhareka, you mean?" He waved his hands in the air. "What would they have said?" He paused, brooding, his eyes averted. "Well done, Gradho, for thinking outside the box...you're a gift to this land!' No! I'd have been met with resentment, finger-pointing, and a premature quashing of an army we clearly need." He strode back to his seat and eased himself into it. "Just so we're clear, my men are Tuscanians, not mercenaries. Their goal is aligned to our cause."

"And their pockets are aligned to the one who fills them!" I interjected.

The elders seemed detached and in a contemplative frame of mind. They tried to stay aloof over the infighting of the outer council. Ralda rested his weight on his stick, in quiet deliberation. As for the councillors, their earlier murmurings unravelled into silence.

I stared studiously at Gradho. "Who commands this infantry?"

He waited a beat before he answered. "Bydrel—"

"Your brother...with allegiance to you?"

"To the land of the Rising Sun god of Light—to the kingdom under the moons—to the mother of the shield."

I was curious, but I didn't press the point. "I don't have time for this. You're right to be in possession of an army, but keeping it from the Dhareka and the Voices of Sequence was wrong, deceitful, and simply disrespectful!"

"It shouldn't be your concern, Dante. You're not part of this council." Gradho's lower jaw tightened. "You don't have the right to be bothered by matters of this land."

I gazed at the flagon sitting next to him. I felt thirsty, but no amount of water would be enough to quench my dry throat. I lifted my gaze to him. "I don't need to be a constituent of the Dhareka." My voice was stern. I'd just about had enough to handle in one moon-day. "I am *the* Larize. I have *every* right to know what's happening in this land *and* beyond."

Gabe was smiling avidly at me. He wasn't the only one. It

was the first time I'd openly embraced my duty. I'd put it off for a long while, but I always knew the time would come when I'd have to step up.

"Spoken like *the* gods-chosen rightful Larizon." With an exhale, Ralda walked over. He slid his hand into his cloak pocket, brought out a small bottle and handed it to me. "Any vengeance you seek for your mother has to wait for another moon-day." He sighed. "Heed my words, Larize. You're walking on fine sand…your strides need to be longer, more precise, and headed in the right direction. Don't go astray. The land needs the chosen one back under our protection."

I nodded.

"Tell me your proposition."

That knocked me back slightly. I didn't have one yet.

Ralda gazed at me, listlessly scrutinizing my silent response. "In your palm is *ahwira* liquid tranquilizer. A few drops will weaken any creature that inhales it. Be careful not to breathe it in, Larize. If it reaches your lungs, death will overtake you. I've made enough errors; do not make me have a handful." His hands shook as he squeezed mine.

"Thank you." After I embraced him in a farewell hug and placed the bottle in my rucksack, I turned to Gradho. "I won't get in your way. Your army is advancing southeast, and I'm heading south to Tregnika through the Jungle of Voices and the Sands of the Dead. Our paths won't cross."

"Larize." He gestured formally by dipping his head as though he meant it. If I didn't know Gradho so well, I'd say he sounded sincere. "I have a few men to spare; perhaps they could accompany you south?"

"How many?"

"Twenty…twenty-five."

I rubbed my chin. "I appreciate the offer…but a such small number will be no match for De-Deganon's men. It's best I do this alone. I'll blend in."

"I don't doubt that—"

"It's a lesser risk," I rephrased. Arguments were exhausting. I was done for the moon-day.

"One man cannot encircle a humongous anthill alone, young Larize," Ralda said, "but if the only option risks the lives of many, the gods have no choice but to hold his hands."

"Well said, old man,"Teethie, one of the elders said, seeming as if he'd just woken up from a light nap. The elders had not left their homes in a long time, which explained their detachment to the conversations happening around them. Still it was frustrating that they were just sleeping and not even attempting to join the discussions. "Larize," Teethie called. "None of us are asleep, my young Larize." He had somehow breached my shield and answered my unspoken question. "Whilst our mouths are shut, our minds are constantly at work linking this precious sequence piece by piece from moon-day one, Alessia's arrival to now. As we speak, the Felradian halkateiy are hard at work churning our sequences and that of our chosen one, and we must use our minds to stay ahead of the game."

I allowed myself a brief smile. In the eyes of the gods, we were one family.

"May the winds of Sequence guide you through the right path," Ralda said, walking me to the door. "Young Larize, outside of the shield…it's you against the forces of darkness." He took a breath. "The gifts of our minds are absolute within the boundary of our ancestors' shield…beyond that, our gifts are as unpredictable as the Njuzathian weather."

At that moment, I was my father's son, fearless. I exiled my anguish to an abyss unknown to men. I had a grave quest for my *lost heart*, one that had the power to change the world. I couldn't afford to harness desperation. I needed resilience to hold her in my arms again, and by the moons, only death would ever part us, and even then, I was certain the moons would be up for a compromise.

17. BLOOD OF MY BLOOD

Under the veil of the night skies, I lay low, unobserved. I squatted on a rooftop of a deserted building adjacent to De-Deganon's castle. Sad to say, I hid, the kind of hiding that a rodent does when a predator is close. The only difference was, I wasn't terrified; I knew I was in over my head. Lessi's life and well-being kept me focused. I had to stay alive for her, and if it meant being disguised like a rodent for some time, so be it!

The sky was clear, littered with twinkling stars, and the moons—a double halo hanging in the moon-night sky—glinted like a pair of salvers. The streets were womb-quiet; only the howl of the wind whistled in the moon-night. Still, the ground below was as hostile as the gnawing pain in the back of my head. Exhaustion and mental fatigue had enveloped me, making my head thump. Not even the full moons could cast beautiful silhouettes over this cursed land—Tregtaria—an ill-starred state.

Armed with my bow and arrow, my sword, a dagger, and a few knives, I could take out a handful of guards, or more at a push, but not a valorous army. That was simply suicidal.

As if that wasn't bad enough, I had no idea where *my heart* was. As soon as I'd crossed the shield, my mindreading prowess had vanished. Now my mind was as void as the hole inside my chest. My plan, the one I didn't quite have, was flawed. Ralda had been right; our minds were elusive beyond the shield. Still, it didn't explain why I could hear voices as a boy and not now.

After scouting the perimeter of the castle, I'd found the perfect spot to view it undetected. For some time now, I watched the guards as they did their rounds. It had gone past midnight when I'd gathered enough information to make my way into the castle unnoticed.

A window on the ground floor was open. The high command, although vigilant were too arrogant to think anyone would be brave enough to storm into De-Deganon's house. During the change of the guards, I planned to dispose of a guard, steal his armour, and walk through the door. Blending in was not an issue. The only problem was I didn't know which room she was held in or if she was in the castle.

Search room by room until I find her...that's foolproof all right!

A flurry of activity at the castle gates caught my attention. I shifted to a crouching position. The high command was leaving the castle. I breathed steadily and searched for one who had a tonne to answer for. It was at that moment that I saw him, his head held higher than the rest. Immediately, I positioned my bow, drew my arrow, and aimed it at his heart. From my position, he didn't have a chance. I could kill him and be done with it!

Squinting, I'd never concentrated that much on a target.

"Phew...phew..." My breathing felt strange to my ears.

What am I doing?

I inhaled deeply and then exhaled. With frustration, I set the bow down. Emotion was a curse in my world. I gritted my teeth. *Kill him now and avenge my mother.* I had a clear line of sight, and by the gods, I had a worthy cause! I hastily grabbed my bow again and drew it at him. Still, I couldn't let go.

I kept sight of him through the tip of my arrow; my hands began to quiver, and a trickle of sweat dribbled down my brow. With a lengthy sigh, I placed my bow on the ground. Inside my head, he was as good as dead. Only I wasn't Tregtarian enough. I wasn't Tuscanian enough, either. I was something in between—an unstirred broth. My chest tightened. Even in my time of serenity, I had bursts of anger that I couldn't control. I had acute urges to crash my arms into something…anything. I was constantly in a fight with myself. It frustrated me! I didn't know *where* I belonged…until Lessi. She saw me for the man I was. She turned my flaws into perfection.

I took another deep breath. *Kill him now and avenge my mother… Let the gods have their vengeance, his life isn't mine to take.* I drew my arrow again, for the third time, and followed him across the lane. *I'll give away my position.*

With that thought, I set my bow down. *Lessi's my priority.*

Instantly, my non-existent plan became a potential strategy. The hole inside my chest galloped. I didn't know why it hadn't crossed my mind before. If there was anyone who knew where Lessi was, my father would. He would take me to her!

So I allowed him to live…for now. I'd never taken a person's life before, and starting now, especially killing the man I once loved with a devotion he couldn't understand, scared the life out of me. I knew what had to be done should the need arose. Kill one to save many, an option the gods would have no choice but to forgive. It was time to return to my roots.

* * *

Nothing could prepare me for facing the man who murdered my mother. My eyes flitted across his dim bedchamber. An enormous bed was set against the far wall with a weapons cabinet for a frame. My father sat in his armchair, a thick rope tied around him. Ralda's potion had sent him into a deep sleep, and temporarily paralysed him from the waist down, enabling me to get to work. This was long overdue. I grabbed a bucket of water that I'd carefully set on the floor next to my mother's chair, and threw it over him. He woke up to a chilling drench of cold water. He jerked his head upwards and met my confrontational gaze. He swallowed hard, blinking a few times, his glance sweeping across his spacious, dimly lit bedchamber.

He was a prisoner in his own home, something that would never sit right with a Tregtarian, let alone *the general* of the ruthless high command.

I smiled cunningly, though not inwardly, to make certain to him I wasn't a Felradian dream but a very real nightmare. There was no love lost for us.

He jiggled in his armchair, attempting to break free of the restraints. I'd tied a thick rope around him…there was no escape.

His head waggled about endlessly in the shadowy chamber. It was quite uncomfortable to watch.

He bellowed out. "What the—"

"Calm down, Father." I leaned forward and placed the water bucket on the floor.

My eyes settled on the red and blue handprint heart my mother and I had painted onto the marbled floor. I must have been eight at the time. She'd spent most of her moon-days in this chamber, a *prisoner* without chains…

I drew in a deep breath to stay focused and perched my right foot on the bucket next to my father's jingwe-hide armchair that he was fettered to, too close for comfort.

"You're not dead yet!" I gave him a slanted smile and slowed my words for emphasis. I needed him to know early on I wasn't back for a family reunion.

I picked my diamond stone, held my dagger at a thirty-degree angle, and sharpened the blade. He eyed me menacingly for some time, breathing heavily. He couldn't put up much of a fight. Ralda's potion ensured that. Nostrils flaring, he turned to the door, but I'd secured it with the strongest Tuscanian bolts I'd brought with me.

One egotistical man—three warriors guarding the interior of his large house—seven guards within the Haurilio walls—seven more outside the perimeter of his gated land—eleven servants. It was ridiculous…lonely, even. For him, it would be a sad end to a life tangled in shadows.

Still it hadn't stopped me from getting to him.

Lines formed between his thick eyebrows. "H-How did you get inside my house?" His bleak, peeved expression was priceless.

"This was my home, once." I watched him piercingly. "I came in the same way I got out."

"The ancient tunnels?" His glance darted around and settled on the ajar secret door to his left.

At least his head was one part of his body he could still use. He tried to wiggle again, to no avail, and his red eyes opened wider. "Boy, what have you done to me!" he thundered, water dripping down his rather unkempt hair.

I continued to sharpen my blade like I intended to use it.

"I shared the under passage with *my son, my blood*, in case of an enemy attack." His voice wobbled. It was strange, but it served as assurance that I'd ruffled him. "And this is how he repays me?"

I looked up from my dagger to meet his gaze. "Where's the enemy, Father?" I said in a low, quiet voice. "All I see, is you and me…all I ever saw was you, me, and Mother!"

"Undo what you did to me, boy, or you'll regret this!" he spit out through his teeth.

We lapsed into threatening silence. His yes hovered across his bedchamber. One thing Tregtarians didn't do was give up. After death, it was up to the gods to silence them.

He lips parted. But he was too arrogant to call for help.

"Guards?" I shook my head. "Don't…. The servants will sleep easy tonight."

"What have you done to my guards?"

"I've assisted them in meeting the gods sooner rather than later," I lied. I'd only knocked out the guard manning the ground floor before spiralling my way to my father's bedchamber.

His gaze followed mine to the chained door. "One man against my warriors? Impossible!"

I smiled for his benefit; inside, I was praying for the guards not to interrupt us. I didn't have enough ahwira potion to drug them all. Trying to engage in a fight with the Haurulio guards was suicide. They had the training, the spirit and the numbers to send me to an early grave. I had to improvise. "What makes you think I came alone?"

"No Tuscanian has the courage to enter my household!" he rasped.

I didn't pursue his line of thinking. "As for the servants... when I'm done with you, they can make arrangements for your burial. Right now, they won't hear your plight, and even *if* they do, they'll probably shove their daggers into you, anyway. You see, *Father*, it's just you, me, and a long overdue moon-day of judgement!"

A curiously confusing smile travelled across his mouth. "Blood of my blood, you've followed your feet," he said calmly, his tone softening.

That took me aback, and I retreated towards his bed, and froze for a heartbeat mid-breath. Everything I'd done since I'd set foot in his home was a direct result of my upbringing: sharpening my blade—threatening to end his life—lying about the guards—terrorising a man in his own home. I'd turned into my father overnight, and he delighted in that.

Instilling fear in someone—anyone—wasn't my way, but it was the only way I knew he'd take me seriously.

Early sounds of dawn buzzed in the air. Bells rang in the distance, and morning birds chirped a greeting to the Sun god of Light. It had taken me half the moon-night to navigate through the web of tunnels that ran underneath Tregnika, and one of them ended in a spiral stairway that led right into his bedchamber. The perks of being *the* high commander.

I strolled towards the oak-framed window and peeked outside. His bedchamber was three floors up. My mother and I used to sit by the balcony, counting the birds in the sky...

"Has your heart brought you home?" he asked.

"Not quite." I turned round and blew onto my dagger.

"You're now a man," he said, wearing a half-smile over his fatigue-ravaged face. The transformation was startling: from the earlier loathing of a Tregtarian high commander to a proud and devoted father. "You're where you belong—"

"You're deluded if you think I'm here because I missed you." I dragged an adjacent chair and lowered myself in front of him.

"Given your hostility so far, I can only wish it. You're my son! That's written in blood by the gods—"

"And my mother! Why couldn't you let her go?" I lost composure and stabbed the dagger into the arm of his chair... reflex...unplanned.

His facial features spasmed violently. "If you had the choice, would you let go of your destiny? She was my life—my intended—my destiny!"

"And the arrow, was it her destiny, too?" My voice rose and cracked.

"The arrow was supposed to miss her. The shot wasn't supposed to be fatal." His eyes twisted into a dark and gloomy red.

"When you play with fire, at some point you'll get burnt. You expect me to believe you didn't mean to shoot at her?"

"Believe what you want." His voice was firm. "The truth is there in your eyes. Unlock it, son. Your mother was the love of my life!"

"Spare me *your* version of the truth!" I said harshly. "We both know it would be different if we'd met in favourable circumstances for you." I plucked my dagger out of the chair.

"I loved Raquel—"

"Love! You took her l-life!" I gripped my dagger tightly, my hand trembling.

"The arrow led to her death?" His eyebrows pulled down over his blood-rimmed eyes.

I swallowed hard. Was it possible he never knew? I didn't know whether to believe him or even if I wanted to believe him; I couldn't. He was the reason my mother was dead. I swallowed a thick lump in my throat. "Your shot was fatal. If your spies spared you the truth...this is it. *Your* destiny took her last breath a few moon-days after *your* arrow went through her!"

Frustrated, he whipped his head around and wiggled about again, failing to rise to his feet. After a few minutes, he became subdued, and his stance changed. For the first time, I saw something that resembled pain in his eyes. "It was a fever," he muttered under his breath. "I didn't know...you have to believe me." He gritted his teeth. "If I'd known—"

"What could you have done?" My blood boiled inside my veins. I sprang up and stabbed the dagger onto the curved wooden pillar. "Rejoiced in your victory?"

"D-Don't assume my calmness for stupidity, son." He scowled. "Why are you here?" His tone was hard. "If it's vengeance you seek, take it now!"

"Killing you would be too easy," I lied. I glanced to the east, a shaft of the first rays of sunlight beamed through my mother's curtains. Her design still hung untainted. She'd tried to find peace where peace didn't exist.

Attempting to calm myself, I paced about for a while, but then I sank into the chair in dejection. "I'll let you be your own death!"

"You've changed," he said. "You were like your mother—"

"D-Don't speak of her!"

He grimaced. "Your love for me was unwavering—"

"You speak of love as if you know what that is. Husbands don't murder their wives for *love*." I swallowed a huge lump of emptiness. "Fathers don't kill the mother of their child for *love*...I know how it is *to* love and *be* loved. You will never experience how that feels!"

He gave me a reproachful look. "Son, I'm sorry we're in this position right now."

I was thrown off balance. Him, apologising? *What am I missing here?*

"There are paths intertwined with destinies I can't share with you, not just yet. Before your betrayal, our destinies were on track." He paused. "You've seen how I live now. Do you think I c-chose this life?" His voice was toned with a pained quake that wasn't like him. "I haven't remarried, son. I…I hoped someday you'd return to me."

"I'm not your wife, Father! You murdered her. She's not coming b-back!"

He let out a huge breath. "I couldn't bear it if you came home and found another woman in your mother's kitchen."

"Come home? So you can feed me to the jingwes?"

"No, I would—"

"Of course, because you'd order your thugs to do it on your behalf!" I snapped.

"Blood of my blood, you were born to ride into the eye of the storm. Your destiny will be fulfilled but not without—"

"Enough about destiny!" My brow creased. The throbbing pain on my left temple was becoming unbearable. "You had a choice! Hiding behind the veil of destiny because you made the wrong decision is petty, even for you."

"Destiny and Sequence are aligned side by side, son!"

"Don't you dare bring Sequence into this," I bellowed. "You know nothing about Sequence."

His hard features tightened. "I know enough. I am the high commander, son, but my family is *command* to me! You're my blood. Despite my ways, you're a part of me." He even sounded honest. I shook my head. He seemed older than I recalled, a few wrinkles ringed his eyes. His wet hair was shorter, dishevelled.

"Father." I took a steadying breath. "I'd like to believe your sincerity, but we're too far gone." Despite my words, in spite of the unforgivable wrongs he'd done, I still felt something other than hate for him. I rubbed the back of my neck, my throat closing up.

"You need to learn to trust again," he said. "Trust begins with blood. Once you've grasped that, the future is yours for the taking."

I rose to my feet and gave my back to him.

"Tell *your father* why you're back."

I whipped my head round and stared right at him, my gaze catching sight of the early morning glow through the double doors.

"Despite your earlier threats, I'm certain you're not here to kill me." His confidence was unsettling. "What can I do to earn your trust and *be* your father once more?"

I took the plunge. "I'm looking for someone. I need to know where she is."

"The human!" he exclaimed, his eyes opening wider.

"Lessi," I corrected him, and swallowed hard.

"A friend of yours?"

"It's not your concern," I said curtly. "Tell me where she is, and you'll never hear from me again."

He brooded. "In De-Deganon's house of houses, of course."

"That I know. I need specific information, which wing, floor—chamber—how many guards—"

"You're risking your life for a mere human?" he groaned.

"My motives aren't your concern!" My voice was cold.

"Perhaps you can enlighten me. I can't figure out why a little human causes a stir wherever she goes." He eyed me suspiciously. "De-Deganon has her on a tight leash. She's a reminder of *the forgotten*. You'll not get to her undetected."

The air froze around us. "Let me figure that out."

"You'll be dead by dusk!"

"If that's my destiny, it's already written…but before then, I have to see her again."

He gaped at me warily. "You're in love with this *human*?"

What do you know of love? Why can't he just use her name? "Lessi!" A gush of rage enveloped me. "I will not answer that, High-Commander Jizu Haurilio. D-Don't mistake my respect for you and think for one second…I forgive you for taking my mother's life. You stopped being *my father* the moon-day you murdered her."

His red eyes turned fierce with burning anger. "Risking your life for a stranger is not how I raised you!"

I took a slow deep breath. "You don't know me...not anymore. Don't presume to think you know exactly what's going through my mind."

"I know enough! You're making rushed decisions. Your mind is clouded. Son, take a step back, and strategize before getting yourself killed through stupidity!"

If the voice of reason came from someone else other than him, maybe I'd consider.

"Is that an order—"

"Call it what you like! I'm protecting you! I'll be damned if I let you storm into De-Deganon's house to certain death. You know what they do to—"

"*They*, Father? *They?* Should you not be saying *we*?" I raged, my eyes burning with fury. "Why would you exclude yourself from these massacres as if *you* are the saint? You're the high commander; you command those men!"

"One moon-day, you'll understand that all is not as it seems. I did and do what I have done and still do to create a future for you." He was calm now—way too calm.

"For me? Are you out of your mind?" I choked out. His words were odd.

"Everything is to shape a path that is right for my sons—"

I laughed darkly. "Son?" I corrected him.

He grinned. "You were never destined to walk alone.... Had your mother lived, your destiny would have long since been fulfilled. Now you'll go round in circles to reach the summit of the mountain of destiny, my son, but trust that you'll get there."

What am I—ten moon-years old?

"Since you blame destiny for your actions, did destiny end my mother's—"

"Don't mock the winds of destiny, boy! Never lay blame on destiny. Embrace it."

"Your wife is dead," I said coldly. "Do you embrace that?"

At least he looked remorseful. His bedchamber seemed dimmer, quieter. "It was an accident, one I hadn't foreseen." His voice toned down to a whisper.

"Your Felradian dreaming friends didn't let you in on *that* part of the future?"

"Family, not friends…in time you'll realise…your blood is the purest of all."

I shook my head. He'd say and do anything to absolve himself from what he did.

Unexpectedly, a stour erupted from the corridor beyond the chained door. I froze mid-breath. A loud clamour rose from the floors below. They must have found the knocked-out guard. Shouts and shrilling screams filled the air. Before I could react, the door was booted, a rattling sound reverberating as the bolts I'd used to secure the door were tested to the core.

"Intruder! Intruder!" a voice shouted.

The door shook vigorously. My already pounding head thumped so hard it felt like it would split in two. I couldn't work out a plan of action that could save me or get me the information I needed to find my lost heart.

"My commander!" a voice shouted forcefully. "We need to take you to safety!"

My father easily broke through the restraints and jumped to his feet. My world crashed down in front of my eyes, I went into a defensive crouching position. He shot me an unsettling look and loped towards the door. He spread his arms and blocked the door from being beat down.

Thunderstruck, I could only gape at him. "How did you—"

"You allowed your emotions to govern you and lost sight of your captive! Your tranquiliser wore off ages ago. If my commanders see you, I can't protect you," he whispered. "Go!"

Adrenaline quickly replaced shock. I grabbed my rucksack from the bed and clutched it tightly. "Where is she?" Blood pounded in my temples.

"Go home, son. She's not *your* destined!"

"Where is she?" I whispered harshly.

"She's a chink in your armour, boy!"

"My High-Commander, an intruder is within our walls!" a voice shouted. "Open the door!"

The door was booted again with so much force my father had trouble holding it back. The rising noise intensified. The sound of howling dogs filled the air.

I gripped the secret door handle. "F-Father, t-ell me where she is!" I begged. "P-Please—"

"Your death is on you! East wing—De-warrior Dranisha's court—four floors up—three guards inside—a dozen outside," he rushed the words. "Now run!"

18. There's One Greater Than Death and Denser Than Life: Love.

Hurtling down the spiral stairs, I took two steps at a time. My pulse pounded in all my veins. I knew I'd be racing men faster than me. They had the practice, and determination was in their blood. An all-out pandemonium and a tumult of shouting and screaming broke out from the servants as guards roused them from their sleep.

"Find him!" a voice bawled from my father's bedchamber.

I sprinted down the stairs and reached the hatch on the ground floor, gasping for breath.

I lost focus! I hastily flipped the hatch open, slid through, and slumped into the underpass. A veil of darkness met me. I grabbed my lamp from my rucksack and switched it on before taking a left towards the nexus of the tunnels.

In and out strategy...that was the plan! I kicked myself for my drift in concentration. *I wasted valuable time!*

The arched underground passage was long, narrow, and winding. Under a cloud of constant darkness, a complex, four-dimensional web ran under Tregnika...the ancients' design. Tregtarians didn't understand it; no one did. The sleeping ones had been the ones to engineer such a multiplex network.

Scurrying through the succession of tight passages with

one hand gripping the lamp was almost impossible, but needs required it. With deep regret and sadness, I swished my way underground, avoiding the channelling water and *tonzos* as much as I could. The ancients' tunnels were hazardous to manoeuvre at normal pace. On the run, they were a death trap.

"Damn," I cursed as I leapt over a well in the centre of the passage.

Every few metres wells had been dug out, for no logical reason, too. I kept looking over my shoulder; the silence behind me was unsettling.

If they're not behind me, they'll be waiting for me at the egress. I tried to plan, but I was too ruffled to think clearly. *Whichever route I take, I have to reach the exit first.*

Throughout the morning, I shuttled from passage to passage, counting them as I went. Any mishap in tally, and I'd end up where I'd started. The ancients were too clever for their own good. Every so often, a clamour of noise erupted, but I couldn't tell if it was coming from behind me or above ground.

"Twenty-five." Breathing heavily, I stopped, having reached the nexus. Forget my father's confused notions about destiny; mine was what I chose to make of it.

There were only three exits I knew about: my father's house, De-Deganon's house, and the River Gande.

I turned to my left. *West—De-Deganon's house, far too risky. They'll be expecting me.*

With that option off the cards, I glanced to my right. *East—my father's house. They're already on high alert.*

North—follow the flow of water…to the River Gande—the hub of Tregtaria's food source. I'll backtrack to De-Deganon's castle and approach from the east wing…

A scratching sound came from behind me. I had to keep moving and stop thinking, so I pivoted and headed north. The passages were tighter and murkier, and a bad stench filled the air. I increased my pace, relying on my speed to reach the exit first.

For half a moon-day, I trooped from tunnel to tunnel. Inevitably, I tripped, swayed, and tumbled to the concrete, head first.

"Ouch," I groaned. A shatter of glass followed by a tinkering sound and a well of darkness tripled my troubles. My only source of light was dead. A gash sent shots of pain through my leg, but I scrambled up and pitched face-first into the darkness. All I had now were my childhood memories to guide me.

I can do this. I limped my way across the tunnels. Accompanied by darkness, I wasn't sure where I was stepping. At the end of each passage, small rays of light beamed from ventilation holes.

Follow the light…with caution. Come on, Dante, where's your strength? My mind focused on my only mission, and I plodded along.

When a spout of light emerged from the vent ahead, I knew it was the one. A spurt of relief jolted through me, and I quickened my pace, or tried to; the throbbing pain in my leg was excruciating. On approach, I took a breather, fatigued.

A moment later, I lifted the hatch door and peeked out into the open. A quick all-round perimeter check, and I heaved a sigh. To my left was a scatter of shrubs and rocks that edged towards Tregnika. The River Gande was to my right. A double surge of relief washed through me. I was at the right egress. The moons had intervened; the stars had been rewritten.

I leapt up above ground and crouched extra-cautiously as I shut the flap. Oppressive heat met me. Before I'd gathered myself, a splash of water swirled from the river. Mid-stride, I spun halfway and froze.

"Where's the fun in that?" a voice said.

I took a deep breath and collapsed to my knees. I raised my gaze and was eye-to-eye with seven generals of the high command.

"Surely, you can give us a fight, son!" Gidron, my father's right-hand warrior, said. His croaky voice was not one I could easily forget.

I didn't respond. At times, a good fight was not to fight at all but knowing when to lay down your arms and accept that there are forces of destiny that are written in stone. So I did just that. I'd done all I could, given it all I had. It was a good fight.

"Do your worst!" I rasped.

* * *

Lord De-Deganon's chamber was as vile as the occupiers. I stood tall, head held high. If this was my death, I would die standing. "Throw yourself to the ground, or face the lord's wroth!" Gidron barked.

I threw him a defiant stare and then swept my gaze across the *mzinda* chamber of gloom. "I won't take a knee for him!" I grated.

"My good commander's son, still as stubborn as ever..." The narcissistic De-Deganon smiled darkly from his throne. "How *wonderful* to see you again."

"I'm not here to grovel. Do what you must, and be done with it."

"Compelling words from one who's about to meet his makers," De-Deganon said. "In that case, tell your lord what brings you to Tregtaria, after all these moon-years?" He sat high and proud, his eyes bulging out.

My gaze strayed to the high command, to my father. His eyes didn't give anything away. Consequently, he flashed a slanted half-smile! I glared at him. *Betraying your own son—not once but twice!* That was low...even for a vainglorious self-absorbed man.

"Just get on with it!" I snarled. Before I could blink, I took a blow to my head, flopping head-first to the floor.

"My Commander, don't enfeeble him just yet!" De-Deganon bawled. "Killing him now is a wasted opportunity." He sprang to his feet. "I need an audience! And *he* is a high-profile contender! Let's give him an appellation... Death-at-your-doorstep warrior. The cowards will love that...and their lord. Open the gates to the Arena of Glory! At midday tomorrow, a game of death will commence." A pompous grin travelled across his square-jawed face. He turned to my father. "My good Commander Jizu, I'll give your son a glorious death and restore honour to your house. Take him to the stakes. It's a one-way path for traitors!"

* * *

Dante's Chain of Thought

In a Game of Sequence, when you're faced with certain death, there are only two options to you—Zeneshians and humans alike. Be bold, or cry yourself to sleep, but neither makes you a hero, for death is, without question, the master of all life.

Each moon-day that you're alive, you're running from him—death, such is his nature to chase...like a hunt...only this hunter is unyielding, unmerciful, tenacious. For as long as you can, you dodge this unalterable shadow or try to...but relentlessly, death pursues you. You stop, and he, too, takes a breather, watching you from a distance.

You pick yourself up, stagger across the land, running when you can, plodding, crawling, feeling as if your breath is being sucked out of you. Succumbing to your fate, you finally trip and fall. Death stops and appears to feel your pain.

Again, not wanting to concede defeat, you find your willpower. You wobble to your feet. At that time, the rain is thumping so hard you feel each bruise. A moment after, the sun is scorching the life out of you, but still, you carry on. Why? Because you have a path to follow, a destination to reach, a Sequence to fulfil. With hope and faith, you aim to make your life worth something.

Inevitably, death catches up, for he is the result of living. What eats you up and threatens to kill you before death has done his final deed is regret.

What could I have done differently? What did I do with the time I was given to live? You forage for answers. In those final moments, when you get into that empty space and invisible walls are caving in, what makes you strong is one greater than death and denser than life. Love. To live is to love–loving is living! There's a sequence to life, love, and death, and regardless of how hard one tries, no one can escape it!

So you cling to those precious memories, feeling the warmth of each thread of love, praying to all your gods for love to conquer death once and for all, hoping your journey to the land of no return is a downhill glissade and not a clamber uphill!

It was in that space that I now found myself.

Regardless of my impending doom, I was content. In Lessi, I'd found, lived, and felt love. Dying in search for her now didn't seem like a failure; it was a tragic success. She was my beginning–my end–my life. Now also, she would be my death–my complete circle of life.

Facing death in search of my heart seemed the right way to go...the only way to go! Without her, I was a bare shell–deflated and hollow. All that was left was a burning emptiness that bubbled through my throat and torched my eyes. The pain inside my chest scorched the life out of me, forcing me to release it. But unleashing it meant hurting someone...anyone. So I bottled it for as long as I could because I had a heart...once. But now my heart had been safely guarded by my only love, and she'd keep it safe perpetually. I wasn't dying. I'd live endlessly in her heart. She had an impervious place for me–this was living!

And before I met my demise, I would unleash the dormant Tregtarian in me. I would fight with everything I had until my last breath. Giving up a fight–any fight was not in me. I was born a warrior and wreathed in the vile curses of my father's blood. I could kill with my eyes shut. I could end a man's life with one strike. I was as good a fighter as death, himself! I had to find it within me to resurrect my bad blood, and fight for good...for Lessi.

Giving up on her was not an option. Never a

consideration. Giving up on us was impossible. I wouldn't lay down like a coward. I wouldn't beg for my life. I wouldn't yield. Death would eventually come for me. That was a given. Until then, I had a battle on my hands. Just before the gong of midday, I shut my eyes to the land and waited for my fate. The doors opened. It wasn't yet time to say good-bye. It was time to fight!

PART V

Alessia – Destined to Live, Love, and be Loved

19. Death by Glory

"Alee, wait up!" Jad said for the umpteenth time now. It was getting quite exhausting. Fortunately, the sun was beginning to pierce through the darkness, and I had a date with Sequence. By sunset, Jad and I would be in Tregnika and I'd be in Dante's arms. How? I didn't know yet. All I knew was Sequence had a lot to answer for...should it choose to deviate from that plan.

Streaks of red and orange sliced the horizon and, with it, a dawning hope for a reunion that was anointed by the Star gods and the Sun god of Light herself. It had been a long night!

"We've been through this, Jad." My voice bounced back from the edges of the dense Jungle of Voices. "Don't turn this into a battlefield."

"Turn what? This...between us? You'd better wear your shield, Alee, this isn't over!"

"Like I said a day ago, and the one before, I'm done talking." By then, I'd settled down to a steady plod but didn't stop.

"So am I." He hauled me back and spun me round in one hasty movement before squeezing my shoulders. "You're not dying on my watch!" He emphasised each word. "Do you understand that?"

"Is that a threat?"

"A warning." His red eyes sent a bitter challenge across the little distance between us. "One you should take seriously."

I took two deep breaths and waved a leaf from his red shock of hair before resting my hand on his shoulder. "Jad, this protection thing you've got going on will get you killed before me. Can you drop it…please?"

He broke away and gave his back to me. "Fine. I'm not planning on dying today, either." He swivelled, stepped forward, and stood right in front of me. "I'll only drop it when you start acting sensibly." He lifted my chin to force a face-off. "Thinking is one thing you're not doing!"

"And you are?" I stormed, swatting his hand away.

"I'm being rational. Are you?"

"Following me across the land to our possible deaths…is that you thinking this through?" I challenged him. "I could have gotten you across the shield, Jad, to freedom. And yet you chose this." My throat suddenly grew dry.

"You wouldn't last a moon-day or half in this terrain on your own!" He gritted his teeth, his sotto voice fading into the trees. "Shall I remind you about the sand-snakes?"

My leg muscles tightened, and my thoughts drifted back to two nights ago, in the Tregtarian semi-desert.

* * *

In the early hours of the morning, Jad gently poked my shoulder arousing me from the depths of oblivion. "Be very still," he mouthed, hovering over me stealthily. "Don't move."

"Why," I asked.

"Just don't make a sound." His gaze darted sideways, his eyes glowing a dark hazy-red in the shadowy desert.

A rush of panic went through me. Something was wrong. Jad's expression was too serious, forehead creased, his breath burst in and out, his actions meticulous. My heart hesitated for a second before threatening to leap out of me.

"On the count of three," he mouthed again, side-stepping gingerly to my left. "Stand up and walk slowly towards me. Please, don't make a sound."

"Why," I whispered urgently. "Just tell me, already."

"Alee, you're lying in a snake—"

At his words, overwhelming panic mixed with deep-rooted fear coiled around me, long before the horrid snakes could get to me, squeezing my insides, strangling my throat, clutching at my heart. What happened after was a true Alessia classic. A stupid classic that could have killed us both…yet it was inevitable, I reacted the only way I knew how to.

Did I wait for him to finish his sentence? No. Did I do as I had been told? No.

Did I stay calm and composed? No. I cried so loud, my insides were on the way out.

Going against everything he'd said, I leaped up screaming, and jumped right into his arms. He caught me. In the dim-light of twilight, I flicked my gaze to the ground. Dozens of weird-looking, fur-covered snakes slithered around the sand, raising a plume of dust into the air. Dread clutched at my heart with frozen claws. I shivered. In panic, my heart attempted a painful escape through my burning throat.

Jad hit the ground running with me in his arms. How he managed to hold it together, keep me afloat, and run over the wretched creatures with piercing green eyes that darted about in search of a victim to sink their fangs into, is still a mystery. I squeezed my eyes shut, and clung to Jad like my life depended on him. Before my heart had left me forever, Jad plunged into a pool of water still holding me tightly in his arms. "We're safe in the oasis," he said.

I flung my eyes open, my breath short and choppy. He let go of me and my feet touched the bottom of the pool. I shook uncontrollably. Jad kept his arms around me, calming me. "I'm s-sorry," I found my voice from somewhere, trembling. "I'm so sorry. Are you o-okay?"

"I'm fine." He breathed and drew back. "What part of do not make a sound did you not understand?" he bellowed, a flash of anger crossing his face.

"The part about the snakes," I shivered from both fear and a deep chill that had enveloped me. The early morning desert air was nippy enough for me to see my breath.

Then unexpectedly, laughter replaced anger. Jad's bubbling laugh rose into the air. "It's so hard being angry with you... Do you know that? They are blind sand-snakes, Alee. Those piercing green eyes don't see a thing. The desert-snakes seek heat in the moon-night, and that's why they found a warm home in you. You woke them up when you yelled like—"

"You wanted me to stay quiet when I was about to be attacked?"

"Sound is what triggers them to attack."

"How was I supposed to know that?"

"I told you, didn't I? Your instructions were clear. Don't make a sound?" He smiled, shaking his head. In an instant humour turned to seriousness, his face clouding over. "Watch out! There's one right behind you!"

My heart leaped out of my rib cage attempting to break free, then plunged back inside after hitting the walls of my freezing chest. With a splash, I flew towards Jad. Fear squeezed my stomach threatening to cause an unprecedented wave of nausea.

Jad wound his arms around my waist, only to roar in booming laughter like he'd never laughed before. He buoyed me up in the waters, making fun of me. I realised then, there was no snake near me. There was never a threat in the waters. The threat was him. "You're jumping at your own shadow now?" he teased.

"It's not funny, Jad," I smacked him hard on the shoulder, my teeth chattering. "You scared the life out of me, so I could come running to you?" I drew back and slid out of his arms.

"It's the only way I was certain you'd come running to me."

"So that's what you do in your spare time, is it?" I yelled. "You go around the kingdom, scaring young, vulnerable girls so they can come running to you!" I edged farther away from him, a stark, bewildered feeling coming over me.

He smiled, a thoughtful smile seeming to grasp that there was some truth in my words. "Girls? No. Only *one* girl... *the* girl...young maybe. Vulnerable? I wouldn't call you that. Someone with a mind that's capable of melting matter, I'm the one at risk here." He raised his eyebrows awaiting a comeback. All he got was a faint smile. "What you persistently fail to see is when you run, I run after you." He'd kept his gaze steady, his maroon-red eyes glinting and holding me captive for a moment. "Wherever you go, I go." His voice turned a corner, bringing a strange feeling in me. "Besides, you're kind-of cute when you squeal!"

I stifled a laugh, feigned a glaring look, and tried so hard to keep my angry face, but failed. Instead, I burst into a bubble of laughter, and watched the glow of the moons create elongated shadows of us in the pool.

"Laughter is the first cure for fear," he said, satisfied with his tease.

"And the second?"

"Beauty of the gods--being in love." He swung a casual glance at the sky.

"What?" I jerked back. "That doesn't make sense."

"Look up," he said. I lifted my gaze to the night skies. The gigantic dual moons stared right at us, reflecting the waters in an alluring light. Even in the heart of Tregtaria, the moons were as captivating as they were in my motherland. A galaxy of stars surrounded them, flickering and dancing about in merriment, like they were in a twinkle dance of twilight.

"This pool is named the Oasis of Light." He settled his gaze on the environs of the pool embosomed in a scatter of olive and palm groves. "It's the most refreshing and spiritual body of water in the Tregtarian desert. Nothing can touch you here? Not even the sand-snakes venture in--you are safe in the waters."

At his words, my mind drifted to Ralda's words. I wasn't safe in the waters. I wasn't safe anywhere. But one thing had been clear, I was safe with Jad. "The water is believed to have some healing properties."

I spun around, swirling my arms in the clear-cool water. "You could have just left me in the sand to die, but you didn't. You risked your life...again. Why?"

"It's too early for goodbye's, Alee. Our farewell will come... not just yet. You are sort-of stuck with me now." He gave me one of his usual contagious smiles, before his expression turned serious. "I will throw myself in the snake pit first before anything can bite you," he said.

* * *

I looked at Jad with heartfelt regret. He was right; I did need him. It wasn't just because he made me feel safe. It was everything else. He was great company...at times. Three days we'd been trudging through the forest...three days we'd been arguing. From dawn to dusk, sunset to sunrise, the same argument hung around us like a furtive shadow. Even when we'd agreed to chat about anything else, we'd found ourselves haunted by the same gnawing wrangle that sent us into warranted silence.

"I'm on a journey, Jad." I held his hand lightly. "I know that now. My mum sacrificed her life, her home, for me."

I cast my eyes to the birdless sky, seeking her seal of approval, only the canopy of trees was so dense I could hardly see the sky. *Mum, I hope you're watching me from the best seat in heaven.*

I blew a kiss to the heavens and turned back to Jad. "I'm destined to bring peace to the worlds, to do things I never thought were possible. Don't you get it, Jad? I'm here to rebuild the lands, to fix what's broken, to love where no love exists."

"And returning to the land of goons to save one person makes this all okay?" His neat eyebrows pulled down slightly over his olive-toned skin that shimmered with the first light's glow.

"I can't do any of the things I'm destined to do without him."

The shadowy trees swayed lackadaisically to the whistling wind like they concurred.

He placed his hands on my shoulders gently, smiled, and then muttered, "Alee, you've done weird and wonderful things already without him."

"He's always with me, Jad! Even when I can't see him. Our families share an ancient bond, a Foretold Sequence of Hearts. Dante's on the other side of my Sequence of First and Forever and he's waiting for me."

He brusquely let go of my shoulders and moved away. "There's no such thing."

"You have little faith, Jad," I said. "It's real. Wait till you meet him."

"I've met him before, remember, and his mother the moon-night they escaped." He bit his lip, thoughtful.

"Briefly. And as the story goes, his mother gave you a dia-mond necklace as a thank you to keep you quiet. I remember, Jad. Contrary to what you might think, I was attentive," I said. On one of our nights in the wilderness one conversation had led to another and we had spoken about Dante, my love for him and his love for me.

Jad didn't believe in the Sequence of First and Forever. His words were: "It's as strange as it is ridiculous." His last memory of Dante was seeing him wielding a sword and guiding his mother through a hatch on the ground floor of the Haurulio residence.

I smiled. "That's hardly long enough to know someone. Wait till you see Dante with me. He and I are meant for each other. Everyone can see it."

"Your confidence is worrying."

"Either that or I cry," I said, unable to conceal the quake in my voice. "And I'm done crying!"

By mid-morning, we'd followed the tree line to the north,

which took us to the Sands of the Dead—Taria, the outskirts of Tregnika. The dense forest had been replaced by barren, fruitless, and arid land. Thick sheets of dust formed a gooey layer around us.

"The air is denser here. It'll subside farther inland," Jad said, ripping a piece of cloth from his cloak and placing it over my mouth and nose. "This will keep you quiet for a while." He winked at me playfully.

I nudged him in the stomach with my elbow. A burst of laughter escaped from his lips before he covered his mouth and nose, too.

We reached Taria at midday. Astonishingly, hundreds of people roamed the winding streets. A multitude of red-bricked houses with tiny brown doors and windows were scattered around the streets. Creatures that looked like rats scurried everywhere, my stomach turning at the sight. I didn't realise I was a bit squeamish until then. The creatures were in competition with Tarians. An absolute infestation. I darted over them unsuccessfully and almost lost my balance.

"Tonzos are monstrous at this time of moon-day," Jad commented, making his way with ease.

How do you live amongst such an infestation?

"You get used to it after a while," he answered my unspoken question.

"Now I see why you're always so irritable," I teased.

He laughed for a bit before his eyes turned piercing. "Try growing up here and see if your mind will be as beautiful as you are…" Suddenly, he stopped and put out his hand. "Allow me."

"Jadherey," a hurried whisper came from behind us.

We swivelled around simultaneously. A bald middle-aged man was bursting out of a small house. A waft of boiled cabbage and smoke seeped into the air from the open door. "Where in the moons' name have you been?" he asked with a look of concern. "The lord has a price on your head!"

"It's hardly news, Ezra," Jad said simply, hugging the man in a warm embrace.

"What did you do? Lord De-Deganon demands your head on a plate." He gave me a sidelong glance. "And who's she?"

"A friend." Jad reached for my hand. "Don't worry about my head, Ezra," he teased. He found time for humour, even when everything was bleak. "Where's everyone headed?"

"To the games, of course."

"What games?" Jad furrowed his brows.

I blinked, my stomach twisting and churning. Somehow, I didn't think any kind of games here would be nice and friendly.

"The Games of Death at the arena. The high command opened the doors two moon-days ago." A swift, hot breeze blew dust into the air and Ezra wiped his face.

Jad's mouth fell open. "The Arena of Glory?"

Ezra's red eyes lit up fervently. "Oh, you should see it. It's a magnificent structure. It seats thousands of people. The lord put out *the* show at the opening ceremony. Today, everyone who's anyone will be there. I need the best seat. Are you... there are De-Deganon's spies everywhere. You'll need to come in disguise, of course. Bring your friend!"

"Perhaps another time. I need some information." Jad lowered his voice. "High-Commander Jizu's son, do you know where he's being held?"

"Held?" He sounded shocked, and my heart thumped. "Which land are you living in...Young Haurilio is the star of the show. Read this!" Ezra slid his hand into his robe pocket and brought out a brown piece of paper. He uncrumpled it, excitement evident in his touch. With fear causing the letters to swim on the page, I struggled to read over Jad's shoulder:

BORN TO A TREGTARIAN WARRIOR.
MOTHERED BY A TUSCANIAN SORCERESS.
YOUR LORDSHIP IS PROUD TO PRESENT
DEATH-AT-YOUR-DOORSTEP WARRIOR:
DANTE ERAJION OF HOUSE HAURILIO.

"They're forcing him to fight!" I grimaced in horror, unable to read the rest. *He's my Dante! Not a warrior.*

"He fights to live. Just yesterday he slayed three warriors in one moon-day! One man. One sword. One fight. He is his father's son!" Ezra gushed. "His mother was a Tuscanian sorceress, and he is the living Sequence of death!"

I shuffled back a few steps. Tears flooded my eyes, and I shuddered. A tight knot formed in the pit of my stomach. My hand slipped from Jad's. My legs grew too numb to hold me up, and my knees buckled. I crumbled to the ground, out of breath. *No. No. No!*

Tonzos scuttled about me like we were family. For someone who was done crying, I was bawling. Crying was not done with me.

Jad hastened to his knees. "We can't make a scene here! There are too many eyes," he whispered against my shoulder, holding me lightly in his arms. "We need a plan."

"T-Take me to him," I muttered through the silent sobs.

"In time." He pecked me on my forehead. "Ezra, I need your help!"

"Anything for you, my friend," he answered.

I looked up. Ezra's dazed gaze pierced through me "You are the h-human?" His voice cracked, and shock registered in his eyes. He shifted his attention to Jad. "Jadherey, what have you done?"

"It can't be undone now, Ezra." Jad licked his lips. "Meet me at the Arena in one moon-hour," he said. "I have a plan, but there's something I need to do first."

***

"Is this the way, Jad?" I asked ten minutes into our journey. Hordes of people plodded along in the opposite direction to us. I reached for Jad's arm. "Where are you taking me?"

"We're re-routing, that's all." He guided me forward. "Keep moving. I need to collect something." He gestured with his arm.

About fifty yards away, a quirky-shaped stone-and-wood building complete with a solid thatched roof stood in my line of sight. Thick timber-framed windows with glass inserts oozed character that reminded me of 11th to 12th century buildings in my home county of Norfolk. The big and bold inscription read Shabheenie La Meleki.

"You're taking me to a tavern?" I halted, brow furrowed. "Are you out of your mind?"

"I don't intend to have a drink, Alee." He swung his gaze around, keeping a guarded eye in case someone was watching us.

"You need to collect something from a tavern filled with drunk people and who knows what else?"

"It's the safest place to keep something precious. It's everything I have," he said in a quiet voice. "Keep your head under cover." He fixed my hood, emotion chiselled onto his face. "We'll get to Dante before the moon-day is gone." He swallowed hard.

He steered me across the winding street to the front of the tavern. Loud cackles, laughs, and voices rose into the air. The high windows obstructed me from seeing inside. We strode in through an arched door so small Jad had to duck his head to avoid hitting the timber beam. A wall of noise struck me. Tumult.

"We want our bre-ew!" a horde of men yelled. "Brew! Brew! Brew!" They hit their fists against the wooden tables.

"No one gets a swallow until I say!" a young woman bellowed from atop the counter.

Dressed in a tight-fitting Basque bodice and full-length wavy skirt, she was eye-catching. Her striking bosom caught my eye. Hair flowing in waves over her bare shoulders, eyes a lighter shade of golden-red, she was fearless…and stunning.

"This is my shabheenie. You drink when I say!" she rasped.

"I brought my silver chalice, woman!" a man drawled in a piercing voice.

"I don't care whether you brought a dozen chalices or one. No one gets a drop until I say!" she roared like a ferocious lioness.

My pulse jumped. I wished I had that kind of stamina.

"Brew! Brew. Brew!" Chants lifted into the air.

"What's going on?" I said to Jad as loudly as I could manage. "Why can't she just give them what they want?"

"You've never been in a tavern before?" He swung an arm around me and steered me to the side of the counter.

"Is she the tavern-keeper?"

"The one and only Rizo of Shabheenie La Meleki," Jad said with adoration, his gaze on her. The young woman meant something to him.

In a trickle, she spotted us. She froze and then quickly relaxed her facial features. "One more brew, and you're out of here!" Her voice bounced off the stone walls.

Impatient groans and sneers lifted. "One is not enough!" a man roared.

"I don't care," she rasped. "That's all you're having." Eyes squinting, she turned to her left where a group of four men sat behind some large instruments. "Jeejay…music!" She jumped off the counter and briskly strode towards Jad and me.

The musical instruments were spectacular. One man played a balloon-shaped stringed instrument that was partly covered by animal hide. The other three men pounded some mallets over a peculiar instrument made of wooden planks with resonators attached to the bottom. As the loud and pounding music rose into the air, clapping and singing quickly followed suit. Jad grabbed my arm and steered me to the side door. The tavern-keeper nodded to Jad and unlocked the wooden door in silence. She grabbed a lamp and led us down a narrow, dimly lit, winding stairwell that went into the cellar.

Inside the cellar, dozens of wooden barrels were scattered around the shadowy enclosure. I sucked in a breath of damp air, hands folded in front of me.

"My Jadherey." She threw her arms around Jad and hugged him close. "You shouldn't be here."

"I had to come." Jad held her for a tad longer and drew back, slanting a look in my direction.

"Is she your lady?" The tavern-keeper turned her attention to me, a curious smile gracing her face. Her eyes glinted. "Your human lady?"

Jad puffed a laugh, and I wondered what he had told her. "Alee, this is Rizo."

"Hello," I greeted, my voice low.

"You're the girl who's worth Jadherey's head?"

I didn't know what to make of her comment so I smiled and swung Jad a glance. He favoured me with a reassuring and light grin.

"I see," Rizo said, beaming. She took a couple of steps towards me and pulled me in a warm embrace. "You look like you could use a hug." She held me close, and snuggly, a welcome respite. "My Jadherey's friends are my friends, too. You're welcome here. Anytime."

"Thank you." Heartened by her kind words, I held onto her. She was spot on. I needed this.

Jad tapped Rizo on the shoulder. "We don't have much time. Do you have it?"

"Close to my heart, always." Rizo pulled back and slid her hand into her bosom. "It's the safest place to keep something precious," she said to me, having noticed my raised brows. She brought out a red pouch, fixed her bodice, and handed the pouch to Jad.

"I wonder what else you're storing in there," Jad joshed. I couldn't help but smile.

"A lady never tells." Rizo flashed a warm smile. "Both pieces are there…good as new." Her gaze wandered over me and settled on my face. "I see why you need this, now." She nodded, musing. "Don't do anything reckless. I must say, she's a perfect fit."

"I'm sorry. Perfect fit for what?" I switched my attention to Jad.

"Rizo," Jad hastened to say, a secretive smile on his face, "thank you...for everything." He was hiding something, that was evident. I let out a heavy sigh. I thought we were past secrets. I was wrong.

"Is this goodbye?" Rizo asked.

Jad swallowed hard. "It's never goodbye for us." He placed the pouch in his pocket.

"Always a good moon-day!" Rizo swung her arms around Jad.

There was something special and sad about their farewell. I hated goodbyes, and this one wasn't any different. It touched me as though it was my own.

After we'd left the tavern, we trod along the streets in surreal hush. Jad's silence worried me. "Rizo is lovely," I started, hoping to break the ice shield that Jad had built around himself. "Why didn't you tell me you had a girlfriend?"

"She's not my girlfriend." He kept his gaze focused ahead.

"There's nothing to be embarrassed about," I teased, poking him in the ribs.

"No embarrassment, Alee. She's not my girlfriend." He rubbed his jaw. "She's a friend who does some favours for me."

"She gives you favours?" My voice rose. "What kind of favours?"

"My moons! Not those kinds, surely." His eyes flashed mercury-red. "She's not that...not to me." He was quiet for some time. "Don't," he said suddenly.

"What did I say?" I jested. "You're a mind reader now?"

"I know what you're thinking!" He stole an arm on my lower back and guided me through clusters of small crowds that jeered as they strolled merrily to the games. Most had already made their way. "Why in the moons' name would you think she's my girlfriend?"

"Because you're so secretive about whatever she gave you."

"You have your secrets." He flashed an endearing smile. "I have mine."

"Well, it's not everyday you meet someone who gives your best friend a precious keepsake dug out of her stunning bosom."

He burst into a chuckle, but then his expression changed from amusement to concern. Eyebrows pulled down, his lips tightened. "You're not funny when you're sad."

"I can handle my sadness, Jad," I said, trying so hard to find a balance between my broken heart and staying strong. "Just admit it, will you?"

The muscles in his jawline contracted. "I'm not admitting to anything."

"Just say it. You'll feel better for it. Besides, I need something to cheer me up."

He halted. "Me having a girlfriend would cheer you up?" His eyes pulled back, lips pressed into a thin line.

"Why shouldn't it?" I asked, concerned. "It's nice to know you have someone who cares for you."

Silence descended until he broke it. "I don't need someone to care for me, Alee." A troubled frown crept up his forehead.

My throat ached. All his life, all he had was himself, and perhaps Rizo. Not family. Not love. Not true happiness. "Everyone needs someone, Jad. Even you."

"I don't need someone else," he reiterated. Something about the sadness in his voice invoked a torrent of emotion in me. "I have you."

I averted my gaze, suddenly tearful. His words at the Ruins of the Walter Walkers and at the shield flooded my mind. *If happiness could be bought, I would have sold everything I have for a slice of happiness with you.*

"I'm refusing to cry," I whispered. "Please don't make me."

"My lady," he teased, lowering his head to whisper in my ear, "it's your tears that tell me in enough words...you care."

* * *

The Arena of Glory was a circular, white-washed, concrete-and-stone structure—a stupendous edifice. Rewind the clock to 81 AD, and I'd be facing the Roman Coliseum twice the size. An enormous and impressive building but nothing more than a death zone: a place to kill, die, or watch death in action.

Gleam and gloom was suffocating me. The blazing sun hid in the clouds. It was a humid, dull, and dingy day in Tregtaria; even the Sun god of Light couldn't stomach the sight. A huge, sky-blue velarium stretched over the arena like a curtain. Surely they didn't need it today; the sun wasn't intending to show its face.

"This is where history and names are created," a man gushed as he bustled into the arena. "Today, Sequences will be redefined, new destinies forged, and stars will be rewritten."

"History never recalls you or me, my friend. We're mere spectators," another said, jostling his way ahead of us. "Onlookers will always be just that—observers."

Jad and I wore beige cloaks with matching cowls. The disguise wasn't perfect, but our options were limited. As we made our approach, a deafening noise arose from the audience. Strange excitement lingered in the air, disturbingly dire and sickening. Jad, Ezra, and I paced in through the threatening, deep-red iron gates. Armoured warriors patrolled the area in numbers. Fortunately, they were too occupied with their arrogance to take notice of us, but that didn't stop Jad being super cautious.

I stood on my toes to whisper into his ear, "If you keep glancing around, you'll look suspicious."

He tightened his arm that was draped around me. "Just stay close to me." His gaze darted about the rusty limestone-adorned six floors of the arena. He seemed amazed at the colossal structure but too vigilant to raise any attention.

We trod through the hordes of surging crowd, all eager to enjoy the unthinkable. They had a sickening obsession with the games. Obsession about death. Death by obsession. It hung in the air. The noise intensified in the seating area. Roars of laughter, chants, and the beating of gongs and drums bounced off the Tregnika's buildings surrounding the arena.

I focused on my feet, only looking up when necessary. From the inside, the arena was grander, colossal…sadly impressive. It was almost impossible to see beauty in death, so everything that was wrong with it was wrong. This was not how I'd planned to see Dante again. Not like this! My heart, now a lump of ice, was slowly sinking into my stomach as I strode up the steps to our seats in the inner cavea of the gigantium arena. I flopped into my position in dejection. The semi-circular chairs were inclined to ensure we got a perfect view. A view of death!

"Stay here. I'll be right back," Jad said.

"You're leaving me?" I darted a worried glance around my new neighbours garbed in multi-coloured tunics and robes. They were excitable, oblivious to my exchange with Jad.

"Not forever. You'll be safe. No one knows who you are," he whispered. "I need to tie up some loose ends, that's all." He clasped my hands. "Alee, I can't lose you…not today!"

The firmness of his tone stunned me to silence.

"Whatever happens, stay in this seat." He eyed me carefully, like I might vanish into the crowd. "Don't move!"

I nodded, too subdued to put up a fight.

He turned and dashed down the stairs with Ezra.

Under the disguise of a beige, tattered cloak, I took in thousands of tiered seats brimming with the zealous crowd. Wagons of food and snacks dotted around the arches to the crowd's pleasure. Strange scents wafted through the air.

My seat was right at the edge, with Jad's empty seat next to mine. This was not a football match; it was a game of death. The blaring of trumpets and the beating of drums were so deafening, a head-splitting migraine was moments away.

My stomach twisted nervously at the thought of being alone in an arena bursting with a buzzing crowd. It was as surreal as it gets. Every second Jad was away was a second too long.

Jad, where are you? I tapped my feet on the concrete floor. It had been over an hour. I tried to regulate my breathing, unsuccessfully, hoping I wasn't getting a panic attack not that I'd had any of those in the past; this was unprecedented.

You're taking too long. I placed my head in my hands and tried to shut myself off from my surroundings. The crowd grew restless, impatient. The games should have started by now. Too many things were happening at once. I didn't know what to take in first, or even if I wanted to. The searing atmosphere, the piercing war cry from the warriors on the arena floor, and the subsequent cheers from the throngs were an ear-splitting multitude of noises inside my head.

It's so loud I can't hear myself think!

Seeking a distraction, I stared into the distance. The high command, heads held high, took their seats in their box, one of the eight arches of the arena walls. Guarded by imposing ivory and gold statues of the ancient gods, the lord's stage was adorned with colourful wreaths of flowers. Garbed in handsome armoury attire, the high command relished every second of their tyranny.

With a heavy breath, I settled my eyes on Lord De-Deganon, only to drop my gaze when I observed De-warrior Dranisha ease herself next to him. I couldn't stomach her today, or any day. High Commander Jizu swaggered about the box.

My heart lurched. *What kind of a man watches his own son fight to the death?* Now I understood why Dante despised him.

Jad, where are you? I looked around again, my fingers locking into each other. I shut my eyes and brought my hands to my ears. It was so loud, trying to block out the noise with my hands was of no use. Subsequently, the noise turned to surreal hush. I glanced up under lowered lashes. Everyone had taken his or her seats. The air was denser, strange, stuffy...toxic. I straightened, my heart thumping.

The silence was quickly replaced by a thunderous, dragged-out throaty voice that reverberated around the cavea of the arena.

"Today, on the mighty moon-day of the gods...in the sanctified Arena of Glory, your lordship is proud to give you a game of games, a death of deaths, and a show of shows in true Tregtarian honour!"

Tumultuous cheers from the crowd followed the announcer's trumpet from atop the stands.

Jad, where are you? A feeling of nausea brew within me even though the sandy arena floor was tidy, smoothed, with no signs of blood or filth you'd expect at such an event.

Soon, though...

"Introducing the first contender...born to our very own high commander!" He dipped his head slightly to High-Commander Jizu, who sat in Lord De-Deganon's box. "Some say he's a Tuscanian god; others call him the unbeatable. The *truth*, people of Tregtaria...he was mothered by a Tuscanian Sorceress...and now lives as your very own gods-given-death-at-your-doorstep warrior...the one, the only...Dante Erajion of house *Haurilio*!"

At the sound of his name, a deep feeling of dread rose up from the pit of my tummy. The usual flutters and butterflies I always had when I heard his name were replaced by stomach cramps, hot flashes, and feeling as if I was about to choke on my breath. This was not the way I'd envisaged seeing him again. *Not like this!*

Four massive warriors stood on the west side of the arena floor about a hundred metres from me. They drew a huge, iron cage door up, making my heart leap. I sprung up on wobbly legs and immediately sloped back into my seat. A deep roar erupted from the crowd. As I gasped for air that was suddenly in short supply, I glimpsed him.

Dante!

My breath caught in my throat. He emerged from an

underground passage, all alone. Seeing him again, from a distance, surrounded by thousands of people, broke my aching heart. A chilling cold slithered down my spine, and I shuddered.

He strode into the centre, his sword in his right arm, shield in his left, gaze fixed to the ground.

That's not your walk. What have they done to you?

A cry of pain tore from my trembling lips. *"Dante! Dante-e-e-e!"* But the clamorous mob and the penetrating sound of trumpets blaring the arena swallowed my voice.

He looked like a soldier returning from the thick of battle, and yet, his fight was still pending. He lifted his gaze. *Oh my God!* My stomach knotted. His eyes glowed a deep red, a hue I'd yet to see. An impending sense of doom overcame any hope I had of a happy reunion.

I can't do this. I can't breathe! I took long, deep breaths, or tried to. *I can't breathe! I can't be without you!* I fanned myself with shaky hands. *Dante?* I turned to telepathy. *Can you hear me?* Silence. *Dante, please answer me.* The mind thing was of no use in the land of the warriors. I knew that, but I had to try. It didn't work. Heat brewed inside me. I had an urgent need for some air, and I knew exactly where to get it. I sprang to my feet, and my cloak slipped to the ground. The walls caved in; the arena contracted around me; the noise subsided.

Thinking, not thinking, knowing I had to get to him, I dragged in shreds of non-existent air. *You have to know I'm here.* My vision hazy, I leapt onto the aisle, and right into Jad's arms.

"I'm sorry I took so long." He ushered me back toward my seat and then crouched, out of breath.

I darted a tearful, breathless glance at him.

"Sit," he demanded.

I complied without questioning. A tingling sensation rushed through my legs. I needed to run...but I couldn't find my strength, now.

"Breathe," he urged, taking the seat next to me.

"I need some air...I'm too h-hot." I cooled myself with my

hands, my heart pounding to the beating of the gongs around the arena. I squeezed my eyes shut and attempted to summon that thing that resided in the inner me. *You'll come out now, or...*

"Dan-te...Dan-te...Dan-te..." the crowd chanted his name, the noise suffocating me.

I couldn't concentrate, and the thing wouldn't come out. Instead, I was overcome by the urge to flee but found myself helplessly frozen in my seat.

"It's not the heat, Alee. Just breathe...look around you," he muttered against my shoulder. "Dante's a warrior...a damn good one, I'm told. He's already won three fights. He'll win this fight. The high command may not believe in him, but my people do...you should, too." He held my face in his hands. "Half a moon-day, that's all I ask. Can you survive half a moon-day for me...for him?"

"He's injured, Jad." I cast my gaze at Dante and he winced. "He's too weak to fight."

"Are you seeing what I'm seeing? He's strong...he doesn't have an ounce of weakness in him. A few bruises...not life-threatening."

I gulped. "He needs to know I'm here—w-we're here—for him."

"The plan is in place. It's a solid plan...Ezra is a good man. We'll get to Dante tonight." His calm voice was reassuring. "He needs to win one more fight, and you," he said, wiping droplets of tears that had escaped my eyes, "need to try and not do anything stupid...like run onto the arena floor to certain—"

"...Bugan of Dugaria-a-a-a-a-a!" the announcer declared.

An armoured warrior barrelled into the arena on a chariot drawn by horned animals similar to the ones that had transported me from the shield. He circled the arena a few times before leaping off the chariot, much to the crowd's pleasure.

My breath hitched as I held onto what was left of my heart. The warrior brandished his sword, circling Dante and stepping around him in a move that was too quick and impossible to follow. My heart sank deeper, squeezing my stomach to destruction.

"Bugan's trying to unsettle Dante before the fight…don't worry. More fool him, he's wasting his energy!" Jad said into my ear.

Dante removed his breastplate and tossed it to the side.

"Why is he taking off his protection?" My cry turned into a wail absorbed by the crowd's cheers when I noted a cut across his chest.

"Calm down. I'm sure he has a good reason for it." Jad drew in a long and ominous breath and clasped my hand in his. "That armour is wearing him down. It's too heavy and too tight. He's better off without it."

"Why are you so calm?" I raised my voice so loud I hit the dark side of composure.

It was a long while before he answered. "The way I see it, if you lose *him*, I lose *you*…and it's too early in our moon-day for good-byes. It w-won't be today!" His expression shadowed for a second before he quickly perked up. "He's already won three fights… he'll win this one!"

"I c-can't watch him fight, Jad."

"You don't have to. Come here," he urged, as he opened his arms for me and pressed my cheek against his chest. "Close your eyes…breathe. It'll all be over soon."

"Your friend is a tad squeamish!" a loud voice came from behind us.

"Just fastidious about how she'd like to spend her afternoon." Jad made gentle, circular strokes across my back.

"You're in the wrong place, princess!" the man shouted, his voice competing with the deafening chants now magnified by the stamping of feet on the concrete.

"Death by Glo-ry! Death by Glo-ry! Death by Glo-ry!"

From chanting Dante's name to chanting Death by Glory when it was plainly death by the sword…I questioned the crowd's logic. There was nothing glorious about a man's death, and when that man held the key to my heart…

I forced my eyes shut and allowed the horror to happen around me. I couldn't think of anything worse than having him die in front of my eyes.

So I summoned that thing again—the inner me, that force that chose to come out on its own terms. *Not today…today you will come out, and save him,* I commanded it from inside my head. *It's my turn to make decisions. Come out. Come out!*

I was answered with only silence.

A tinkering sound like a smash of metal resounded. Subsequent cheers from the bloodthirsty crowd signalled that the fight had begun. My knuckles clenched into Jad's shirt, and I kept my eyes tightly shut. A continuous crescendo of strange sounds from the arena floor lifted into the air. I felt each clunk and every rattle of metal rather than heard it. I flinched, too frightened to open my eyes.

At one point, I briefly snapped my eyes open and noticed Bugan charging at Dante with his sword upheld. I recoiled against Jad's chest, shutting my eyes for a second, only to open them again immediately after. Dante dodged the strike, swung, and took a backswing at Bugan.

Bugan blocked it with his shield and smiled. They took another swing, and their swords caught each other in the air. Bugan was out for blood…that was it for my nerves.

Come out now!

When the thing didn't answer, I turned to the gods. My fingers crossed against Jad's chest. *Save him, please. I'll do anything you ask,* I prayed.

Every now and again, the air rang with a tinkering sound, a thud, and a load of weird sounds I tried to shut out. I quailed into Jad's arms.

Then I heard Jad shout out. "Get up! Get up, Dante. Get up!"

Something was wrong. I clutched onto Jad's shirt so tightly it bunched together.

In a minute the suspense became insufferable. I snapped my eyes open. Dante was lying inertly on the ground. A wrench of pain tore at my heart. "Dante!" I yowled. "You'll not die on me! Get up and f-fight!" My voice choked on a sob as a stabbing burst of pain shot through me.

Lessi! His voice echoed inside my head, startling me. Instantaneously, he rolled to the side at lightning speed.

"I'm here, Dante. I'm here!" I squeezed Jad's thigh, my gaze fixed on the love of my life. "You'll not die today!" I murmured to myself. "Fight! For us! For your *sequence*, my *sequence*, our *sequence*, for anything…just fight!" I sprang up.

In a lightning speed manoeuvre that had the crowd on their feet, Dante used his foot to kick his sword into the air. A whirl of sand rose with the sword as Dante caught it with his right arm and tossed it towards Bugan in a daring, arcing shot that pierced through Bugan's armour. Bugan staggered, dropped to a knee, tried to stand up, but tumbled again. He landed on his back, to the crowd's pleasure.

Dan-te! Dan-te! Dan-te!" the crowd chanted his name, this time filling my heart with overwhelming joy. He owned the crowd, and the entire arena…one man…my Dante, a proud yet nerve-wracking moment. *You've done it!*

I turned to Jad, grabbed his forearm, and leaned against it. "He's done it!"

"I can see now why you're obsessed with the guy," he teased.

For the first time all afternoon, I had a good old laugh.

Dante paced the arena floor to the crowd's cheers. Suddenly, he winced, and I gaped. He looked fatigued. His fight was over…I could sense that.

At that time, Lord De-Deganon gave a thumbs-down gesture, surely signalling for Dante to kill Bugan, who lay still and dripping blood on the sand.

"Kill, kill, kill!" the crowd echoed the same sentiment.

With his sword in one hand, Dante bent down on one knee, stabbed his sword into the ground, and held onto it.

The crowd went into baffled numbness.

"I am done killing for you! I am not a slayer. I am not your entertainment." Dante shook his head, his voice booming into the air. "I don't kill for you! I don't kill for anyone! I don't kill for pleasure! If you want him dead, come down and do it yourself!" he rasped, his eyes fixed at the lord's stage.

He stunned me, Jad, too. "What is he doing?" Jad questioned me as if *I* was inside Dante's head. "He's just signed his death warrant!"

Paralysed by shock, I could feel myself grow pale.

Lord De-Deganon sprang to his mighty feet and jolted to the edge of his box. "How dare you defy my command in *my* land! My kingdom!" he grated. "If death is what you seek, death is what you'll get!"

My heart lurched, and my chest grew tight and hot.

Lord De-Deganon barked an order to a servant, who jumped to his feet and burst out of the box.

"No, no, no!" Anxiety racked through me.

"Kill! Kill Kill!" the crowd roared wildly, their fists raised in the air. "Dan-te! Dan-te..." They turned the name of my love into a rhythmical slogan so he could end another man's life! *What's wrong with these people?*

"Just kill the goon!" Jad said angrily, his expression taut with frustration.

"He's given up!" I cried, almost shaking the life out of Jad's arms. "He wants to die! Why? I'm here. I'm here!" Then a thought struck me. Our sequence was pure. My heart to his heart. My mind to his mind. He was Tuscanian first, not Tregtarian. "He's not a killer, Jad," I whispered. I was his balance. He felt me. I felt him.

"He's killed before, Alee," Jad bellowed. "Why can't he do it now?"

"He won't end a man's life in my presence," I cried.

"That doesn't make sense." He breathed. "How can you be certain?"

"It's Sequen—"

"You tame the Tregtarian in him!" Jad bellowed.

"I don't know, Jad!" I cried. "I d-don't know anymore."

"Does he even know that you're here?"

"I don't think so…but he can feel me. He can sense me." I darted a glance around. "I'm here, Dante. I'm here." *Find it within you to kill him and save yourself. Please don't give up.*

"Then you will be his death, Alee."

The announcer's voice trumpeted across the arena, "He defied a direct command, now he'll meet certain death…but not before we've given you a final showdown!"

The eager crowd roared in applause.

"Introducing nature's perfectly engineered predator, the ultimate killer, so majestically beastly, each with the strength of four combined warriors… Some say they're telepathic; others say they're reincarnated Tuscanians for they attack with precision—timing—coordination." His stentorian voice resounded across the arena as the crowd wailed in jubilation and anticipation. "They remain undefeated and unconquerable. They have an insatiable hunter's appetite. Your lordship is pleased to give you the indomitable jingwes of Dzundaria-a-a-a-a."

The beating of the drums and the cheering of the crowd filled the air.

Jad flinched too noticeably for my sanity, totally freaking me out.

"No one survives the jingwes. He'll not survive this!" he said again, like I hadn't heard him the first time.

Thunderstruck, I watched as an armoured warrior hauled a cart in from the underground passage. My broken heart sank. Huge trap doors were thrown up, and the crowd cheered uproariously at the emergence of a pack of seven buffalo-sized, zebra-striped beasts! Their shaggy manes were so long it was nothing like I'd ever seen.

I shuddered, my gaze switching back and forth between Dante and the new arrivals. He didn't twitch, still kneeling, awaiting his death. They'd stolen his hope; now his life was about to suffer the same fate. A deep howling sound echoed around the arena floor—the roar of a predator.

Not whilst I still breathed!

At that moment, I realised that Jad was holding me in a tight grip…restraining me.

"Let me go, Jad!" I said fiercely, staring at the pack of jingwes cantering across the east side of the arena floor at an easy gait. Their tawny eyes darted about the arena stands, overwhelmed by the crowd's cheers.

"Don't do this!" He tightened his hold.

It was fortunate I couldn't see the thing that resided in the inner me. I wanted to squeeze it out and shake the life out of it for betraying me. *You spared my life so I can watch him die? No! Now you'll watch me die!*

"Let me go!" I growled, kicking him with both legs.

"You can handle it, you said! Is this you *handling* it?"

"I'm handling it the only way I know how. Let me go!"

"No! He's dying, Alee! Accept i-tt!" His voice broke. "I'm sorry. All I'm saying is he's here for you…what good is it if *he* dies for you, *you* for him, and *I* for you?" His eyes blazed with fierce anger.

If gravity can't hold me down, neither can you! "There's no good in this hell!" I rasped.

In desperation, I did something foreign to me but totally necessary…and I felt terrible for it. I hastily lowered my head and sunk my teeth into Jad's arm.

That jolted him. "Ouch! A-Alee!" The angry bitterness in his voice pierced my heart, but he loosened his grip for a microsecond.

That was all I needed.

I ducked, slipped under his arm, and hurdled over the arch of the stairs. I ran desperately, flying over stairs, my heart beating audibly against my ribs. The noise from the crowd intensified as my boots hit the terraces.

My heart in crash-landing mode, I was dimly aware of Jad blitzing behind me, yelling—shouting—pleading for me to stop. In the distance, on the west side of the arena, I glimpsed a figure leaping onto the arena floor.

Tan-tan! That's suicide! Then again, I was on the same path. At the back of my mind, I could hear the crowd's monotonous chants as they stamped their feet on the ground.

A huge commotion erupted as the spectators took in Tan-tan's daring move. To the east, the jingwes seemed to be strategizing, gazing back and forth between the hordes and their targets, their heads whipping around in unison. From the west, Tan-tan sprinted towards a stunned Dante, who was now on his feet.

In a moment of bittersweet surrender, I took a lurch into a two-metre drop, and landed on my back on the arena floor. I rolled onto my front as grains of sand attached to me. The crowd cheered on, the sound deafening. Something snapped in me. I didn't stop to feel the pain.

From the corner of my eye, I glimpsed the menacing jin-gwes charging towards me. Hunched, muscles rippling, their white coat with black stripes ignited in the daylight. I realised then I'd given them the go-ahead to attack. With my racing heart in my palms, I scrambled to my feet and gazed upon the love of my life.

Lessi! Dante spun round. His expression froze in a blood-less, heartrending mask. He raced, albeit with a limp, towards me. Tan-tan sprinted closely behind. With each stride, Dante's face contorted with incredulous, bewildered agony, anger, and something else I couldn't work out.

From behind me, I heard someone jump onto the arena floor. I cast a brief glance behind. Jad was sprinting towards me, his huffing breath in tune with my breathing. My heart sank deeper. *How many people have to die today?*

In less than a minute, Dante and I covered the distance between us. A metre from him, I leapt off the sand and thrust myself into his arms. My body crashed into his. With an incredible bout of strength, he caught me, buoyed me up in a bittersweet moment that sent the crowd into a tremendous roar.

"L-Lessi, what are you—"

"I c-can't watch you die! I w-won't do it!" I trembled and buried my head in his shoulders, as he cradled me tightly. By then, I had exhausted all my adrenaline, and yet it was in his arms that I returned to life, however briefly.

At that exact time, the dribbling jingwes swooped up in unison, howling and panting, their claws mere metres from us. Dante pitched me to the ground and lay over me. My hero, my protector...in life and in death. I could never live in a world without him!

"I'm s-sorry," he said, and kissed my brow with fiery intensity. His voice was crisp and beautiful, just as I remembered. "I'm so sorry!"

"I love you!" I pulled him down and buried my head in his neck. "I love you!"

If those were to be my last words, they were the only ones I'd rather say.

Breathing heavily, I awaited the inescapable death by torturous ripping and shredding. I could almost feel the impending pain, but I had comfort in knowing it would be both short-lived and a thousand times more bearable than losing him.

I clutched onto him and waited, breathing into him, him into me. Hot, scorching tears burned through my eyes...a strange air surrounded us. The wait was agonisingly long. Seconds turned to minutes—chants were replaced by silence—my heart stopped pounding. *Why is it so quiet? Are we dead?*

20. BUBBLE OF LOVE - FUSION OF FIRE AND FROST

In the surreal silence that followed, a heat wave shot through my eyes, a sign I was alive but not dying soon enough. I emitted a jarring shrill in agony, my hands unwittingly coming to cover my eyes.

"Lessi!" Dante's breath came short and sharp against my neck.

I snapped my eyes open, hoping we'd vanished into safety. Sadly, the Arena of Glory, ringed by tiers of stands, was bursting with the astonished faces of my foes...Tregtarians. *Why are we still alive?*

A fire erupted inside my eyes, and I squeezed them shut. I yowled in baffled agony.

Dante held my face in his hands. "Lessi...talk to me!"

His voice sounded strange. Something was off. It sounded like we were in a vacuum. Suddenly, it went quiet...stealthily still and devoid of all noise. My eyes healed. The fire subsided as quickly as it ignited, and I went numb.

"I'm f-fine," I mumbled, perplexed. I brought my hands to my ears. *Why the silence?*

A sudden burst of laughter echoed from Tan-tan. "Mother of Sequence! Bubble of love...unbelievable! Dan, are you seeing this? Aless... Amazing! You built us a shield!" He laughed again, the kind only one who had faced the shroud of death and found life could emit. "Our personal shield! Dan, tell me you're seeing this!"

Dante sprang to his feet and helped me up. "Tan…you laugh in the face of death! That move you made…never do it again!" His voice boomed into the air.

"Don't you see, Dan? They can't touch us!" Tan-tan said. "Aless, are you seeing this?"

Still hazy with the untoward events, I glanced at Tan-tan before my gaze settled on a heap of burning ash about four metres away from where we stood. I gasped, my hands coming to my stomach. Thick, dark smoke bellowed into the sky. An unpleasant, pungent smell lingered in the air. The jingwes had suffered death by incineration!

Squinting, I rubbed my eyes, questioning my eyesight. *I didn't do this. I couldn't have done this…* A ring of fire blazed into the ground, etched around us like someone had dug an oval into the sand, poured some fuel, and ignited a fire.

The swoosh of arrows sounded. I spun round. Despite blurry vision, I noticed a flurry of arrows whooshing towards us. Holding my breath, I cowered in terror.

"Aless, don't duck for cover…*you* are the cover!" Tan-tan said.

In surreal stupefaction, dozens of warriors wielding weapons raced towards us, only to come to a halt beyond the ring of fire. Why they would run towards the circle of fire instead of away from it was true Tregtarian instinct.

Dante caught me by the arm. "Are you all right?"

Dazed by the barrage of arrows bouncing off an invisible ball, I managed a nod, trembling. My pulse raced. He seemed on point with the unfolding events.

My mind dawdled, my body equally sluggish. The crowd in the arena went into a state of frenzied confusion…their faces said it all.

Still, I expected an outcry—screams—shouts—anything from the throngs to assure me this wasn't a dream. Instead, the air was dense with the sound of silence. A soundless carnage had erupted beyond the ring, yet inside, we were at peace.

A continuum of air floated about us with no distinction or separation. Through me, our ancestors, or maybe *I* had built us a mini Tuscania within the home of our enemies.

"Why is it so quiet?" My voice was barely above a whisper.

"We can't hear them, and they can't hear us, either," Dante said.

"A soundproof *hot* shield!" Tan-tan marvelled.

The shield, it burns... In a heartbeat, I felt like an arrow shot through my brain. "Oh my God, Jad!" I dropped to my knees and punched the ground. "No, no, no!" *How can I forget! How did I forget!*

Fresh tears of pain broke through, and a bone-chilling cold froze my eyes. A freezing whirlwind swept around me. To my bafflement, the shield of fire subsided, and in its place, jagged ice peaks encircled us like a wreath of frost.

"Jad!" I wailed. Seconds after, I went into a state of nihility where everything went cold and black. "I can't see!" I cried, waving my hands in the air...reaching out. My eyes felt cold, freezing cold. "Dante, I can't see!"

The soft whisper of clothing and then the brushing of shifting sand sounded as loud as a gunshot. Arms wrapped around me, Dante cradling me from behind. "You've lost your vision?" he asked, with a tremor in his voice.

"I've lost Jad. I can't see...Jad!" I sobbed, still waving my hands in the air in a frantic search. "I killed him...I burnt Jad...the shield...he was right behind m-me..."

Dante spun round with me in my arms. Suddenly, he stopped. "He's here, Lessi. Jad is here!" He breathed.

Hands cupped both sides of my face. "Hey...shhh, you're done crying...remember?" Jad consoled. "I'm fine. Freaked out, but all here."

"W-Why did you wait so long to respond when I called?" I threw the question at him. "I thought you were d-dead."

He puffed a broken laugh. "You can't kill me off that easily, Alee."

"W-Why did you run?" I covered his hands with mine, my voice ragged with sobs.

"Are we *really* going to do this in this bizarre Fusion of Fire and Frost!" he said playfully. When I leaned towards him, he wrapped his arms around me. "I couldn't miss out on all this action," In the eye of death, he teased.

I sobbed a laugh, waved my hand back, and reached for Dante's arm. "Dante, you've met Jad!" Definitely not the way I'd envisaged the introduction, but that had to do, for now.

Dante planted a gentle kiss on top of my head in silence.

"I have something for you." Jad opened up my palm and placed a cool object into it.

I ran my free hand over it and gasped. "The jewel of the ocean! You found it!" I threw my arms around him in gratitude.

"Larumia is you," he whispered. "You can't return home without it."

Amid the commotion surrounding us, we, thanks to the gifts passed down by our ancestors, were in our own little bubble of fire and frost, shielded by our love for each other. I allowed myself a smile. It wasn't yet time to raise the white flag.

"I feel left out of this party...Aless," Tan-tan said.

"Tan-tan!" I dropped my arm from Jad and waved my hands towards Tan-tan, but because I still couldn't see, I had my bearings all wrong.

He came from behind and spun me round before pulling me up to my feet. "Come here, you!" He gave me a bear hug. "The Moon gods love you, Aless...he missed you, you know. You'll break a few hearts...but mend them again, I'm sure." He pecked my cheek.

"We need to go!" Dante took me from Tan-tan's arms. "Lessi, how long can you hold this shield?" he asked with urgency.

"I don't know." Gloom seemed tenfold. "I can't see."

"Neither can they," Jad's voice came from behind me. "We can sit it out until the goons exit the arena and walk right out."

Dante turned round with me in his arms. "It's too risky.

At some point, her mind will tire…we have to be out of here before then."

"What's happening?" I asked, my stomach churning.

Dante hesitated. "The shield has made us invisible to them. I think they can't see us when you can't see them. They're searching for us even though we're right here."

"Hand me the sword. I'll lead the way!" Jad said.

Dante didn't answer. A heavy silence descended. Maybe being stripped of my vision was why it seemed more pronounced.

My arm tucked securely behind Dante's back, I slid my free hand up his chest. A chill settled in my gut. "You're bleeding."

"It's a flesh wound, Lessi," he said.

"The injured leading the blind…I don't think so. Dante, the sword!" Jad insisted.

I felt Dante's body tense up. *What's going on?*

"Dante." I lifted my chin. Obviously a silent exchange was going on. I wished I could see the warmth in their eyes; sadly, I only saw varying shades of darkness.

"De-Deganon's servant!" Dante said, voice bursting with surprised horror. He had just picked up on who Jadherey was.

"Not anymore!" Jad said calmly.

"You were there with De-Deganon in my father's house the moon-night my mother and I escaped." It wasn't a question, more of a firm statement.

"I didn't tell on you." Jad's voice was even. "I didn't say a word about your escape."

"He's all right, Dante," I said. "Jad was Lord De-Deganon's servant. He's a friend."

It seemed a long time before Dante spoke. "You trust him?" Dante breathed into my neck.

"With my life," I declared. "Jad will get us home."

"That responsibility is *mine!*" Dante's voice wobbled and frosted the edges of my heart.

"I know," I said, "but you're hurt. Let *him* take us home. He's coming home with us!"

"He won't make it across the shield," Tan-tan said.

"He will. The shield will not harm h-him." My voice cracked. "He saved me. The shield will save him."

Before Dante could object, a torrential deluge poured over us, cleansing the land anew. I coiled against Dante's chest. Although made of a fusion of fire and frost, the shield wasn't waterproof.

He grasped me in his arms. "Can you walk?"

I nodded, but truthfully, I had no idea where I was placing my feet. I was drained. I wasn't me anymore. I didn't feel like me. The innermost me had decided to come out after all. Now *she* was sapping the energy out of me and taking over.

Suddenly, we were moving briskly, trudging and sludging through the mud. Dante bolstered me, limping. In less than a minute, my legs gave way. I felt my eyelids shut…I remember the rain being violent—unusual—biblical. How easy it would be to drift into oblivion. I'd done it so many times now there was a pattern—it was when *she* chose to come out. This wasn't my fight anymore; it was *hers*.

"I've got her. Keep moving!" Dante said as if from far away. By then, my feet were no longer on the ground…my consciousness was slipping into unknown realms.

Everything became a blur. I wasn't D'Artagnan, but I had three musketeers, no three *gisbornias* protecting me. Gloom closed around me. When I finally plunged into magnified darkness, I drifted into a state of lassitude, losing all sense of time, direction, and existence.

* * *

Seconds felt like minutes—minutes translated to hours. All I could see was a blank canvas, dark and stripped of all colour. Not too long after, I tripped and stepped over Dante's foot, at least I thought it was Dante's foot.

"Sorry," I said tearfully, fatigued and disorientated. An intense vulnerability settled in.

Dante swept his arms around me, lifting me off the ground and cradling me in his arms. I buried my head in his shoulders. A zephyr wind, cool and refreshing, ruffled my hair. I clung to him and absorbed his warmth, but at the back of my mind, I knew he was hurt.

"You're hurt. Let me walk," I whispered against his neck.

"No can do! I'm not losing any of my toes!" Jad answered.

I would've shot back with a jerk if I wasn't too zonked to move a muscle. "Jad," I exclaimed, raising my voice as loud as I could. Sadly, it was just above a whisper.

"Hey, beautiful," he muttered under his breath.

"Did I just step over your foot?" I asked.

"Impossible. Your feet haven't touched the ground in a long time," he answered.

I realised then, I had been dreaming. It took me a few seconds to open my eyes. Unfortunately, I was met by a sea of darkness. I wearily swept my gaze around anyway, hoping for anything... but nothing. A tingle touched my brow. Instantaneously, Jad blew some warm air onto my forehead.

"What is it?" The smell of wildflowers breezed through the air.

"A peculiar yet pretty fly," he answered.

"A butterfly!" I squinted. My heartbeat accelerated. A throbbing pain had found a home behind my eyes, and I couldn't it shake off. "We made it?"

"Yup. We did."

This was epic, and yet his voice was toned down.

"H-How did we get here?" I asked. "W-What happened?"

He planted a kiss on my forehead. "Do you prefer the long story or Jad's version?"

"Jad's version will do just fine...for now."

I felt him smile against my brow. "Thanks to this invisible shield you have going on, I beat the hell out of those goons.

I got my sweet revenge after all." He chuckled. "Thinking of it now, it was side-splitting to see those thugs flying to the ground without the faintest clue of where the blow was coming from…" He paused. "You still can't see?"

"It's all dark, Jad." A cool wind blew soft tendrils of my hair.

"Don't worry. I'll just have to be your eyes from now on."

I couldn't help but smile. The air felt fresh against my skin. "Where's Dante and Tan-tan? How long have I been asleep?" Each word was a drain to my energy reserves.

"Slow down…you call *that* sleeping? You have tonnes to answer for." I felt his breath on my forehead, his voice seeming closer than before. "I'll let you off for now until you're yourself again."

"I'm not me?"

"You're you…just different."

"I must look awful…" I raised my face to the sun; its warmth was comforting.

"You look perfect, just…fragile. This can't wait, though. Why didn't you tell me Dante is the Larize of the Favoured Kingdom under the Moons?" he whispered.

"I didn't think it mattered."

"It mattered all right," he said after a moment, "especially when you decided to blank out after the arena and left me to answer for myself. When we reached your ancestors' shield, imagine my surprise when I found out it was *his* decision whether I enter *his* land or not."

"It's the shield's decision."

"The shield is you…remember? I suppose even *the* Larize is under your command." He paused. "It took some persuasion to get him to risk your life and hand you over to me so I could walk right through the daisies. As long as I had you in my arms, I wouldn't burn…that was the plan, right?"

I nodded with a faint smile. "Where is he?"

"He's right behind us, keeping an eye and all. In case you're wondering why it's me and not him right now…it's been him all the way. But he's still injured, and I have to earn my keep somehow, so I'm giving him a rest from carrying you. You're kind of heavy, you know that, right?" he teased.

"Remind me to punch you when I'm feeling up to it." I almost let out a laugh. "Is Tan-tan with him?"

"He's gone ahead to alert your people and bring some ewies. They'll meet us halfway...wherever that is." He turned round and called, "She's awake!"

Seconds later, the air around me felt different. The smell of fresh flowers infused the air with a promise of honeysweet calm. Jad set me down, and I swivelled into Dante's arms. "Dante," I exclaimed wearily.

Wordlessly, Dante lifted me bodily into his arms as if I weighed nothing more than a feather. I pressed my face against his neck and clung to him tightly with my eyes shut. "Don't tire yourself. I can walk," I whispered.

Who was I kidding?

"We're staying here, now. Tan is on his way back." He was quiet for a short while. "Zaira says hello."

A heartfelt smile graced the corners of my mouth. "We're within range?" I tried to concentrate, but seconds later, I gave up. "I can't hear her voice. It's just empty silence."

"You're exhausted. Get some rest. She'll be here soon."

"She's riding out?" An image of Zaira galloping across the Tuscanian forest presented itself to my mind. Grandma oozed elegance every time, and to imagine her riding at speed was as strange as it was comforting to me.

"Without seeking to overwhelm you, Lessi, the whole kingdom is riding out, with trumpets blaring, to bring you home." He brushed his lips against my cheek.

"I'll give you a moment." Jad's footsteps faded into the distance.

Dante lowered himself onto the ground with me in his arms, and I was suddenly aware of the masculine contours of his body, the steady beat of his heart, the smile that overwhelmed my senses…at least that was the picture inside my head.

I imagined gazing helplessly into his eyes…recalling the various shades of red that dazzled me. The lustrous stream of his red shock of hair, his beautiful bronzed skin…

I don't want to forget.

Slowly, I brought my hands to his face, traced his sturdy jaw, and brushed my hands across his lips. Momentarily, I thought about stealing that first kiss but immediately backtracked. I was too fatigued to give it justice. Most importantly, I needed to look into his eyes when we took that first step.

What if I never see again? I stifled my anxiety for less than a second but being in his arms brought out a vulnerability in me only he could cure. I yearned for his protection—warmth—love—more than I did anything else.

I was the shield…but *he* was my armour.

"Dante," I whispered. "I'm scared!"

"Why, Lessi?" His otherwise velvet voice was ragged with bafflement.

"Of never getting to see you again." Hopeless tears welled in my eyes.

His cool hand smoothed the hair softly from my face. "This is only short-term. It'll soon come to pass. W-What you did… for us took a phenomenal amount of energy. Rest is what you need."

He slid his hands to my eyes, gently shutting my eyelids before placing a couple of warm kisses on each eye that generated a fountain of more tears.

A scent of fresh pine and a strong fragrance of wildflowers breezed through the air. "Tell me what you see!" I clung to him with a sob.

His arms folded tightly around me, but he didn't answer right away. "We're surrounded by a scatter of pine cones. Ahead is a winding forest lane, guarded by a cluster of ancient trees with an array of colourful purple, pink, and white flowers. They appear to be at least a thousand moon-years old yet are still untouched." He swallowed. "Above, the Sun god of Light is filtering through the leaves and flowers, emitting a greenish light over us…" His lips brushed the top of my head. "Most importantly, I see you," he whispered, his warm breath sweet against my hair.

I smiled. "And I feel you!"

For a long time, we cradled in silence. My head rested on his knee whilst my body nestled into his. Talking was a drain to my already depleting energy reserves, as was staying awake, so we were as still as hibernating Njuzathians, waiting for our people to take us home.

The air seemed cooler than before, and a little chill slithered across my spine. I shivered and snuggled closer to him. My head safely hidden against his chest, I was slowly drifting back to sleep. "Is Zaira close?" I asked, my voice fading away.

It was a while before he answered. "She rides ahead of everyone, Blamorey inches back, and Gradho not too far behind."

"Can you do something for me?" It felt as if my mind was flitting away, too.

He exhaled sharply. "Anything." His voice quivered; something was off. I didn't know what it was.

"Can you ask Zaira to keep Gradho away from Jad?"

It was a moment before he answered. "Not a problem!" He rested his chin on my head.

"Thank you," I mouthed. "Could you send three messages to Zaira for me?"

"Absolutely." There was an unsettling quake to his voice.

My throat dried up. "Tell her…I love her."

"Noted." He smoothed the hair off my face, his hand a tad shivery.

"And…I miss her."

His muscles flexed against my body, and then he swallowed hard. "D-Done." His voice was tinged with sadness.

"And that I-I really, really need a bath…" My voice trailed off.

He almost choked a laugh, his arms tightening around me. A droplet of moisture fell onto my cheek, and he hastened to wipe it off.

"Is it raining?" I mouthed.

He heaved a huge sigh instead.

"Dante?" Gathering the little strength I had left, I brought my hand to his face. I gasped. The wetness of his cheek invoked a torrent of emotion in me. *Don't hold back for my benefit,* I thought, hoping he could hear me. *If angels can cry, so can you. I'll love you through all the tears and smiles.*

He took my hand in his, and cradled it against his chest, a sign he was inside my head. For some time, a sad silence enveloped us until his voice echoed inside my head. *In the arena, I killed men, Lessi. Without you, I lost myself. I lost my ways. I lost us.*

It's impossible to lose us, I thought, and hoped he could hear. *Don't let what happened in the arena eat you up. I won't let you. You did what you did to survive. You had to fight to live.*

That was not fighting. He gripped my hand tightly. *I ripped those men apart and made sure their deaths were as gruesome as I could manage. I had no pity—no regret—no mercy. De-Deganon loved me for it. My father saw himself in me. It bought me a few moon-days to live. But on that final fight, I sensed you...inside. I couldn't do it. You're the best part of me...the only unsullied ray of light that resides inside me. You fight off the vile Tregtarian curse of my blood. You make me a better man, Lessi. Please hold on for me. I'll prove my love to you. I'll prove my worth. I'll prove my all...*

Tears coursed down my cheeks. *I'm barely hanging on.* My chest ached, and my body went cold. *But I'll hold on with everything I have for you. I won't let go.*

Despite not seeing, I was sure the tears in his eyes could only dim the effulgence that shone through them, but in the wake of our destiny—of our sequence, I knew without a shred of doubt, they'd shine brighter than the brightest star.

"You're safe now," he whispered, an unaccustomed emotion lingering to his tone. He brought his cheek to mine, and a flood of warmth rushed through me. "I'll make it right! I promise!" He planted the softest, gentlest, and most prolonged kiss on my cheek, inches from the corner of my lips.

Before long, his kiss floated me off to yet another dreamless sleep...where darkness was tenfold, stark, and bereft of colour.

21. WAKE UP ALREADY!

"She sleeps so soundly you'd think her life was trouble-free." Dante's honeyed voice, crisp, beautiful... and my wakeup call!

Dante. My heart skipped. I attempted to get up, only my body wasn't cooperating. Seconds later, I replayed his words, and a pang of panic shot through me. *I'm asleep?*

"The heart of the shield resides in her." Zaira's soft and velvety voice was like music.

Grandma! I called. *Grandma!*

"It's too huge a weight for her to carry," Dante went on to say.

Dante!

"That's why she has you," Zaira said.

They can't hear me! A double shot of panic went through me. *I can't see them...they can see me. So I am asleep...strange...odd, even.*

Dante took my hand. His skin felt cool to my hot palm. "She looks so delicate... fragile—"

"And yet so strong," Zaira reassured. "I see her mother in her. She will regain consciousness."

A knock at the door startled me. The door creaked, and a set of footsteps got louder until there was silence. "You think it's today?" Gradho's orotund voice was ear-splitting; if he couldn't wake me up, no one could. I felt the urge to cover my ears, but my hands were too heavy for me.

"Any time now!" Dante said.

"It's been seven moon-days," Gradho pointed out to my bafflement. "And she has the ancient gene, after all. Perhaps she's in hibernation?"

Seven days? Oh my God! No wonder I'm so hungry!

"She'll not sleep for three hundred moon-years, Gradho, surely." Dante seemed so calm. I, on the other hand, was teetering on the brink of a terror-filled panic attack.

What? Three hundred moon-years... No, no, no! That won't do. I have to wake up. Wake up, Alessia! Wake up!

"You don't know that for certain," Gradho's powerful voice screamed inside my head. "This is revolutionary...unprecedented. There's no telling if, when, or what she'll do when she wakes up. For all *we* know, she could have amnesia!"

Gradho, stop talking! A heavy silence descended. Prolonged... quiet...haunting. *Why are you all so quiet now? Did you hear me? Dante?*

He stroked the back of my hand.

"Don't give me the look, Larize," Gradho finally said. "I'm only preparing you for such an eventuality. She may not remember you."

Forget Dante... seriously? Gradho, what world are you living in? I've got to wake up. I tried to roll sideways but failed. *Baby steps...* I wiggled my toes. I gasped. It worked!

"She's flickering her eyelids. Have some faith," Dante said to my relief.

I'm close. It's working. I wriggled my fingers.

"Have you tried reaching out to her?" Gradho asked.

"Of course. We all have," Dante answered, annoyance in his tone.

"Her mind may have since bid farewell...only her shell resides now. No one has yet returned from the *gondol*...The moons may have already laid claim on her."

Hey, I'm still here, okay? In some creepy form of sleep paralysis or something...right?

"Drop it, Gradho!" Dante snapped. "Your theories are ill

advised. There's no place for them here! Your efforts in trying to rescue Lessi may have earned you a seat in this house, but don't seek to make me revoke that decision."

If words could slice, I was certain Gradho was feeling the pain.

"I apologise, Larize," Gradho hastened to say. "My tongue ran away with my words."

An all-round thoughtful silence was cut short by an all-too-familiar voice inside my head. *Tan-tan...if I were you, I'd watch your new red-eyed friend... It's the way he looks at her...I don't trust him.* Gradho's voice seemed thunderous now.

Tone down! I thought.

Give it a rest Gradho, Tan-tan answered, his voice sounding ten times louder, too. *You've been told to shut up...that includes your mind, too.*

The mind thing! So I can penetrate their shields... how is that possible?

What I want to know is how did a Tregtarian survive zera-pe-ladha's mini shield and then cross the shield of our ancestors unharmed, and how in the moons' name is he shielding his mind? Gradho asked. *I can't read anything from him. Not even the Voices of Sequence can.*

If you're really peed off about it, just ask him, Tan-tan bit back.

My heart raced. *Jad's here.*

You were there, you tell me. There was a tiny pause. *If you're not sharing, fine. My problems are miniature compared to the Larize's.*

Your point?

The Tregtarian servant calls her Alee!

Again, your point? Tan-tan's voice sounded frustrated.

No one else refers to her as Alee, and he does. Don't you think it's beyond strange? I don't trust him.

You don't trust anyone.

Granted. Still, the new arrival is a real headache for Dante, now isn't he? Seven moon-days and he's yet to leave her side... they've enjoyed each other's company all right!

Ah! I screamed. This was like eavesdropping. *Get out of my head!*

They must pray she wakes up soon…anymore time together—

Gradho, stop talking…thinking…whatever, just stop! I cried. *Alessia, wake up already!*

Suddenly, it happened; my eyes fluttered open. The voices vanished. My vision returned, and what a beautiful sight met my eyes! I blinked a few times. I was in my mum's bedroom, my room…home. When I turned my head sideways, my world tilted on its axis. Dante knelt next to my bed, holding my hand over white silk covers. *Dante!*

His eyes held mine. They were stunningly glowing, like they were reading into my soul. His urbane look drew me to him, but I didn't move, and I couldn't look away, either. I just stared. He was it—whatever *it* was—he was it. My heart skipped.

He stroked the back of my hand. Even a hand as steady as his shook with nervous excitement. "D-Do you remember me, Lessi?" he asked.

I dropped his hand in a jiff and threw my arms around him. "Are you kidding me?" I laughed, tightening my hold.

"Lessi! Thank the moons!" he breathed with relief, wrapping his arms around me.

His familiar hold…his unmistakable touch brought a burst of warmth to my face. Through my silk nightgown, I felt the muscles of his stomach contract, his chest heaving in tune with his breathing. For a minute, we cuddled.

You held on… his mind found mine.

With everything I had. I kept my head buried in his arms, loving the feel of him against me.

He pulled back slightly and held my face in his hands. *Still holding on.*

Never letting go! I tilted my head to lean into his hands.

Make time for me…tonight? He pulled away, too quickly for my failing sanity.

A swift, cool breeze blew from the open window, bringing

a sweet flowery aroma into my room. My family stood by the edge of my bed. Five sets of anxious eyes gazed back at me, faces wreathed in smiles. An infusion of blue teary eyes concocted with a couple of red, vibrant scorchers and a dash of hazel filled the room. My eyes strained as I beamed at them.

Zaira, in an immaculate long emerald chiffon dress, took three strides towards me, her sea-blue greenish eyes glistening with each step.

"Grandma!" I cried in delight.

Dante edged away to make room for her.

"Welcome back, velici!" She kissed my cheek and wrapped her arms around me in a warming embrace. Home had never felt so good. Neither of us moved—the emotion flowing through us couldn't be rushed. "I knew you'd come back. I never lost hope, velici," she said with feeling. She drew back and held my face in both her hands. "I adore you…I missed you…I made sure all your requests were taken care of…all of them. Now that you're awake, you can have that bath all to yourself."

I laughed, and so did she. A slight feeling of déjà vu crept up on me from my first day in Zeneshia. My room was as I remembered: white with circular turquoise panels.

From the corner of my eye, I saw Tan-tan step forward. He reached for my hand and placed a light kiss. "You were *so* hot out there." He threw an upwards glance at Dante.

"Tan, surely you can phrase that better," Dante warned with a bantering smile.

"The gods love you, Aless," Tan-tan said with a beaming grin. "Thank you!"

"No. Thank *you* for bringing me home!" I said.

Gradho, in a heavenly-blue robe, was next to inch closer. He took both my hands in his and squeezed them. "For a young girl, you have quite an unparalleled flair. I hear you put on *the* show in the South!" He paused, watching me studiously. "You've lost too much weight, zera-pe-ladha."

"Nice to see you too, Gradho," I said.

"I'm just stating the obvious." He dropped a kiss on my hands before stepping aside.

I smiled. He was weirdly odd but a reminder that I was home.

A sparkle shimmered in Jad's eyes.

Why are you just standing there? "Jad!" I called.

He flashed a whimsical smile, the one I always returned with an automatic beam. Suddenly, he breezed towards me and snuggled me up into his arms. For a moment, we were all very quiet. I barely noted the curious looks from my family, but I could sense a difference to the air. It would take some time for anyone to understand or begin to unravel the bond between Jad and me.

"There's too much love going around," he whispered. "I'm feeling strangely gooey inside."

I burst into a light chuckle. "You've met my family now. Loving is what we do." I gave him a soft kiss on the cheek. I turned to Zaira. "Grandma, can he—"

"He has a home with us, velici," Zaira said with an immaculate gesture.

"Thank you." Jad seemed oddly too agreeable.

Gradho cleared his throat. "I'm happy to offer my residence, too." He cast a sideways glance at Jad. "I own a huge demesne. You'll have your own space, of course...I get him off your hands and—"

"Gradho! Jadherey has a home with *us*!" Zaira said sharply.

Gradho raised a quizzical eyebrow. "Larize, you concur?"

All heads turned to Dante, who seemed a bit caught off guard. He shot a penetrating look at Gradho, his eyes ablaze with something between bafflement and uncertainty. Gradho grinned knowingly. For a while, they faced each other. They were having a telepathic private moment; that was evident.

As they settled matters with their minds, my gaze hovered over the bright, vivacious vases of flowers laid out on the windowsill, and I smiled contentedly. Zaira had brought the outdoors in…the cascading waterfall in the corner of my room was adorned with a spray of flowers that hung freely over the surround. Tregtaria was just a memory.

Soon after, Dante strode towards me and perched himself on the bed. I shifted slightly and rested my back on him. His cotton shirt felt soft against my skin.

He turned to Jad. "I speak from the heart, and for the land, when I say we owe you *more* than a home for protecting our most precious gift…our most cherished sequence…when we couldn't."

His eyes glinting with amusement, Gradho cleared his voice.

"When *I* couldn't…" Dante took a breather. "The land is indebted to you. Tuscania is your home now. Where you choose to lay your head is up to you. Rest assured, you have a home in all our houses for as long as you wish." He stroked my bare shoulders gently as he spoke. "For now, I think you'll agree with my assumption…you'd rather be wherever *she* is."

"I wouldn't have it any other way." Jad reached for my hand and squeezed it tightly, and a sudden, heart-warming aware-ness of being home washed through me.

"Bravo! Since we're all in agreement," Gradho said, "how about a party in true Tuscanian fashion?"

"Let her catch her breath." Zaira nodded at me. *It's your decision, velici.*

"Whilst she's doing that, I'll be organising the best party the land has ever seen. We'll host it here, of course. Zaira's gardens are perfect at this time of the moon-year." Gradho strode towards me and knelt next to my bed before holding my hand in his. "Say yes, zera-pe-ladha. Something to perk you up. There's been a stench of bad air since you've been gone. The Voices of Sequence need a drink or two to stay awake." He grinned, as if he knew he'd got his point across. "The army I sent across the shield to Sanchuri atunya came back unscathed.

They merely watched as Tregtarians and Felradians knocked each other out. The moons favour us, zera-pe-ladha. It's time we get the land together and celebrate. The land demands it."

Leaning against Dante's arm, I smiled gratifyingly. "Since the land demands it…I can't deny it."

"I'll make the arrangements," Dante said to my astonishment. He didn't seem like the party planner type. "It's the least I can do."

"Larize, allow me!" Gradho hastily rose to his feet. "You have your hands full."

"No, I don't!"

"Believe me, *you* do!" Gradho raised an eyebrow.

Dante frowned and sharpened his gaze. They were having another telepathic moment.

Seconds later, Dante emitted a low laugh and then made quite an effort to compose his expression. "Gradho, don't you have a party to organise!" Dante yielded. The gleam of amusement in his eyes made me wonder what had just transpired.

I've been gone two seconds, and you and Gradho are best buddies now? I teased telepathically. Something was different, strange. It boggled my mind.

I've since lost all taste for arguments. Today and forever is all about you.

You flatter me.

Make time for me tonight, and I'll do much more than flatter you!

Gradho clapped his hands with delight. "Jadherey, you're coming?"

No! I protested inwardly. Jad rubbed his jaw, then nodded hesitantly.

"You'll have to leave this room at some point," Gradho said firmly, raising his brows. "She's awake now. I doubt she's going anywhere."

Jad slanted me a concerned look, swivelled and took one step towards the door but halted. My heart leaped. He turned round, his face a mask of worry. In a trickle, he took three loping strides back in my direction. I flashed a warm smile, anticipating his actions. Gently, he swung his arms around me like I'd just risen from the dead. He held me once again in a tight and emotional hug that summoned tears from my eyes.

I returned his embrace, and whispered, "Hey, what is it?"

"Are you sure you're all right?"

"I'm fine. I'm more than fine. I'm great. You, however, I'm not so sure."

He sighed. Seconds later he drew back. My family watched. I couldn't read their minds. Gradho made an impatient groan. Tan-tan and Dante had some telepathic communication going on. And Grandma was merely smiling.

"I'll survive." Jad swallowed hard. Something was eating at him. But I wasn't going to allow that. I wanted more for him. He deserved more.

"You always survive, Jad. You've always done." I held his hands in mine. "This time, you won't just survive, you'll live." I cast a sideways glance at Zaira. "Grandma always says, we live to gain, we live to lose, ultimately, we live. It's your turn to live, now."

"My moons!" Gradho exclaimed. "Zaira, your granddaughter is turning into you." He beamed. "Her time away did her some good. What a fine prodigy she's become."

Grandma flashed a sincere smile of satisfaction. "She's blossomed into the rarest flower that she is. An original flower of Sequence." She picked an osiria rose from the vase and brought it to her nose. "Whilst our neighbouring Felradians are relentlessly churning the wheels of the future, our flower is in bloom." She strode to the bed and handed me the rose. "They started the game of Sequence. What the future doesn't tell them is…you'll end it."

"Grandma," I said, touched. She had so much confidence in me. "Thank you."

"Well said, Zaira. However, this flower of Sequence needs

a party," Gradho said. "Jadherey, I have just the job for you?" Gradho wasn't taking no for an answer.

"Gradho, delegating is not organising," Dante said to my relief. "Allow Jadherey to settle in first."

"But…" Gradho hesitated then agreed almost immediately. "Yes, Larize." He dipped his head and quickly strode out of the room.

"Jadherey," Zaira said. "Amerey is waiting in the hallway. She'll show you to your room." She gave a maternal smile.

"See you later," Jad said, raking his hand through his ruffled hair. There were undertones of weariness in his voice. He was free. A free man. Now he had a home.

"I'll come with you," Tan-tan said.

I smiled reassuringly at Jad, and he flashed a reluctant smile back before the pair strode out of my room.

"How about a warm, long and scented bath before your granddad and Veremy return?" Zaira swiftly made her way towards the dressing room. "They'll not want to leave your side."

Instantly Dante stood and bent over to kiss my cheek. "Find time…tonight." Subtle amusement lingered in his voice.

* * *

Just before dinner, I ventured to the *Veela*-Guest Wing of house Serenius to see if Jad had settled in all right. The bright winter-white halls adorned with a spray of flowers, a huge contrast to the armour-decorated Tregtarian corridors, was a much-needed reminder that everything would be just fine… for him.

A familiar sense of family, love, and serenity washed through me as I strode down the long and spacious hallway lined with white wooden doors. The floor-to-ceiling glazed windows to my right brought the beauty of nature in, capturing neat rows of green hedges and red-leafed jajaja trees in bloom that added an enchanting and dramatic touch to the landscape. I turned left and peeked into the guest parlour. It was empty. Tuscanians were never late for anything…certainly not dinner. This time, they were a tad early because this dinner was special. We were hosting a Tregtarian! Not only that…I was back home.

I took a moment to savour Grandma's stunning garden from three levels up. The garden floor was sprinkled with blooms and blossoms that lifted with the passing of an ocean breeze and flitted into the backdrop of the Blue Ocean of Sequence. I glanced to the heavens. The sky was a dome of blue, a ribbon of hazy fog carving the horizon in a stupendous coating of colour. *Home.*

A shuffle of feet sounded from behind me. Daphne, carrying an ivory basket in her hands, took hesitant steps backwards and forwards along the hall adjacent to Jad's room. Grandma had allocated the finest room on the Veela floor to Jad. Located on the curvature of the South and West facing Veela Wings, the circle-shaped room had beautiful views of the ocean, gardens, and the sky.

"Daphne," I called from a few metres away.

She jumped and almost toppled the vase of carnations that sat to her left.

"You've still not given it to him?" My brow furrowed.

Daphne let out a sigh and gently swung the basket in her hands. Grandma and I had neatly laid out a folded set of midnight-blue towels, a pair of trousers, shirt, robe, scented candles, and eucalyptus and vanilla incense sticks for Jad. Daphne was meant to deliver them to him an hour ago.

"Did he refuse you?"

"Me? No. Shh. The door is open," she whispered, bringing her free hand to her mouth. She crossed to my side with haste and craned her head towards Jad's room, her dark lengthy hair flowing in waves over her shoulders. "He didn't refuse me. Neither did he refuse the basket of goodies. How could he?

Our guest is asleep…on the floor." Her lips parted. "I came earlier and waited for him to wake up. He didn't. So I went away, and I've just returned. He's still asleep, Alessia. On the *floor!*"

My heart lurched, and I swung her a warm smile. "He doesn't bite, you know," I said teasingly.

"I know, but…he's a Tregtarian and he's in our h-home." Her voice quivered slightly.

"He's not a threat, Daphne." I took the basket from her shaky hands. "He's a friend, and a good man. He just needs a break."

I'm sure he does, but sleeping on the floor is weird. The bed is right next to him. She half-smiled, eyebrows raised. "Too strange… I'll leave you to it." She threw her arms around me. With the basket between us, the awkward and strange embrace invoked a burst of laughter. *It's good to have you home.* Seconds later, she breezed down the hall and out of sight.

Jad's bedroom door was slightly ajar. I pressed the basket against my stomach, nudged the door so it opened wider and let myself in. The heavy cinnamon drapes were shut. I strode in lightly and tried to make my footsteps as quiet as a whisper. I halted by the foot of the bed in the centre of the room. Jad nestled on the marble floor, next to the window, asleep. His tattered cloak was wrapped around him, yet a king-sized bed sat next to him, undisturbed and untouched.

Jad, why are you doing this to yourself? My heart sank. I drew in a deep breath and gently laid the basket on the bed. I strode to his side and kneeled. Grandma had said he hadn't slept in seven days. Out of everyone, he'd had it tough. He was in a foreign kingdom, and the one person who should have been there for him had been stuck in some deep sleep.

You're not comfortable. I hesitantly reached out for his arm and drew back. *You can't possibly be comfortable like this.* After minutes of agonising about whether to wake him or not, I lay down sideways next to him, an arm's length away. A cold chill rose from the marble floor and pierced unmercifully through me. Perhaps lying on the floor was a bad idea. I outstretched my hand and placed it on Jad's shoulder.

He awoke, and his gaze met mine. "Alee," he whispered, eyes twinkling in the dim-lit room.

"The bed is not to your taste?" I teased, smiling. A deep chill slithered down my spine.

A warm smile radiated from his lips and spilled into his eyes. "My lady, the floor is not your place. Never your place." His voice was low and cool. He pushed back his hair from his clean-shaven face. A fresh masculine scent of lime and cocoa filled the air.

"Neither is it yours, Jad." My lips pressed tight. "Did you fall off the bed?"

A light chuckle escaped his lips, and a twinkle of mischief glinted his eyes. "No. Did *you*? What are you doing sleeping with a servant?"

"You really need to rephrase that, Jad!" I wriggled to make myself a bit more comfortable on the cold floor. It wasn't easy.

He took a short pause. "My lady, why are you lying on the floor next to a servant?" He slowed down his words. "Better?"

"It's not as if it's the first time."

"Everything is different now. We're not in the wilderness. You're home."

I merely beamed, heartened. Jad was a constant glow, a bright shimmer, a gift to my heart from the moons. Every time he grinned, he propelled me to smile, too.

"If your family see you like this, they'll think you're broken, Alee." The warmth of his voice was like a burst of light on a dark night.

"It's your fault," I whispered. "You broke me."

He puffed a laugh. "With a very blunt object." He regarded me for some time. "Look at you. You're lolling on the marble in your grand dress."

"Granted. That wasn't one of my brightest ideas," I agreed.

"You're obviously not grasping how uncomfortable the floor is. If you can somehow see it in my discomfort instead… It's my turn to take care of you now."

"Lounging on the marble is taking care of me?"

A feeling of deja vu swept over me. "I want you to feel at home," I said earnestly. "If you want to continue sleeping on the floor, that's exactly where you'll find me."

"You'd do that?" He released a disbelief yet appreciative sigh, at least that's what it seemed like.

"In a flash, Jad. I'd do that for you until you see the bed and this land for what it is…*comfort.*"

"Just to prove a point?" He flashed a sincere smile. "I've slept on the floor all my life, Alee. The bed takes some getting used to."

The honesty in his tone made me tearful. Chill bumps popped out of my arms. The freezing cold struck me hard. I shivered and sucked in a shaky breath. "With or without your permission, I'm demanding your comfort."

"You're trembling." He hurriedly reached out for my arm.

"I'm so cold." I wriggled restlessly. "I've no idea why I can't regulate my body temperature. D-Do you not feel the cold?"

He jerked back. "Alee, get up."

"You f-first."

Hastily, he sprung to his feet and pulled me up. With speed, he grabbed the throw from the bed and flung it over my shoulders. "What were you thinking?" His jaw tightened.

My teeth chattered. The chill penetrated deeper.

"You're not yet fully recovered." He drew me into his arms for a miniscule and drew back. He breathed. "You don't seek or demand someone's comfort by neglecting your own." He ran his hands across my bare arms and caressed them. "That was one of the most ill-thought out decisions you've made, and you've made quite a few."

"Whatever it takes," I stated. "You were such a comfort to me, and now I'm here for you." My throat grew thick. "Why haven't you been sleeping in seven days?"

He raised his dark brows, taken aback. "I couldn't."

"You haven't even made it to the dining room."

"Someone's been talking." A faint smile crept up his lips.

"Rightly so, Jad. Spending seven days in one room watching me sleep is creepy." I playfully rolled my eyes.

The laughter lines on the corners of his eyes deepened.

I crossed to the window and parted the cinnamon drapes, flooding the room with sunlight.

"Spending seven moon-days ensuring my lady is not dying on me is commitment." His voice was crisp and firm. "Eternal loyalty, Alee."

"Now you make it seem like a pledge," I murmured.

With my back to him, I opened the window, and a fresh ocean breeze wafted in, lifting the loose tendrils of my hair. I inhaled the profusion of scented flowers that drifted gently into the room and beamed. The twitter of ocean-birds was like a welcome song of home sweet home. I snuggled under the throw, wrapping it around my shoulders tightly.

"You were not asleep, Alee," Jad said, and I spun to meet his troubled gaze. He stood close to me. "You were gone." His voice was ragged with emotion. "You were just going to leave me here on my own."

"In a kingdom full of people, Jad." I blinked. "Good people."

"They don't trust me." He raked his hair back.

"They don't know you like I do." I moved sideways, loped around him, and strode to the bed. "They need time." I tossed the throw onto the bed, grabbed the basket, and turned round to find Jad smiling.

"To what do I owe this great honour?" He dipped his head playfully.

"A gift for you." I curtsied, holding the basket against my stomach. "To welcome you to my home."

"Towels and candles?" His voice rose, and a tentative smile played on his lips.

"And a change of clothes." I feigned seriousness but couldn't hold it for long and burst into light laughter. "Honestly, I saved one of the dreyziz the slightly daunting task of handing these directly to you," I said truthfully, "but Grandma and I packed it."

"The dreyziz are afraid of me?" His eyes locked onto mine and rooted me to the spot.

"I wouldn't exactly say that. They're simply mesmerised that you're the first full-blooded Tregtarian to cross our ancestors' shield, and no one can read your mind. You've made history."

Silence enveloped us, broken only by the whistling ocean breeze. Tantalising fragrances of exotic flowers and sea water perfumed the air.

Jad surveyed me for an interval. "You look grand in red." His eyes sparkled.

I nodded a silent thank you. "And you need to dress for dinner."

He swallowed hard. "I've never attended or sat at a formal dinner as a guest before." His lips thinned into a hard line. "I've always been the help. Serving is all I know."

My throat ached. His whole life had been one chore after another. "It'll be fine. I'm sitting next to you." I kept my voice even.

"You've seen the sitting plan?" He quirked a curious brow.

"Seen?" I shook my head. "I prepared it."

"How many are coming?" A shadow crossed his face.

"Twenty." I paused. "Okay, twenty-four of the gentlest Tuscanians ever."

"Your grandmother spoils you." His eyes danced with subtle amusement.

"Hey." I raised my voice. "You've been here how long?"

"A joke, Alee." He chuckled. Seconds after, his expression switched to seriousness. "You're loved...greatly," he murmured.

"So are you." I strolled towards the door and whirled around. "You need to change," I instructed. "We can't be late for dinner."

He slanted me a half-smile that I returned with a beam and then reached for the door.

"Alee," he called.

I turned to him.

He stood by the window, his gaze on me. "I'm pleased you're still you."

It took a few seconds for his words to sink in. "You're worried that now I'm home I'm just going to throw you away at the first chance I get?"

"You have an entire kingdom running after you. I'm simply an insignificant dot in an ocean of crystal-clear waters." His eyes tightened. "Soon, I might end up being a thorn in a sea of flowers. You don't need me."

A hush fell over us.

"Jad." I dredged up a smile. Inside, I was hurting for him—with him. He was lost in a world he didn't feel he belonged. I understood that feeling because I felt it too when I first came here, but now I understood that Tuscania was my world, and one day he would understand that, too. "I need you more now than before. I'll promise you three things, okay? I'll not fish you out and feed you to the sharks. I'll not let you sink or drown. I'll not turn blind to your presence," I said with great resolve. "I'll swim with you. I don't care how deep the waters are; I'm swimming with you."

"And if I can't swim?" He raised amused eyebrows.

"Then I'll carry you." I chuckled. "You're impossible. All I'm trying to say is being back home is exactly what it is. *Home*. But I will never forget you...us...or what we went through together. Not for the kingdom. Not for anything. Not for anyone. You're stuck with me and my family, now." I eased myself onto the bed and crossed my legs like my shrink used to do. "Why are you this worried, anyway? I'm the one who worries, not you."

"This time, I have a myriad of reasons for my worries, and she's worth all the worries in the Four Kingdoms." His voice was low.

My stomach curled, my heart lurching at his words. I breathed and sprung up. "Tell you what you need—"

"What I need..." He hesitated, looked away briefly, and then settled his gaze on me. "Would you mind if I request a hug?" he asked in a cool voice.

Lines formed on my forehead. "From me?" I darted a glance around to make a point.

"I don't see anyone else here, Alee." A corner of his mouth twitched.

My eyes widened, and my lips parted. "Jad...you carried me halfway across the vastness of Tregtaria to bring me to safety, yet you're requesting a hug?"

"What would you have me do, Alee?" His expression shadowed.

"Claim it." The words tore free from my lips.

A sparkle shone in his eyes. "Just like that."

"You're as good as my brother, Jad." I brought my hand to my chest. "You have a permanent place inside my heart. You've never asked before. What's changed—"

"Everything." Something flashed in his eyes, but before I could put a name to it, it was gone. He took a couple of long strides to my side, slipped his strong arms around my waist, and swooped me into a warming cuddle. The urgency of his embrace made me burst into light laughter. He buoyed me up and cradled me close.

"If that's your claim, it was way too rushed." I laughed. "Careful not to squeeze my insides out."

"You're forgetting one fundamental truth, Alee. I was born and raised a servant," he whispered. "Nothing comes freely to me."

"You were born a servant, but from now on, you'll live like a Larize because of the goodness of your heart." My eyes misted.

He let out a low growl, seemingly in disapproval.

"You'll be happy, here. I promise."

Lessi, everything all right? Dante's mind found mine.

324

My pulse gave a mighty leap. I had missed his voice inside my head.

He stood by the entrance, hands tucked deep in his trousers, a gentle look gracing his face. "Do you need a moment?"

"No, we're good." I beamed. "Jad is feeling a bit homesick."

Jad lowered my feet to the floor, and I slid out of his arms. He dipped his head slightly at Dante. "Larize."

"Nostalgia. It will soon come to pass." Dante strode in and focused his attention at me. "Gradho is beginning to grumble. Are you ready for dinner?"

"Jad needs to change."

"I'll be as quick as I can manage, Larize," Jad said apologetically.

"We'll wait for you in the hallway." I cast him a sideways and reassuring glance.

Dante softly took my hand and led me out of the room and into the hallway, closing the door behind us. We stood by the floor-to-ceiling glazed windows facing the ocean. The sky was a cloak of cerulean, without a wisp of a cloud in the air. The dual moons hung low, in competition with the beaming Sun god of Light. Dante slipped an arm to my waist and drew me close. I had missed his touch.

"Jadherey is struggling to settle in," he said after prolonged silence.

"Everything is strange for him," I answered, my gaze fixed at the ocean. "Despite my reassurance, he's worried I might abandon him now that I'm back home."

"Surely he must know that's not in you." He swallowed hard. "You're different...with him." His voice was controlled.

I tucked my hand into his and leaned against him. An enormous sense of well-being flooded through me.

"You're happy," he said.

"I'm happy he's found his freedom, that he has a home now."

"You feel responsible for him?" His eyes clouded with concern.

"It worries you?" I asked.

"You have a huge responsibility to this land, to our people, to me…what's one more person?" He flashed a smile. "I'm sure you can manage."

"You should have seen the life he led, Dante. No one should ever live like that. I want him to be happy. He deserves happiness."

"He'll find his own sequence to happiness, Lessi…if he hasn't already." He reached for my free hand, raised it to his lips, and placed a long and lingering kiss that made my pulse jump. *We all did.* His voice sounded inside my head. *The moons favour him, too.*

I smiled my heart to him. "Are you okay?"

He slanted me a half-smile. No, he wasn't. His eyes were a deep-red, their usual shimmer non-existent. "I need time with you…alone."

I ducked under his arm, rested my head against his chest, and curled my hands around him. Heaven. The warmth of his body engulfed me and brought a familiar wave of security. *We could skip dinner and just run.*

He held me snug and tightened his grip around me. *The thought has crossed my mind.*

The soothing sound of his breathing and the velvet tone of his voice resurrected a fluttering feeling inside me, something only he could command. I soaked in his embrace, loving everything about him and hoping with all my heart that our time apart was just a factor of our sequence, that our Sequence of First and Forever would never die.

Just make time for me tonight, please, he said. *I need you.*

* * *

That evening, following dinner, Zaira and I had a long chat. An intoxicating aroma of exotic blossoms mixed with seawater that wafted gently from beyond the glaze sweetly infused the sunroom. The panoramic views still baffled my senses. It was simply an unending spectrum of vibrant colours.

Everything was as it should be—flawless. The glorious Tuscanian sun had yet to dip. Its rays cast a soft amber glow across my skin. I felt warm, serene, and reposed...a feeling now foreign to me. Over a bowl of Araya deri's vegetable soup, Zaira had dropped a few tears...something one didn't see every day from the Lady of Composure. In the end, they were happy tears. I shed some myself.

A buzz of activity filled the house. House Serenius was alive with people streaming in and out. A shower of gifts, food, and offerings poured in continuously. Gradho bustled about self-importantly, in party-planning mode. I dreaded to think what he had in store. The two-dozen dreyziz and dreyris were working around the clock to keep the house functioning in sequence, the way of our people.

Just as we were chatting about Prince Charming, *the* Zeneshian Adonis approached quietly and stood by the doorway. I looked up, marvelling at his stamina. A few scratches and bruises remained visible, a reminder that he'd tasted death and survived, but no cut could make him look less flawless.

He was dressed casually in blue slacks and a white shirt, seeming too cool for my deep-red silk dress I'd chosen specifically to match his eyes. His shoulder-length hair he'd let loose, just the way I liked it. My heart skipped. I hadn't seen him since dinner—three hours ago, *I know*—and I missed him.

He had a quiet sadness hanging over him, though, like he blamed himself for everything. Lucky for him, I wasn't having that.

I set my bowl on the table and turned to Zaira. "May I, Grandma?"

"Go to him, velici. Go!" Her eyes held a gentle softness.

I dropped a light kiss on her cheek, flew towards Dante, threw myself with delight into his arms, and wound my arms around him. He gave a startled laugh as he whisked me off my feet and swung me around a few times.

Zaira burst out laughing. "I'm off to bed," she said, pacing towards us.

"The sun is not even set yet, Grandma," I said, still in Dante's arms.

"But the moons are already peeking at us." She patted my shoulder. "The more reason to get my beauty sleep. Don't stay up too late!"

With so many people in the house, all wanting to hear about our time in Tregtaria, Dante and I had to sneak out using the back door so we could get some alone time. We strode hand in hand across the boardwalk towards my favourite place in the gardens: *Lessi's utopia above the sea*—my special place. That's where he'd first made his feelings known to me.

As we took in the shimmering deep blue of the Tuscanian waters that stretched before us, any concerns relating to whether we could reignite what we had following our long absence from each other seemed rather unnecessary now. We sat on the bench, marvelling at our second chance at life.

"Lessi, I'm so sorry about everyth—"

"Shh." I placed my hands on his lips and smiled. "We've been through hell and back. I won't let you blame yourself."

A silence descended, bar the sound of whispering waves as they kissed the shore. The oceanic blue in our line of view was wonderfully appealing. There were gobs to discuss and things to catch up on, but neither of us knew where to begin. I leaned against his arm, and he cuddled me. We stared at the great vault of the sky; the moons hung very low, and the Sun god of Light hadn't even sunk yet. It was a perfect summer evening.

"Are you all right?" he finally asked, his voice breaking.

I nodded.

"Inside?" His jaw tightened.

"A little bruised." I lifted my chin and smiled. "I'll survive." I tried to lighten the air, but he was too concerned to play along.

"Did they…hurt you?" He swallowed hard. "Were you—"

"Dante, I'm fine." I half-pulled back to look into his eyes. "I'm here…with you. I'm okay."

"I need to know, Lessi." His voice grew quieter, his red eyes shimmering. "I have to know," he said, almost like he was pleading.

My eyes glistened. "Okay," I said after a moment. I owed him that. I lifted my feet off the ground and nestled comfortably into his arms. His arm automatically encircled me like he was protecting me from an unknown force.

I had to go back to a place my heart and mind would rather shut out…a path I never wanted to walk again. He needed closure, and I needed him to take that journey with me.

"It'll be easier if I take you there." I blinked, and a solitary tear trickled down. "First the Nadeira, then Tregtaria…We can't keep on racing with Sequence. Sequence is us…" I breathed against his neck, trusting my mind to open up for him.

He kissed the top of my head.

I rewound the clock for him. It was like an invisible light switch. A little flick of my thoughts, and it switched on. I unlocked this dark chapter in our lives, one last time, so he and I could have some peace.

I allowed the heart-wrenching memories to flood my mind from the moment I opened the notelet in Ralda's house in the woods…my journey into Tregtaria…Lord De-Deganon's dungeon…Dranisha's uncanny hospitality…the three-pinned scary as hell men…my precious time with Jad…the Ruins of the Water Walkers…Home Shield Home…the Jungle of Voices…the Sands of the Dead…the Arena of Glory…

Every now and again, he flinched, stiffened, and held me tighter. I could feel the contours of his firm muscles through my dress. There was something incredibly fulfilling about being in his arms. I felt him inside my head, but it wasn't intrusive or forced. It was like our minds were one. Our thoughts were aligned. Our hearts were in sync.

Then it was over.

He planted a heartfelt and powerful kiss on my forehead. "I'm so sorry I wasn't there for you." He ran his free hand through his windblown hair. "If I could take away the pain you—"

"It's over, Dante." I shook my head for emphasis. "Let it go." I looked up and found myself gazing into his stunning red-eyes, relishing the fact that what we had between us was priceless and stupendously beautiful.

In my people's ways, our Sequence of Hearts was remarkably timeless—faultless—flawless. Now I understood exactly why people always said the best things didn't cost anything. I jumped into the ocean and landed in his gentle and strong arms. Freedom of choice gave me freedom of hearts. He had given me his love without expecting anything in return. His love for me was free, and so was mine for him!

We sat in agreeable silence, watching the waves dance methodically against the shore. The colour of the sea kept changing from a subtle baby blue to a deeper shade of blue with the passing of a cloud. His arm was comfortably draped around my shoulders whilst my head rested on him.

"Lessi," he said after a while.

He glanced up to the sky, and I followed suit. The majestic aglow moons stared down at us from the east. They still hung very low. Strangely, the sun didn't seem in a rush to go to sleep either.

Swiftly, he rose up, pivoted, and went down on one knee. I smiled curiously. He flashed one of his usual dazzles and put out his hand, palm up. I reached for it slowly, drinking into his vinous-red eyes, a distinct red that reminded me of Aunt Kate's centuries-old vintage wine, made and stilled to perfection. Our hands interlaced.

Oh my God! My mouth opened slightly. "What are you doing?" I whispered.

"I'm kneeling," he said simply. The gentle breeze lifted soft tendrils of his red shock of hair, but this time, he kept his hands locked onto mine.

"I can see you're kneeling," I said in a low voice. "Why?" By then, I'd totally figured out what he was about to do, and I did an Alessia classic—I panicked! I was neither prepared nor expecting it. Not today. Not now.

His wine-red eyes sparkled like they translated the moons' glow through them. "Marry me." The honeyed tone in his voice sent heat streaking through my body.

I gasped. For a few heartbeats, there was absolute stillness from both of us. I couldn't tear my gaze away from the nadirs of his sanguine eyes. *This is not happening!*

"Marry me, Lessi!" he said again.

I'd heard him the first time, clearly, too. It was taking me longer than normal to process. Not a muscle twitched on his face as he gazed into my eyes, making my heart beat in a frenzy.

"Is it Tuscanian tradition to kneel when you propose?" The question was out before I could stop it. I appreciated the similarity with my home world.

"I ask you to marry me, and instead you ask me if it's tradition to kneel?" he teased.

I fell in love with him all over again but I reserved my answer all the same, savouring the moment. I didn't want it rushed, and from the look in his eyes, he didn't either. I breathed.

With a staggering smile, he held both my hands against my lap. "No, we do it differently. I picked up one or two things from your mind when you kindly allowed me inside your head…I thought it may be easier if I did something familiar."

A tremulous smile formed on my lips. I opened my mouth to speak, but no words could give justice to what I was feeling. My eyes flooded with a torrent of emotion. I hadn't foreseen or forethought this. *Not now—not today—not right now.*

"This isn't working," he said after a long while. "I thought I'd have *some* answer by now!"

I smiled playfully and glanced at the sea waves that scintillated with the sun's reflection.

"If you keep me waiting any longer, I'll be inclined to reactivate the olden ways," he said. "I guarantee you'll be my wife at the break of dawn!"

"Is that so?" I teased, settling my gaze back at him. "Tell me more!"

There was a change in him. His eyes revealed a staggering determination that I'd yet to see. "About what exactly?"

A cool ocean breeze swept over us, refreshing and uplifting. My gaze wandered from Dante's stunning red eyes to the swathes of blue silk in the distance and back to him. I smiled, taking in the hypnotic and fragrant scent of sea, home, and Dante, an infusion like no other.

"The ancient ways of courting, proposals, and…things like that," I said in a low voice.

He kneaded my hands for some time. "Care to be more specific?" He edged closer such that my knees were now pressed against him.

"Everything…" My voice toned to a mere whisper.

He seemed even closer, his head inches from mine. In a heartbeat, a burst of heat flashed across my face. He ran an enticing fingertip down my cheek. "Just the ancient ways or the modern ways, too?" he whispered.

I didn't answer; I was too flustered to my find my voice. I'd missed this feeling. My heart was beating against my ribs so hard I was melting.

"We could sample both, and after, you can tell me what you prefer," he said.

I swallowed before I could speak. I knew then that I'd started something, and I had no idea how it would end. Still, I was right to ask. He'd just asked me to marry him…but he hadn't kissed me yet, *really* kissed me. Of course I was entitled to know that at the least, and everything else.

I could kiss him, I supposed…but I couldn't risk breaking any traditions. There were too many customs, and I'd just scratched the surface. I didn't want him to hate me for it.

Despite the stronger breeze and the whistling wind rippling around us, I was too warm now.

Slowly he brought his hands to my waist. "I'm waiting."

I wriggled closer, and swept my arms around his neck. "S-Start with the ancient ways."

He dropped his gaze for a second and then beamed. "In the olden moon-days, there was no courting. If we'd lived four hundred moon-years ago, I would have made you my wife long before you could say my name," he said with a dazzling smile, the one I could never tire of. "My proposal would have been a one-directional calling to your heart that you couldn't refuse. All I had to do was lurk around you for as long as it took to know your schedule more than you. On a moon-night like this, I'd have hungrily come for you, found you sitting right here... unaware of how your life was about to change. I'd approach you from behind and grab you, and before you could cry for help, I'd carry you over my shoulder and run away with you towards my home."

"That's kidnapping!"

He laughed. "It was tradition. The correct term is *Musreta Setara*. The trick was to get you to spend the moon-night with me in my room." A note of amusement sounded in his voice.

"In your bedroom?"

He nodded. "By sunrise, if you were still locked in, you'd be given to me as a wife for life."

"That's unfair!" A thought came to me. "Does it mean we... they would have..." Oh boy, I didn't know how to say this.

He laughed again. "Not necessarily. It was assumed, but who knows? One thing could have led to another." He bit his lip.

"But what if I—she—didn't feel the same for him?"

"Are you trying to tell me something?" he teased, taking my hands from his neck and holding them against his chest.

"No...I mean, her, back in the day!"

"Oh, Lessi, when will you stop worrying about everyone

else?" He kissed my hands. "You're concerned about our ancestors' love lives now?"

"Someone has to." I paused briefly. "Was it forbidden to…"

"Don't worry about that!"

"About what?" I turned defensive.

"Any of it," he said. My look of shock made him smile. "Lessi, j-just don't worry…"

A myriad of thoughts and emotions danced in his eyes, sending my pulse racing. The warmth of his smile was like a light glowing inside my heart.

I took a deep breath. "Seriously, what did she have to do if she didn't like the guy?"

"She'd need to use everything within her powers to leave that room before dawn. At daybreak, their fates were sealed."

"Oh! Like maul him with her nails…or scream?"

He burst into light laughter before his expression sort of shadowed. "This is becoming the longest proposal to date. At this rate, you'll be married off to the land before me." He held a steady, firm gaze.

"You're serious!"

"The land loves you. I won't risk it claiming you anymore than it's already done." His tone was smooth and beseeching. "Marry me!"

I held my answer just a tad longer. Honestly, he and I both knew my answer. He didn't even need to ask. But he asked all the same. Besides, he was delightfully charming in that state. "I've spent nights at your home with you…doesn't it make me your wife already?"

"Not without intent." He paused in contemplation. "You seem hung up on our ancestors' ways. If I were to run away with you right now, clearly the intent is there. That would make you my wife at sunrise," he teased.

"You think I can't fight you?"

"I'd like to see you try," he said playfully.

"Well, seeing that I've got the upper hand…and you're still

recovering from being 'death-at-your doorstep warrior'...I'm certain I'll have no problems keeping you at arm's length." I pecked him softly on the cheek.

"I'm pretty sure I can hold you down!"

He slid his arms around my waist and held me tightly, tantalising all my senses. A nervous thrill of excitement slithered across my spine. Carefully, he scooped me into his arms and rose to his feet.

"What are you doing?" I whispered again.

"You obviously need some persuasion." He dropped a kiss onto my forehead. "And you asked for it!" With that, he took off with me in his arms.

22. ETERNITY -
FOUNTAIN OF DIAMONDS

Still reeling from the shock of my kidnapping, I shut my eyes so I could feel, think, and see just *him with me*. I was delighting in this abduction. Against my better judgement, I was thrilled. His heartbeat raced methodically against mine, its rhythm beating through my pulse. I lay my head comfortably on his chest, my arms encircled around his neck. All the while his sturdy arms held me tightly against him. This was heaven!

I wouldn't dream of mauling him with my nails or asking him to take me home…for *home* was wherever *he* was. *What does this make me?* I allowed myself a small, mischievous smile. My concern, my only humongous concern, was what would happen once we reached house Hantaria. *Will we? Will he…go all the way? Do I need some preparation? Am I really going to be his wife by daybreak? Oh God!* A pang of panic shot through me.

Before I'd mentally prepared myself or organised my thoughts enough to know what was expected of me, he skidded to a halt. I exhaled.

"We're here," he said in a fervent whisper.

Already! My heart lurched. A panic attack was not cool and so unromantic! I took a deep breath and opened my eyes. The sight that met my eyes was profoundly majestic; it threatened to blind me. Blinded by beauty…Oh my goodness, it seemed possible, now.

"Dante!" I muttered in wonder.

My earlier worries flitted away like fading stardust. He gently set me down, brought his hands to my shoulders, and pulled me closer so my back was pressed against him.

A tongue of lush land spread across the meadow. A magnificent three-tier waterfall cascaded over luminous stones that twinkled like millions of tiny, polished diamonds. A lustrous glow of red, blue, and yellow emanated from the sparkling falls. It was simply a stunning, splashing rainbow of wonder.

"Where are we?" I asked. My gaze swept across nature's staggering landscape. In the dying light of sunset, the pool below was varnish-clear...serene...a divine phenomenon.

"Home," he said simply, his warm breath sweet on my neck. He made gentle strokes across my arms; I slowly melted into him.

Vibrant, moss-covered trees peeked from the sides in competition with forest-green fronds that spread across the environs.

I turned my head slowly and glanced back at him.

"You didn't think I was abducting you to my uncle's home... did you?" he asked, a pleasant smile lingering on his lips.

"With that speed...I didn't know *what* to think," I said.

He laughed lightly. Then his eyes deepened, and he spun me round. "The Fountain of Diamonds is my gift to you...for loving me!"

I wowed internally. If we were anywhere else but Zeneshia, I'd have simply regarded that as a wind-up! The waters were laced with a kaleidoscope of colourful threads that continuously bounced off the glittery stones.

"The Fountain of Diamonds?" I repeated in stunned amazement, my mouth slightly open. "Oh, Dante...are they *real* diamonds?"

He nodded and turned round, amused.

I smiled in enchantment. "Where I come from, you're meant to put a diamond on my finger...not give *all* of this to me." *It can't be real.* Somehow, I came short of pinching myself.

He gave me a reassuring smile. This was no wind-up.

I'd known for a while now that Tuscania was bursting with unimaginable riches. Diamonds—emeralds—sapphires… more like *The Hidden City of Jewels*, only that Tuscanians didn't value them with greed. On earth, people died every day for those stones, and in those quantities, I couldn't comprehend what they would do. Blood diamonds—thieving—smuggling… Here, similar stones lay in undisturbed serenity as part of the land—a gift from the Star gods of the Four Oceans.

His hand closed firmly around mine. "You are the only *diamond* I see—a rare gem. This is just a token of my steadfast love for you, as is the stone behind the falls, but nothing compares to you!"

"I won't know what to do with all of this," I whispered.

"When the time comes, you will," he reassured.

He gently drew me towards him, and my heart lurched in anticipation. Apart from the quaint scenery, something else hung in the air, something fizzing, bubbling and sizzling, waiting to gush out and envelope us.

"Let's take a walk," he said.

"Into the pool?" I settled my gaze on the mystical pool. To its right sat an equally stunning raised platform that appeared like it was suspended in air. *Extraordinary!* Under the arch of the falls, a cave opened up and stretched into vast space.

"Close," he said.

We strode hand in hand around the most breath-taking body of water I'd ever laid eyes on. Bubbles of spray sprinkled over us. Sprouting flowers were hemmed into the edges like a delicate work of art. With each step, goose bumps mixed with adrenaline made my heart feel like I was shuttling into space.

Once we reached the bottom of the overhang, he stopped. Carefully, he wound his arms around me and buoyed me onto the raised platform. A second later, he joined me on the ledge. I stood in awe at perfection…from all angles. Forget Tregtaria; we were on top of the world!

At close proximity, the waterfall swished joyfully over the drape of colour. The tropical feel and the aura were like a hallucinatory drug, one that would stick to me for life, but nothing was complete without my most amazing love. To me, he would never do wrong.

He stood next to me, as we watched nature's splendour like an uncut movie that continued into perpetuity. It was an unquestionable true scenic wonder!

"Look up, Lessi," he said into my ear.

I followed his gaze to the night skies and then back at him. His wine-red eyes held a fierce intensity, a calling to my soul; it was impossible to look away for long.

"Whilst the dual moon gods are in the sky for a purpose— to enlighten our world and guide our paths—one thing they did right was place you, Lessi, as divine as you are, in my path." He slid his hand to my cheek, holding his striking ruby gaze. "Our sequences were merged so you and I can never lose sight of one another."

The clasp of his hand was cool and firm, like ice on fire. I was hot, but a shiver of excitement shot through me, my heart lurching crazily at his words.

"Surrounding us is just a piece of land, but what stands out is the way each facet compliments another. Without the land, the sky has no bounce. The moons and the stars bounce off the sun for light. Every aspect was designed to fit neatly into each other...like a glove." His tone was silky—smooth—enthralling.

My eyes misted in tune with the light scatters of mist enveloping us like a protective sheath of comfort, love, and bliss.

"This land is not awe-inspiring without the waterfall... neither is the waterfall without the land. Both water and land are in perfect *alignment*, such as I feel *you* are to me," he said.

I wowed inwardly again whilst an incredibly refreshing scent of minerals wafted through the air, making my stomach dance.

"The world above and below the seas have remained a myth

in both our worlds for far too long. Surely that myth can now be laid to rest, for you, my love…you cross all mythical, magical, and scientific boundaries of men and creatures alike." He held my hands against his chest, meaning every word.

I wanted to jump up and down with elation, but it was too precious a moment to spoil, so I stifled a jump and smiled, wondering how I could be this lucky to have him in my life.

"The moons aligned to the sun at just the right time to sweep the tide that brought you across the Four Oceans of the Surging Tide and into my world. If I had to live a millennium longer to find you, it would have been worth every moment. I would grow old in pursuit of a love like this, for there's nothing else I'd rather have but *you*."

A gentle spray of water filtered over us, dousing us in small doses. My heart was racing a marathon. A simple, artless yes wasn't going to be enough. It was so last year. I had to think… fast!

"I am not Dante without Lessi. Everything right now is in perfect position: the moon gods with the star gods, the Sun god of Light with the sky, the land with the water…you and I, we're one." He placed a slow kiss on my hands, still intertwined with his. "You saved *my* life, Lessi…in ways that go against the natural order of life. There are so many rules on what I can and can't do with you as we are. The gods know I've broken a few… allowing me to love you without restriction…I promise…this is the last time I'll ask you to save me one more time…from disobeying my gods, our ancestors' ways, and the rules of my land."

"Oh, Dante!" I couldn't hold back anymore.

"Will you be my wife?"

I nodded wordlessly, too touched to speak. *Who would deny such a proposal?*

"I know you're young," he hastened to add. "You need time to—"

I brought my hand to his lips. "You're stealing my lines." I breathed, or tried to, my breath catching.

He laughed gently, his eyes shimmering a deep red.

"This land, Zeneshia...the kingdom under the moons brought a fairy tale to my life, and *you* make it real. I'm not too young to love, neither am I too young to know I'm in love with you." I kept my hand on his lips. "I always knew it was going to be all or nothing for me. And I found *all* and more, abundantly more, in you. I don't need time to feel anything else other than what I feel for you. I love you, Dante...so much that I would marry you yesterday or right now...Yes, I'll *be* your wife...in Sequence, in life, in love, and in death."

He gently took my face into his hands and gazed into my eyes for a long while, savouring the magical moment, as I was.

"If you really want to do the ancient kidnap thing, right now, I won't stop you. I won't fight you." My voice was so low. "I'll run ahead of you...to give you absolute assurance that I can't wait to be your wife."

His wine-red eyes danced. The glint was hypnotising. In the seconds that followed, the burbling waterfall seemed to be listening to us, except we were as quiet as the sleeping ones. The moons' glow caught the waterfall's explosion of colour, dazzling my already compromised senses. His heartbeat was strong against mine. The ragged sound of our breathing felt strange.

Slowly, he brushed a loose strand of my hair before tucking it behind my ear. Momentarily, he slid his arms on the curve of my waist and pulled me nearer, so close I was pressed against him. I could sense a difference to this touch.

"I've been waiting too long." He stared deep into my eyes. A second after, he gently cupped my cheek with his palm, and unhurriedly leaned towards me until his lips were inches away from mine. The warmth of his breath brushed against my lips. I dared not breathe. *This is it.* For a few seconds, he enticed my senses with a promise of unbridled passion yet to come.

Just as the waiting became unbearable, we simultaneously closed the tiny gap between us. His mouth opened over mine, and naturally mine opened, too. Softly, he pressed his lips against mine and instantly took my non-existent breath away.

Like I had been born for just that one moment, I responded to a long yet slow, gentle yet passionate, and much awaited *real* first kiss. It was as amazingly sweet as a whisper, as refreshing as a serein, and as caressing as a gentle breeze on a faultless summer's day.

Suddenly, a gust of wind blew over us, bringing with it a deluge of water from the waterfall! In seconds, we were soaked. We burst into light laughter before his arms folded around me. With one fluid movement, he pulled me into the cave. He kissed me again, long and hard, long and light, long and fluttering. It was an exploration for me as it was for him. His lips were warm and sensual—a seamless fit for mine!

I was completely lost to the world. Vaguely aware of the fine shreds of mist spraying over us, in the heat of the moment, I don't quite remember how I ended up lying down... He half-lay over me, pressing me gently onto the ground. His lips on mine and mine on his, I was double-dosed with a foreign sensation. I allowed my eyes to close in contentment, relishing the moment, absorbing the power and passion of our love. Instantaneously, I unwittingly got inside his head and gasped.

Dante! My breath caught. Fiercely, I yanked him tightly against me.

It was one thing being consumed by my own desire, quite another feeling his love for me; it was an explosion of endearment! For a second, I was confused. *Is this natural? Am I meant to feel what he's feeling? Does he know I'm inside his head? Is he feeling it, too?*

For *that* brief moment, I was engulfed by his intense yearning. An incredibly surreal feeling overpowered me. I could attempt to control *my* feelings, but *his* were too overwhelming. I succumbed to the pull of emotion, unable to think of anything other than us.

Lessi! His voice echoed, loud and sweet inside my head. *I can't stop!*

He felt it, too! *I know…Neither can I.*

At that juncture, we broke off the kiss—and the world stopped. Only the glowing pearl discs casting rays of light, creating silhouettes over the land, hovered above us, like shining stars.

"You knew this would happen?" I asked, breathless, hands curved around his neck. Our faces were only inches apart, him inside my head, me inside his, then us.

"The Sequence of First and Forever has its own perks," he murmured.

"A perk of Sequence," I whispered in awe, running my fingers gently through his hair, loving everything about the amazing world of Sequence. "If this is one of the perks of Sequence…" I licked my lips. "What else should I look forward to?"

He smiled handsomely, still hovering over me. "Everything carved by the hand of Sequence gets better," he said, and dropped a light kiss on my lips, "sweeter," he added, and fluttered another on my bottom lip, "and superior," he finished, and lowered his lips to cover mine in one sweep. *With time,* he completed his words telepathically. He gently drew back, eyes glinting. "We can't possibly anticipate Sequence's next move."

He rolled to my side and gathered me in his arms. I buried my head in his chest, relishing every second of being in his arms again. In comfortable silence, he made calming strokes across my arm, making my stomach dance as if flurries of butterflies were fluttering around my insides. His chest reverberated against my cheek, warm and lulling.

"Is there a limit to us, to Sequence, to what we might… together?" I shifted my head and looked up.

His eyes sparked golden-red, the kind that teased of the fury of a blazing fire yet oozed nothing more than cosy warmth on a faultless evening. "When the Sequence is this strong, there's no limit to what we might experience when our hearts, minds, and bodies are aligned," he said softly in a honeyed voice.

"It's magical?" I breathed, blinking more times that I intended.

"It's Sequence," he said in a low and mellifluous voice, his heart beating steadily against my palm.

"You call it Sequence. I call it magic. How about we settle for a compromise?" I teased, smiling. "Magical Sequence?"

"Sounds about right," he whispered into my hair.

I lay my head back on his chest. "Tell you what…I'm so in love with Sequence right now I could kiss him." My voice was barely above a whisper.

"Him?" He gently slid his hand to my cheek and tilted my chin so I could look up into his eyes. Then he raised his eyebrows. "I don't think you want to be kissing any other man right now, Lessi." He rolled me over and brushed the hair gently off my neck, leaving a trail of warm shivers along my neckline. He kissed me yet again, telling me in more ways than one, he was the one. This time, it was full of passion and bursting with emotion that invoked a thrilling sensation in me.

Her? I asked telepathically.

His low laugh echoed inside my head. *No, Lessi! Not him and not her.*

It? I tantalised him further.

He let out a low growl. "How much I had missed you."

What he did next, I didn't expect or anticipate. He gently rose to his feet with me securely curled up in his arms and lifted me to him. His warm breath caressed my cheek, searing a honeyed trail in its wake.

"You're not reconsidering the ancient kidnap thing now," I just had to ask, "are you?"

He burst into outright laughter, tightened his arms around me, and whispered, "I've decided to put Sequence's limits to the test." He kissed the tip of my nose and drew back.

"Now?" Curiosity made my voice crack.

He brought his lips to mine. Inevitably, I pulled him just a fraction closer, and in a heartbeat, I slipped involuntarily inside his head. My stomach contracted. My breath caught. I clutched onto him, consumed by his love for me. It was one of the most surreal experiences of our love. A cloak of warmth enveloped me, squeezing me into a feeling of helplessness. I was drenched yet fizzing with bubbling heat that coiled around me relentlessly. As he deepened the kiss, my body gave way.

"Dante!" I gasped and drew him hard against me. *I'm floating. I'm flying. I'm falling. I'm not in control.*

I've got you. His honeyed voice reached out to me. *Don't fight it, Lessi. You wanted to be inside my head—inside my heart—now you are. I need you to feel my undying love for you.*

So I felt it—the surreal and magical connection between us—the flame of our Sequence—the fire of passion that resided inside of him—they all radiated in bountiful heat waves around me. Overwhelmed by his emotion, I wriggled farther into his arms and allowed him to transport me to the unfathomable depths of his heart. I knew he loved me, I knew he adored me, but this profundity of his love was mind-boggling. Seeing and experiencing how much I meant to him blew me away. Hot scorching tears brimmed my eyes and inevitably cascaded down my cheeks.

Instantly, he drew back. "You're crying, my love."

"Happy tears," I whispered. "I didn't know just how much."

He lowered himself to the ground with me in his arms. "Now you know."

I nodded and snuggled up in his arms, unable to find words to express what I had just experienced. "The fire?" I whispered. "Does it burn?"

"It's alight for you. When I'm with you, it's bearable. It's warm, simply warm, but when you're gone, it burns me from the inside out."

"This connection between us—me being inside your head, you being inside mine…is it why you never kissed me before?"

"I suspected that this would happen." A tinge of amusement sounded in his mellow voice. "It's an inevitable pull of Sequence I couldn't risk. Heart to heart, mind to mind, the possibilities are endless. I was afraid that if it were too soon, we wouldn't be able to…"

"You thought I couldn't handle it?" I teased.

"Not you. Me."

I raised my brows. "So now you're not afraid?"

He didn't answer right away. "The only fear that keeps me awake every moon-night is the fear of losing you."

"You're a death-at-your-doorstep warrior." I bit my lip. "You're dauntless."

"I have a weakness for you," he whispered. "I can't bear it if I ever lose you again."

I drew in a deep and satisfied breath, relishing the magic of our love. "Is there anything that Sequence can't do?"

He was quiet for some time and then shifted and curved his arm around my waist. "Truthfully, I don't know. All I know is that right here, right now, Sequence is in our favour."

I stared into his stunning eyes and saw everything that brought out the best in me. He was a guy of quiet sophistication, extraordinary intelligence, and, simply put, the apotheosis of the most perfect boyfriend. His strength of character radiated to me. There was enough courage, devotion, and endearment in him that filled my heart and consumed my whole.

"Marry me!" A faint smile played on his lips.

"I said yes already," I whispered.

The night turned quiet—not a haunting silence, but a serene silence. With a smile of satisfaction, he pulled away and lolled on his back. A split-second later, he wound his arms around me and rolled me over so I half-lay on top of him.

"It's time we let the land know!" He couldn't conceal his mirth.

"Too late…" I couldn't resist kissing him again. "The land already knows," I breathed the words into his mouth.

Sometime later, I rested my head on his chest and gazed at the stelliferous night skies abounded with thousands of flickering and dancing stars. It was an extraordinary thing to love someone and to be fortunate enough to feel them loving you, too! Like an open book, we were just at the incunabulum. The future was ours for the taking!

This was where we both wanted to be, together, in an aligned and perfectly symmetrical Sequence of Hearts forever! We could stay lost in that moment for eternity and never need to find anything else, other than what we already had. A complete feeling of belonging graced me...I was home.

It was in *this* home that I found everything...my freedom, a haven, and, above all, a love that could only be dreamt of. A love that was based on a mutual understanding of the rarity of our bond. A love that was pure, honest, and beauteous. A destined serendipity built on the values of a solid Sequence of First and Forever. A steadfast devotion to each other, one that never wilted or shrivelled with time or separation.

Love between our worlds once divided by the deep, unfathomable Four Oceans of the Surging Tide. It defied the greatest scientists' theories. It defied the designs of the manipulators of sequences. It challenged the odds. It was magical. It could only be love known, kneaded and dispensed by the silent Moon gods of the night sky.

* * *

The story continues in Volume Three:
The Heart of the Ocean Series—SeQuence Entangled.

The Heart of the Ocean Series

Lose yourself in the sensational YA fantasy romance series that captures the magical Sequence of first and forever love.

* * *

Enthralling, romantic, and totally enchanting, The Heart of the Ocean Series will whisk you to the kingdom under the moons, where fantasy and romance merge into a magical fusion of steadfast love.

Don't miss the third instalment of the sensational series.

**Book Three, SeQuence Entangled,
will be available Spring/Summer 2017!**

TOP PICK FROM
SeQUENCE ENTANGLED

The

Three Hundred Moon-Year
Treaty Of Peace

between

The Ancient Gods-Chosen
Masters Of All Lands

Njuzathians

and

Tuscanians

and

The Others

No being, Tuscanian or Njuzathian, shall use the powers of the mind to shift, transform, or alter the course of the lands, nor shall he use his powers to adjust, refine, or modify his Sequence or that of others.

* * *

For the sake of completeness and clarity, and to avoid discombobulation, this includes mindless, warmongering Tregtarians and futuristic, we-dream-it-all Felradians.

* * *

To use the gods-given powers of the mind beyond the boundaries of one's land is forbidden!

To use the gods-given powers for personal gain is prohibited!

To use the gods-given powers to alter the Sequence of others is outlawed!

* * *

In simplified terms, attempting to fly when one doesn't have wings is banned!

*Breach one...it's forgotten.

*Breach two...it, too, shall be forgiven.

*Breach three...you'll wish you'd stopped at one!

Three violations are an absolute breach of this agreement. After which, the consequences will be felt by every generation thereto.

* * *

Njuzathia agrees to follow the course of nature, regardless of the unfair nature of fate and this somewhat pointless treaty, and agrees under duress to sleep for three hundred moon-years.

* * *

Shall the treaty be breached in any capacity, shape, or form in the three hundred moon-years of Njuzathian sleep, Njuzathia will awake and become rightful masters of the world below and above the seas.

Signed at Ngupori Jiromu 10, 3567

Master Ze Zedka (Njuzathia)

_____

Z

Larizon Trezia E (Tuscania)

_____

T

Dear Reader,

I hope you enjoyed SeQuence Aligned!

If you did, I would appreciate it if you could take a few minutes of your time to write a review. Positive reviews are the best way to thank an author for writing the book you loved. It doesn't have to be long (unless you really are a lover of words). A few words, a sentence and a star rating will be more than sufficient. This will help others decide whether this book is for them. I treasure your feedback.

Thanks so much for reading!

Would you like to get involved?

It would mean the world to me, and the SeQuence characters if you could help create a buzz and hopefully bring them to life. There are various little and big ways to get involved. Below are a few ways:

Write a review.

Interview the characters.

Ask the author.

Twitter: Join the hashtag #Sequencebook
@GameofSequence @authorlorraineM

Facebook: Join the Facebook Group
Lorraine M.L.M Books Street Team

STAY UP-DATED

Want to know when I release new books? Here are some ways to stay up-dated:

Join my mailing list at:
http://eepurl.com/b-3fXn

Like me on Facebook:
www.facebook.com/authorlorraineM

Follow me on Twitter:
www.twitter.com/authorlorraineM

About the author

Lorraine M.L.M writes young adult romantic fiction. Her love for reading prompted her passion for writing. She loves all genres of romance but has a special and inherent interest in Sci-Fi and Fantasy/Romance in particular uplifting and thought provoking fiction.

Looking Ahead:

She's currently writing the rest of the books in **The Heart of the Ocean Series.**
    In addition, she's also writing the following:
    YA Contemporary Romance novel
    YA Sci-Fi adventure/Romance trilogy
    YA Paranormal/Romance Serial

When she's not writing, she can be found gazing into the distance thinking about writing.

ACKNOWLEDGEMENTS

Writing SeQuence and SeQuence Aligned is one of the best things I ever decided to do! The journey has been long, tedious yet liberating. Sometimes my resolve dwindled, and I'd fail to see the end of the sequence. But I didn't give up. And given the choice, I'd happily do it all over again.

First, I'm indebted to my family for enduring countless conversations about this book, from characterisation, naming, plotting and everything "SeQuence." They weathered the storm with me. Through the dark cloud they showed me the horizon. In the sunshine they held my hand and laughed with me. In the rain, they danced alongside me and willed me forward. This book is a co-production. I didn't do it alone.

First and foremost, I'd like to give special thanks to my entire family, (Dad M, Mum L, Mainini Q & T, Husband Simba, Children N & N, Brother Syd, Sis-in-law B, Cousins (too many fabulous cousins to mention), wonderful uncles and aunts, friends who are as good as family...) Your unwavering support resides inside my heart and will never fade. Deepest thanks to you..

Special mention to my Dad, Moses C. M (Sekuru a Tatata) who has always believed in me. Your joy is my jubilation. To my Mum, Loveness B. M (Asele), you're the best mother any daughter could ever ask for.

To my cheerleaders for life, Natasha and Nathan, you cheered me on and believed in me. You were the first ones to call it out. "Mummy is an author! Dante is at the door! Alessia is at the door!" Screams! To my husband, Simba…thanks for all your outstanding help and patience. It's been a long journey.

Thank you a million times over to Mbuya aRumbi for fuelling my imagination. Zeneshia would not be the same without you.

Special gratitude to my amazing friends, "angels of words and wisdom," Critique and Beta Buddies, you guys rock! Profound thanks to the Romantic Novelists Association and the anonymous reader who critiqued SeQuence Aligned. I'll forever be grateful. More thanks goes to Lee Ann. You made me believe in myself and encouraged me to find my voice. I thank you from the bottom of my heart.

Additional heartfelt thanks to the wonderful Nicole Zoltack. You're simply amazing! To the lovely, Katy Haye, I can't thank you enough. You've been a huge help and I'll forever be grateful. More thanks goes to my fabulous cover designer, Jane Dixon Smith. Thank you for designing the most stunning SeQuence and SeQuence Aligned covers. You took Zeneshia out of my head and brought it to life. I also want to say huge thanks to Maria Gandolfo -- I Renflowergrapx for illustrating the most wonderful map of Zeneshia. You're truly gifted.

To my SeQuence Launch Team, thank you from the bottom of my heart for taking this journey with me. You believed in me--in the story--in the characters and for that I'm most thankful. One step at a time, we'll get there. To my work colleagues (you know who you are) thanks so much for your ongoing support. Special mention to Andy Starkings…thanks for being one of the first people to like my Facebook posts. It hasn't gone unnoticed. I appreciate your support.

With thanks!

CPSIA information can be obtained
at www.ICGtesting.com
Printed in the USA
LVOW07s0001300617
539826LV00001B/15/P